The Thousand a

A Companion to the "

Miss Pardoe

Alpha Editions

This edition published in 2023

ISBN : 9789357945189

Design and Setting By
Alpha Editions
www.alphaedis.com
Email - info@alphaedis.com

INTRODUCTION.

The Compiler of the graceful little volume which I have the pleasure of introducing to the public, has conferred an undeniable benefit upon the youth of England by presenting to them a collection of Oriental Tales, which, rich in the elements of interest and entertainment, are nevertheless entirely free from the licentiousness which renders so many of the fictions of the East, beautiful and brilliant as they are, most objectionable for young and ardent minds. There is indeed no lack of the wonderful in the pages before us, any more than in the Arabian and Persian Tales already so well known: but it will be seen that the supernatural agency in the narratives is used as a means to work out totally different results. There is, in truth, scarcely one of these Tales which does not inculcate a valuable moral lesson; as may be seen by reference to "The Powder of Longevity," "The Old Camel," and "The Story of the Dervise Abounadar" among several, others.

The present collection of Eastern Stories has been principally derived from the works of different Oriental Scholars on the Continent, and little doubt can be entertained of the genuineness of their origin; while they have been carefully selected, and do honour to the good taste of their Compiler. An acknowledgment is also due to him for his adherence to the good old orthography to which we have all been accustomed from our childhood, in the case of such titles as "Caliph," "Vizier," "Houri," "Genii," &c.; as, however critically correct and learned the spelling of Mr. Lane may be in his magnificent version of the "Thousand and One Nights," and however appropriate to a work of so much research and value to Oriental students, it would have been alike fatiguing and out of character to have embarrassed a volume, simply intended for the amusement of youthful readers, by a number of hard and unfamiliar words, difficult of pronunciation to all save the initiated; and for the pleasure of the young requiring translation fully as much as the narrative itself.

In one of the Tales there will be at once detected a portion of the favourite old story of Aladdin's Lamp, in the subterranean gem-garden discovered by the handsome youth; while in another, mention is made of the already-familiar legend of the hidden city of Ad, so popular among the ancient Arabs[1]; but these repetitions will cease to create any surprise when it is remembered that the professional story-tellers of the East are a wandering race, who travel from city to city, exhibiting their talent during seasons of festivity, in the palaces of the wealthy and the public coffee-houses. Those admitted to the women's apartments are universally aged crones, whose volubility is something marvellous; and they are always welcome guests to the indolent beauties, who listen to them for hours together without a symptom of weariness, as they pour forth their narratives in a monotonous voice strangely displeasing to European ears. The men, while reciting their tales, indulge in violent gesticulations and contortions of the body, which appear to produce great delight in their audience. Since they generally travel two or three in company; and, save in rare cases of improvisation, their stock of narrative is common to all, it is their ambition so individually to embellish, heighten, and amplify their subject-matter, as to outshine their competitors; and it is consequently to this cause that the numerous variations of the same Tale which have reached Europe must be attributed.

[1] Most of our readers will also recognize in the Story of the Princess Schirine the groundwork of one of Hans Andersen's beautiful Danish Tales, "The Flying Trunk."

Taken altogether, there can be no doubt that the "Thousand and One Days" merit the warm welcome which I trust awaits them.

J. P.

LONDON, FEB. 1857.

I.

THE STORY OF HASSAN ABDALLAH; OR, THE ENCHANTED KEYS.

Theilon, caliph of Egypt, died, after having bequeathed his power to his son, Mohammed, who, like a wise and good prince, proceeded to root out abuses, and finally caused peace and justice to flourish throughout his dominions. Instead of oppressing his people by new taxes, he employed the treasures, which his father had amassed by violence, in supporting learned men, rewarding the brave, and assisting the unfortunate. Every thing succeeded under his happy sway; the risings of the Nile were regular and abundant; every year the soil produced rich harvests; and commerce, honoured and protected, caused the gold of foreign nations to flow abundantly into the ports of Egypt.

Mohammed determined, one day, to take the census of the officers of his army, and of all the persons in public situations whose salaries were paid out of the treasury. The vizirs, to the number of forty, first made their appearance and knelt in succession before the sovereign. They were, for the most part, men venerable from their age, and some of them had long beards of snowy whiteness. They all wore on their heads tiaras of gold, enriched with precious stones, and carried in their hands long staves as badges of their power. One enumerated the battles in which he had been engaged, and the honourable wounds he had received; another recounted the long and laborious studies he had pursued, in order to render himself master of the various sciences, and to qualify himself to serve the state by his wisdom and knowledge.

After the vizirs, came the governors of provinces, the generals, and the great officers of the army; and next to them the civil magistrates, and all who were entrusted with the preservation of the peace and the awarding of justice. Behind these walked the public executioner, who, although stout and well-fed, like a man who had nothing to do, went along as if depressed with grief, and instead of carrying his sword naked on his shoulder, he kept it in its scabbard. When he came into the presence of the prince, he threw himself at his feet, and exclaimed, "O mighty prince, the day of justice and of munificence is at last about to dawn on me! Since the death of the terrible Theilon, under whose reign my life was happy and my condition prosperous, I have seen my occupation and its emoluments diminish daily. If Egypt continue thus to live in peace and plenty, I shall run great danger of perishing with hunger, and my family will be brought to misery and ruin."

Mohammed listened in silence to the complaints of the headsman, and acknowledged that there was some foundation for them, for his salary was small, and the chief part of his profits arose from what he obtained from criminals, either by way of gift, or as a rightful fee. In times of trouble, quarrelling, and violence, he had lived, in fact, in a state of ease and affluence, while now, under the present prosperous reign, he had nothing better than the prospect of beggary before him.

"Is it then true," exclaimed the caliph, "that the happiness of all is a dream? that what is joy to one, may be the cause of grief to another? O executioner, fear not as to your fate! May it, indeed, please God that, under my reign, your sword,—which is almost as often an instrument of vengeance as of justice,— may remain useless and covered with rust. But, in order to enable you to provide for the wants of yourself and your family, without the unhappy necessity of exercising your fatal office, you shall receive every year the sum of two hundred dinars."

In this way all the officers and servants of the palace passed before the notice of the prince; he interrogated each on the nature of his occupation and his past services, on his means of existence, and on the salary which he received. When he found that any one held a situation of a painful and difficult nature, for which he was inadequately remunerated, the caliph diminished his duties and increased his pay; and, on the other hand, when he found the contrary to be the case, he lessened the salary and increased the duties of the office. After having, in this way, performed many acts of wisdom and justice, the caliph observed, among the officers of the civil service, a sheik, whose wrinkled countenance and stooping figure indicated his great age. The caliph called him up, in order to inquire what was his employment in the palace, and the sum which it yielded him.

"Prince," the old man replied, "my only employment is to take care of a chest that was committed to my charge by your father, the late caliph, and for attending to which he allowed me ten pieces of gold a month."

"It seems to me," replied Mohammed, "that the reward is great for so slight a service. Pray what are the contents of this chest?"

"I received it," replied the sheik, "in charge forty years ago, and I solemnly swear to you that I know not what it contains."

The caliph commanded the chest to be brought to him, which was of pure gold, and most richly adorned. The old man opened it. It contained a manuscript written in brilliant characters on the skin of a gazelle, painted purple and sprinkled with a red dust. Neither the prince, however, nor his ministers, nor the ulemas who were present, could decipher the writing. By the caliph's order, the wise men of Egypt were summoned, as well as others from Syria, Persia, and India, but to no purpose; not one was able to interpret the mysterious characters. The book remained open for a long time, exposed to the gaze of all, and a great reward was offered to any one who could bring forward a person of sufficient learning to read it.

Some time after this, a savant who had left Egypt in the reign of Theilon, and had now returned after a long absence, chanced to hear of the mysterious book, and said that he knew what it was, and could explain its history. The caliph immediately admitted him to an audience, and the old man addressed him as follows:

"O sovereign ruler, may the Almighty prolong your days! Only one man can read this book, its rightful master, the sheik Hassan Abdallah, son of El-Achaar. This man had travelled through many lands, and penetrated into the mysterious city of Aram, built on columns, from which he brought this book, which no one but himself could read. He made use of it in his experiments in alchemy, and by its aid he could transmute the most worthless metals into gold. The caliph Theilon, your father, having learned this, commanded the sage to be brought before him, with a view of compelling him to reveal the secret of his knowledge. Hassan Abdallah refused to do so, for fear of putting into the hands of the unjust an instrument of such terrible power; and the prince, in a rage, laid hold of the chest, and ordered the sage to be thrown into prison, where he still remains, unless he has died since that time, which is forty years ago."

On hearing this, Mohammed immediately despatched his officers to visit the prisons, and, on their return, learned with pleasure that Hassan was still alive. The caliph ordered him to be brought forth and arrayed in a dress of honour; and, on his appearing in the audience chamber, the prince made him sit down beside him, and begged him to forgive the unjust treatment which his father had caused him to undergo. He then told him how he had accidentally discovered that he was still alive; and at last, placing the mysterious book before him, said,

"Old man, if this book could make me the owner of all the treasures of the world, I would not consent to possess it, since it only belongs to me by injustice and violence."

On hearing these words, Hassan burst into tears.

"O God," he exclaimed, "all wisdom proceeds from Thee! Thou causest to arise from the same soil the poisonous and the wholesome plant. Every where good is placed by the side of evil. This prince, the support of the feeble, the defender of the oppressed, who has conferred on me the happiness of spending my remaining years in the light of day, is the son of the tyrant who plunged Egypt in mourning, and who kept me for forty years in a loathsome dungeon. Prince," added the old man, addressing Mohammed, "what I refused to the wrath of your father, I willingly grant to your virtues: this book contains the precepts of the true science, and I bless Heaven that I have lived long enough to teach it to you. I have often risked my life to become the master of this wonderful book, which was the only article of value that I brought from Aram, that city into which no man can enter who is not assisted by Heaven."

The caliph embraced the old man, and, calling him his father, begged him to relate what he had seen in the city of Aram.

"Prince," replied Hassan, "it is a long story, as long, nearly, as my whole life."

He then proceeded as follows.

Story of the Enchanted Keys

THE STORY OF HASSAN ABDALLAH.

I am the only son of one of the richest inhabitants of Egypt. My father, who was a man of extensive knowledge, employed my youth in the study of science; and at twenty years of age I was already honourably mentioned among the ulemas, when my father bestowed a young maiden on me as my wife, with eyes brilliant as the stars, and with a form elegant and light as that of the gazelle. My nuptials were magnificent, and my days flowed on in peace and happiness. I lived thus for ten years, when at last this beautiful dream vanished. It pleased Heaven to afflict me with every kind of misfortune: the plague deprived me of my father; war destroyed my dear brothers; my house fell a prey to the flames; my richly-laden ships were buried beneath the waves. Reduced to misery and want, my only resource was in the mercy of God and the compassion of the faithful whom I met while I frequented the mosques. My sufferings, from my own wretched state of poverty, and that of my wife and children, were cruel indeed. One day when I had not received any charitable donations, my wife, weeping, took some of my clothes, and gave them to me in order to sell them at the bazaar. On the way thither I met an Arab of the desert, mounted on a red camel. He greeted me, and said,

"Peace be with you, my brother! Can you tell me where the sheik Hassan Abdallah, the son of El-Achaar, resides in the city?"

Being ashamed of my poverty, and thinking I was not known, I replied,

"There is no man at Cairo of that name."

"God is great!" exclaimed the Arab; "are you not Hassan Abdallah, and can you send away your guest by concealing your name?"

Greatly confused, I then begged him to forgive me, and laid hold of his hands to kiss them, which he would not permit me to do, and I then accompanied him to my house. On the way there I was tormented by the reflection that I had nothing to set before him; and when I reached home I informed my wife of the meeting I had just had.

"The stranger is sent by God," said she; "and even the children's bread shall be his. Go, sell the clothes which I gave you; buy some food for our guest with the money, and if any thing should remain over, we will partake of it ourselves."

In going out it was necessary that I should pass through the apartment where the Arab was. As I concealed the clothes, he said to me, "My brother, what have you got there hid under your cloak?"

I replied that it was my wife's dress, which I was carrying to the tailor.

"Show it to me," he said. I showed it to him, blushing.

"O merciful God," he exclaimed, "you are going to sell it in order to get money to enable you to be hospitable towards me! Stop, Hassan! here are ten pieces of gold; spend them in buying what is needful for our own wants and for those of your family."

I obeyed, and plenty and happiness seemed to revisit my abode. Every day the Arab gave me the same sum, which, according to his orders, I spent in the same way; and this continued for fifteen days. On the sixteenth day my guest, after chatting on indifferent matters, said to me, "Hassan, would you like to sell yourself to me?"

"My lord," I replied, "I am already yours by gratitude."

"No," he replied, "that is not what I mean; I wish to make you my property, and you shall fix the price yourself."

Thinking he was joking, I replied, "The price of a freeman is one thousand dinars if he is killed at a single blow; but if many wounds are inflicted upon him, or if he should be cut in many pieces, the price is then one thousand five hundred dinars."

"Very well," answered my guest, "I will pay you this last-mentioned sum if you will consent to the bargain."

When I saw that he was speaking seriously, I asked for time in order to consult my family.

"Do so," he replied, and then went out to look after some affairs in the city.

When I related the strange proposal of my guest, my mother said, "What can this man want to do with you?" The children all clung to me, and wept. My wife, who was a wise and prudent woman, remarked,

"This detestable stranger wants, perhaps, to get back what he has spent here. You have nothing but this wretched house, sell it, and give him the money, but don't sell yourself."

I passed the rest of the day and the following night in reflection, and was in a state of great uncertainty. With the sum offered by the stranger I could at least secure bread for my family. But why wish to purchase me? What could he intend to do? Before next morning, however, I had come to a decision. I went to the Arab and said, "I am yours." Untying his sash, he took out one thousand five hundred gold pieces, and giving them to me, said, "Fear not, my brother, I have no designs against either your life or your liberty; I only wish to secure a faithful companion during a long journey which I am about to undertake."

Overwhelmed with joy, I ran with the money to my wife and mother; but they, without listening to my explanations, began weeping and crying as if they were lamenting for the dead.

"It is the price of flesh and blood," they exclaimed; "neither we nor our children will eat bread procured at such a cost!"

By dint of argument, however, I succeeded at length in subduing their grief; and having embraced them, together with my children, I set out to meet my new master.

By order of the Arab I purchased a camel renowned for its speed, at the price of a hundred drachms; I filled our sacks with food sufficient for a long period; and then, mounting our camels, we proceeded on our journey.

We soon reached the desert. Here no traces of travellers were to be seen, for the wind effaced them continually from the surface of the moving sand. The Arab was guided in his course by indications known only to himself. We travelled thus together for five days under a burning sun; each day seemed longer to me than a night of suffering or of fear. My master, who was of a lively disposition, kept up my courage by tales which I remember even now with pleasure after forty years of anguish; and you will forgive an old man for not being able to resist the pleasure of relating some of them to you. The following story, he said, had been recounted to him by the basket-maker himself, a poor man whom he had found in prison, and whom he had charitably found means to release.

THE STORY OF THE BASKET-MAKER.

I was born of poor and honest parents; and my father, who was a basket-maker by trade, taught me to plait all kinds of baskets. So long as I had only myself to care for, I lived tolerably well on the produce of my labour; but when I reached twenty years of age, and took a wife, who in a few years presented me with several children, my gains proved insufficient to maintain my family. A basket-maker earns but little; one day he gets a drachm, the next he may get two, or perhaps only half a drachm. In this state of things I and my children had often to endure the pangs of hunger.

One day it happened that I had just finished a large basket; it was well and strongly made, and I hoped to obtain at least three drachms for it. I took it to the bazaar and through all the streets, but no purchaser appeared. Night came on and I went home. When my wife and children saw me return without any food, they began to cry and to ask for bread, but as I had none to give them, I could only weep with them: the night was long and sorrowful. At daybreak my wife awoke me, saying, "Go, and sell the basket at any price you can get for it, were it only half a drachm." I set out, and perambulated the streets and squares, but night came on again without my finding a purchaser. My wife burst out into a great rage. "What!" she said, "do you still bring back this basket? Do you wish to see us die with hunger?"

I assured her that I had tried every means, but in vain, to sell the basket. She then took some articles of her own, and told me to go and sell them, and procure some bread for the children. I did as she said, and my famished family partook of a miserable repast, which my depressed state of mind prevented me from sharing with them. I slept little that night; and as soon as it was day I performed my devotions, and prayed to God to come to my assistance. I then went out again with my unsaleable basket, with which I made many weary and fruitless rounds through the whole city. At noon, overwhelmed with fatigue and famished with hunger, I sat down at the door of a mosque, where the voice of the muezzim was calling the faithful to prayer. I entered to implore of God's goodness that I might be able, by his assistance, to sell the basket. Prayer being ended, the faithful left the mosque, and I found myself alone with a venerable Persian, named Saadi, who seemed lost in contemplation. Rising to go away, he passed near me, and noticing how pale I was, he said, "Friend, you are too much addicted to wine, and your health suffers from it."

"My lord," I replied, "do not believe it; I have never tasted wine; my weakness and paleness arise from my not having had any food for the last two days."

I then related to him my life, my occupation, and my wretched state. Whilst listening to me the stranger shed tears; and when I had finished speaking, he said, "God be praised, my brother! for I can put an end to your troubles: take this," putting a purse of gold into my hands; "run to the market, and buy meat, bread, and fruits for the refreshment of yourself and family. What I have given you will last you for a year to come; and in exchange, I only ask you to meet me here, at the same day and hour, every year." So saying, he departed.

I could scarcely think but that I had been dreaming; the purse, however, proved that I was indeed awake. I opened it, and found in it a hundred pieces of gold! Overjoyed, I ran to the bazaar, and, in pursuance of the orders of the benevolent donor, I purchased enough, not only to satisfy the calls of hunger, but also food of such a nourishing nature, as had never entered my house before. The whole I put into my basket, and hastened to return home. Having reached the door, I listened, being curious to know what was going on. My children were uttering lamentations, and their mother was endeavouring to quiet them by repeating, for the hundredth time, her advice, to be quiet, and not to weep, for that their father would be sure to return with something to eat. I then entered the room, exclaiming, that God had heard them, and had sent them a plentiful supply for a long time to come. But when I showed them the purse and its contents, my wife shouted out, "What! have you then killed and robbed some one? Are we to become the object of the inquiries and suspicions of the police?"

I then related my fortunate meeting with the old man, and while embracing me with tears of joy, and a conscience at ease, my family partook, with me, of a plentiful repast, at the same time invoking blessings on our unknown benefactor.

For a whole year I lived happily in this manner. The day fixed upon by the stranger having arrived, I went to the mosque, after having attired myself in a becoming manner. The Persian came and seated himself beside me. When prayers were ended, and all the worshippers had departed, he turned towards me and said, with a smiling look,

"O my brother! how has the time passed with you since our last interview?"

"Thanks to your generosity, my lord," I replied, "my life has been spent in a tranquil and happy manner."

The stranger then questioned me as to my courage, address, and love of travelling; and to all his questions I replied in a satisfactory manner, and, in my turn, asked him if I could be of any service to him.

"Noureddin," he replied, "I intend setting out on a journey, and I wish you to accompany me as my servant. I shall employ you in a respectable and becoming manner; and if you show yourself obedient and devoted to my interests, you will have no reason to repent it. The journey will last two months; look, here are thirty dinars; buy provisions, that your family may want for nothing during your absence. In eight days you must bid adieu to your wife and children, and come to meet me here, bringing a supply of rice and dates, and arming yourself with a yatagan, to defend yourself in case of our being attacked."

I then went to my wife, and told her what the stranger required of me. "He is our benefactor," she replied; "it is your duty to obey him." I spent the eight days in laying in a store of food for my family and for the journey, and on the appointed day, after embracing my wife and children, I went to the mosque, where I found the Persian. The muezzim having proclaimed the hour of prayer, we joined in it; and afterwards I followed him to a desert place, where were two fine horses well harnessed and yoked, which we unloosed and mounted, and then set out on our journey.

After having traversed deserts and mountains during a whole month, we arrived at a fertile plain, watered by a fine river, whose peaceful and limpid waters winding about a thick forest, formed it into peninsula: a pavilion, with a golden cupola, seemed to rise out of this mass of verdure, and shone in the sun's rays as if it had been on fire.

The Pavilion with the golden cupola

The Persian now said to me, "Noureddin, enter this forest, and give me an account of what you see." I obeyed, but I had scarcely walked an hour, when I saw two huge lions with manes erect. Seized with alarm, I drew back, and running away reached my master out of breath, who only laughed at my fears, and assured me that I was needlessly afraid of the monsters. He wanted me to return, but I refused, and he was obliged to come back along with me. Having approached the lions, the Persian charmed them by some magical words, on which they became as submissive as lambs, remained motionless, and permitted us to pass. We journeyed on for many hours in the recesses of the forest, meeting, to my great dread, with what appeared to be troops of horsemen, sword in hand, and giants, armed with clubs, ready to strike us. All these fantastic beings disappeared at the sight of my master, and we reached at last the pavilion which crowned the forest.

My master then said to me, "Go, Noureddin, to this pavilion; remove the belt of iron chains which fastens the gates, while I go and pray to the great Solomon to be propitious to our enterprise." I did as he commanded me; but when I let the chains fall, a frightful noise was heard, which made the earth shake under my feet. More dead than alive, I returned to the Persian, who, having finished his prayer, entered the pavilion. At the end of an hour he came out, bringing a book with him written in the sacred language. He began to read it; and when he had finished, with his countenance radiant with delight he exclaimed, "O thrice fortunate Saadi! thou possessest at last this holy book,—the sum of wisdom, the mirror of the good and the terror of the wicked! May the perusal of this garden of roses lead the children of Adam back to that original innocence from which they have so fatally departed! Hearken to these maxims and sentences, worthy to be the guides of mankind from the shepherd to the king:—

'He who learns the rules of wisdom without conforming his life to them, is like the man who tills his field but never sows any seed therein.

'Virtue does not consist in acquiring the riches of this world, but in attaching all hearts by benefits and good offices.

'If you are insensible to the sufferings of the unfortunate, you do not deserve the name of a man.

'It is better to be loaded with chains for having told the truth, than to be freed from them by means of a lie.

'A wicked person that accuses you of licentiousness should be made to blush, in his turn, by your virtues and your innocence.

'Man should remember that he is born of the earth, and that his pride will one day come to an end in it.

'Crystal is found every where; but nothing is more rare than the diamond, and hence the difference in their value.

'Instruction only bears fruit in so far as it is assisted by your own endeavours.

'The discipline of the master is of greater benefit to the child than the indulgence of the father.

'So long as the tree is young it is easy to fashion it as you please; but when it has been permitted to grow, nothing but fire can straighten it.

'Woe to the man of might, who devours the substance of the people! At last some dire calamity will, of a surety, overtake him.

'The most awful spectacle at the day of judgment will be, says the prophet, to see pious slaves in paradise, and hard and merciless masters in hell.

'Do you ask whether the ant beneath your feet has a right to complain? Yes; just as much right as you would have if crushed to atoms by an elephant.

'Encouragement towards the wicked is a wrong done to the good; and the severest attack on virtue is to be indulgent to crime.

'The perpetrator of an unjust action dies, but his memory is held in everlasting abhorrence. The just man dies, and his good actions bear fruit unto eternity.

'Be assured that thou wilt be rewarded if thine actions are good, whether thou wearest the dress of the dervise or the crown of the king.

'Would a king have nothing to fear from his enemies, let him live in peace with his subjects.

'O my brother! the world forsakes us all. Fix thy heart on the Creator of the universe, and all will be well with thee.

'What signifies it, whether we die in a stable or on a throne?

'At your morning and evening prayer be able to say, Almighty God, be pleased to remember Thy servant, who has never forgotten Thee!'

"My ambition is satisfied," resumed the Persian, "by the possession of this book; but a fortune of that description would be no fortune to you, Noureddin. You stand in need of a material treasure; and this sacred volume tells me where we ought to look for it. Quick! Mount your steed, and let us proceed so long as Solomon favours us." Leaping into our saddles, therefore, we set off at full gallop, and entering the desert, journeyed thus for two days and a night.

On the evening of the second day we arrived at a city situated on a high mountain, and surrounded with white walls which shone like silver. We passed the night under the trees of an adjoining wood; and next day, having offered up our prayers, looked about for some way of entering the city, the gates of which were shut, and within which there reigned a perfect stillness. My master went round the walls, and in his examination of them he discovered a stone slab, in which was fastened an iron ring. We endeavoured to move the slab, but could not. The Persian then ordered me to take the horses and to fasten them to the ring with our sashes; and by this means we succeeded in removing the stone, which discovered the entrance to a subterraneous passage. My master said to me, "Noureddin, follow me; by this passage we shall get into the city." On leaving the subterraneous passage we heard a noise like that which might be produced by the loud puffing of the bellows of a forge, and we supposed for a moment that the city was inhabited. This strange noise was nothing else than the hissing of two winged serpents, which advanced towards us at a frightful pace. With the sacred book in his hand the Persian advanced to meet them, and with one touch of this talisman laid them prostrate on the ground.

This obstacle being overcome, we traversed the whole city, admiring its squares, houses, mosques, and palaces. But what had become of the inhabitants? By what scourge had they been cut off, or what reason had induced them to quit so beautiful a city? How long ago was it inhabited? My mind was lost in conjectures about what seemed so far beyond my comprehension, and my master made no reply to the questions which I addressed to him. At length we stopped at the open railing of some gardens surrounding an enormous palace, which surpassed all that the imagination could conceive. Bushy thickets; orchards covered with flowers and fruits; enamelled meads, watered by murmuring streams; parterres planted with the rarest and most variegated flowers, every where met the eye. The Persian sat down under the shadow of a tree, opened the book, and commenced reading, and when he had finished ordered me to enter the palace. I reached it by a staircase that could only have been constructed by the hands of genii; it was formed of the most rare and costly marble, as were also the statues which were placed at the sides. After having walked through many spacious and magnificent apartments richly adorned, I entered a subterranean hall, still larger and more splendid. A hundred crystal lustres, brilliant with gold and precious stones, and lit up with thousands of wax-lights, shed a refulgence more dazzling than the day. Its walls were covered with paintings, in which the spirit of evil strove in vain for the mastery over the spirit of good, and a long series of the statues of justly-renowned dead princes were ranged all around. Vacant pedestals, waiting to receive monarchs still living, whose names were inscribed on them, were also to be seen. In the centre of this subterranean apartment, a throne of gold arose, incrusted with pearls and rubies. On this throne an old man was reposing, with a countenance pale as death, but whose open eyes shone with a supernatural brilliancy. I saluted him respectfully, but he made no gesture. I spoke to him, and he made no reply. Seized with astonishment and fear, I returned to my master and told him what I had seen.

"God be praised!" he said, "we are now near the end of our enterprise. Return, Noureddin, to the old man; go up to him fearlessly, and bring to me the chest on which his head rests."

I obeyed, and on my return to the subterranean hall I drew near to the throne, to which three silver steps led up. When I placed my foot on the first step the old man stood up; in spite of my surprise I ascended the second step, when, seizing a bow, he placed a keen-pointed arrow in it, and aimed it at me. Without any consideration of my benefactor's orders, I jumped backwards and took to flight anew. When the Arab saw me, he said, "Is this what you promised me? cowardly man, come with me, and you will find inestimable riches!" I then conducted him to the place where the old man was to be found. When my master was near the throne, he ascended the first step, and the old man arose; at the second step he took his bow and arrow; and at the third he shot it at my master, who received it on the sacred book, from which it rebounded as from a steel cuirass, and fell broken on the ground. The old man fell back motionless on the throne, and his eyes ceased to shine. My master then laid hold of the mysterious chest of which he had spoken to me, and took from it the magic key which opened subterranean recesses where heaps of pearls, diamonds, and rubies were deposited. The Persian allowed me to take as much as I pleased. I filled my trousers and the folds of my robe and turban with the finest pearls, the largest diamonds, and many other kinds of precious stones. As Saadi the Wise passed by all these treasures without looking at them, I said to him, "O my lord, why do you leave here all this wealth, and take away with you, as the reward of so many fatigues, an article of so little value? The book of wisdom is now useless; what man is there who does not think himself wise?"

"My son," replied the old man, "I am near the end of my career, and my life has been spent in the search after true wisdom. If I have done nothing to improve mankind, God, when I appear before Him, will reckon with me not only for the evil I shall have done, but also for the good I may have neglected to do. As for you, who have a wife and children, I approve of your wishing to provide for their future condition."

We left the enchanted city and its treasures, which I greatly regretted not being able to carry away. When we reached the open country, I looked back to gaze upon the palace and city, but they had disappeared, at which I expressed my astonishment to my master, who replied, "Noureddin, do not seek to fathom the mysteries of knowledge, but be contented to rejoice with me at the success of our journey." We then directed our faces towards Bagdad, and at the end of a short time arrived there, without meeting with any thing else worth relating. My family were rejoiced at my return and at the good fortune I had so unexpectedly met with. The old man abode with us for some time, which he employed in reading the Gulistan and in giving me useful counsels as to my future conduct.

"Noureddin," he said, "you are the possessor of great wealth; know how to make a good use of it; always remember the wretched condition in which I found you in the mosque; beware of bad company and pretended friends and flatterers; avoid covetousness, and be charitable toward the poor; remember the uncertainty of riches, and how Providence often punishes those who give way to ingratitude and pride." Besides his good advice, he would often relate to me instructive histories by way of example, and I shall not tire you too much if I repeat one of them to you.

THE STORY OF THE DERVISE ABOUNADAR.

A dervise, venerable from his age, fell ill at the house of a woman who was a widow, and who lived in a state of great poverty in the outskirts of Balsora. He was so affected by the care and zeal with which she had nursed him, that at the time of his departure he said to her, "I have noticed that your means are sufficient for yourself alone, and are not adequate for the additional support of your only son, the young Mujahid; but if you will entrust him to my care, I will do my utmost to repay through him the obligations which I am under to your care."

The good woman received the proposal with pleasure, and the dervise took his departure with the young man, stating, at the same time, that they were to be absent two years on a journey. While travelling in various countries the widow's son lived in opulence with his protector, who gave him excellent instructions, attended to him in a dangerous illness which he had, and, in short, treated him in every respect as if he had been his only son. Mujahid often said how grateful he was for such kindness, and the old man's constant reply was, "My son, gratitude is shown by actions, not words; at the proper time and place we shall see how you estimate my conduct towards you."

One day, in their journeyings, they reached a place out of the beaten road, and the dervise said to Abdallah, "We are now at the end of our travels; I am about to cause the earth to open and allow you to enter a place where you will find one of the greatest treasures in the bosom of the globe; have you courage sufficient to descend into this subterranean recess?" Mujahid declared that he might be depended upon for his obedience and zeal. The dervise then lighted a small fire, into which he threw some perfumes, and when he had pronounced some prayers the earth opened, and the dervise said to the young man, "You can now enter; remember that it is in your power to render me a great service, and that the present occasion is perhaps the only one when you can prove to me that you are not ungrateful. Do not allow yourself to be dazzled by all the wealth which you will find, but think only of getting possession of an iron chandelier with twelve branches which you will see near a door; lose no time in bringing it to me." The youth promised to attend to all that was required of him, and plunged into the subterraneous recess full of confidence in himself. Forgetting, however, what had been so expressly enjoined upon him, while he was busy filling his pockets with the gold and diamonds spread around in prodigious quantities, the entrance by which he had descended was closed. He had, however, the presence of mind to lay hold of the iron chandelier which the dervise had urged him to bring away; and although he was now, by the closing of the entrance, placed in circumstances which were enough to appal a stouter heart, he did not abandon himself to despair. While trying to discover some way of escape from a place which was likely otherwise to be his grave, he saw but too plainly that the opening had been closed upon him on account of his not having strictly followed the dervise's orders; and reflecting on the kindness and care with which he had been treated, he bitterly reproached himself for his ingratitude. At length, after a busy search and much anxiety, he was fortunate enough to discover a narrow passage that led out of this dark cavern. The opening was covered over with briers and thorns, through which he managed to struggle, and thus recovered the light of day. He looked around him every where for the dervise in order to deliver the chandelier to him, but in vain; he was not to be seen.

Unable to recognize any of the places where he had been, he walked at random, and was very much astonished to find himself, after a short time, at his mother's door, from which he had thought himself at a great distance. In reply to her inquiries respecting the dervise, he frankly told her all that had happened, and the danger he had encountered in order to gratify the fancy of the dervise; and then he showed her the riches with which he was loaded. His mother concluded, on seeing all this wealth, that the dervise only wanted to try his courage and obedience, and that he ought to take advantage of his good luck, adding, that such was no doubt the intention of the holy man.

While they gazed on these treasures with avidity, and framed a thousand dazzling projects for spending them, the whole vanished suddenly from their eyes. Mujahid then reproached himself again for his ingratitude and disobedience; and looking at the iron chandelier which alone remained of all his treasure, said, "What has happened is just. I have lost what I had no wish to render back; and the chandelier, which I desired to give to the dervise, remains with me,—a proof that it belongs to him, and that the rest was improperly obtained." So saying, he placed the chandelier in the middle of his mother's small house.

When night came on, Mujahid thought he would put a light in the chandelier, by way of turning it to some use. No sooner had he done this, than a dervise immediately appeared, who, after turning round, vanished, and threw a small coin behind him. Mujahid, whose thoughts were occupied all next day with what he had seen the evening before, wished to see what would be the event if he placed a light in each of the twelve branches. He did so, and twelve dervises immediately appeared, who, after wheeling round, also became invisible, each of them at the same time throwing down a small coin. Every day Mujahid repeated the same ceremony with the same success; but he could only make it occur once in twenty-four hours. The moderate sum with which the dervises supplied him daily was sufficient for the subsistence of himself and his mother, and for a long time this was all that he desired. By and by, however, his imagination began to feast itself with the idea of the riches of the cavern, the sight of those which he had once thought to be safe in his possession, and the schemes which he had formed as to the use to be made of his wealth; all these things had left so deep an impression on his mind, that he found it impossible to rest. He resolved, therefore, if possible, to find out the dervise, and to take him the chandelier, in the hope of obtaining the treasure by bringing to the holy man an article for which he had shown so strong a desire.

Fortunately Mujahid recollected the dervise's name, and the name of the city, Magnebi, where he dwelt. He set out on his journey as soon as possible, bidding farewell to his mother, and taking the chandelier with him, which supplied him every evening, after being lit, with the means of supporting himself, without having occasion to resort for assistance to the compassion of the faithful. When he reached Magnebi, his first inquiry was after the house where Abounadar lodged. He was so well known, that the first person he met could tell him his residence. On arriving at the house, or rather palace, he found fifty porters keeping watch at the door, each of them bearing a wand with a golden apple for its handle. The courts of the palace were crowded with slaves and domestics; indeed, no prince's residence ever displayed greater splendour. Mujahid, struck with astonishment and admiration, was reluctant to proceed further. "Either," said he to himself, "I have described the person whom I wanted imperfectly, or those to whom I spoke must have wished to make a mock of me, observing that I was a stranger. This is not the residence of a dervise, but of a king."

Mujahid was in this state of embarrassment when a man came up to him and said, "You are welcome, Mujahid; my master, Abounadar, has been long expecting you;" and so saying, he conducted him into a magnificent garden, where the dervise was seated. Mujahid, struck with the riches which he saw every where around him, would have thrown himself at his feet, but Abounadar would not permit him, and interrupted him when he was about to make a merit of bringing back the chandelier which he presented to him, by saying, "You are an ungrateful wretch. Do you think to impose upon me? I know all your thoughts; and if you had known the worth of this chandelier, you would never have brought it to me. I shall now make you acquainted with its true use." In each of the branches of the chandelier he now placed a light; and when the dervises had turned round, Abounadar gave each of them a blow with a stick, and immediately they were converted into twelve heaps of sequins, diamonds, and other precious stones. "Look," he said, "at the use to be made of this wonderful chandelier. My only reason, however, for wishing to place it in my cabinet, was on account of its being a talisman composed by a sage whom I revered; and I shall be always happy to show it to persons who visit me. To prove to you," he continued, "that curiosity is the only reason which induced me to procure the lamp, take the keys of my cellars, open them, and judge for yourself of the extent of my opulence, and say if I should not be the most insatiably avaricious of all men, not to be contented with what I have." Mujahid took the keys, and made a survey of twelve magazines so filled with every description of precious stones, that he was unable to tell which of them most deserved his admiration. Regret at having restored the chandelier, and at not having discovered its uses, now wrung his heart intensely. Abounadar seemed not to perceive this, but on the contrary loaded Mujahid with caresses, kept him for some days in his palace, and desired his servants to treat him as they would himself. On the evening before the day fixed for his departure, Abounadar said to him, "Mujahid, my son, I think, from what has occurred, that you are now cured of the frightful sin of ingratitude; however, I owe you something for having undertaken so long a journey for the purpose of bringing to me an article which I wished to possess. You may now depart; I will detain you no longer. To-morrow you will find at the gate of my palace one of my horses to carry you home. I will make you a present of it, together with a slave who will bring you two camels loaded with gold and precious stones, which you can select for yourself from among my treasures."

During the night Mujahid was restless and uneasy, and unable to think of any thing except the chandelier and its wonderful qualities. For a long time he said to himself, "It was in my power; Abounadar would never have obtained it but for me. What risks did I not encounter in the subterranean cave in order to secure it! Why is it that he is now the fortunate owner of this treasure of treasures? Is it not owing to my fidelity, or rather folly, in bringing it to him, that he now profits by the trouble and danger I underwent in the long journey I had to make? And what does he give me in return? only two miserable camels loaded with gold and precious stones, when in a moment the chandelier could supply me with ten times as much! It is Abounadar who is ungrateful, and not I who am so. What injury shall I do him by taking the chandelier? Not any; for he is rich, and wants nothing more."

These ideas determined him, at last, to do all in his power to get possession of the chandelier; and it was not difficult to do so. He knew where to find it, and having taken it, he placed it at the bottom of one of his sacks which he had filled with the treasure given to him, and put the sack, along with the others, on the back of one of the camels. His only desire now was to get away, and after having hurriedly bid farewell to the generous Abounadar, he took his departure, with his slave and camels.

When now at some considerable distance from Balsora, he sold his slave, not wishing to retain him as a witness of his former poverty, or of the source of his wealth. He purchased another, and went straight to his mother's house, whom he scarcely noticed, so absorbed was he with his treasures. His first care was to place the camels' luggage in a secure place; and, in his impatience to feast his eyes with solid riches, he placed lights in the chandelier without delay. The twelve dervises made their appearance, and he bestowed on each of them a blow with all his might, being afraid of not complying sufficiently with the laws of the talisman; but he had not noticed that Abounadar, when striking them, held his stick in his left hand. Mujahid naturally held his in his right hand, and the dervises, instead of being changed into heaps of treasure, drew from beneath their robes formidable bludgeons, with which they all belaboured him so long and so severely, that they left him nearly dead, after which they disappeared, carrying with them the camels and all their burdens, the horse, the slave, and the chandelier.

Thus, for not being contented with a large fortune honestly acquired, Mujahid fell into a state of misery from which he never recovered—a suitable punishment for his ingratitude and avarice.

The old man at last took his leave of us, and returned to Schiraz, his native place, bearing with him the blessings of all my family.

After Saadi's departure, I unhappily neglected to follow his good advice. I purchased a new and splendid residence, where I lived in great splendour and luxury. Instead of being grateful to Heaven for its bounty, I became proud and insolent. I entertained and feasted all the gay companions I could meet with, while I refused to give alms, and drove the needy from my door; in short, I spent my money rapidly, and made the worst possible use of what I had so mysteriously acquired. My treasure soon began to run low; still I lived in the same profuse extravagance, until at last all was spent, and I found that, for some time, I had been living upon credit. The truth could no longer be concealed, and, being unable to meet the demands upon me, I had to sell off the whole of my property. A small sum would have sufficed to release me, so that I might again return to my trade, and, for this purpose, I appealed for assistance to my former friends and companions. Not one of these, however, would come forward in my behalf. The produce of the sale of my house and effects was insufficient to pay my debts, and I was consequently thrown into prison, where I have remained for three years, my family, in the mean time, living upon the casual alms of the faithful. The aid you have rendered me will suffice to set me free, and I am now resolved to labour with diligence, in order to repair, as far as possible, my past folly.

Shooting at the Enchanted Keys

CONTINUATION OF THE STORY OF HASSAN ABDALLAH.

In this manner our journey was beguiled, and on the sixth day, in the morning, we entered on an immense plain, whose glittering soil seemed composed of silver dust. In the middle of the plain arose a lofty pillar of granite, surmounted by a statue of copper, representing a young man, whose right hand was stretched out open, and to each of whose fingers was suspended a key; the first was of iron, the second of lead, the third of bronze, the fourth of copper, and the fifth of gold.

This statue was the workmanship of an enchanter, and each key was a talisman; whoever was led by accident or his own free will into this desert, and became possessed of these keys, inherited the destiny attached to them. The first was the key of calamities, the second of physical sufferings, the third of death, the fourth of glory, and the last of knowledge and wealth.

I was ignorant of all these matters; but my master had become acquainted with them from a learned Indian, who had also informed him that the keys could only be obtained by shooting them down with arrows. The Arab planted his foot near to the column, and then fixing an arrow in his bow, which was of a foreign make, he shot it towards the statue, but, whether from want of skill or intentionally, the arrow did not reach halfway. He then said to me, "Hassan, you have now an opportunity of discharging your debt to me, and of purchasing your liberty. You are both strong and skilful; take this bow and arrows, and bring me down those keys." I took the bow, and perceived that it was of Persian workmanship, and made by a skilful hand. In my youth, I had accustomed myself to this exercise, and had acquired great reputation in it. Desirous of displaying my attainments, I bent the bow with all my strength, and with the first arrow I brought down the first key. Overjoyed, I took it up, and presented it to my master. "Keep it," he said; "it is the reward of your skill." With a second arrow, I brought down the leaden one. The Arab would not touch it, and I took it, and put it in my belt, along with the other. With two other arrows, I brought down two more keys—the copper key and the golden key. My companion took them up, uttering exclamations of delight.

"O Hassan," he said, "God be praised! blessed be he who trained your arm and practised your eye to such accuracy. I am proceeding happily towards the accomplishment of my object."

I was about to aim at the last key—that of death, and had raised my bow for that purpose, but he forbade me, and struck my arm to prevent my shooting. In doing this, he caused the arrow to fall and pierce my foot, producing a painful wound. Having dressed it as well as he could, he assisted me to mount my camel, and we thereupon continued our journey. After three days and nights of laborious travelling, we arrived in the neighbourhood of a small wood, where we stopped to spend the night. I set about looking for water, and some refreshing fruits, and particularly some with whose good qualities I was acquainted, but I could find nothing eatable. At last I discovered in the crevice of a rock a small spring, which invited me, by its clear and limpid waters, to refresh myself; but stooping down to drink, I heard the voice of my companion shouting to me not to taste the water, for that it was poisoned. "What matters it," I said, "whether I die of thirst or of poison?"

"This water," he said, "comes from the infernal regions, and passes through the mass of sulphur, bitumen, and metals that feed the fires in the centre of the earth; and if you drink, you will in all probability fall a victim to your imprudence."

Although bitter, the water was so clear and fresh, that without heeding what he said, I drank some of it, and feeling refreshed for the time, I agreed to proceed on our journey, but I had scarcely gone on a hundred paces, when I was attacked by the most racking pains, and with many exclamations and cries to Heaven for help, I endeavoured to moderate the speed of my camel, who was following his companion at a brisk pace. My tortures became so great, that I called aloud to the Arab, and begged him to stop; he consented, when I dismounted and walked for some time, which partly relieved me. The Arab chid me for my disobedience to his commands, and taking out a small phial from his pocket, gave me a few drops of a cordial, which in a short time completely cured me.

Towards evening we came near a high mountain, where we stopped to take a little rest. The Arab said, "God be praised, to-day will not be a fast day with us! by experience I have learned to collect a healthy and refreshing nourishment from a quarter where you would only find poison." He then went to a bush with leaves of a very thick and prickly nature, and having cut off some of them with his sabre, and stript them, of their skins, he extracted from them a yellow and sugary substance, similar in taste to figs, and I partook of the food until I was quite satisfied and refreshed. I was beginning to forget my sufferings, and hoped to pass the night in peaceful slumber, but when the moon arose my master said to me, "I expect you to perform a signal service for me; you have to ascend this mountain, and when at the summit, you must wait for sunrise; then, standing up and turning towards the East, you must offer up your devotions and descend; but take care, and do not allow yourself to be overtaken by sleep, for the emanations which arise from the ground in this place are extremely noxious, and you may suffer severely from them."

Although overwhelmed with fatigue and pain, I obeyed the Arab's orders, remembering that he had given bread to my children; and that, perhaps, should I refuse, he would abandon me in this savage wilderness. I ascended the mountain and reached the summit about midnight. The soil was bare and stony; not a shrub, not a blade of grass was to be found upon it. The extreme cold, together with fatigue, threw me into such a state of torpor that I could not resist lying down on the earth and falling asleep. I awoke at the rising of the sun to fulfil my instructions. I stood up with difficulty; my aching limbs refused to support my body; my head hung down as if made of lead, and I was unable to lift up my paralyzed arms. Making a painful effort, and holding myself up towards the East, I invoked the name of God. I then endeavoured to descend the mountain, but it was so steep, and my weakness was so great, that at the first step my limbs tottered under me, and I fell, and rolled down the mountain with frightful rapidity; stones and thorns were the only obstacles to my descent, and they tore my dress and my skin, causing me to bleed at every pore. At length I reached the bottom of the hill, near to where my master was stretched on the ground, tracing lines on it with such attention, that he did not observe in what a state I was. "God be thanked and praised," he said, without noticing me; "we were born under a happy planet; every thing succeeds with us! Thanks to you, Hassan, I have just discovered what I wanted, by measuring the shadow projected by your head from the summit of the mountain. Assist me to dig where I have stuck my lance." He raised his head, and seeing me extended on the earth, motionless, came up to me, and exclaimed, "What! in disobedience to my orders you have slept on the mountain, and imbibed its unwholesome vapours into your blood! Do not despair, however, I will cure you;" and he took from his pocket a lancet, with which, before I could offer any resistance, he made small incisions in different parts of my body, from which I bled profusely. He then dressed my wounds and bruises carefully, and I felt a little better. Seeing that I was too weak to assist him, he began to dig in the earth himself at the place which he had marked. He soon exposed to view a tomb of white marble, which he opened; it contained some human bones, and a book written in letters of gold on the skin of the gazelle.

My master began reading it with attention: at length his pale brow became lit up with pleasure, and his eyes sparkled with delight.

"Hassan Abdallah," he said to me, "this book teaches me the way to the mysterious city; we shall soon enter into Aram, built on columns, where no mortal has ever as yet penetrated; it is there that we shall find the principle of earthly riches, the germ of the metallic mines which God has placed in the centre of the earth."

"My lord," I replied, "I share with you in your joy; but this treasure is of little or no advantage to me; I would rather, I assure you, be poor and in good health at Cairo, than rich and in wretchedness here."

"Ungrateful man!" he exclaimed; "I am labouring for your advantage as well as for my own, intending to share with you the fruit of our journey, as I have done until now."

"True," I said, "but, alas! all the ill fortunes and calamities fall to me." However, after some further assurances on the part of the Arab, I became pacified, and the same day, after having laid in a stock of fruits, we reascended our camels, and continued our journey towards the East.

We journeyed thus for three days and nights. The fourth day in the morning we perceived in the horizon the appearance of a large mirror, which reflected the sunbeams. On drawing near we saw that it was a river of quicksilver; it was crossed by a bridge of crystal, without balustrades, but so narrow and slippery that no man in his senses would think of attempting to pass it. My master told me to unsaddle the camels, to let them feed at liberty, and to prepare woollen slippers with thick and soft soles for both of us; and having ordered me to walk behind him without looking to the right hand or to the left, he crossed the bridge with a firm step, and I followed him trembling.

After we had crossed the river and proceeded for some hours, we found ourselves at the entrance of a gloomy valley. It was surrounded on all sides with black rocks, hard as iron, and here and there on the ground were spread human bones, bleached by time. Through the dark foliage of the shrubs which grew there might be seen the undulating and scaly forms of serpents gliding along. I retreated hastily from this den of horror, but could not discover the spot at which I had entered, the rocks seeming every where to rise up like the walls of a great cavern.

I began to weep, and said to my companion, "You have led me on to death by the path of suffering and misery; I shall never see my wife and children again. Why have you torn me away from my poor but peaceful home?"

"Hassan," he said to me, "be a man! Have patience; we shall soon get out of this horrible place. Wait a few moments, and I will show you how we may escape." So saying, he sat down on the ground, and, opening the mysterious book, began turning over the pages and reading in it as calmly as if he had been sitting in his own house. After a short time he called to me, and said, "My friend, call up your courage, your task is easy; you are a skilful marksman; take this bow and arrows; examine the valley until you meet with a huge serpent with a black head, kill him and bring his head and heart to me."

"Alas!" I said, weeping, "is this indeed a thing so easy for me? Why will you not do it yourself? We are too fortunate not to be molested by these monsters; why should we go in search of them?" Upon this he started up with a fierce aspect, and, drawing his sword, swore that he would kill me that instant if I did not obey him.

"Do you see all these bones?" he said. "They are the bones of men who disobeyed me, and who died in consequence by my hand." Trembling, I took the bow and arrows, and went among the rocks where the serpents were to be found. Selecting one which appeared to me to answer the description given me, I took aim at its head, and, invoking the assistance of Heaven, discharged my arrow. The serpent, mortally wounded, sprung up, and twisting and contorting itself in a frightful manner, fell dead on the ground. When I was certain that he was dead, I took my knife, cut off his head, and took out his heart. With these bloody trophies I returned to my master, who received me with a smiling countenance. "Forgive me," he said, "for employing threats towards you; in reality I was anxious to save you from a miserable fate. The men to whom these bones belonged died here of hunger by their own fault; they proved deficient in courage, and I was compelled, in spite of myself, to abandon them to their fate."

"Now," he continued, "come and assist me to make a fire."

I collected dry leaves and small branches of trees, of which he made a small heap; then turning an enchanted diamond towards the sun, which was then in its meridian, a ray of light issued from the precious stone which set the materials in a blaze. He next drew from under his robe a small iron vase and three phials; the first, of ruby, contained the elements of winds; the second, of emerald, contained a ray of moonlight; and the third, which was of gold, contained the blood of a ph[oe]nix. All these substances he placed in the vase, and added the heart and brain of the serpent. He then opened the book and put the vase on the fire, pronouncing at the same time some words which to me were unintelligible. When he had finished, he uncovered his shoulders, as the pilgrims do at their departure, and dipping a portion of his garment in the mixture, handed it to me, desiring me to rub his back and shoulders with it. As I did so I observed the skin swell out and wings spring forth, which, visibly increasing in size, soon reached the ground. The Arab spread them and began to rise in the air. Fear of remaining in this doleful place lent me courage, and laying hold with all my might of the end of his girdle, I was borne up along with him, and in a few moments we bade farewell to the black rocks of this fatal valley. Presently, as we pursued this aërial tour, we found ourselves soaring above an immense plain, surrounded by a precipice of crystal, tinged with azure and purple. The earth seemed formed of golden dust, and the pebbles upon it looked like precious stones. Before us were the lofty walls of a city crowded with magnificent palaces and delicious gardens. Lost in admiration of this glorious scene, the Arab forgot to keep his wings moving, and we descended rapidly towards the ground, which I of course reached first, he falling upon me. I then perceived his wings gradually diminish, and by degrees wholly disappear. When I noticed this to him, he replied, that, unfortunately, science was limited in its powers; it enabled him to construct wings of great power, but could not avail for their preservation beyond a certain time. "To become the possessor," said he, "of the ingredients which you saw me employ in forming these wings, I have spent thirty years of my life, the lives of many men, and money sufficient for a king's ransom. The wings helped me but for a few moments, long enough, however, for my purpose; they have borne me to glory and fortune. Rejoice, Hassan Abdallah; behold Aram, the city built on columns, the mysterious city!"

The Escape of Hassan Abdallah and the Arab from the Enchanted Valley

We then approached the walls; they were built of alternate layers of bricks of gold and silver. The battlements were of marble, cut and sculptured by the hands of genii. There were eight gates in the walls,—the number of the gates of paradise; the first was of silver, the second of gold, the third of agate, the fourth of coral, the fifth of pearl, the sixth of topaz, the seventh of emerald, and the eighth of ruby.

The Arab informed me that this city had been built by the famous enchanter Tchedad, the son of Aad, who had exhausted upon it all the treasures of earth, sea, and sky. He wanted in his pride to rival the glory of the Almighty by this piece of workmanship; but God, to punish him, struck him and his family with lightning at the very instant he and they were solemnly taking possession of the palace. An impenetrable veil hangs over the city ever since, and no one has been able to discover it.

We went forward, invoking the name of God; the streets were lined with palaces adorned with columns of marble, agate, and all kinds of costly materials; streams of odoriferous waters embalmed and refreshed the atmosphere; trees of a wondrous form furnished a delicious shelter from the rays of the sun, and in their branches birds of song produced concerts of ravishing sweetness. The very air that one breathed seemed to fascinate the mind, and to lift it up to heaven.

The Arab, taking me by the hand, conducted me towards the palace of Tchedad; its construction, in point of art and splendour of adornment, was unspeakably magnificent. Terraces, formed of coloured crystal, were supported on a thousand columns of gold. In the midst of the palace was an enchanted garden, where the earth, breathing of musk, bore fruits and flowers of marvellous richness and beauty. Three rivers surrounded the garden, flowing with wine, rose-water, and honey. In the centre of the garden there was a pavilion, whose dome, formed of a single emerald, overshadowed a throne of gold covered with pearls and rubies. On the throne there was a small chest of gold; the Arab opened it, and found in it a red powder. "Throw away this dust," I said, "and fill the casket with precious stones."

"Poor fool that you are," he replied; "this dust is the source of all the riches of the world; it is red sulphur. A small portion of it is sufficient to change into gold the basest metals. With it I can build palaces, found cities, purchase the life of men and the admiration of beautiful women. I can even, if I please, cause myself to become prince and king; but I cannot by it prolong my life a single day, or efface an hour from my by-past existence. God alone is great! God alone is eternal!"

Whilst he thus spoke, I employed myself in collecting precious stones and pearls, filling with them my girdle, pockets, and turban.

"Unhappy man!" he cried, "what are you doing? You will bring down upon us the vengeance of Heaven. We are only permitted to touch this casket; and if we should attempt to carry out of the valley a leaf from one of these trees, or a stone from off the ground, instantaneous death would be our lot."

I immediately emptied my pockets, much to my regret, and followed my master, not however without often turning my head aside to look at the incalculable riches spread around me. Fearing that I should fall a prey to the seductions of wealth, my master took me by the hand and led me out of the city. We quitted it by the path by which we came, but more slowly than we approached. When we arrived at the crystal precipice it opened before us, and we passed through it; when we had done so, we looked about in vain for the wonderful plain and the city,—they could no longer be seen. We found ourselves on the brink of the river of quicksilver, and crossed the bridge. Our camels were feeding on the flowery herbage, and I ran to mine with delight, as to an old friend. After refastening our girths, we mounted and set out on the road to Egypt. We were three months in reaching Cairo. During all this time I suffered many privations; my health was destroyed, and I endured every kind of evil. From some fatality, the cause of which was unknown to me at the time, I alone was exposed to all the accidents of the journey, while my companion continued in health and comfort, passing safely through every danger. I discovered afterwards that all my misfortunes arose from my having in my possession the enchanted keys. This was one day towards the close of our journey, when the Arab confessed to me that he was aware of this fatal quality of theirs, and that it was in order to free himself from it that he purchased me. When I wanted to throw away the accursed keys, he withheld me. "Patience and resignation," said he, "and these virtues only, can exhaust their evil influence, and for your own sake I would advise you to keep them to the end. All will turn out eventually for your good."

A few days after receiving this communication we arrived at Cairo, and I immediately ran to my home, the door of which was open and broken, and the interior occupied by crowds of famished and prowling dogs, who had taken up their abode there. A neighbour, who heard me calling out in an agony of despair, opened her door, and said to me, "Hassan Abdallah, is that you? Well may you be astounded! Know that some time after your departure,—that is, about five months ago,—some thieves, knowing that you were absent, and that there was no male slave left to take care of your house, broke into your house during the night, insulted the women, and went off with all the property that you had left. Your mother died a few days after, in consequence. Your wife, in her destitution, resolved to go to Alexandria, to her brother. The caravan which she accompanied was attacked by the Arabs of the desert, who, being enraged at the resistance they met with, put all to the sword without mercy."

On hearing these sad tidings, I shed many tears, and returning to the Arab, accused him with being the cause of all my misfortunes. "God is the author and end of all things," he said to me, and then, taking me by the hand, led me along with him. It appeared that on the same day he had hired a magnificent palace, to this he now compelled me to repair and reside with him; and for my consolation, he told me that he would share with me the treasures of science, and teach me to read in the book of alchemy.

Here we resided a long time: whenever his costly fancies caused him to be in want of money, he used to have several hundred-weight of lead conveyed secretly to him, and when it was melted he threw some small portions of red sulphur into it, and in a moment the vile metal was changed into the purest gold. In the midst of all this luxury, I continued ill and unhappy; my feeble body was unable to support the weight, or to endure the contact of the rich clothes and the precious stuffs with which I was covered. The most delicate food was served up to me in vain, and the most delicious wines; I only felt disgusted and disinclined towards them all. I had superb apartments, beds formed of sweet smelling and costly woods, and divans of purple; but sleep, in spite of all, was a stranger to my eyes.

I called on death, but he refused to come to me. The Arab, on the other hand, passed his time in pleasure and feasting.

The palace gardens extended to the banks of the Nile; they were planted with the rarest trees, brought at a great expense from India, Persia, China, and the isles. Machines, constructed with great skill, raised the water of the Nile, and caused it to fall in fresh and brilliant jets into marble reservoirs,

"'Mid orange groves and myrtle bowers, that breathed a gale of fragrance round,"

mingled with the perfume of jasmines and roses; there were silken pavilions, embroidered with gold, and supported on pillars of gold and silver; brilliant lamps, enclosed in globes of crystal, shed over all a light soft and effulgent as that of the moon.

There, on each returning night, the Arab received his companions, and treated them with the utmost magnificence. His liberality made every one who approached him his friend, and they styled him the Great, the Magnificent.

He would sometimes come to see me at the pavilion, where my illness compelled me to remain, a solitary prisoner. On one such occasion, he paid me his visit after a night of pleasure, early in the morning. He was heated with wine, his face red, and his eyes shining with a strange lustre. He sat down beside me, and taking hold of my hand, began singing, and when he had concluded, shut his eyes, leaned his head on his breast, and appeared to fall asleep. Alarmed at length at his unnatural stillness, I leaned over to him; his breathing had ceased, he had expired.

Perceiving that all help was useless, I began to rummage his pockets, his girdle, and his turban, in the hope of finding the keys of happiness and of wisdom, but could not discover them. I thereupon, in spite of my bad state of health, and without losing a moment, laid hold of the casket containing the book of alchemy and the red sulphur; and considering that I might lawfully regard myself as the legitimate proprietor, I carried it secretly to my former house, which I had previously caused to be rebuilt and provided with new furniture.

Returning to the palace just as I had left it, I began to cry aloud, and to ask for help; the slaves and servants ran immediately to know what was the matter, and I then sent them to bring the best physician, even the caliph's, if he could be found. When the medical men came they declared that the stranger had died by the will of God. I then gave orders for the funeral.

His body, attired in the richest vestments, was placed, exposed to view, in a coffin of aloe-wood, lined with gold. A cloth of a marvellously fine tissue, which had been manufactured for a Persian prince, served for a coverlet. Fifty servants, all dressed in mourning attire, bore, in turns, the coffin on their shoulders; and every good mussulman who passed by, hastened to lend his assistance, if it were only by a helping hand.

A considerable number of women, hired for the purpose, followed the bier, uttering plaintive cries.

The keepers of the mosque sung sacred verses, and the crowd repeated, "God is God! There is no God but God! He alone is eternal." In this order, accompanied by numerous friends whom the Arab had made by his generosity, we proceeded to the cemetery, southward of the city, and near to the gate of Bab-el-Masr (the gate of victory). I gave a purse of gold to a skilful architect, with orders to raise a tomb to the memory of my master.

Returning to the palace, it fell to my lot, of course, to preside at the funeral repast. This painful duty was scarcely over, when I saw some officers from the caliph arrive, who were commanded by his order to take possession of the wealth contained in the palace, and which belonged to him, as a stranger's heir. I was driven away, and left the palace, taking with me, in appearance, nothing but the dress which I wore, but, in reality, the owner of an inestimable treasure.

Betaking myself to my house, I resolved to live there an unknown and peaceful life, passing the time in the study of the sciences, and only using the red sulphur to impart benefit to others in secret.

A curious and jealous neighbour having ascended the terrace of my house one evening, and seen me at work, effecting the transmutation of the lead into gold, told my secret to his wife, who repeated it at the bath, and next morning all Cairo was acquainted with it.

The report reached the ears of the caliph, Theilon, who sent for me, and told me that he knew I possessed the great secret of knowledge, and that if I would share it with him, he would overwhelm me with honours, and associate me with him in rank. I refused to the impious man the distinguished favour which God had denied to him. Transported with rage, he caused me to be loaded with chains, and thrown into a gloomy dungeon; and being baffled in his attempts to penetrate my secret, he placed the casket and the book under the care of a person on whose fidelity he could depend, hoping to force the secret from me by the sufferings which he made me endure. In this state I have lived for forty years. By my persecutor's orders, I have been made to undergo all kinds of privations and tortures, and only knew of his death by my being relieved from punishment.

This morning, when kneeling on the ground at my devotions, I put my hand on a strange and hard substance. Looking at it, I perceived that it was the fatal keys which I had years ago buried under the floor of my dungeon. They were so worn by rust and damp, that they crumbled into powder in my hand, and I then thought that God intended to have pity upon me, and that my afflictions were about to end, either by death or the alleviation of my sufferings. A few moments after, your officers came and set me at liberty.

"Now, O king!" continued the old man, "I have lived long enough, since I have been permitted to approach the greatest and most upright of monarchs."

Mohammed, overjoyed at performing an act of justice, thanked Heaven for having sent him such a treasure, and being desirous to prove its reality, he caused one thousand hundred-weight of lead to be melted in immense caldrons; and having mixed some of the red powder in the fiery mass, and pronounced over it the magical words dictated to him by the old man, the base metal was instantly changed into pure gold.

The caliph, in order to propitiate the favour of Heaven, resolved to employ this treasure in the building of a mosque which should transcend by its magnificence every other in the world. He collected architects from all the neighbouring countries, laid before them the plan of a vast edifice, unfettered by the difficulties or expense of its execution.

The architects traced out an immense quadrangle, the sides of which faced the four cardinal points of the heavens. At each corner a tower of prodigious height was placed, of admirable proportions; the top of the structure was surrounded with a gallery and crowned with a dome of gilt copper. On each side of the edifice one thousand pillars were raised, supporting arches of an elegant curve and solid construction, and on the arches terraces were laid out with balustrades of gold of exquisite workmanship. In the centre of the edifice an immense pavilion was erected, whose construction was of so light and elegant a nature, that one would have thought it reached from earth to heaven. The vault was inlaid with azure-coloured enamel and studded with golden stars. Marbles of the rarest kinds formed the pavement, and the walls consisted of a mosaic formed of jasper, porphyry, agate, mother-of-pearl, sapphires, rubies, and other precious stones. The pillars and arches were covered with arabesques and verses from the Koran, carved in relief, and painted. No wood was employed in the building of this wonderful edifice, which was therefore fire-proof. Mohammed spent seven years in erecting this celebrated mosque, and expended on it a sum of two millions of dinars.

Although so old, Hassan Abdallah recovered his health and strength, and lived to be a hundred years of age, honoured with the esteem and the friendship of the caliph.

The mosque built by the caliph Mohammed is still to be seen at Cairo, and is the largest and the finest of all the mosques of that great city.

One day, very shortly after the completion of the mosque, the caliph and Hassan Abdallah were absent for three days on a journey. Mohammed communicated to no one but his first vizir his intention; but on his return he assembled his whole court, and informed them that the object of the expedition had been to bury the casket, with the book and the powder, where it was impossible they could ever be discovered. "I have done," added Mohammed, "what I could to consecrate this wonderful treasure, but I would not trust even myself any longer with so dangerous a temptation."

II.

SOLIMAN BEY AND THE THREE STORY-TELLERS.

Soliman Bey, passing one day along a street in Cairo, saw three common-looking men seated at the door of a coffee-house and sipping their cup of mocha. From their dull and meaningless looks he conjectured that they were under the influence of haschich[2]. After looking at them attentively, the bey saluted them, and was pursuing his way, when he suddenly found himself obliged to stop, as a long train of camels, heavily laden, blocked up the street and prevented him from passing on. The bey, having nothing better to do, amused himself by scrutinizing attentively the eaters of haschich, who were old men. A warm discussion seemed to be going on among them; they raised their arms, vied with each other who should cry the loudest, and made the strangest possible grimaces; but owing to the distance at which he stood, he was unable to hear what they said. On his return home, being curious to know the subject of their dispute, he sent his officer to beg these three originals to wait upon him.

[2] An intoxicating drug, like opium.

When they arrived, he said to them, "What were you disputing about, my friends, when I passed you?"

"May Allah prolong your days!" replied one of them; "we were disputing about which of us it was to whom the salutation belonged that your highness addressed to us, for each of us took that honour to himself."

The bey burst out laughing. "I greeted," he said, after a moment's reflection, "him among you who did the greatest number of foolish things while intoxicated by the haschich."

"It was I, my lord," they all at once exclaimed.

"Stop," replied the bey; "let each of you tell me one of the tricks played him by the haschich, and the honour of my greeting shall be his who shall have committed the greatest act of folly; and do you begin," added the bey, pointing to one of the men.

THE FIRST STORY-TELLER.

"Be it known to you, my lord," said the first story-teller, "that a short time ago I had in my purse a thousand piastres, which were enough for my expenses, and I was contented with my lot. One day, however, I had been taking a walk, and on my return I sat down to rest and chewed a bit of haschich, took my coffee, and lit my pipe; in two or three hours my head began to buzz. I went out again and walked about the streets. In front of a coffee-house I noticed some men collected round an *improvisatore*, who was singing and accompanying himself on the timbrel. I sat down in the circle and asked for coffee. I lighted my pipe and commenced listening. The improvisatore depicted a young girl. Oh, how beautiful she was! it was impossible not to love her. Compared with her Iyleika[3] was but as a star in the presence of the sun, and Ablia[3] but as the dirt of the street. I was so captivated by his description of the beautiful girl, that when he ceased I gave him all the money I had about me.

[3] Personages who figure in Arabian legends.

"Next day, at the same hour, while the haschich was boiling in my brain, I ran to the coffee-house, where the improvisatore was commencing the continuation of his yesterday's story. He now told how paladins and padishahs disputed for the possession of my adorable Haridée, and how she disdained their love and refused their offers. I became more distracted this time than before, and the improvisatore got from me twice as much as he did the day before. I gave him all that I had, even to the last farthing.

"Next day I never left my little seat at the *café*. The improvisatore struck his tambourine this time with more vehemence while singing the charms of the beautiful Haridée. He then began to relate how Haridée was in love with a certain worthless fellow. At this it was impossible to tell what I felt; the hydra of jealousy devoured my heart and poured a maddening poison through my veins. I became as one deprived of all sense and feeling. But stop; the parents have separated the lovers and plunged them in an ocean of tears. I again breathed more freely, and emptied my pockets to fill the purse of the improvisatore.

"Thus were passed many days in succession. The flame of love and the stings of jealousy tormented me without ceasing. The haschich did its part unremittingly, and threw me at one moment into fire, and at another into ice and snow, hurling me from the height of bliss into the depths of misery. My fortunes fell with me, and I soon became totally destitute. But my thoughts were otherwise taken up than with eating or drinking; my love for Haridée had become the only source to me of life and action. In this way, with empty stomach and purse, I went one day to the *café* after having paid a few paras for a little haschich. I listened—the voice of the improvisatore trembled; in truth he wept, and grief was depicted on his features.

"'What has happened?' I asked, drawing near to him.

"'Poor Haridée!' he replied.

"'What is the matter? What has taken place?' I exclaimed.

"'She is dead!' he muttered.

"I wept, I tore my clothes, and fled I scarce knew where. When the first transports of my despair had subsided, I saw pass before my eyes, still under the influence of the haschich, the funeral of Haridée. The mournful cry of 'There is no God but God, and Mahomet is his prophet,' echoed in my ears, amidst the outcries and the lamentations of the women. I ran like a madman from street to street, while the crowd followed on my path with the coffin of Haridée, and the frightful groans and cries burst forth louder and louder on my ears. At length, worn out, and sore all over, I fell down in a state of complete unconsciousness, and when I came to myself, I perceived that I was at the threshold of my own home. I arose, and endeavoured to recal past events, which as they woke up in my memory caused me to feel the utmost surprise. My purse was empty, my heart broken, and the blood was flowing down my face, for in my fall I had cut open my head. After remaining a whole day in the house, I took a small piece of haschich and went to a coffee-house near at hand, where my friend the landlord poured me out a cup of mocha, and gave me a pipe. It was there that I met my two friends, and received from you, my gracious lord, a look, and a nod."

"This story is not a bad one," replied Soliman Bey, "but do not too hastily take to yourself the honour of my greeting; let me hear first what the others have to say."

THE SECOND STORY-TELLER.

"Know, my lord," replied the second, "that I was formerly a rich and respected merchant, with a beautiful wife and fine children. My life was like a morning of spring-time—clear, peaceful, and balmy. But haschich has ruined the structure of my happiness, and destroyed it from the roof to the foundations. One day when I had imbibed a little of this fatal poison, I was reclining, after the labours of the day, on my sofa, sipping from time to time a mouthful of coffee, and inhaling a whiff of perfumed *latakia*. My wife was occupied at my side in embroidery, and my children were at play in the room, which they made ring again with their shrill voices. At length, my brain becoming overpowered by the vapours of the haschich, the thickening fancies began to chase each other in quick succession, and my imagination at length became morbidly excited. The cries of my children seemed insupportable to me. I ordered them several times to be quiet, but the brats, wild with their games and noise, paid no attention to me. At last I lost patience, laid hold of my stick, and rapped angrily on the floor, ordering them sternly to be quiet. In the midst of this fit of anger, I stopped short, all of a sudden. The floor of my apartment emitted a hollow sound, as if there were a vault beneath it. The haschich suggested to me that there might be hidden treasure down below. 'Oh, oh,' I said to myself, 'I must not be in a hurry. If I should discover the treasure in my wife's presence, she will foolishly run and trumpet it about to all our neighbours. What good would that do? Let me consider, then, what I shall do to get her away.' Intoxicated as I was, there was no need to deliberate long. I darted from my seat, exclaiming, 'Woman! thou art separated from me by a triple divorce!'[4]

[4] This is the legal form of pronouncing a divorce among the Mahometans.

"My wife became pale as death. She threw aside her embroidery, and rose up.

"'What is the matter, my dear husband? What has happened? Of what have I been guilty?'

"'Don't say a word! And hasten this moment to leave the house, with your children.'

"'But pray inform me, my lord and master, when and how I have given you any cause of complaint? We have now lived together twelve years in perfect peace and harmony, and never been but on the most affectionate terms; tell me.'

"'No more explanations,' I replied; 'here are a thousand *grouches*[5]. Go to your room, and take of the furniture as much as you require, and return to your father's house.'

[5] A small coin, in circulation in Turkey, about the value of eighteenpence of our money. It is probably from the same root as the German *groschen*.

"Sadly and sorrowfully she thereupon proceeded to collect her wearing apparel, uttering mournful cries and lamentations, and taking her children with her, left the house.

"'Now!' I exclaimed, with satisfaction, 'now, I am quite alone.'

"'Silence, Abou-Kalif,' whispered the haschich to me; 'don't be in such haste. Suppose you find this treasure, who knows but that at the first meeting of haschich-eaters, you will disclose your discovery to all the world. Put yourself to the proof beforehand, by some effectual means, and thus find out if your tongue have sufficient self-command to keep still, and not say one word too much.'

"Faithful to the voice of my inward monitor, I arose, and taking from my chest the sum of five hundred grouches, went to pay a visit to the vali[6].

[6] The public executioner.

"'Here,' said I to him, 'take this money, and give me on the soles of my feet five hundred blows with a leathern thong, and, while laying them on, ask me if I have seen, found, or discovered any thing?'

"The man was extremely surprised at my request, and refused to comply with it; but the people about him said that my body was my own, and that I was at liberty to dispose of it as I thought proper. 'Take his money,' they said to him, 'and give him a hearty flogging.'

"The vali, shrugging his shoulders, gave the signal; I was laid on the ground, my feet were tied together, and the lash whistled and sung on my bare feet. At each blow, the question I had suggested was asked, and I replied in the negative. This system of question and answer went on till the last blow. Fairly exhausted with the pain, I fell down the moment I attempted to stand up. I therefore crawled along on my knees, and reached my ass, on whose back I managed, somehow or other, to raise myself, and thus reached my home.

"A few days' rest having restored me in some measure, I resolved to prosecute my search for the hidden treasure. But the haschich, to which I had not forgotten on that day to pay my usual respects, stopped me in my intention. 'O Abou-Kalif,' it muttered in my ear, 'you have not yet put yourself sufficiently to the proof. Are you now in a fit state to resist all attempts to make you disclose your secret? Submit to another trial, my good fellow!' This suggestion was all-powerful, and I submitted forthwith. I drew from my strong-box one thousand grouches, and went to the aga of the Janissaries. 'Take this money,' I said to him, 'and give me in exchange for it a thousand stripes with a thong on the bare back; asking me between the blows, Have you seen any thing? have you found any thing? have you discovered any thing?' The aga did not keep me waiting long for a reply,— and having pocketed the money, bestowed upon me most faithfully the full complement of the lashes desired.

"At the conclusion of the whipping my soul seemed hovering on my lips, as if about to leave my mutilated body, which was quite prostrated by the infliction. I was obliged to be carried to my ass, and it was many days before I could set my feet to the ground. When I had recovered a little, I recollected all the details of the strange adventure which had brought upon me the acute anguish that I felt in every part of my body; and the more I reflected on the matter, the more vividly I saw the fatal consequences that would follow from too much confidence in the suggestions inspired by the haschich. I cursed the hateful ideas produced by the vapours of this drug, and promised myself that I would amend my ways, and repair, as far as possible, my injustice to my wife. But at the very moment when this praiseworthy resolution arose in my brain and diffused its odours there, like a fresh-opening flower, my hand, from the strength of habit, sought for the tin box that lay under my pillow, and drew from it a white particle, which I placed in my mouth, as if to mock all the weak efforts of my will. In fact, while my mind was occupied in planning a final rupture with the perfidious hempen-seed, my enemy stole in on me like a midnight robber by night, imposed his yoke, and overthrew completely all my good intentions. Unwittingly I found myself again in the power of the enemy. 'Well, Abou-Kalif,' he said, 'arise. The precautions you have taken are sufficiently severe; it is time to set to work, and not allow the favourable moment to escape, otherwise you may repent it.' In this manner spake the delusive poison working within me, and I was wholly in its power, incapable of resistance. I rose from my bed with a frightful pain in my back and sides, dragged myself along towards the mysterious flag-stone, and with my heart beating violently, and my brain cloudy and obscured, I set to work to raise the stone, which speedily yielded to my efforts. In a state of the highest excitement, I sat down on the edge of the cavern with my legs hanging down into it, and my hands leaning on its sides; I scarcely dared to look downwards. The haschich, however, pushed me forwards, and seemed to press on my shoulders. My hands at last yielded, and I fell down. O my sovereign and master, do not ask where I found myself; enough that I felt myself stifled. The noisome matter into which I had fallen up to the chin, being disturbed and agitated, had emitted exhalations which fairly suffocated me. I strove to cry out, but in vain. I fainted, and lost all consciousness.

"Meanwhile, whilst I, pursued by the fatal influence of the haschich, had fallen over the edge of the precipice, where I was now struggling, my disconsolate wife had begged her father to allow her to make inquiry respecting me. 'I know,' she said, weeping, 'that a sudden attack of madness has seized him, and that the real cause of his sending me away, as well as of all the evil that has just befallen us, is the haschich. Let no curse fall upon him. No doubt my husband will change his conduct with regard to me, as I cannot reproach myself with any thing; I will therefore go and see what has happened to him.' 'Well, my child, you may go,' replied her father; 'I shall not seek to hinder you.' She went, and knocked at the door, but no one replied. She then inquired of the neighbours if Abou-Kalif was at home; they said they had not seen him leave the house for the last week. On being told this, she had the door burst open, and, followed by a crowd of neighbours of both sexes, searched for me for a long time in vain. At last, however, I was discovered, half dead and stifled. They pulled me out, cleansed and sweetened me, and attired me in a fresh suit of clothes; after which I left the house to breathe the fresh air and recover myself. It was not long, however, before the haschich regained its old dominion over me, and led me to the coffee-house, where you saw me, and condescended to honour me with your greeting."

"Not quite so soon," exclaimed the bey, holding his sides with laughter; "your story is also a very good one, but before I award to you the honour of my salutation, I must hear what your other companion has got to say."

THE THIRD STORY-TELLER.

"Sovereign and master," commenced the third eater of haschich, "no longer ago than a week I was so happy and satisfied with my lot, that in truth I would not have exchanged it even for your own. I had a house filled with every comfort, plenty of money, and a wife who was a miracle of beauty. One day this charming better half of myself, after having passed all the day in the bath, returned from it looking so clean, fresh, and rosy, that my head, where the haschich which I had been taking for the last hour and a half was breeding disorder, became on fire and was lost. My eyes grew intoxicated with my wife, as if I had then beheld her beauty for the first time, and my heart bounded like the holy waves of the Nile during a storm.

"'Dear cousin,' I cried, for she was my cousin as well as my wife, 'how captivating you are to-day! I am over head and ears in love with you again!'

"At this instant the haschich suggested to me to divorce her immediately in order to contract a new marriage and taste again the bliss of a first union. No sooner said than done; I pronounced the prescribed phrase, and the next day I celebrated a new marriage with her[7]. When the festivities were over, I conducted my relations and guests to the door, which, from absence of mind, I had forgotten to shut.

[7] The Mahometans may immediately take back the woman whom they had divorced, but a fresh marriage ceremony must take place.

"'Dear cousin,' said my wife to me when we were alone, 'go and shut the street door.'

"'It would be strange indeed if I did,' I replied. 'Am I just made a bridegroom, clothed in silk, wearing a shawl and a dagger set with diamonds, and am I to go and shut the door? Why, my dear, you are crazy; go and shut it yourself!'

"'Oh indeed!' she exclaimed; 'am I, young, robed in a satin dress, with lace and precious stones, am I to go and shut the court-yard door? No, indeed, it is you who have become crazy, and not I. Come, let us make a bargain,' she continued; 'and let the first who speaks get up and bar the door.'

"'Agreed,' I replied, and straightway I became mute, and she too was silent, while we both sat down, dressed as we were in our nuptial attire, looking at each other, and seated on opposite sofas. We remained thus for one—two—hours. During this time thieves happening to pass by, and seeing the door open, entered and laid hold of whatever came to their hand. We heard footsteps in the house, but opened not our mouths; the robbers came even into our room, and saw us seated, motionless and indifferent to all that took place. They continued therefore their pillage, collecting together every thing valuable, and even dragging away the carpets from beneath us; they then laid hands on our own persons, which they despoiled of every article worth taking, while we, in the fear of losing our wager, said not a word.

"Having thus cleared the house, the thieves departed quietly, but we remained on our seats, saying not a syllable. Towards morning a police officer came round on his tour of inspection, and, seeing our door opened, walked in. Having searched all the rooms and found no one, he entered the apartment where we were seated, and inquired the meaning of what he saw. Neither my wife nor I would condescend to reply. The officer became angry, and ordered our heads to be cut off. The executioner's sword was just about to perform its office, when my wife cried out, 'Sir, he is my husband, spare him!'

"'Oh, oh!' I exclaimed, overjoyed and clapping my hands, 'you have lost the wager; go, shut the door.'

"I then explained the whole affair to the police officer, who shrugged his shoulders and went away, leaving us in a truly dismal plight. Immediately after I went to a coffee-house, where you deigned to honour me with a salutation."

At the conclusion of this story the bey, who was ready to die with laughter, exclaimed, "This time it is you who are in the right; you are truly entitled to my respects."

III.

THE STORY OF PRINCE KHALAF AND THE PRINCESS OF CHINA.

Prince Khalaf was the son of an aged khan of the Nagäi-Tartars. The history of his time makes honourable mention of his name. It relates that he surpassed all the princes of the age in beauty, in wisdom, and in valour; that he was as learned as the greatest doctors of his age; that he could fathom the deepest mysteries of the commentaries on the Koran; and that he knew by heart the sayings of the prophet: it speaks of him, in short, as the hero of Asia and the wonder of the East.

This prince was the soul of the councils of his father Timurtasch. When he gave advice, the most accomplished statesmen approved it, and could not sufficiently admire his prudence and wisdom. If, moreover, it were necessary to take up arms, he was immediately seen at the head of the troops of the state, seeking out the enemy, engaging them and vanquishing them. He had already won several victories, and the Nagäis had rendered themselves so formidable by their repeated successes, that the neighbouring nations did not venture to quarrel with them.

Such was the prosperous state of affairs in the khan's dominions, when an ambassador from the sultan of Carisma arrived at the court of Timurtasch, and demanded in the name of his master that the Nagäis should henceforth pay him a yearly tribute; he added that in default he would come in person, with an overwhelming force, and compel them to submit, at the same time depriving their sovereign of his crown as a punishment for his refusal. On hearing this arrogant message, the khan immediately assembled his council in order to decide whether to pay the tribute rather than risk a war with so powerful an enemy, or whether to treat his menaces with contempt and prepare to repel the invaders. Khalaf, with the majority of the council, were of the latter opinion, and the ambassador being dismissed with a refusal, took his departure for Carisma.

The khan lost no time in sending deputies to the neighbouring nations, in order to represent to them that it was to their interest to unite with him against the sultan of Carisma, whose ambition now exceeded all bounds, and who would undoubtedly exact the same tribute from them if he should succeed in conquering the Nagäis. The deputies succeeded in these negotiations; the neighbouring nations and tribes, and amongst them the Circassians, engaged to join in the proposed confederation, and to furnish among them a quota of fifty thousand men. On this promise, the khan proceeded to raise fresh troops, in addition to the army which he already had on foot.

While the Nagäis were making these preparations, the sultan of Carisma assembled an army of two hundred thousand men, and crossed the Jaxartes at Cogende. He marched through the countries of Ilac and Saganac, where he found abundance of provisions; and had advanced as far as Jund, before the army of the khan, commanded by prince Khalaf, was able to take the field, in consequence of the Circassians and the other auxiliary troops not having been able sooner to join him. As soon as these succours arrived, Khalaf marched direct towards Jund, but he had scarcely passed Jenge Kemt, when his scouts informed him that the enemy was close at hand, and was advancing to attack him. The young prince immediately ordered his troops to halt, and proceeded to arrange them in order of battle.

The two armies were nearly equal in numbers, and the men who composed them equally courageous. The battle which ensued was bloody and obstinate. The sultan did all that a warrior skilled in the conduct of armies could do; and the prince Khalaf, on his side, more than could be expected from so young a general. At one time the Nagäi-Tartars had the advantage, at another they were obliged to yield to the Carismians; at last both parties, alternately victors and vanquished, were obliged by the approach of night to sound a retreat. The combat was to have recommenced in the morning; but, in the mean time, the leader of the Circassians went secretly to the sultan, and offered to abandon the cause of the Nagäis, provided the sultan would pledge himself, on oath, never to exact tribute from the Circassians upon any pretence whatever. The sultan having consented, the treaty was confirmed, and the Circassian leader, instead of occupying his place next day in the army of the khan, detached his troops from the Nagäis, and took the road back to his own country.

This treachery was a terrible blow to prince Khalaf, who, seeing himself now much weakened in numbers, would have withdrawn for the time from the conflict; but there was no possibility of retreat. The Carismians advanced furiously to the charge, and taking advantage of the ground which allowed them to extend their lines, they surrounded the Nagäis on all sides. The latter, notwithstanding that they had been deserted by their best auxiliaries, did not lose their courage. Animated by the example of their prince, they closed their ranks, and for a long time firmly sustained the terrible onset of their enemies. At last, however, resistance became hopeless, and Khalaf, seeing all hope at an end, thought of nothing but his escape, which he fortunately succeeded in effecting. The moment the sultan was apprised of his flight, he sent six thousand horsemen to endeavour to capture him, but he eluded their pursuit, by taking roads that were unknown to them; and after a few days' hard riding through unfrequented and unknown tracts, arrived at his father's court, where he spread sorrow and consternation, by the disastrous tidings he brought.

If this piece of news deeply afflicted Timurtasch, the intelligence he next received drove him to despair. An officer who had escaped from the battle, brought word that the sultan of Carisma had put to the sword nearly all the Nagäis, and that he was advancing with all possible speed, fully resolved to put the whole family of the khan to death, and to absorb the nation into his own kingdom. The khan then repented of having refused to pay the tribute, but he fully recognized the force of the Arab proverb, "When the city is in ruins, what is the use of repentance?" As time pressed, and it was necessary to fly, for fear of falling into the hands of the sultan, the khan, the princess Elmaze (diamond), his wife, and Khalaf, made a selection of all their most precious treasures, and departed from the capital, Astracan, accompanied by several officers of the palace, who refused to abandon them in their need, as well as by such of the troops as had cut their way through the ranks of their enemies with the young prince.

They directed their march towards Bulgaria; their object being to beg an asylum at the court of some sovereign prince. They had now been several days on their journey, and had gained the Caucasus, when a swarm of some four thousand suddenly poured down upon them from that range. Although Khalaf had scarcely a hundred men with him, he steadily received the furious attack of the robbers, of whom numbers fell; his troops, however, were by degrees overpowered and slaughtered, and he himself remained in the power of the bandits, some of whom fell upon the spoil, whilst others butchered the followers of the khan. They only spared the lives of that prince, his wife, and his son, leaving them, however, almost naked in the midst of the mountains.

It is impossible to describe the grief of Timurtasch when he saw himself reduced to this extremity. He envied the fate of those whom he had seen slain before his eyes, and giving way to despair, sought to destroy himself. The princess burst into tears, and made the air resound with her lamentations and groans. Khalaf alone had strength to support the weight of their misfortunes; he was possessed of an indomitable courage. The bitter lamentations which the khan and his wife uttered were his greatest trouble. "Oh, my father! Oh, my mother!" said he, "do not succumb to your misfortunes. Remember that it is God who wills that you should be thus wretched. Let us submit ourselves without a murmur to his absolute decrees. Are we the first princes whom the rod of justice has struck? How many rulers before us have been driven from their kingdoms, and after wandering about for years in foreign lands, sharing the lot of the most abject of mortals, have been in the end restored to their thrones! If God has the power to pluck off crowns, has He not also the power to restore them? Let us hope that He will commiserate our misery, and that He will in time change into prosperity the deplorable condition in which we now are."

Prince Khalaf holding back his father

With such arguments he endeavoured to console his father and mother, and to some extent succeeded; they experienced a secret consolation, and at last allowed themselves to take comfort. "So be it, my son," said the khan, "let us bow to Providence; and since these evils which encompass us are written in the book of fate, let us endure them without repining." At these words the royal party made up their minds to be firm under their misfortunes, and proceeded to continue their journey on foot, the robbers having taken their horses. They wandered on for a long time, living upon the fruits they found in the valleys; but at length they entered upon a desert, where the earth yielded nothing upon which they could subsist, and now their courage deserted them. The khan, far advanced in years, began to feel his strength fail him; and the princess, worn out with the fatigue of the journey she had made, could scarcely hold out any longer. In this predicament, Khalaf, although wofully tired himself, had no resource but to carry them by turns on his shoulders. At last all three, overwhelmed by hunger, thirst, and weariness, arrived at a spot abounding with frightful precipices. It was a hill, very steep, and intersected with deep chasms, forming what appeared to be dangerous passes. Through these, however, seemed to be the only way by which to enter upon the vast plain which stretched out beyond; for both sides of the hill were so encumbered with brambles and thorns, that it was impossible to force a way through. When the princess perceived the chasms, she uttered a piercing cry, and the khan at length lost his patience. He rushed furiously forward. "I can bear this no longer," said he to his son; "I yield to my hard destiny; I succumb to so much suffering. I will throw myself headlong into one of these deep gulfs, which, doubtless, Heaven has reserved for my tomb. I will escape the tyranny of wickedness. I prefer death to such a miserable existence."

The khan, yielding himself up to the frenzy which had taken possession of him, was on the point of throwing himself down one of the precipices, when prince Khalaf seized him in his arms and held him back. "Oh, my father!" said he, "what are you doing? Why give way to this transport of fury? Is it thus that you show the submission you owe to the decrees of Heaven? Calm yourself. Instead of displaying a rebellious impatience of its will, let us endeavour to deserve by our constancy its compassion and favour. I confess that we are in a deplorable state, and that we can scarcely take a step without danger amidst these abysses; but there may be another road by which we can enter the plain: let me go and see if I can find one. In the mean time, my lord, calm the violence of your transports, and remain near the princess; I will return immediately."

"Go, then, my son," replied the khan, "we will await you here; do not fear that I will any longer give way to despair."

The young prince traversed the whole hill without being able to discover any path. He was oppressed with the deepest grief; he threw himself on the ground, sighed, and implored the help of Heaven. He rose up, and again searched for some track that would conduct them to the plain. At length he found one. He followed it, returning thanks to Heaven for the discovery, and advanced to the foot of a tree which stood at the entrance of the plain, and which covered with its shade a fountain of pure transparent water. He also perceived other trees laden with fruit of an extraordinary size. Delighted with this discovery, he ran to inform his father and mother, who received the news with the greater joy, since they now began to hope that Heaven had begun to compassionate their misery.

Khalaf conducted them to the fountain, where all three bathed their faces and their hands and quenched the burning thirst which consumed them. They then ate of the fruits which the young prince gathered for them, and which, in their state of exhaustion from want of food, appeared to them delicious. "My lord," said Khalaf to his father, "you see the injustice of your complaints. You imagined that Heaven had forsaken us; I implored its succour, and it has succoured us. It is not deaf to the voice of the unfortunate who put their whole trust in its mercy."

They remained near the fountain two or three days to repose and recruit their wasted strength. After that they collected as much of the fruit as they could carry, and advanced into the plain, hoping to find their way to some inhabited place. They were not deceived in their expectations; they soon perceived before them a town which appeared large and splendidly built. They made their way to it, and having arrived at the gates, resolved to remain there and wait for night, not wishing to enter the town during the day, covered with dust and perspiration, and with what little clothing the robbers had left them, travel-worn and rent with brambles. They selected a tree which cast a delicious shade, and stretched themselves upon the grass at its foot. They had reposed there some time, when an old man came out of the town and directed his steps to the same place, to enjoy the cool shade. He sat down near them after making them a profound obeisance. They in turn saluted him, and then inquired what was the name of the town. "It is called Jaic," replied the old man. "The king, Ileuge-Khan, makes it his residence. It is the capital of the country, and derives its name from the river which flows through it. You must be strangers since you ask me that question." "Yes," replied the khan, "we come from a country very far from here. We were born in the kingdom of Chrisnia, and we dwell upon the banks of the Caspian Sea; we are merchants. We were travelling with a number of other merchants in Captchak; a large band of robbers attacked our caravan and pillaged us; they spared our lives, but have left us in the situation in which you see us. We have traversed mount Caucasus, and found our way here without knowing where we were directing our steps."

The old man, who had a compassionate heart for the distress of his neighbour, expressed his sympathy for their misfortunes, and, to assure them of his sincerity, offered them shelter in his house. He made the offer with such cordiality, that, even if they had not needed it, they would have felt some difficulty in refusing.

As soon as night set in he conducted them to his home. It was a small house, very plainly furnished; but every thing was neat, and wore the appearance rather of simplicity than of poverty. As the old man entered he gave some orders in an undertone to one of his slaves, who returned in a short time followed by two boys, one of whom carried a large bundle of men's and women's clothes ready made, the other was laden with all sorts of veils, turbans, and girdles. Prince Khalaf and his father each took a caftan of cloth and a brocaded dress with a turban of Indian muslin, and the princess a complete suit. After this their host gave the boys the price of the clothes, sent them away, and ordered supper. Two slaves brought the table and placed upon it a tray covered with dishes of china, sandal, and aloe-wood, and several cups of coral perfumed with ambergris. They then served up a repast, delicate, yet without profusion. The old man endeavoured to raise the spirits of his guests; but perceiving that his endeavours were vain, "I see clearly," said he, "that the remembrance of your misfortunes is ever present to your minds. You must learn how to console yourselves for the loss of the goods of which the robbers have plundered you. Travellers and merchants often experience similar mishaps. I was myself once robbed on the road from Moussul to Bagdad. I nearly lost my life on that occasion, and I was reduced to the miserable condition in which I found you. If you please I will relate my history; the recital of my misfortunes may encourage you to support yours." Saying this, the good old man ordered his slaves to retire, and spoke as follows.

THE STORY OF PRINCE AL ABBAS.

I am the son of the king of Moussul, the great Ben-Ortoc. As soon as I had reached my twentieth year, my father permitted me to make a journey to Bagdad; and, to support the rank of a king's son in that great city, he ordered a splendid suite to attend me. He opened his treasures and took out for me four camel-loads of gold; he appointed officers of his own household to wait upon me, and a hundred soldiers of his guard to form my escort.

I took my departure from Moussul with this numerous retinue in order to travel to Bagdad. Nothing happened the first few days; but one night, whilst we were quietly reposing in a meadow where we had encamped, we were suddenly attacked so furiously by an overwhelming body of Bedouin Arabs, that the greater part of my people were massacred almost before I was aware of the danger. After the first confusion I put myself at the head of such of the guards and officers of my father's household as had escaped the first onslaught, and charged the Bedouins. Such was the vigour of our attack, that more than three hundred fell under our blows. As the day dawned, the robbers, who were still sufficiently numerous to surround us on all sides, seeing our insignificant numbers, and ashamed and irritated by the obstinate resistance of such a handful of men, redoubled their efforts. It was in vain that we fought with the fury of desperation; they overpowered us; and at length we were forced to yield to numbers.

They seized our arms and stripped off our clothes, and then, instead of reserving us for slaves, or letting us depart, as people already sufficiently wretched, in the state to which we were reduced, they resolved to revenge the deaths of their comrades; and were cowards and barbarians enough to slaughter the whole of their defenceless prisoners. All my people perished; and the same fate was on the point of being inflicted on me, when making myself known to the robbers, "Stay, rash men," I exclaimed, "respect the blood of kings. I am prince Al Abbas, only son of Ben-Ortoc, king of Moussul, and heir to his throne." "I am glad to learn who thou art," replied the chief of the Bedouins. "We have hated thy father mortally these many years; he has hanged several of our comrades who fell into his hands; thou shalt be treated after the same manner."

Thereupon they bound me; and the villains, after first sharing among them all my baggage, carried me along with them to the foot of a mountain between two forests, where a great number of small grey tents were pitched. Here was their well-concealed camping ground. They placed me under the chief's tent, which was both loftier and larger than the rest. Here I was kept a whole day, after which they led me forth and bound me to a tree, where, awaiting the lingering death that was to put an end to my existence, I had to endure the mortification of finding myself surrounded by the whole gang, insulted with bitter taunts, and every feeling miserably outraged.

I had been tied to the tree for some considerable time, and the last moments of my life appeared fast approaching, when a scout came galloping in to inform the chief of the Bedouins that a splendid chance offered itself seven leagues from thence; that a large caravan was to encamp the next evening in a certain spot, which he named. The chief instantly ordered his companions to prepare for the expedition; this was accomplished in a very short time. They all mounted their horses, and left me in their camp, not doubting but at their return they would find me a corpse. But Heaven, which renders useless all the resolves of men which do not agree with its eternal decrees, would not suffer me to perish so young. The wife of the robber chief had, it seems, taken pity on me; she managed to creep stealthily, during the night, to the tree where I was bound, and said to me, "Young man, I am touched by thy misfortune, and I would willingly release thee from the dangers that surround thee; but, if I were to unbind thee, dost thou think that thou hast strength enough left to escape." I replied, "The same good God who has inspired thee with these charitable feelings will give me strength to walk." The woman loosed my cords, gave me an old caftan of her husband's, and showing me the road, "Take that direction," said she, "and thou wilt speedily arrive at an inhabited place." I thanked my kind benefactress, and walked all that night without deviating from the road she had pointed out.

The next day, I perceived a man on foot, who was driving before him a horse, laden with two large packages. I joined him, and, after telling him that I was an unfortunate stranger, who did not know the country, and had missed my way, I inquired of him where he was going. "I am going," replied he, "to sell my merchandise at Bagdad, and I hope to arrive there in two days." I accompanied this man, and only left him when I entered that great city; he went about his business, and I retired to a mosque, where I remained two days and two nights. I had no desire to go forth into the streets; I was afraid of meeting persons from Moussul, who might recognize me. So great was my shame at finding myself in this plight, that far from thinking of making my condition known, I wished to conceal it, even from myself. Hunger at length overcame my shame, or rather I was obliged to yield to that necessity which brooks no refusal. I resolved to beg my bread, until some better prospect presented itself. I stood before the lower window of a large house, and solicited alms with a loud voice. An old female slave appeared almost immediately, with a loaf in her hand, which she held out to me. As I advanced to take it, the wind by chance raised the curtain of the window, and allowed me to catch a glimpse of the interior of the chamber; there I saw a young lady of surpassing beauty; her loveliness burst upon my vision like a flash of lightning. I was completely dazzled. I received the bread without thinking what I was about, and stood motionless before the old slave, instead of thanking her, as I ought to have done.

I was so surprised, so confused, and so violently enamoured, that doubtless she took me for a madman; she disappeared, leaving me in the street, gazing intently, though fruitlessly, at the window, for the wind did not again raise the curtain. I passed the whole day awaiting a second favourable breeze. Not until I perceived night coming on, could I make up my mind to think of retiring; but before quitting the house, I asked an old man, who was passing, if he knew to whom it belonged. "It is," replied he, "the house of Mouaffac, the son of Adbane; he is a man of rank, and, moreover, a rich man and a man of honour. It is not long since he was the governor of the city, but he quarrelled with the cadi, who found means of ruining him in the estimation of the caliph, and thereby caused him to lose his appointment."

With my thoughts fully taken up by this adventure, I slowly wandered out of the city, and entering the great cemetery determined to pass the night there. I ate my bread without appetite, although my long fast ought to have given me a good one, and then lay down near a tomb, with my head resting on a pile of bricks. It was with difficulty that I composed myself to sleep: the daughter of Mouaffac had made too deep an impression upon me; the remembrance of her loveliness excited my imagination too vividly, and the little food I had eaten was not enough to cause the usual tendency to a refreshing sleep. At length, however, I dozed off, in spite of the ideas that filled my imagination; but my sleep was not destined to be of long duration; a loud noise within the tomb soon awoke me.

Alarmed at the disturbance, the cause of which I did not stay to ascertain, I started up, with the intention of flying from the cemetery, when two men, who were standing at the entrance of the tomb, perceiving me, stopped me, and demanded who I was, and what I was doing there. "I am," I replied, "an unfortunate stranger, whom misfortune has reduced to live upon the bounty of the charitable, and I came here to pass the night, as I have no place to go to in the town." "Since thou art a beggar," said one of them, "thank Heaven that thou hast met with us; we will furnish thee with an excellent supper." So saying, they dragged me into the tomb, where four of their comrades were eating large radishes and dates, and washing them down with copious draughts of raki.

They made me sit near them, at a long stone that served as a table, and I was obliged to eat and drink, for politeness' sake. I suspected them to be what they really were, that is to say, thieves, and they soon confirmed my suspicions by their discourse. They began to speak of a considerable theft they had just committed, and thought that it would afford me infinite pleasure to become one of their gang; they made me the offer, which threw me into great perplexity. You may imagine that I had no desire to associate myself with such fellows, but I was fearful of irritating them by a refusal. I was embarrassed, and at a loss for a reply, when a sudden event freed me from my trouble. The lieutenant of the cadi, followed by twenty or thirty *asas* (archers) well armed, entered the tomb, seized the robbers and me, and took us all off to prison, where we passed the remainder of the night. The following day, the cadi came and interrogated the prisoners. The thieves confessed their crime, as they saw there was no use in denying it; for myself, I related to the judge how I had met with them, and, as they corroborated my statement, I was put on one side. The cadi wished to speak to me in private, before he set me free. Accordingly, he presently came over to me, and asked what took me into the cemetery where I was caught, and how I spent my time in Bagdad. In fact, he asked me a thousand questions, all of which I answered with great candour, only concealing the royalty of my birth. I recounted to him all that had happened to me, and I even told him of my having stopped before the window of Mouaffac's house to beg, and of my having seen, by chance, a young lady who had charmed me.

At the name of Mouaffac I noticed the eyes of the cadi sparkle, with a curious expression. He remained a few moments immersed in thought; then, assuming a joyous countenance, he said, "Young man, it depends only on thyself to possess the lady thou sawest yesterday. It was doubtless Mouaffac's daughter; for I have been informed that he has a daughter of exquisite beauty. Though thou wert the most abject of beings, I would find means for thee to possess the object of thine ardent wishes. Thou hast but to leave it to me, and I will make thy fortune."

I thanked him, without being able to penetrate his designs, and then by his orders followed the aga of his black eunuchs, who released me from the prison, and took me to the bath.

Whilst I was there, the judge sent two of his *tchaous* (guards) to Mouaffac's house, with a message that the cadi wished to speak to him upon business of the greatest importance. Mouaffac accompanied the guards back. As soon as the cadi saw him coming he went forward to meet him, saluted him, and kissed him several times. Mouaffac was in amazement at this reception.

"Ho! ho!" said he to himself, "how is this, that the cadi, my greatest enemy, is become so civil to me to-day? There is something at the bottom of all this."

"Friend Mouaffac," said the judge, "Heaven will not suffer us to be enemies any longer. It has furnished us with an opportunity of extinguishing that hatred which has separated our families for so many years. The prince of Bozrah arrived here last night. He left Bozrah without taking leave of his father the king. He has heard of your daughter; and from the description of her beauty which he has received, he has become so enamoured of her, that he is resolved to ask her in marriage. He wishes me to arrange the marriage,— a task which is the more agreeable to me, as it will be the means of reconciling us."

"I am astounded," replied Mouaffac, "that the prince of Bozrah should have condescended to confer upon me the honour of marrying my daughter; and that you of all men should be the chosen means of communicating this happiness to me, as you have always shown yourself so anxious to injure me."

"Let us not speak of the past, friend Mouaffac," returned the cadi; "pray let all recollection of what we have done to annoy each other be obliterated in our happiness at the splendid connexion which is to unite your daughter with the prince of Bozrah; let us pass the remainder of our days in good fellowship."

Mouaffac was naturally as good and confiding as the cadi was crafty and bad: he allowed himself to be deceived by the false expressions of friendship that his enemy displayed. He stifled his hatred in a moment, and received without distrust the perfidious caresses of the cadi. They were in the act of embracing each other, and pledging an inviolable friendship, when I entered the room, conducted by the aga. This officer, on my coming out of the bath, had clothed me with a beautiful dress, which he had ready, and a turban of Indian muslin, with a gold fringe that hung down to my ear, and altogether my appearance was such as fully to bear out the statements of the cadi.

"Great prince," said the cadi as soon as he perceived me, "blessed be your feet, and your arrival in Bagdad, since it has pleased you to take up your abode with me. What tongue can express to you the gratitude I feel for so great an honour? Here is Mouaffac, whom I have informed of the object of your visit to this city. He consents to give you in marriage his daughter, who is as beautiful as a star."

Mouaffac then made me a profound obeisance, saying, "O son of the mighty, I am overwhelmed with the honour you are willing to confer upon my daughter; she would esteem herself sufficiently honoured in being made a slave to one of the princesses of your harem."

Judge of the astonishment that this discourse caused me. I knew not what to answer. I saluted Mouaffac without speaking; but the cadi, perceiving my embarrassment, and fearing lest I should make some reply which would destroy his plot, instantly took up the conversation.

"I venture to submit," said he, "that the sooner the marriage contract is made in presence of the proper witnesses the better." So saying, he ordered his aga to go for the witnesses, and in the mean time drew up the contract himself.

When the aga arrived with the witnesses, the contract was read before them. I signed it, then Mouaffac, and then the cadi, who attached his signature the last. The judge then dismissed the witnesses, and turning to Mouaffac said, "You know that with great people these affairs are not managed as with persons of humble rank. Besides, in this case you readily perceive that silence and despatch are necessary. Conduct this prince, then, to your house, for he is now your son-in-law; give speedy orders for the consummation of the marriage, and take care that every thing is arranged as becomes his exalted rank."

I left the cadi's house with Mouaffac. We found two mules richly caparisoned awaiting us at the door; the judge insisted upon our mounting them with great ceremony. Mouaffac conducted me to his house; and when we were in the court-yard dismounted first, and with a respectful air presented himself to hold my stirrup,—a ceremony to which of course I was obliged to submit. He then took me by the hand and conducted me to his daughter, with whom he left me alone, after informing her of what had passed at the cadi's.

Zemroude, persuaded that her father had espoused her to a prince of Bozrah, received me as a husband who would one day place her upon the throne,— and I, the happiest of men, passed the day at her feet, striving by tender and conciliating manners to inspire her with love for me. I soon perceived that my pains were not bestowed in vain, and that my youth and ardent affection produced a favourable impression upon her. With what rapture did this discovery fill me! I redoubled my efforts, and I had the gratification of remarking that each moment I made advances in her esteem.

In the mean time Mouaffac had prepared a splendid repast to celebrate his daughter's nuptials, at which several members of his family were present. The bride appeared there more brilliant and more beautiful than the houris. The sentiments with which I had already inspired her, seemed to add new lustre to her beauty.

The next morning I heard a knock at my chamber-door; I got up and opened it. There stood the black aga of the cadi carrying a large bundle of clothes. I thought that perhaps the cadi had sent robes of honour to my wife and myself, but I was deceived.

"Sir adventurer," said the negro in a bantering tone, "the cadi sends his salutations, and begs you to return the dress he lent you yesterday to play the part of the prince of Bozrah in. I have brought you back your own old garment, and the rest of the tatters, which are more suited to your station than the other."

I was astounded at the application; my eyes were opened, and I saw through the whole malicious scheme of the cadi. However, making a virtue of necessity, I gravely restored to the aga the robe and turban of his master, and retook my own old caftan, which was a mass of rags. Zemroude had heard part of the conversation; and seeing me covered with rags, "O heavens!" she exclaimed, "what is the meaning of this change, and what has that man been saying to you?"

"My princess," I replied, "the cadi is a great rascal, but he is the dupe of his own malice. He thinks he has given you a beggar for a husband, a man born in the lowest grade, but you are, indeed, the wife of a prince, and my rank is in no way inferior to that of the husband, whose hand you fancy you have received. I am to the full the equal of the prince of Bozrah, for I am the only son of the king of Moussul, and am heir to the kingdom of the great Ben-Ortoc; my name is Al Abbas." I then related my history to her, without suppressing the least circumstance. When I had finished the recital,

"My prince," said she, "even were you not the son of a great king, I should love you none the less; and, believe me, that if I am overjoyed to learn the circumstance of your exalted birth, it is but out of regard to my father, who is more dazzled by the honours of the world than I; my only ambition is to possess a husband who will love me alone, and not grieve me by giving me rivals."

I did not fail to protest that I would love her, and her alone, all my life, with which assurance she appeared delighted. She then summoned one of her women, and ordered her to proceed with all speed and secrecy to a merchant's, and buy a dress, ready made, of the richest materials that could be procured. The slave who was charged with this commission acquitted herself in the most satisfactory manner. She returned speedily, bringing a magnificent dress and robe, and a turban of Indian muslin as handsome, even handsomer, than what I had worn the previous day, so that I found myself even more gorgeously dressed than on the occasion of my first interview with my father-in-law. "Well, my lord," said Zemroude, "do you think the cadi has much reason to be satisfied with his work? He thought to heap reproaches on my family, and he has bestowed upon it an imperishable honour. He thinks that we are now overwhelmed with shame. What will be his grief when he knows that he has conferred such a benefit upon his enemy? But before he is made aware of your birth, we must invent some means of punishing him for his wicked designs against us. I will take that task upon me. There is in this city a dyer, who has a daughter most frightfully ugly. I will not tell you further," she continued, checking herself. "I will not deprive you of the pleasure of the surprise. I shall only let you know that I have conceived a project which will drive the cadi nearly mad, and make him the laughingstock of the court and the city."

She then dressed herself in plain clothes, and covering her face with a thick veil, asked my permission to go out, which I granted her. She went alone, repaired to the cadi's house, and placed herself in one corner of the hall, where the judge gave audience.

He no sooner cast his eyes upon her, than he was struck with her majestic figure; he sent an officer to ask who she was, and what she desired. She answered that she was the daughter of an artisan in the town, and that she wished to speak to the cadi on important private business. The officer having borne her answer to the cadi, the judge made a sign to Zemroude to approach, and enter his private apartment, which was on one side of the court; she complied, making a low obeisance. When she entered the cadi's private apartment, she took her seat upon the sofa, and raised her veil. The cadi had followed her, and as he seated himself near her, was astonished at her beauty.

"Well! my dear child," said he, patronizingly, "of what service can I be to you?"

"My lord," she replied, "you, who have the power to make the laws obeyed, who dispense justice to rich and poor alike, listen, I pray you, to my complaint, and pity the unfortunate situation in which I am placed."

"Explain yourself," replied the judge, already moved, "and I swear by my head and my eyes that I will do every thing that is possible, ay, and impossible, to serve you."

"Know then, my lord," replied Zemroude, "that, notwithstanding the attractions which Heaven has bestowed upon me, I live in solitude and obscurity in a house, forbidden not only to men, but even to women, so that even the conversation of my own sex is denied me. Not that advantageous proposals were at one time wanting for my hand; I should have been married long ago, if my father had not had the cruelty to refuse me to all who have asked me in marriage. To one he says, I am as withered as a dead tree; to another, that I am bloated with unnatural fat; to this one, that I am lame, and have lost the use of my hands; to that one, that I have lost my senses, that I have a cancer on my back, that I am dropsical; in fact, he wishes to make me out a creature not worthy the society of human beings, and has so decried me, that he has at length succeeded in making me the reproach of the human race; nobody inquires about me now, and I am condemned to perpetual celibacy."

When she ceased speaking she pretended to weep, and played her part so well that the judge allowed himself to be deceived.

"What can be the reason, my angel," said he, "that your father prevents your marrying? What can his motive be?"

"I know not, my lord," replied Zemroude; "I cannot conceive what his intentions can be; but I confess my patience is exhausted. I can no longer live in this state. I have found means to leave home, and I have escaped to throw myself into your arms, and to implore your help; take pity on me, I implore you, and interpose your authority, that justice may be done to me, otherwise I will not answer for my life."

"No, no," replied he, "you shall not die, neither shall you waste your youth in tears and sighs. It only remains with yourself to quit the darkness in which your perfections are buried, and to become this very day the wife of the cadi of Bagdad. Yes, lovely creature, more fair than the houris, I am ready to marry you, if you will consent."

"My lord," replied the lady, "even were not your station one of the most dignified and honourable in the city, I could have no objection to give you my hand, for you appear to be one of the most amiable of men; but I fear that you will not be able to obtain the consent of my father, notwithstanding the honour of the alliance."

"Don't trouble yourself upon that point," replied the judge, "I will pledge myself as to the issue; only tell me in what street your father lives, what his name is, and what his profession."

"His name is Ousta Omar," replied Zemroude; "he is a dyer, he lives upon the eastern quay of the Tigris, and in front of his door is a palm-tree laden with dates."

"That is enough," said the cadi; "you can return home now; you shall soon hear from me, depend upon my word."

The lady, after bestowing a gracious smile upon him, covered her face again with her veil, left the private chamber, and returned to me.

"We shall be revenged," she said, laughing gaily; "our enemy, who thought to make us the sport of the people, will himself become so."

The judge had scarcely lost sight of Zemroude, ere he sent an officer to Ousta Omar, who was at home. "You are to come to the cadi," said the man, "he desires to speak with you, and he commanded me to bring you before him." The dyer grew pale at these words, he thought that some one had lodged a complaint against him before the judge, and that it was on that account the officer had come to fetch him. He rose, however, and followed in silence, but in great uneasiness.

As soon as he appeared before the cadi, the judge ordered him into the same chamber where he had had the interview with Zemroude, and made him sit upon the same sofa. The artisan was so astonished at the honour paid him, that he changed colour several times.

"Master Omar," said the cadi, "I am glad to see you; I have heard you spoken very well of this long time past. I am informed that you are a man of good character, that you regularly say your prayers five times a day, and that you never fail to attend the great mosque on Friday; besides, I know that you never eat pork, and never drink wine nor date-spirits; in fact, that whilst you are at work one of your apprentices reads the Koran."

"That is true," replied the dyer; "I know above four thousand *hadits* (sayings of Mahomet), and I am making preparations for a pilgrimage to Mecca."

"I assure you," replied the cadi, "that all this gives me the greatest pleasure, for I passionately love all good mussulmen. I am also informed that you keep concealed at home a daughter of an age to marry; is that true?"

"Great judge," answered Ousta Omar, "whose palace serves as a haven and refuge for the unfortunate who are tossed about by the storms of the world, they have told you true. I have a daughter who is old enough, in all conscience, to be married, for she is more than thirty years old; but the poor creature is not fit to be presented to a man, much less to so great a man as the cadi of Bagdad; she is ugly, or rather frightful, lame, covered with blotches, an idiot; in a word, she is a monster whom I cannot take too much pains to hide from the world."

"Indeed," said the cadi, "that is what I expected, master Omar. I was certain that you would thus praise your daughter; but know, my friend, that this blotchy, idiotic, lame, frightful person, in short, this monster, with all her defects, is loved to distraction by a man who desires her for his wife, and that man is myself."

At this speech the dyer seemed to doubt whether he were awake; he pinched himself, rubbed his eyes, and then looking the cadi full in the face, said,

"If my lord, the cadi, wishes to be merry, he is master; he may make a jest of my child as much as he pleases."

"No, no," replied the cadi, "I am not joking, I am in love with your daughter, and I ask her in marriage."

The artisan at these words burst into a fit of laughter. "By the prophet," cried he, "somebody wants to give you something to take care of. I give you fair warning, my lord, that my daughter has lost the use of her hands, is lame, dropsical."

"I know all about that," replied the judge, "I recognize her by her portrait. I have a peculiar liking for that sort of girls, they are my taste."

"I tell you," insisted the dyer, "she is not a fit match for you. Her name is Cayfacattaddhari (the monster of the age), and I must confess that her name is well chosen."

"Come, come!" replied the cadi, in an impatient and imperious tone, "this is enough, I am sick of all these objections. Master Omar, I ask you to give me this Cayfacattaddhari just as she is, so not another word."

The dyer, seeing him determined to espouse his daughter, and more than ever persuaded that some person had made him fall in love with her upon false representations for fun, said to himself, "I must ask him a heavy *scherbeha* (dowry): the amount may disgust him, and he will think no more of her."

"My lord," said he, "I am prepared to obey you; but I will not part with Cayfacattaddhari unless you give me a dowry of a thousand golden sequins beforehand."

"That is rather a large sum," said the cadi, "still I will pay it you." He immediately ordered a large bagful of sequins to be brought, a thousand were counted out, which the dyer took after weighing them, and the judge then ordered the marriage contract to be drawn out. When, moreover, it was ready for signature, the artisan protested that he would not sign it except in the presence of a hundred lawyers at least.

"You are very distrustful," said the cadi; "but never mind, I will satisfy your wishes, for I don't intend to let your daughter slip through my fingers." He thereupon sent immediately for all the neighbouring doctors, alfayins, mollahs, persons connected with the mosques and courts of law, of whom far more crowded in than the dyer required.

When all the witnesses had arrived at the cadi's, Ousta Omar spoke thus,

"My lord cadi, I give you my daughter in marriage, since you absolutely require me to do so; but I declare before all these gentlemen that it is on condition, that if you are not satisfied with her when you see her, and you wish afterwards to repudiate her, you will give her a thousand gold sequins, such as I have received from you."

"Well! so be it," replied the cadi, "I promise it before all this assembly. Art thou content?" The dyer replied in the affirmative, and departed, saying that he would send the bride.

He had scarcely left the house before the enamoured judge gave orders to have an apartment furnished in the most splendid manner to receive his new bride. Velvet carpets were laid down, new draperies hung up, and sofas of silver brocade placed round the walls, whilst several braziers perfumed the chamber with delicious scents. All was at length in readiness, and the cadi impatiently awaited the arrival of Cayfacattaddhari. The fair bride, however, not making her appearance so speedily as his eagerness expected, he called his faithful aga, and said, "The lovely object of my affections ought to be here by this time, I think. What can detain her so long at her father's? How slow the moments appear which retard my happiness!" At length his impatience could brook no longer delay, and he was on the point of sending the aga to Ousta Omar's, when a porter arrived carrying a deal case covered with green taffeta.

"What hast thou got there, my friend," inquired the judge.

"My lord," replied the porter, placing the box on the ground, "it is your bride; you have only to take off the covering and you will see what she is like."

The cadi removed the cloth and saw a girl three feet and a half high: she had a lank visage covered with blotches, eyes sunk deep in their sockets and as red as fire, not the least vestige of a nose, but above her mouth two horrid wide nostrils like those of a crocodile. He could not look at this object without horror; he hastily replaced the cover, and, turning to the porter, cried,

"What am I to do with this miserable creature?"

"My lord," replied the porter, "it is the daughter of master Omar, the dyer, who told me you had married her from choice."

"Merciful heavens!" exclaimed the cadi, "is it possible to marry such a monster as that?"

At that moment the dyer, who had foreseen the surprise of the judge, arrived.

"Wretch," said the cadi, "what dost thou take me for? Thou certainly hast an amazing amount of impudence to dare to play me such a trick as this. Dost thou dare thus to treat me who have it in my power to revenge myself on my enemies; me who, when I please, can put the like of thee in fetters? Dread my wrath, wretch! Instead of the hideous monster which thou hast sent me, give me instantly thy other daughter, whose beauty is unparalleled, or thou shalt experience what an angry cadi can do!"

"My lord," replied Omar, "spare your threats, I beg, and don't be angry with me. I swear by the Creator of the light that I have no other daughter but this. I told you a thousand times that she would not suit you; you would not believe—whose fault is it?"

The cadi at these words felt his soul sink within him, and said to the dyer,

"Master Omar, a damsel of the most exquisite loveliness came here this morning and told me that you were her father, and that you represented her to the world as a perfect monster, indeed so much so, that no one would ask her in marriage."

"My lord," returned the dyer, "that girl must have been playing you a trick; you must have some enemy."

The cadi bent his head on his bosom, and remained some time in deep thought.

"It is a misfortune that was destined to befal me; let us say no more about it; have your daughter taken back home; keep the thousand sequins you have got, but don't ask for any more, if you wish us to be friends."

Although the judge had sworn before witnesses that he would give a thousand sequins more if Omar's daughter did not please him, the artisan did not dare to endeavour to compel him to keep his word, for he knew him to be a most vindictive man, and one who would easily find an opportunity of revenging himself upon any one he disliked, and was, of course, afraid to offend him. He thought it better to be content with what he had received.

"My lord," said he, "I will obey you, and relieve you of my daughter, but you must, if you please, divorce her first."

"Oh! true," said the cadi; "I have not the least objection; be assured that shall soon be done."

Accordingly, he instantly sent for his naib, and the divorce was made out in due form, after which master Omar took leave of the judge, and ordered the porter to bear the wretched Cayfacattaddhari back home.

This adventure was speedily noised all over the city. Every body laughed at it, and warmly applauded the trick which had been played upon the cadi, who could not escape the ridicule in which the whole city indulged at his expense. We carried our revenge still further. By Mouaffac's advice, I presented myself before the prince of the faithful, to whom I told my name and related my story. I did not suppress, as you may imagine, the circumstances which put the malice of the cadi in so strong a light. The caliph, after listening to me with the greatest attention, received me very graciously. "Prince," said he, "why did you not come at once to me? Doubtless you were ashamed of your condition, but you might, without a blush, have presented yourself before my face, even in your wretched state. Does it depend upon men themselves to be happy or unhappy? Is it not Allah that spins the thread of our destiny? Ought you to have feared an ungracious reception? No! You know that I love and esteem king Ben-Ortoc, your father; my court was a safe asylum for you."

The caliph embraced me, and conferred on me a *gulute* (robe of honour) and a beautiful diamond which he wore on his finger. He regaled me with excellent sherbet, and when I returned to my father-in-law's house, I found six large bales of Persian brocade, gold and silver, two pieces of damask, and a beautiful Persian horse richly caparisoned. In addition, he reinstated Mouaffac in the government of Bagdad; and as to the cadi, by way of punishment for his malicious attempt to deceive Zemroude and her father, he deposed him, and condemned him to perpetual imprisonment, and, to crown his misery, ordered him as a companion in his confinement the daughter of Ousta Omar.

A few days after my marriage, I sent a courier to Moussul, to inform my father of all that had happened to me since my departure from his court, and to assure him that I would return shortly, with the lady whom I had married. I waited most impatiently for the return of the courier; but, alas! he brought me back news which deeply afflicted me. He informed me that Ben-Ortoc having heard that four thousand Bedouin Arabs had attacked me, and that my escort had been cut to pieces, persuaded that I no longer lived, took my supposed death so much to heart that he died; that prince Amadeddin Zingui, my cousin-german, occupied the throne; that he reigned with equity; and that, nevertheless, although he was generally beloved, the people no sooner learned that I was still alive, than they gave themselves up to the greatest joy. Prince Amadeddin himself, in a letter which the courier placed in my hands, assured me of his fidelity, and expressed his impatience for my return, in order that he might restore the crown to me, and become the first subject in my dominions.

This news decided me to hasten my return to Moussul. I took my leave of the prince of the faithful, who ordered a detachment of three thousand cavalry of his own guard to escort me to my kingdom, and, after embracing Mouaffac and his wife, I departed from Bagdad with my beloved Zemroude, who would almost have died of grief at the separation from her parents, if her love for me had not somewhat moderated the violence of her sorrow. About halfway between Bagdad and Moussul, the vanguard of my escort discovered a body of troops marching towards us. Concluding at once that it was a body of Bedouin Arabs, I immediately drew up my men, and was fully prepared for the attack, when my scouts brought me word, that those whom we had taken for robbers and enemies were, in fact, troops from Moussul, who had set out to meet me, with Amadeddin at their head.

This prince, on his part, having learned who we were, left his little army to meet me, accompanied by the principal nobles of Moussul. When he reached the spot where I was awaiting him, he addressed me in the same tone in which his letter had been couched, submissively and respectfully, whilst all the nobles who accompanied him assured me of their zeal and fidelity. I thought it my duty to show my entire confidence in them, by dismissing the soldiers of the caliph's guard. I had no reason to repent of this step; far from being capable of forming any treacherous design, prince Amadeddin did all in his power to give me proofs of his attachment.

When we came to Moussul, our safe and auspicious arrival was celebrated by gifts to the mosques, abundant alms to the poor, fêtes, and an illumination of the palace gardens with lamps of a thousand different colours. The people in general testified the delight they felt at my return by acclamations, and for a space of three days gave themselves up entirely to great rejoicings. The booths of the itinerant merchants, and the bazaars, were hung within and without with draperies, and at night they were lit up by lamps, which formed the letters of a verse of the Koran, so that every shop having its particular verse, this holy book was to be read entire in the city; and it appeared as though the angel Gabriel had brought it a second time in letters of light to our great prophet.

In addition to this pious illumination, before each shop were placed large dishes, plates of pillau, of all sorts of colours, in the form of pyramids, and huge bowls of sherbet and pomegranate juice, for the passers-by to eat and drink at pleasure. In all the cross streets were to be seen dancers, displaying their graceful evolutions to the sounds of drums, lutes, and tambourines.

The different trades formed a procession, consisting of cars decorated with tinsel and many-coloured flags, and with the tools used in their trades; and after traversing the principal streets, defiled to the music of pipes, cymbals, and trumpets, before my balcony, where Zemroude was sitting by my side, and after saluting us, shouted at the top of their voices, "Blessing and health to thee, Apostle of God, God give the king victory."

It was not enough for me to share these honours with the daughter of Mouaffac, my study was to find out every thing that would afford her any pleasure. I caused her apartments to be adorned with every thing most rare and pleasing to the sight. Her suite was composed of twenty-five young Circassian ladies, slaves in my father's harem; some sang and played the lute exquisitely, others excelled on the harp, and the rest danced with the greatest grace and lightness. I also gave her a black aga, with twelve eunuchs, who all possessed some talent which might contribute to her amusement.

I reigned over faithful and devoted subjects; every day I loved Zemroude more and more, and she as ardently reciprocated my attachment.

My days passed thus in perfect happiness, till one day a young dervise appeared at my court. He introduced himself to the principal nobles, and gained their friendship by his pleasing and agreeable manners, as well as by his wit and his happy and brilliant repartees. He accompanied them to the chase, he entered into all their gaieties, and was a constant guest at their parties of pleasure. Every day some of my courtiers spoke to me of him as a man of charming manners, so that at last they excited in me a desire to see and converse with the agreeable stranger. Far from finding his portrait overdrawn, he appeared to me even more accomplished than they had represented him. His conversation charmed me, and I was disabused of an error into which many persons of quality fall, namely, that men of wit and high sentiment are only to be met with at court. I experienced so much pleasure in the company of the dervise, and he seemed so well suited to manage affairs of the greatest importance, that I wished to appoint him my minister, but he thanked me, and told me he had made a vow never to accept any employment, that he preferred a free and independent life, that he despised honours and riches, and was content with what God, who cares for the lowest animals, should provide for him; in a word, he was content with his condition.

I admired a man so much raised above worldly considerations, and conceived the greatest esteem for him; I received him with pleasure each time he presented himself at court; if he was among the crowd of courtiers my eyes sought him out, and to him I most frequently addressed myself; I insensibly became so attached to him, that I made him my exclusive favourite.

One day during a hunt, I had strayed from the main body of my followers, and the dervise was alone with me. He began by relating his travels, for although young he had travelled extensively. He spoke of several curious things he had seen in India, and, amongst others, of an old Bramin whom he knew. "This great man," said he, "knew an infinity of secrets, each more extraordinary than the former. Nature had no mystery but what he could fathom. He died in my arms," said the dervise, "but as he loved me, before he expired he said, 'My son, I wish to teach you a secret by which you may remember me, but it is on condition that you reveal it to no one.' I promised to keep it inviolate, and on the faith of my promise he taught me the secret."

"Indeed!" said I, "what is the nature of the secret? Is it the secret of making gold?"

"No, sire," replied he, "it is a greater and much more precious secret than that. It is the power of reanimating a dead body. Not that I can restore the same soul to the body it has left, Heaven alone can perform that miracle; but I can cause my soul to enter into a body deprived of life, and I will prove it to your highness whenever you shall please."

"Most willingly!" said I, "now, if you please."

At that moment there passed by us most opportunely a doe; I let fly an arrow, which struck her, and she fell dead. "Now let me see," said I, "if you can reanimate this creature."

"Sire," replied the dervise, "your curiosity shall soon be gratified; watch well what I am about to do."

He had scarcely uttered these words, when I beheld with amazement his body fall suddenly without animation, and at the same moment I saw the doe rise with great nimbleness. I will leave you to judge of my surprise. Although there was no room left to doubt what I beheld, I could hardly believe the evidence of my senses. The creature, however, came to me, fondled me, and after making several bounds, fell dead again, and immediately the body of the dervise, which lay stretched at my feet, became reanimated.

I was delighted at so wonderful a secret, and entreated the dervise to impart it to me.

The Dervise and the Prince

"Sire," said he, "I deeply regret that I cannot comply with your desire; for I promised the dying Bramin not to disclose it to any one, and I am a slave to my word."

The more the dervise excused himself from satisfying my wishes, the more did I feel my curiosity excited.

"In the name of Allah," said I, "do not refuse to comply with my entreaties. I promise thee never to divulge the secret, and I swear by Him who created us both never to employ it to a bad purpose."

The dervise considered a moment, then turning to me said,

"I cannot resist the wishes of a king whom I love more than my life; I will yield to your desire. It is true," added he, "that I only gave a simple promise to the Bramin. I did not bind myself by an inviolable oath. I will impart my secret to your highness. It consists only in remembering two words; it is sufficient to repeat them mentally to be able to reanimate a dead body."

He then taught me the two magic words. I no sooner knew them, than I burned to test their power. I pronounced them, with the intention to make my soul pass into the body of the doe, and in a moment I found myself metamorphosed into the animal. But the delight I experienced at the success of the trial was soon converted into consternation; for no sooner had my spirit entered into the body of the doe, than the dervise caused his to pass into mine, and then suddenly drawing my bow, the traitor was on the point of shooting me with one of my own arrows, when, perceiving his intention, I took to flight, and by my speed just escaped the fatal shaft. Nevertheless, he let fly the arrow at me with so true an aim, that it just grazed my shoulder.

I now beheld myself reduced to live with the beasts of the forests and mountains. Happier for me would it have been if I had resembled them more perfectly, and if in losing my human form, I had at the same time lost my power of reason. I should not then have been the prey to a thousand miserable reflections.

Whilst I was deploring my misery in the forests, the dervise was occupying the throne of Moussul; and fearing that, as I possessed the secret as well as himself, I might find means to introduce myself into the palace, and take my revenge upon him, on the very day he usurped my place he ordered all the deer in the kingdom to be destroyed, wishing, as he said, to exterminate the whole species, which he mortally hated. Nay, so eager was he for my destruction, that the moment he returned from the hunting expedition, he again set out at the head of a large body of followers, intent upon the indiscriminate slaughter of all the deer they might meet.

The people of Moussul, animated by the hope of gain, spread themselves all over the country with their bows and arrows; they scoured the forests, over-ran the mountains, and shot every stag and deer they met with. Happily, by this time I had nothing to fear from them; for, having seen a dead nightingale lying at the foot of a tree, I reanimated it, and under my new shape flew towards the palace of my enemy, and concealed myself among the thick foliage of a tree in the garden. This tree was not far from the apartments of the queen. There, thinking upon my misfortune, I poured forth in tender strains the melancholy that consumed me. It was one morning, as the sun rose, and already several birds, delighted to see its returning beams, expressed their joy by their minstrelsy. For my part, taken up with my griefs, I paid no attention to the brightness of the newborn day; but with my eyes sadly turned towards Zemroude's apartment, I poured forth so plaintive a song, that I attracted the attention of the princess, who came to the window. I continued my mournful notes in her presence, and I tried all the means in my power to render them more and more touching, as though I could make her comprehend the subject of my grief. But, alas! although she took pleasure in listening to me, I had the mortification to see, that instead of being moved by my piteous accents, she only laughed with one of her slaves, who had come to the window to listen to me.

I did not leave the garden that day, nor for several following, and I took care to sing every morning at the same spot. Zemroude did not fail to come to the window; and at length, by the blessing of Providence, took a fancy to have me. One morning she said to her female attendants, "I wish that nightingale to be caught; let birdcatchers be sent for. I love that bird; I doat upon it; let them try every means to catch it, and bring it to me." The queen's orders were obeyed; expert birdcatchers were found, who laid traps for me, and, as I had no desire to escape, because I saw that their only object in depriving me of my liberty was to make me a slave to my princess, I allowed myself to be taken. The moment I was brought to her she took me in her hand, with every symptom of delight. "My darling," said she, caressing me, "my charming bul-bul, I will be thy rose; I already feel the greatest tenderness for thee." At these words she kissed me. I raised my beak softly to her lips. "Ah! the little rogue," cried she laughing, "he appears to know what I say." At last, after fondling me, she placed me in a gold filigree cage, which an eunuch had been sent into the city to buy for me.

Every day as soon as she woke I began my song; and whenever she came to my cage to caress me or feed me, far from appearing wild, I spread out my wings, and stretched my beak towards her, to express my joy. She was surprised to see me so tame in so short a time. Sometimes she would take me out of the cage, and allow me to fly about her chamber. I always went to her to receive her caresses, and to lavish mine upon her; and if any of her slaves wished to take hold of me, I pecked at them with all my might. By these little insinuating ways I endeared myself so much to Zemroude, that she often said if by any mishap I were to die, she should be inconsolable, so strong was her attachment to me.

Zemroude also had a little dog in her chamber, of which she was very fond. One day, when the dog and I were alone, it died. Its death suggested to me the idea of making a third experiment of the secret. "I will pass into the body of the dog," thought I, "for I wish to see what effect the death of her nightingale will produce upon the princess." I cannot tell what suggested the fancy, for I did not foresee what this new metamorphosis would lead to; but the thought appeared to me a suggestion of Heaven, and I followed it at all risks.

When Zemroude returned to the room, her first care was to come to my cage. As soon as she perceived that the nightingale was dead, she uttered a shriek that brought all her slaves about her. "What ails you, madam?" said they in terrified accents. "Has any misfortune happened to you?"

"I am in despair," replied the princess, weeping bitterly; "my nightingale is dead. My dear bird, my little husband, why art thou taken from, me so soon? I shall no more hear your sweet notes! I shall never see you again! What have I done to deserve such punishment from Heaven?"

All the efforts of her women to console her were in vain. The dervise had just returned from his murderous expedition, and one of them ran to acquaint him with the state in which they had found the queen. He quickly came and told her that the death of a bird ought not to cause her so much grief; that the loss was not irreparable; that if she was so fond of nightingales, and wanted another, it was easy to get one. But all his reasoning was to no purpose, he could make no impression upon her.

"Cease your endeavours," she exclaimed, "to combat my grief, you will never overcome it. I know it is a great weakness to mourn so for a bird, I am as fully persuaded of it as you can be, still I cannot bear up against the force of the blow that has overwhelmed me. I loved the little creature; he appeared sensible of the caresses I bestowed on him, and he returned them in a way that delighted me. If my women approached him, he exhibited ferocity, or rather disdain; whereas he always came eagerly on to my hand when I held it out to him. It appeared as though he felt affection for me, he looked at me in so tender and languishing a manner, that it almost seemed as though he was mortified that he had not the power of speech to express his feelings towards me. I could read it in his eyes. Ah! I shall never think of him without despair." As she finished speaking her tears gushed out afresh, and she seemed as if nothing could ever console her.

I drew a favourable omen from the violence of her grief. I had laid myself down in a corner of the room, where I heard all that was said and observed all that passed without their noticing me. I had a presentiment that the dervise, in order to console the queen, would avail himself of the secret, and I was not disappointed.

Finding the queen inaccessible to reason, and being deeply enamoured of her, he was moved by her tears, and instead of persevering in fruitless arguments, he ordered the queen's slaves to quit the room and leave him alone with her. "Madam," said he, thinking that no one overheard him, "since the death of your nightingale causes you so much sorrow, he must be brought to life. Do not grieve, you shall see him alive again; I pledge myself to restore him to you; to-morrow morning, when you wake, you shall hear him sing again, and you shall have the satisfaction of caressing him."

"I understand you, my lord," said Zemroude; "you look upon me as crazed, and think that you must humour my sorrow; you would persuade me that I shall see my nightingale alive to-morrow; to-morrow you will postpone your miracle till the following day, and so on from one day to another; by this means you reckon on making me gradually forget my bird; or, perhaps," pursued she, "you intend to get another put in his place to deceive me."

"No, my queen," replied the dervise, "no; it is that very bird which you see stretched out in his cage without life; this very nightingale, the enviable object of such poignant grief; it is that very bird himself that shall sing. I will give him new life, and you can again lavish your caresses upon him. He will better appreciate that delight, and you shall behold him still more anxious to please you, for it will be I myself who will be the object of your endearments; every morning I will myself be his fresh life in order to divert you. I can perform this miracle," continued he; "it is a secret I possess; if you have any doubts upon it, or if you are impatient to behold your favourite reanimated, I will cause him to revive now immediately."

As the princess did not reply, he imagined from her silence that she was not fully persuaded he could accomplish what he professed; he seated himself on the sofa, and by virtue of the two cabalistic words left his body, or rather mine, and entered into that of the nightingale. The bird began to sing in its cage to the great amazement of Zemroude. But his song was not destined to continue long; for no sooner did he begin to warble than I quitted the body of the dog and hastened to retake my own. At the same time running to the cage, I dragged the bird out and wrung his neck. "What have you done, my lord?" cried the princess. "Why have you treated my nightingale thus? If you did not wish him to live, why did you restore him to life?"

"I thank Heaven!" cried I, without paying any regard to what she said, so much were my thoughts taken up with the feeling of vengeance which possessed me at the treacherous conduct of the dervise, "I am satisfied. I have at length avenged myself on the villain whose execrable treason deserved a still greater punishment."

If Zemroude was surprised to see her nightingale restored to life, she was not the less so to hear me utter these words with such fierce emotion.

"My lord," said she, "whence this violent transport which agitates you, and what do those words mean which you have just spoken?"

I related to her all that had happened to me, and she could not doubt that I was truly Al Abbas, because she had heard that the body of the dervise had been found in the forest, and she was also of course well acquainted with the order which he had given for destroying all the deer.

But my poor princess could not recover the shock her sensitive love had sustained. A few days after she fell ill, and died in my arms, literally frightened to death by the imminence of the danger from which she had just been so happily rescued.

After I had bewailed her, and erected a splendid tomb to her memory, I summoned the prince Amadeddin.

"My cousin," said I, "I have no children, I resign the crown of Moussul in your favour. I give the kingdom up into your hands. I renounce the regal dignity, and wish to pass the rest of my days in repose and privacy." Amadeddin, who really loved me, spared no arguments to deter me from taking the step I proposed, but I assured him that nothing could shake my resolution.

"Prince," said I, "my determination is fixed, I resign my rank to you. Fill the throne of Al Abbas, and may you be more happy than he. Reign over a people who know your merit, and have already experienced the blessings of your rule. Disgusted with pomp, I shall retire to distant climes, and live in privacy; there freed from the cares of state, I shall mourn over the memory of Zemroude, and recall the happy days we passed together."

I left Amadeddin upon the throne of Moussul, and, accompanied only by a few slaves, and carrying an ample supply of riches and jewels, took the road to Bagdad, where I arrived safely. I immediately repaired to Mouaffac's house. His wife and he were not a little surprised to see me, and they were deeply affected when I informed them of the death of their daughter, whom they had tenderly loved. The recital unlocked the fountains of my own grief, and I mingled my tears with theirs. I did not stay long in Bagdad, I joined a caravan of pilgrims going to Mecca, and after paying my devotions, found, by chance, another company of pilgrims from Tartary, whom I accompanied to their native country. We arrived in this city; I found the place agreeable, and took up my abode here, where I have resided for nearly forty years. I am thought to be a stranger who was formerly concerned in trade, and whose time is now passed in study and contemplation. I lead a retired life, and rarely see strangers. Zemroude is ever present to my thoughts, and my only consolation consists in dwelling fondly upon her memory and her virtues.

CONTINUATION OF THE STORY OF PRINCE KHALAF AND THE PRINCESS OF CHINA.

Al Abbas, having finished the recital of his adventures, thus addressed his guests:

"Such is my history. You perceive by my misfortunes and your own, that human life is but as a reed, ever liable to be bent to the earth by the bleak blasts of misfortune. I will, however, confess to you that I have led a happy and quiet life ever since I have been in Jaic; and that I by no means repent having abdicated the throne of Moussul; for in the obscurity in which I now live, I have discovered peaceful and tranquil joys which I never experienced before."

Timurtasch, Elmaze, and Khalaf bestowed a thousand flattering encomiums upon the son of Ben-Ortoc; the khan admired the resolution which had caused him to deprive himself of his kingdom, in order to live in privacy in a country of strangers, where the station which he had filled in the world was unknown. Elmaze praised the fidelity he displayed towards Zemroude, and the grief he experienced at her death. And Khalaf remarked, "My lord, it were to be wished that all men could display the same constancy in adversity which you have done, under your misfortunes."

They continued their conversation till it was time to retire. Al Abbas then summoned his slaves, who brought wax-lights in candlesticks made of aloe-wood, and conducted the khan, the princess, and her son to a suite of apartments, where the same simplicity reigned that characterized the rest of the house. Elmaze and Timurtasch retired to sleep in a chamber appropriated to themselves, and Khalaf to another. The following morning their host entered the chamber of his guests as soon as they were up, and said,

"You are not the only unfortunate persons in the world; I have just been informed that an ambassador from the sultan of Carisma arrived in the city last evening; that his master has sent him to Ileuge-Khan, to beg of him not only to refuse an asylum to the khan of the Nagäis, his enemy, but if the khan should endeavour to pass through his dominions, to arrest him. Indeed, it is reported," pursued Al Abbas, "that the unfortunate khan, for fear of falling into the hands of the sultan of Carisma, has left his capital and fled with his family." At this news, Timurtasch and Khalaf changed colour, and the princess fainted.

The swoon of Elmaze, as well as the evident trouble of the father and son, instantly caused Al Abbas to suspect that his guests were not merchants.

"I see," said he, as soon as the princess had recovered her senses, "that you take a deep interest in the misfortunes of the khan of the Nagäis; indeed, if I may be permitted to tell you what I think, I believe you are yourselves the objects of the sultan of Carisma's hatred."

"Yes, my lord," replied Timurtasch, "we are, indeed, the victims for whose immolation he is thirsty. I am the khan of the Nagäis, you behold my wife and my son; we should, indeed, be ungrateful, if we did not discover our position to you, after your generous reception, and the confidence you have reposed in us. I am encouraged even to hope, that by your counsels you will aid us to escape from the danger which threatens us."

"Your situation is most critical," replied the aged king of Moussul; "I know Ileuge-Khan well, and, as he fears the sultan of Carisma, I cannot doubt that, to please him, he will search for you every where. You will not be safe, either in my house or in any other in this city; the only resource left you, is to leave the country of Jaic as speedily as possible, cross the river Irtisch, and gain, with the utmost diligence, the frontiers of the tribe of the Berlas."

This advice pleased Timurtasch, his wife, and son. Al Abbas had three horses instantly got ready, together with provisions for the journey, and giving them a purse filled with gold; "Start immediately," said he, "you have no time to lose, by to-morrow, no doubt, Ileuge-Khan will cause search to be made for you every where."

They returned their heartfelt thanks to the aged monarch, and then quitted Jaic, crossed the Irtisch, and joining company with a camel-driver, who was travelling that way, arrived after several days' journey in the territories of the tribe of Berlas. They took up their quarters with the first horde they met, sold their horses, and lived quietly enough as long as their money lasted; but, as soon as it came to an end, the misery of the khan recommenced. "Why am I still in the world?" he began to exclaim. "Would it not have been better to have awaited my blood-thirsty foe in my own kingdom, and have died defending my capital, than to drag on a life which is only one continued scene of misery? It is in vain that we endure our misfortunes with patience; for, in spite of our submission to its decrees, Heaven will never restore us to happiness, but leaves us still the sport of misery."

"My lord," replied Khalaf, "do not despair of our miseries coming to an end. Heaven, which decrees these events, is preparing for us, I doubt not, some relief which we cannot foresee. Let us proceed at once," added he, "to the principal horde of this tribe. I have a presentiment, that our fortunes will now assume a more favourable aspect."

They all three proceeded accordingly to the horde with whom the khan of Berlas resided. They entered a large tent which served as a refuge for poor strangers. Here they laid themselves down, worn out with their journey, and at a loss at last to know how to obtain even the necessaries of life. Khalaf, however, quietly slipt out of the tent, leaving his father and mother there, and went through the horde, asking charity of the passers-by. By the evening he had collected a small sum of money, with which he bought some provisions, and carried them to his parents. When they learned that their son had actually solicited charity, they could not refrain from tears. Khalaf himself was moved by their grief, but cheerfully remarked, nevertheless, "I confess that nothing we have yet endured has appeared to me more mortifying than to be reduced to solicit alms; still, as at present I cannot procure you subsistence by any other means, is it not my duty to do it, in spite of the mortification it costs me? But," he added, as though struck with a sudden thought, "there is still another resource—sell me for a slave, and the money you will receive will last you a long time."

"What do you say, my son?" cried Timurtasch, when he heard these words. "Can you propose to us that we should live at the expense of your liberty? Ah! rather let us endure for ever our present misery. But if it should come to this, that one of us must be sold, let it be myself; I do not refuse to bear the yoke of servitude for you both."

"My lord," said Khalaf, "another thought strikes me; to-morrow morning I will take my station among the porters; some one may chance to employ me, and we may thus earn a living by my labour." They agreed to this, and the following day the prince stationed himself among the porters of the horde, and waited till some one should employ him; but unfortunately no one wanted him, so that half the day passed and he had not had a single job. This grieved him deeply. "If I am not more successful than this," thought he, "how am I to support my father and mother?"

He grew tired of waiting among the porters on the chance of some person wanting his services. He went out of the encampment and strolled into the country, in order to turn over in his mind undisturbedly the best means of earning a livelihood. He sat down under a tree, where, after praying Heaven to have pity on his perplexity, he fell asleep. When he woke he saw near him a falcon of singular beauty: its head was adorned with a tuft of gaudy feathers, and from its neck hung a chain of gold filigree-work set with diamonds, topazes, and rubies. Khalaf, who understood falconry, held out his fist, and the bird alighted on it. The prince of the Nagäis was delighted at the circumstance. "Let us see," said he, "what this will lead to. This bird, from all appearance, belongs to the sovereign of the tribe." Nor was he wrong. It was the favourite falcon of Almguer, khan of Berlas, who had lost it the previous day. His principal huntsmen were engaged at that moment in searching every where for it with the greatest diligence and uneasiness, for their master had threatened them with the severest punishments if they returned without his bird, which he loved passionately.

Prince Khalaf returned to the encampment with the falcon. As soon as the people of the horde saw it, they began to cry out, "Ha! here is the khan's falcon recovered. Blessings on the youth who will make our prince rejoice by restoring him his bird." And so it turned out, for when Khalaf arrived at the royal tent, and appeared with the falcon, the khan, transported with joy, ran to his bird and kissed it a thousand times. Then addressing the prince of the Nagäis, he asked him where he found it. Khalaf related how he had recovered the falcon. The khan then said to him, "Thou appearest to be a stranger amongst us; where wast thou born, and what is thy profession?"

"My lord," replied Khalaf, prostrating himself at the khan's feet, "I am the son of a merchant of Bulgaria, who was possessed of great wealth. I was travelling with my father and mother in the country of Jaic, when we were attacked by robbers, who stripped us of every thing but our lives, and we have found our way to this encampment actually reduced to beg our bread."

"Young man," replied the khan, "I am glad that it is thou who hast found my falcon; for I swore to grant to whomsoever should bring me my bird, whatever two things he might ask; so thou hast but to speak. Tell me what thou desirest me to grant thee, and doubt not that thou shalt obtain it." "Since I have permission to ask two things," returned Khalaf, "I request in the first place that my father and mother, who are in the strangers' tent, may have a tent to themselves in the quarter where your highness resides, and that they may be supported during the rest of their days at your highness's expense, and waited on by officers of your highness's household; secondly, I desire to have one of the best horses in your highness's stables and a purse full of gold, to enable me to make a journey which I have in contemplation." "Thy wishes shall be gratified," said Almguer; "thou shalt bring thy father and mother to me, and from this day forth I will begin to entertain them as thou desirest; and to-morrow, dressed in rich attire, and mounted on the best horse in my stables, thou shalt be at liberty to go wherever it shall please thee. Thy modesty, the filial love which is imprinted upon thy features, thy youth, thy noble air, please me; be my guest, come and join my festivities, and thou shalt listen to an Arabian story-teller, whose knowledge and imaginative powers instruct and amuse my tribes."

The khan and the son of Timurtasch presently seated themselves at a table loaded with viands, confectionary, fruit, and flowers; gazelle venison, red-legged partridges, pheasants, and black cock were displayed as trophies of the skill of the hunter king. The Arab stationed near the khan awaited his orders. "Moustapha," said the khan at length, turning to the Arab, "I have been extolling thy knowledge and wit to my guest; surpass thyself, and let him see that I have not exaggerated. He shall give thee a subject; treat it in such a manner as to deserve his praise."

"I am curious," said the prince, "to hear of China; I ask thee to instruct me concerning the government of that important kingdom, and to give me an insight into the manners and customs of its people."

The Arab reflected a moment, and then, prefacing his recital with a few general remarks, proceeded to depict in glowing colours this celestial empire, whose civilization dates back to the remotest ages of the world. He described its extent as equal to one-half of the habitable globe; its population as so numerous that it might be counted by hundreds of millions; he spoke of cities, each of which alone brought a revenue to their crown, which surpassed that of entire kingdoms; of those gigantic works, the canals, whose extent equalled the course of the largest rivers, which traversed the vast empire. And he foretold that a time would come when Tartar warriors should scale that very wall which the terror of their arms had caused to be built, and should again reconquer the whole of that wealthy tract. He then began his story as follows.

THE STORY OF LIN-IN.

A CHINESE TALE.

At Wou-si, a town dependent upon the city of Tchang-tcheou, in the province of Kiang-nan, there resided a family in the middle sphere of life. Three brothers composed the family; the name of the eldest was Lin-in (the jasper); the second Lin-pao (the precious); the youngest Lin-tchin (the pearl); this last was not yet old enough to marry; the other two had taken wives to themselves. The wife of the first was named Wang; the wife of the second Yang; and both possessed every grace which can constitute the charm of woman.

Lin-pao's engrossing passions were gambling and wine; he evinced no inclination to good. His wife was of a similar disposition, and depraved in her conduct; she was very different from her sister-in-law Wang, who was a pattern of modesty and propriety. So although these two women lived together on neighbourly terms, there was but little real sympathy between them.

Wang had a son named Hi-eul, that is to say, "the son of rejoicing." He was a child of six years old. One day having stopped in the street with some other children, to look at a great procession in the neighbourhood, he was lost in the crowd, and in the evening did not return to the house.

This loss caused the deepest sorrow to his parents. They had handbills posted up, and there was not a street in which they did not make inquiries, but all to no purpose; they could gain no intelligence respecting their darling child. Lin-in was inconsolable; and giving way to the grief that overwhelmed him, he sought to fly from his home, where every thing brought back the remembrance of his dear Hi-eul. He borrowed a sum of money from one of his friends to enable him to carry on a small trade in the neighbourhood of the city and the adjacent villages, hoping that in one of these short excursions he might be able to recover the treasure he had lost.

As his whole thoughts were taken up with his child, he took little pleasure in the circumstance that his trade flourished. He nevertheless continued to pursue it during five years, without making long journeys from home, whither he returned every year to spend the autumn. At length, being utterly unsuccessful in discovering the least trace of his son after so many years, and concluding that he was lost to him for ever, and finding moreover that his wife Wang bore him no more children, as he had now amassed a good sum of money, he determined to divert his thoughts from painful recollections by trading in another province.

He joined the company of a rich merchant travelling the road he had fixed upon; and the merchant, having observed his aptitude for business, made him a very advantageous offer. The desire of becoming wealthy now took possession of him, and diverted his thoughts from their accustomed channel.

Within a very short time after their arrival in the province of Chan-si every thing had succeeded to their utmost wishes. They found a quick sale for their merchandise, and the profits arising from it was considerable. The payments, however, were delayed for two years in consequence of a drought and famine which afflicted the country, as well as by a tedious illness by which Lin-in was attacked. They were detained altogether three years in the province; after which, having recovered his money and his health, he took his departure to return to his own country.

He halted one day during his journey near a place named Tchin-lieou to recruit his strength, and strolling round the neighbourhood accidentally came upon a girdle of blue cloth, in the form of a long, narrow bag, such as is worn round the body, under the dress, and in which money is usually kept; as he took it up, he found the weight considerable. He retired to a quiet spot, opened the girdle, and found it contained about two hundred täels.

At sight of this treasure he fell into the following train of reflection: "My good fortune has placed this sum in my hands; I might keep it and employ it for my own use without fearing any unpleasant consequences. Still the person who has dropt it, the moment he discovers his loss, will be in great distress, and will return in haste to look for it. Do they not say that our forefathers dared scarcely touch money found in this way; and if they picked it up, only did so with a view of restoring it to its owner? This appears to me a very praiseworthy custom, and I will imitate it, the more so as I am growing old and have no heir. Of what benefit would money got by such means be to me?"

Whilst thus reasoning, he had wandered to some distance from the spot where he had found the money; he now, however, retraced his steps to the place, and waited there the whole day, to be ready in case the owner should return. Nobody came, however, and the next day he continued his journey.

After five days' travelling, he arrived in the evening at Nan-sou-tcheou, and took up his quarters at an inn where several other merchants were staying. The conversation having turned upon the advantages of commerce, one of the company said, "Five days ago, on leaving Tchin-lieou, I lost two hundred täels, which I had in an inside girdle. I had taken it off, and placed it near me whilst I lay down to sleep, when a mandarin and his cortége chanced to pass by. I hastened to get out of the way for fear of insult, and in my hurry forgot to take up my money. It was only at night, as I was undressing to go to bed, that I discovered my loss. I felt sure that as the place where I lost my money was by the side of a well-frequented road, it would be useless to delay my journey for several days in order to look for what I should never find."

Every one condoled with him on his loss. Lin-in asked him his name and place of abode. "Your servant," replied the merchant, "is named Tchin, and lives at Yang-tcheou, where he has a shop and a large warehouse. May I be so bold in return to inquire to whom I have the honour of speaking?" Lin-in told him his name, and said that he was an inhabitant of the town of Wou-si. "My shortest road there," added he, "lies through Yang-tcheou; and, if agreeable to you, I shall have much pleasure in your company so far."

Tchin acknowledged this politeness in a becoming manner. "Most willingly," said he; "we will continue our journey together, and I esteem myself very fortunate in meeting with such an agreeable companion." The journey was not long, and they soon arrived at Yang-tcheou.

After the usual civilities, Tchin invited his fellow-traveller to his house, and on their arrival there immediately ordered refreshments to be brought. Whilst they were discussing their meal, Lin-in managed to turn the conversation on the subject of the lost money.

"What," he asked, "was the colour of the girdle which contained your money, and of what material was it made?"

"It was of blue cloth," replied Tchin; "and what would enable me to identify it is, that at one end the letter Tchin, which is my name, is embroidered upon it in white silk."

This description left no doubt as to the owner. Lin-in, therefore, rejoined in a cheerful tone, "If I have asked you all these questions, it was merely because passing through Tchin-lieou, I found a belt such as you describe." At the same time producing it, he added, "Look if this is yours." "The very same," said Tchin. Whereupon Lin-in politely restored it to its owner.

Tchin, overwhelmed with gratitude, pressed him to accept the half of the sum which it contained; but his entreaties were in vain, Lin-in would receive nothing. "What obligations am I not under to you?" resumed Tchin; "where else should I find such honesty and generosity?" He then ordered a splendid repast to be brought, over which they pledged each other with great demonstrations of friendship.

Tchin thought to himself, "Where should I find a man of such probity as Lin-in? Men of his character are very scarce in these days. What! shall I receive from him such an act of kindness, and not be able to repay him? I have a daughter twelve years old; I must form an alliance with such an honest man. But has he got a son? On this point I am entirely ignorant."

"My dear friend," said he, "how old is your son?"

This question brought tears into the eyes of Lin-in. "Alas!" replied he, "I had but one, who was most dear to me. It is now eight years ago since my child, having run out of the house to see a procession pass by, disappeared; and from that day to this I have never been able to learn any thing of him; and, to crown my misfortune, my wife has not borne me any more children."

Upon hearing this, Tchin appeared to think for a moment, then, continuing the conversation, said, "My brother and benefactor, of what age was the child when you lost him?" "About six years old," replied Lin-in. "What was his name?" "We called him Hi-eul," returned Lin-in. "He had escaped all the dangers of the small-pox which had left no traces upon his countenance; his complexion was clear and florid."

This description gave the greatest pleasure to Tchin, and he could not prevent his satisfaction from displaying itself in his looks and manner. He immediately called one of his servants, to whom he whispered a few words. The servant, having made a gesture of obedience, retired into the interior of the house.

Lin-in, struck by the questions, and the joy which lit up the countenance of his host, was forming all sorts of conjectures, when he saw a youth of about fourteen years of age enter the room. He was dressed in a long gown, with a plain though neat jacket. His graceful form, his air and carriage, his face with its regular features, and his quick and piercing eyes, and finely arched black eyebrows, at once engaged the admiration and riveted the attention of Lin-in.

As soon as the youth saw the stranger seated at table, he turned towards him, made a low bow, and uttered some respectful words; then approaching Tchin, and standing modestly before him, he said in a sweet and pleasing tone, "My father, you have called Hi-eul; what are you pleased to command?" "I will tell you presently," replied Tchin, "in the mean time stand beside me."

The name of Hi-eul, by which the youth called himself, excited fresh suspicions in the breast of Lin-in. A secret sympathy suddenly forced itself upon him; and by one of those wonderful instincts of nature which are so unerring, recalled to his recollection the image of his lost child, his form, his face, his air, and manners; he beheld them all in the youth before him. There was but one circumstance that made him doubt the truth of his conjectures, and that was his addressing Tchin by the name of 'father.' He felt it would be rude to ask Tchin if the youth really were his son; perhaps he might truly be so, for it was not impossible that there might be two children bearing the same name, and in many respects resembling each other.

Lin-in, absorbed in these reflections, paid little attention to the good cheer placed before him. Tchin could read on the countenance of Lin-in the perplexing thoughts that filled his mind. An indescribable charm seemed to attract him irresistibly towards the youth. He kept his eyes constantly fixed upon him, he could not turn them away. Hi-eul, on his part, despite his bashfulness and the timidity natural to his age, could not help gazing intently upon Lin-in; it seemed as though nature was revealing his father to him.

At length Lin-in, no longer master of his feelings, suddenly broke the silence, and asked Tchin if the youth really was his son.

"I am not," replied Tchin, "really his father, although I look upon him as my own child. Eight years ago, a man passing through this city, leading this child in his hand, addressed me by chance, and begged me to assist him in his great need. 'My wife,' said he, 'is dead, and has left me with this child. The impoverished state of my affairs has compelled me to leave my native place, and go to Hoaingan to my relations, from whom I hope to receive a sum of money, to enable me to set up in business again. I have not wherewith to continue my journey to that town, will you be so charitable as to lend me three täels? I will faithfully restore them on my return, and I will leave as a pledge all that I hold most dear in the world, my only son; I shall no sooner reach Hoaingan, than I will return and redeem my dear child.'

"I felt gratified by this mark of confidence, and I gave him the sum he asked. As he left me he burst into tears, and gave every evidence of the grief he felt in leaving his child. I was, however, surprised that the child did not exhibit the least emotion at the separation; as, however, time wore on, and the pretended father did not return, suspicions began to rise, which I was anxious to set at rest. I called the child, and by various questions I put to him, learned that he was born in Wou-si, that having one day run out to see a procession pass by, he had strayed too far from home, and lost his way, and that he had been trepanned and carried off by a stranger. He also told me the name of his father and mother; indeed, it is that of your own family. I thus discovered that the fellow, so far from being the father of the poor child, was the identical rascal who had carried him off. Not only was my compassion excited, but the boy's pleasing manners had entirely won my heart; I treated him from that time as one of my own children, and I sent him to college with my own son, to study with him. I have often entertained the plan of going to Wou-si, to inquire after his family. But business of some kind always prevented me from undertaking the journey, of which, however, I had never fully relinquished the idea; when, happily, a few moments ago, you chanced in the course of conversation to mention your son, my suspicions were aroused, and upon the extraordinary coincidence of your tale, and the circumstances of which I was acquainted, I sent for your child to see if you would recognize him."

At these words Hi-eul wept for joy, and his tears caused those of Lin-in to flow copiously. "A peculiar mark," said he, "will prove his identity; a little above the left knee you will find a small black spot, which has been there from his birth." Hi-eul pulled up the leg of his trouser, and showed the spot in question. Lin-in, on seeing it, threw himself upon the neck of the child, covered him with kisses, and folded him in his arms. "My child," cried he, "my dear child, what happiness for your father to find you after so many years' absence."

It is not difficult to conceive to what transports of joy the father and son delivered themselves up, during these first moments of pleasure. After a thousand tender embraces, Lin-in at length tore himself from the arms of his son, and made a profound obeisance to Tchin. "What gratitude do I not owe you," said he, "for having received my son into your house, and brought up this dear portion of myself with so much care. But for you we should never have been united."

"My kind benefactor," replied Tchin, rising, "it was the act of disinterested generosity you practised towards me, in restoring the two hundred täels, which moved the compassion of Heaven. It is Heaven that conducted you to my house, where you have found him whom you sought in vain for so many years. Now that I know that good youth is your son, I regret that I have not treated him with greater consideration."

"Kneel, my son," said Lin-in, "and thank your generous benefactor."

Tchin was about to return these salutations, when Lin-in himself prevented him, overcome with this excess of respect. This interchange of civilities being over they resumed their seats, and Tchin placed little Hi-eul on a seat by his father's side.

Then Tchin resuming the conversation, said, "My brother (for henceforth that is the title by which I shall address you), I have a daughter twelve years of age, and it is my intention to give her in marriage to your son, in order that the union may cement our friendship more closely." This proposition was made in so sincere and ardent a manner, that Lin-in did not feel it right to make the usual excuses that good breeding prescribed. He therefore waived all ceremony, and gave his consent at once.

As it was growing late, they separated for the night. Hi-eul slept in the same chamber with his father. You may imagine all the tender and affectionate conversation that passed between them during the night. The next day Lin-in prepared to take leave of his host, but he could not resist his pressing invitation to remain. Tchin had prepared a second day's festivity, in which he spared no expense to regale the future father-in-law of his daughter, and his new son-in-law, and thereby to console himself for their departure. They drank and sang, and gave themselves up fully to the hilarity of the occasion.

When the repast was ended, Tchin drew out a packet of twenty täels, and looking towards Lin-in, said, "During the time my dear son-in-law has been with me, it is possible he may have suffered many things against my wish, and unknown to me; here is a little present I wish to make him, until I can give him more substantial proofs of my affection. I will not hear of a refusal."

"What!" replied Lin-in, "at a time when I am contracting an alliance so honourable to me, and when I ought, according to custom, to make marriage presents for my son, presents which I am prevented from doing at this moment, only because I am travelling, do you load me with gifts? I cannot accept them; the thought covers me with confusion."

"Well!" replied Tchin, "I am not dreaming of offering *you* such a trifle. It is for my son-in-law, not the father-in-law of my daughter, that I intend this present. Indeed, if you persist in the refusal, I shall consider it as a sign that the alliance is not agreeable to you."

Lin-in saw that he must yield, and that resistance would be useless. He humbly accepted the present, and making his son rise from table, ordered him to make a profound reverence to Tchin. "What I have given you," said Tchin, raising him up, "is but a trifle, and deserves no thanks." Hi-eul then went into the house to pay his respects to his mother-in-law. The whole day passed in feasting and diversions; it was only at night that they separated.

When Lin-in retired to his chamber, he gave himself up entirely to the reflections to which these events gave rise. "It must be confessed," cried he, "that by restoring the two hundred täels, I have done an action pleasing to

Heaven, and now I am rewarded by the happiness of finding my child, and contracting so honourable an alliance. This is, indeed, joy upon joy; it is like putting gold flowers upon a beautiful piece of silk. How can I be sufficiently grateful for so many favours? Here are the twenty täels that my friend Tchin has given me; can I do better than employ them towards the maintenance of some virtuous bonzes? It will be sowing them in a soil of blessings."

The next day, after breakfast, the father and son got ready their luggage, and took leave of their host; they proceeded to the quay, hired a boat, and commenced their journey. They had scarcely gone half a league, ere they came in sight of a scene of terrible excitement; the river was full of struggling people, whose cries rent the air. A bark, full of passengers, had just sunk, and the cries of the unfortunate creatures for help were heart-rending! The people on the shore called loudly to several small boats which were near to come to the rescue. But the hard-hearted and selfish boatmen demanded that a good sum should be guaranteed them, before they would bestir themselves. At this critical moment Lin-in's boat came up. The moment he perceived what was going on, he said to himself: "It is a much more meritorious action to save the life of a man, than to adorn the temples and support bonzes. Let us consecrate the twenty täels to this good work; let us succour these poor drowning souls." He instantly proclaimed that he would give the twenty täels amongst those who would take the drowning men into their boats.

At this offer all the boatmen crowded towards the scene of the disaster, and the river was, in a moment, covered with their boats; at the same time, some of the spectators on shore, who knew how to swim, threw themselves into the water, and, in a few moments, all were saved, without exception. Lin-in then distributed amongst the boatmen the promised reward.

The poor creatures, snatched from a watery grave, came in a body to return thanks to their preserver. One amongst them, having looked attentively at Lin-in, suddenly cried out, "What! is that you, my eldest brother? By what good luck do I find you here?"

Lin-in, turning towards him, recognized his youngest brother, Lin-tchin. Then, transported with joy, he exclaimed, clasping his hands, "O wonderful circumstance! Heaven has led me hither to save my brother's life." He instantly reached out his hand to him, and made him come into his boat, helped him off with his wet clothes, and gave him others.

As soon as Lin-tchin had sufficiently recovered, he paid the respects due to an elder brother which good breeding demands from a younger, and Lin-in, having acknowledged his politeness, called Hi-eul, who was in the cabin, to come and salute his uncle; he then recounted all his adventures, which threw Lin-tchin into a state of amazement, from which he was a long time in recovering. "But tell me," said Lin-in, at length, "your motive in coming to this country."

"It is not possible," replied Lin-tchin, "to tell you in a few words the reason of my travels. In the course of the three years which have elapsed since your departure from home, the melancholy news of your death from illness reached us. My second brother made every inquiry, and assured himself that the report was true. It was a thunderbolt for my sister-in-law; she was inconsolable, and put on the deepest mourning. For my part, I could not give credit to the report. After a few days had elapsed, my second brother tried all in his power to induce my sister-in-law to contract a fresh marriage. She, however, steadily rejected the proposal; at length she prevailed upon me to make a journey to Chan-si, to ascertain upon the spot what had become of you; and, when I least expected it, at the point of perishing in the water, the very person I was in search of, my well-beloved brother, has saved my life. Is not this unexpected good fortune, a blessing from Heaven? But believe me, my brother, there is no time to be lost; make all possible haste to return home, and to put an end to my sister-in-law's grief. The least delay may cause an irreparable misfortune."

Lin-in, overwhelmed at this news, sent for the captain of the boat, and, although it was late, ordered him to set sail, and continue the voyage during the night.

Whilst all these events were happening to Lin-in, Wang, his wife, was a prey to the most poignant grief. A thousand circumstances led her to suspect that her husband was not dead; but Lin-pao, who by that reported death became the head of the family, so positively assured her that it was true, that, at last, she had allowed herself to be persuaded into that belief, and had assumed the widow's weeds.

Lin-pao possessed a bad heart, and was capable of the most unworthy acts. "I have no doubt," said he, "of my elder brother's death. My sister-in-law is young and handsome; she has, besides, no one to support her; I must force her to marry again, and I shall make money by this means."

He thereupon communicated his plan to Yang, his wife, and ordered her to employ some clever matchmaker. But Wang resolutely rejected the proposal; she vowed that she would remain a widow, and honour the memory of her husband by her widowhood. Her brother-in-law, Lin-tchin, supported her in her resolution. Thus all the artifices which Lin-pao and his wife employed were useless; and, as every time they urged her on the subject it occurred to her that they had no positive proof of his death, "I am determined," said she, at length, "to know the truth; these reports are often false; it is only on the very spot that certain information can be obtained. True, the distance is nearly a hundred leagues. Still, I know that Lin-tchin is a good-hearted man;

he will travel to the province of Chan-si to relieve my anxiety, and learn positively if I am so unfortunate as to have lost my husband; and, if I have, he will, at least, bring me his precious remains."

Lin-tchin was asked to undertake the journey, and, without a moment's hesitation, departed. His absence, however, only rendered Lin-pao more eager in the pursuit of his project. To crown the whole, he had gambled very deeply, and, having been a heavy loser, was at his wit's end to know where to obtain money. In this state of embarrassment, he met with a merchant of Kiang-si, who had just lost his wife, and was looking for another. Lin-pao seized upon the opportunity, and proposed his sister-in-law to him. The merchant accepted the offer, taking care, however, to make secret inquiries whether the lady who was proposed to him was young and good-looking. As soon as he was satisfied on these points, he lost no time, and paid down thirty täels to clinch the bargain.

Lin-pao, having taken the money, said to the merchant, "I ought to warn you, that my sister-in-law is proud and haughty. She will raise many objections to leaving the house, and you will have a great deal of trouble to force her to do it. Now this will be your best plan for managing it. This evening, as soon as it gets dark, have a palanquin and good strong bearers in readiness; come with as little noise as possible, and present yourself at the door of the house. The young woman who will come to the door, attired in the head-dress of mourners, is my sister-in-law; don't say a word to her, and don't listen to what she may say, but seize her at once, thrust her into your palanquin, carry her to your boat, and set sail at once." This plan met with the approbation of the merchant, and its execution appeared easy enough of accomplishment.

In the mean time, Lin-pao returned home, and, in order to prevent his sister-in-law from suspecting any thing of the project he had planned, he assumed an air of the most perfect indifference, but as soon as she left the room, he communicated his plans to his wife, and, alluding to his sister-in-law, in a contemptuous manner, said, "That two-legged piece of goods must leave this house to-night. However, not to be a witness of her tears and sighs, I shall go out beforehand, and, as it gets dark, a merchant of Kiang-si will come, and take her away in a palanquin to his boat."

He would have continued the conversation, when he heard the footsteps of some person outside the window, and went hurriedly away. In his haste he forgot to mention the circumstance of the mourning dress. It was doubtless an interposition of Providence that this circumstance was omitted. The lady Wang easily perceived that the noise she made outside the window had caused Lin-pao to break off the conversation suddenly. The tone of his voice plainly showed that he had something more to say; but she had heard enough; for having remarked by his manner that he had some secret to tell his wife when he entered the house, she had pretended to go away, but listening at the window had heard these words distinctly, "They will take her away and put her into a palanquin."

These words strongly fortified her suspicions. Her resolution was taken at once. She entered the room, and approaching Yang, gave utterance to her anxiety. "My sister-in-law," said she, "you behold an unfortunate widow, who is bound to you by the strongest ties of a friendship which has been always sincere. By this long-standing friendship I conjure you to tell me candidly whether my brother-in-law still persists in his design of forcing me into a marriage that would cover me with disgrace."

At these words Yang at first appeared confused, and changed colour; then, assuming a more confident expression, "What are you thinking of?" she asked, "and what fancies have you got into your head? If there were any intention of making you marry again, do you think there would be any difficulty? What is the good of throwing oneself into the water before the ship is really going to pieces?"

The moment the lady Wang heard this allusion to the ship, she understood more clearly the meaning of the secret conference of her brother-in-law with his wife. She now suspected the worst, and gave vent to her lamentations and sighs; and yielding to the current of her grief, she shut herself up in her room, where she wept, groaned, and bewailed her hard lot. "Unfortunate wretch that I am," cried she, "I do not know what has become of my husband. Lin-tchin, my brother-in-law and friend, upon whom alone I can rely, is gone on a journey. My father, mother, and relations live far from hence. If this business is hurried on, how shall I be able to inform them of it? I can hope for no assistance from our neighbours. Lin-pao has made himself the terror of the whole district, and every body knows him to be capable of the greatest villany. Miserable creature that I am! how can I escape his snares? If I do not fall into them to-day, it may be to-morrow, or at any rate in a very short time."

She fell to the ground half dead; her fall, and the violence of her grief, made a great noise. The lady Yang, hearing the disturbance, hastened to her room, and finding the door firmly fastened, concluded that it was a plan of her distracted sister-in-law to evade the scheme of the night; she therefore seized a bar which stood by and broke the door open. As she entered the room, the night being very dark, she caught her feet in the clothes of the lady Wang, and fell tumbling over her. In her fall she lost her head-dress, which flew to some distance, and the fright and fall brought on a faint, in which she remained for some time. When she recovered she got up, went for a light, and returned to the room, where she found the lady Wang stretched on the floor, without motion and almost without breath.

At the moment she was going to procure other assistance, she heard a gentle knock at the door. She knew it must be the merchant of Kiang-si come to fetch the wife he had bought. She quickly ran to receive him and bring him into the room, that he might himself be witness of what had occurred; but remembering that she had no head-dress, and that she was unfit to present herself in that state, she hastily caught up the one she found at her feet, which was the lady Wang's head-dress of mourning, and ran to the door.

It was indeed the merchant of Kiang-si, who had come to fetch away his promised bride. He had a bridal palanquin, ornamented with silk flags, festoons, flowers, and several gay lanterns; it was surrounded by servants bearing lighted torches, and by a troop of flute and hautboy-players. The whole cortége was stationed in the street in perfect silence. The merchant, having knocked gently and finding the door open, entered the house with some of those who bore torches to light him.

Upon the lady Yang's appearance, the merchant, who spied at a glance the mourning head-dress, which was the mark by which he was to distinguish his bride, flew upon her like a hungry kite upon a sparrow. His followers rushed in, carried off the lady, and shut her into the palanquin, which was all ready to receive her. It was in vain she endeavoured to make herself heard, crying out, "You are mistaken; it is not me you want." The music struck up as she was forced into the palanquin, and drowned her voice, whilst the bearers flew rather than walked, and bore her to the boat.

The lady Yang carried off in the Palanquin

Whilst all this was taking place, the lady Wang had gradually revived and come to her senses. The great hubbub she heard at the door of the house renewed her fears, and occasioned her the most painful anxiety; but as she found that the noise of music, and the tumult of voices, which had arisen so suddenly died gradually away in the distance, she regained her courage, and after a few minutes summoned up strength to go and inquire what was the matter.

After calling her sister-in-law two or three times without effect, the truth began to dawn on her; and after considering the matter carefully, she could only come to the conclusion that the merchant had made a mistake, and had carried off the wrong lady. But now a fresh cause of uneasiness arose; she dreaded the consequences when Lin-pao should return and be informed of the mistake. She shut herself up in her room, and after picking up the head-pins, the earrings, and the head-dress, which were lying on the floor, threw herself, quite worn out with fatigue and anxiety, on her couch, and endeavoured to get a little sleep, but she was not able to close her eyes all night.

At daybreak she rose and bathed her face, and proceeded to complete her toilet. As, however, she was searching about for her mourning head-dress, some one began making a great noise at the room-door, knocking loudly and crying out, "Open the door instantly!" It was, in fact, Lin-pao himself. She recognized the voice at once. She made up her mind at once what to do; she let him go on knocking without answering him. He swore, stormed and bawled, till he was hoarse. At length the lady Wang went to the door, and standing behind it without opening it, asked, "Who is knocking there, and making such a disturbance?" Lin-pao, who recognized the voice of his sister-in-law, began to shout still louder: but seeing that his storming had no effect, he had recourse to an expedient which proved successful. "Sister-in-law," said he, "I have brought you good news! Lin-tchin, my youngest brother, has come back, and our eldest brother is in excellent health; open the door at once!"

Overjoyed at this intelligence, the lady Wang ran to complete her toilet, and in her haste put on the black[8] head-dress that her sister-in-law had left behind, and eagerly opened the door; but, alas! in vain did she look for her friend Lin-tchin; no one was there but Lin-pao. He entered her room hurriedly and looked round, but not seeing his wife, and perceiving a black head-dress on the head of his sister-in-law, his suspicions began to be excited in a strange manner.

[8] The Chinese mourning colour is white.

"Well! where is your sister-in-law?" he asked roughly.

"You ought to know better than I," replied the lady Wang, "since you had the whole management of this admirable plot."

"But tell me," returned Lin-pao, "why don't you still wear a white head-dress? have you left off mourning?" The lady Wang forthwith proceeded to relate to him all that had happened during his absence.

Just at this moment he caught sight through the window of four or five persons hurrying towards his house. To his utter astonishment he perceived that they were his eldest brother Lin-in, his youngest brother Lin-tchin, his nephew Hi-eul, and two servants carrying their luggage. Lin-pao, thunderstruck at this sight, and not having impudence enough to face them, ran off by the back-door, and disappeared like a flash of lightning.

The lady Wang was transported with joy at her husband's return. But who shall describe her ecstasies of joy when her son was presented to her? She could scarcely recognize him, so tall and handsome had he grown. "Oh!" cried she, "by what good fortune did you recover our dear child, whom I thought we had lost for ever?"

Lin-in gave her in detail an account of his adventures; and the lady Wang related at length all the indignities she had endured at the hands of Lin-pao, and the extremities to which she had been reduced by his scandalous treatment.

Lin-in lavished on his wife encomiums which indeed her fidelity deserved; after which, reflecting on the whole chain of events by which the present meeting had been brought about, he seemed deeply moved, and remarked, "If a blind passion for wealth had caused me to keep the two hundred täels I found by accident, how should I have ever met with our dear child? If avarice had prevented me from employing the twenty täels in saving those drowning people, my dear brother would have perished in the waves, and I should never have seen him; if by an unlooked-for chance I had not met my kind-hearted brother, how should I have discovered the trouble and confusion that reigned in this house in time to prevent its disastrous consequences? But for all this, my beloved wife, we should never have seen each other again. I recognize the special interposition of Providence in bringing about all these things. As to my other brother, that unnatural brother, who has unconsciously sold his own wife, he has drawn upon himself his own terrible punishment. Heaven rewards men according to their deserts; let them not think to escape its judgments.

"Let us learn from this how profitable in the end, as well as good, it is to practise virtue; it is that alone which bestows lasting prosperity upon a house."

In due course of time Hi-eul brought home his bride, the daughter of Tchin. The marriage was celebrated with great rejoicings, and proved a happy one. They had several children, and lived to see a crowd of grandchildren, several of whom became men of learning, and acquired important positions in the state.

CONTINUATION OF THE STORY OF PRINCE KHALAF AND THE PRINCESS OF CHINA.

The prince applauded the narrative of the story-teller; and, dinner being over, he prostrated himself a second time before the khan, and, after thanking him for his goodness, returned to the tent, where Elmaze and Timurtasch were anxiously expecting him. "I bring you good news," said he to them; "our fortune has changed already." He then related to them all that had passed. This fortunate event caused them the greatest pleasure; they regarded it as an infallible sign that the hardness of their destiny was beginning to soften. They willingly followed Khalaf, who conducted them to the royal tent and presented them to the khan. This prince received them with courtesy, and renewed to them the promise he had given to their son; and he did not fail to keep his word. He appointed them a private tent, caused them to be waited on by the slaves and officers of his household, and ordered them to be treated with the same respect as himself.

The next day Khalaf was arrayed in a rich dress; he received from the hand of Almguer himself a sabre with a diamond hilt and a purse full of gold sequins; they then brought him a beautiful Turcoman horse. He mounted before all the court; and to show that he understood the management of a horse, he made him go through all his paces and evolutions in a manner that charmed the prince and all his courtiers.

After having thanked the khan for all his benefits, he took his leave. He then sought Elmaze and Timurtasch; and after some time spent in desultory conversation, proceeded to unfold to them a scheme which for some days past had been agitating his mind. "I have a great desire," said he, "to see the great kingdom of China; give me permission to gratify that wish. I have a presentiment that I shall signalize myself by some splendid action, and that I shall gain the friendship of the monarch who holds that vast empire under his sway. Suffer me to leave you in this asylum, where you are in perfect safety, and where you can want for nothing. I am following an impulse which inspires me, or rather, I am yielding myself to the guidance of Heaven."

"Go, my son," replied Timurtasch; "yield to the noble impulse which animates you; hasten to the fortune that awaits you. Accelerate by your valour the arrival of that tardy prosperity which must one day succeed our misfortunes, or by a glorious death deserve an illustrious place in the history of unfortunate princes."

The young prince of the Nagäis, after having embraced his father and mother, mounted upon his beautiful charger, took a respectful leave of the khan, received from the hand of the princess Elmaze, who came out of her tent for the purpose, the parting cup, and set out on his journey. Historians do not mention that he encountered any thing worthy notice on his route; they only say that, having arrived at the great city Canbalac, otherwise Pekin, he dismounted at a house near the gate, where a worthy woman, a widow, lived. Khalaf reined up his horse here, and on the widow presenting herself at the door, he saluted her and said,

"My good mother, would you kindly receive a stranger? If you could give me a lodging in your house, I can venture to say that you will have no cause to regret it." The widow scrutinized him; and judging from his good looks, as well as from his dress, that he was no mean guest, she made him a low bow, and replied, "Young stranger of noble bearing, my house is at your service, and all that it contains."

"Have you also a place where I can put my horse?"

"Yes," said she, "I have," and called a young slave, who took the horse by the bridle, and led him into a small stable behind the house. Khalaf, who felt very hungry, then asked her if she would kindly send and buy something for him in the market. The widow replied, that she had a maiden who lived with her, and who would execute his orders. The prince then drew from his purse a sequin of gold and placed it in the girl's hand, who went off to the market.

In the mean time, the widow had enough to do to answer the inquiries of Khalaf. He asked her a thousand questions; what were the customs of the inhabitants of the city? how many families Pekin was said to contain? and, at length, the conversation fell upon the king of China.

"Tell me, I pray you," said Khalaf, "what is the character this prince bears. Is he generous, and do you think that he would pay any regard to a young stranger, who might offer to serve him against his enemies? In a word, is he a man to whose interests I could worthily attach myself?"

"Doubtless," replied the widow; "he is an excellent prince, who loves his subjects as much as he is beloved by them, and I am surprised that you have never heard of our good king, Altoun-Khan, for the fame of his justice and liberality is spread far and wide."

"From the favourable picture you draw of him," replied the prince of the Nagäis, "I should imagine that he ought to be the happiest and most prosperous monarch in the world."

"He is not so, however," replied the widow; "indeed, he may be said to be the most wretched. In the first place, he has no prince to succeed him on his throne; a male heir is denied him, notwithstanding all the prayers of himself and his subjects, and all the good deeds he performs to that end. But I must tell you, the grief of having no son is not his greatest trouble; what principally disturbs the peace of his life is the princess Tourandocte, his only daughter."

"How is it," replied Khalaf, "that she is such a source of grief to him?"

"I will tell you," replied the widow; "and, indeed, I can speak upon the subject from the very best authority; for my daughter has often told me the story and she has the honour of being among the attendants on the princess."

"The princess Tourandocte," continued the hostess of the prince of the Nagäis, "is in her nineteenth year; she is so beautiful, that the artists to whom she has sat for her portrait, although the most expert in the East, have all confessed that they were ashamed of their efforts; and that the most able painter in the world, and the best skilled in delineating the charms of a beautiful face, could not express those of the princess of China; nevertheless, the different portraits which have been taken of her, although infinitely inferior to the original, have produced the most disastrous consequences.

"She combines, with her ravishing beauty, a mind so cultivated, that she not only understands all that is usual for persons in her station to know, but is mistress of sciences suited only for the other sex. She can trace the various characters of several languages, she is acquainted with arithmetic, geography, philosophy, mathematics, law, and, above all, theology, she knows the laws and moral philosophy of our great legislator, Berginghuzin; in fact, is as learned as all the wise men put together. But her good qualities are effaced by a hardness of heart without parallel, and all her accomplishments are tarnished by detestable cruelty.

"It is now two years ago since the king of Thibet sent to ask her in marriage for his son, who had fallen in love with her from a portrait he had seen. Altoun-Khan, delighted with the prospect of this alliance, proposed it to Tourandocte. The haughty princess, to whom all men appeared despicable, so vain had her beauty rendered her, rejected the proposal with disdain. The king flew into a violent rage with her, and declared that he would be obeyed; but instead of submitting dutifully to the wishes of her father, she burst into bitter lamentations, because he showed a disposition to force her to comply; she grieved immoderately, as though it were intended to inflict a great injury upon her; in fact, she took it so much to heart that she fell seriously ill. The physicians, who soon discovered the secret of her complaint, told the king that all their remedies were useless, and that the princess would certainly lose her life, if he persisted in his resolution to make her espouse the prince of Thibet.

"The king then, who loves his daughter to distraction, alarmed at the danger she was in, went to see her, and assured her that he would send back the ambassador with a refusal. 'That is not enough, my lord,' replied the princess; 'I am resolved to die, except you grant what I ask you. If you wish me to live, you must bind yourself by an inviolable oath never to try to influence my wishes in this matter, and to publish a decree declaring that of all the princes who may seek my hand, none shall be allowed to espouse me who shall not previously have replied, without hesitation, to the questions which I shall put to him before all the learned men in this city; that if his answers prove satisfactory, I will consent to his becoming my husband, but if the reverse, that he shall lose his head in the court-yard of your palace.'

"'By this edict,' added she, 'of which all the foreign princes who may arrive at Pekin shall be informed, you will extinguish all desire of asking me in marriage; and that is exactly what I wish, for I hate men, and do not wish to be married.'

"'But, my child,' said the king, 'if by chance some one should present himself, and reply to your questions?'—

"'Ha! I do not fear that,' she said quickly, interrupting him; 'I can put questions which would puzzle the most learned doctors; I am willing to run that risk.'

"Altoun-Khan pondered over what the princess demanded of him. 'I see clearly,' thought he, 'that my daughter does not wish to marry, and the effect of this edict will be to frighten away all lovers. I run no risk, therefore, in yielding to her fancies, no evil can come of it. What prince would be mad enough to face such danger?'

"At length the king, persuaded that this edict would not be followed by any bad results, and that the recovery of his daughter entirely depended upon it, caused it to be published, and swore upon the laws of Berginghuzin to see that it was observed to the letter. Tourandocte, reassured by this oath, which she knew her father dare not violate, regained her strength, and was soon restored to perfect health.

"In spite of the decree, the fame of her beauty attracted several young princes to Pekin. It was in vain that they were informed of the nature of the edict; and as every body, but particularly a young prince, entertains a good opinion of himself, they had the hardihood to present themselves to reply to the questions of the princess; and not being able to fathom her deep meaning, they perished miserably one after another.

"The king, to do him justice, appears deeply afflicted with their sad fate. He repents of having made the oath which binds him; and however tenderly he may love his daughter, he would now almost rather he had let her die than have saved her life at such a price. He does all in his power to prevent these evils. When a lover whom the decree cannot restrain comes to demand the hand of the princess, he strives to deter him from his purpose; and he never consents, but with the deepest regret, to his exposing himself to the chance of losing his life. But it generally happens that he is unable to dissuade these rash young men. They are infatuated with Tourandocte, and the hope of possessing her blinds them to the difficulty of obtaining her.

"But if the king shows so much grief at the ruin of the unfortunate princes, it is not the case with his barbarous daughter. She takes a pride in these spectacles of blood with which her beauty periodically furnishes the Chinese. So great is her vanity, that she considers the most accomplished prince not only unworthy of her, but most insolent in daring to raise his thoughts towards her, and she looks upon his death as a just chastisement for his temerity.

"But what is still more deplorable, Heaven is perpetually permitting princes to come and sacrifice themselves to this inhuman princess. Only the other day, a prince, who flattered himself that he had knowledge enough to reply to her questions, lost his life; and this very night another is to die, who, unfortunately, came to the court of China with the same hopes."

Khalaf was deeply attentive to the widow's story.

"I cannot understand," said he, after she had ceased speaking, "how any princes can be found sufficiently devoid of judgment to come and ask the hand of the princess of China. What man would not be terrified at the condition without which he cannot hope to obtain her? Besides, despite what the artists may say who have painted her portrait; although they may affirm that their productions are but an imperfect image of her beauty, my firm belief is that they have added charms, and that their portraits exaggerate her beauty, since they have produced such powerful effects; indeed, I cannot think that Tourandocte is so beautiful as you say."

"Sir," replied the widow, "she is more lovely by far than I have described her to you; and you may believe me, for I have seen her several times when I have gone to the harem to visit my daughter. Draw upon your fancy as you please, collect in your imagination all that can possibly be brought together in order to constitute a perfect beauty, and be assured that even then you would not have pictured to yourself an object which could approach the perfections of the princess."

The prince of the Nagäis could not credit the story of the widow, so overdrawn did he consider it; he felt, nevertheless, a secret pleasure for which he could not account. "But, my mother," said he, "are the questions which the king's daughter proposes so difficult of solution that it is impossible to reply to them to the satisfaction of the lawyers who are judges? For my part, I cannot help thinking that the princes who were not able to penetrate the meaning of her questions, must have been persons of very little ingenuity, if not absolutely ignorant."

"No, no!" replied the widow. "There is no enigma more obscure than the questions of the princess, and it is almost impossible to reply to them."

Whilst they were conversing thus of Tourandocte and her lovers, the girl arrived from the market loaded with provisions. Khalaf sat down to a table which the widow had prepared, and ate like a man famishing with hunger. Whilst thus engaged the night drew on, and they heard shortly in the town the gong of justice. The prince asked what the noise meant. "It is to give notice to the people," replied the widow, "that some person is going to be executed; and the unfortunate victim about to be immolated is the prince of whom I told you, and who is to be executed to-night for not being able to answer the princess's questions. It is customary to punish the guilty during the day, but this is an exceptional case. The king, who in his heart abhors the punishment which he causes to be inflicted upon the lovers of his daughter, will not suffer the sun to be witness of such a cruel action."

The son of Timurtasch had a wish to see this execution, the cause of which appeared so singular to him. He went out of the house, and meeting a crowd of Chinese in the street animated by the same curiosity, he mixed with them, and went to the court-yard of the palace, where the tragic scene was to be enacted. He beheld in the middle of the yard a *schebt-cheraghe*, in other words a very high wooden tower, the outside of which, from the top to the bottom, was covered with branches of cypress, amongst which a prodigious quantity of lamps, tastefully arranged, spread a brilliant light around, and illuminated the whole court-yard. Fifteen cubits from the tower a scaffold was raised, covered with white satin, and around the scaffold were arranged several pavilions of taffetas of the same colour open towards the scaffold. Behind these two thousand soldiers of the guard of Altoun-Khan were stationed, with drawn swords and axes in their hands, forming a double rank, which served as a barrier against the people. Khalaf was looking with deep attention at all that presented itself to his view, when suddenly the mournful ceremony commenced. It was ushered in by a confused noise of drums and bells, which proceeded from the town, and could be heard at a great distance. At the same moment twenty mandarins and as many judges, all dressed in long robes of white woollen cloth, emerged from the palace, advanced towards the scaffold, and after walking three times around it, took their places under the pavilions.

Next came the victim, crowned with flowers interwoven with cypress leaves, and with a blue fillet round his head,—not a red one, such as criminals condemned by justice wear. He was a young prince, who had scarcely reached his eighteenth year; he was accompanied by a mandarin leading him by the hand, and followed by the executioner. The three ascended the scaffold; instantly the noise of the drums and bells ceased. The mandarin then addressed the prince in a tone so loud that he was heard by nearly the whole concourse of people. "Prince," said he, "is it not true that you were apprised of the terms of the king's edict before you presented yourself to ask the princess in marriage? Is it not also true that the king himself used all his endeavours to dissuade you from your rash resolution?" The prince, having replied in the affirmative, "Acknowledge, then," continued the mandarin, "that it is by your own fault that you lose your life to-day, and that the king and princess are not guilty of your death."

"I pardon them," returned the prince; "I impute my death to myself alone, and I pray Heaven not to require of them my blood which is about to be shed."

He had scarcely finished these words, when the executioner swept off his head with one stroke of the sword. The air instantly resounded with the noise of the drums and the bells. Then twelve mandarins took up the body, laid it in a coffin of ivory and ebony, and placed it upon a litter, which six of them bore away upon their shoulders into the gardens of Serail. Here they deposited it under a dome of white marble, which the king had ordered to be erected purposely to be the resting-place of all those unfortunate princes who should share the same fate. He often retired there to weep upon the tombs of those who were buried within it, and tried, by honouring their ashes with his tears, in some measure to atone for the barbarity of his child. As soon as the mandarins had carried away the body of the prince who had just suffered, the people and all the councillors retired to their homes, blaming the king for having had the imprudence to sanction such barbarity by an oath that he could not break. Khalaf remained in the court-yard of the palace in a state of bewilderment; he noticed a man near him weeping bitterly; he guessed that it was some person who was deeply interested in the execution that had just taken place, and wishing to know more about it, addressed him in these words:

"I am deeply moved," said he, "by the lively grief you exhibit, and I sympathize in your troubles, for I cannot doubt that you were intimately acquainted with the prince who has just suffered."

"Ah! sir," replied the mourner, with a fresh outburst of grief, "I ought indeed to know him, for I was his tutor. O unhappy king of Samarcand!" added he, "what will be thy grief when thou shalt be told of the extraordinary death of thy son? and who shall dare to carry thee the news?"

Khalaf asked by what means the prince of Samarcand had become enamoured of the princess of China. "I will tell you," replied the tutor: "and you will doubtless be astonished at the recital I am about to make. The prince of Samarcand," pursued he, "lived happily at his father's court. The court looked upon him as a prince who would one day be their sovereign, and they studied to please him as much as the king himself. He usually passed the day in hunting and playing at ball, and at night he assembled secretly in his apartments the distinguished youth of the court, with whom he drank all sorts of liquors. He sometimes amused himself by seeing the beautiful slaves dance, or by listening to music and singing. In a word, his life was passed in a constant round of pleasure.

"One day a famous painter arrived at Samarcand with several portraits of princesses which he had painted in the different courts through which he had passed. He showed them to my prince, who, looking at the first he presented, said, 'These are very beautiful pictures; I am certain that the originals are under a deep obligation to you.'

"'My lord,' replied the artist, 'I confess that in these portraits I have somewhat flattered the sitters; but I crave permission to tell you that I have one far more beautiful than these, which does not approach the original.' Saying this, he drew from the case which contained his portraits that of the princess of China.

"Scarcely had my master looked at it, when not conceiving that nature was capable of producing so perfect a beauty, he exclaimed that there was not in the world a woman of such exquisite loveliness, and that the portrait of the princess of China was more flattering than the others. The artist protested that it was not, and assured him that no pencil could convey an idea of the grace and beauty which shone in the countenance of the princess Tourandocte. Upon this assurance my master bought the portrait, which made so deep an impression on him, that, leaving the court of his father, he quitted Samarcand, accompanied by me alone, and without informing any one of his intentions, took the road for China, and came to this city. He volunteered to serve Altoun-Khan against his enemies, and asked the hand of his daughter the princess. We were apprized of the severe edict connected with the proposal, but alas! my prince, instead of being dismayed by the severity of the conditions, conceived the liveliest joy. 'I will go,' said he, 'and present myself to answer the questions of Tourandocte; I am not deficient in talent or ready wit, and I shall obtain the hand of the princess.'

"It is needless to tell you the rest, sir," continued the tutor, sobbing; "you may judge by the mournful spectacle you have beheld that the unfortunate prince of Samarcand was unable to answer, as he hoped, the fatal questions of this barbarous beauty, whose delight is to shed blood, and who has already been the means of sacrificing the lives of several kings' sons. A few moments before his death he gave me the portrait of this cruel princess. 'I entrust,' said he, 'this portrait to thee; guard carefully the precious deposit. Thou hast but to show it to my father when thou informest him of my sad fate, and I doubt not that when he beholds so beautiful a face, he will pardon my temerity.' But," added the old man, "let any one else who pleases carry the sad news to the king his father; for my part, borne down by the weight of my affliction, I will go far from hence and Samarcand, and mourn for my beloved charge. This is what you wished to know; and here is the dangerous portrait," pursued he, taking it from beneath his cloak and throwing it on the ground in a paroxysm of rage; "behold the cause of the sad fate of my prince. O execrable portrait! why had my master not my eyes when he took thee into his hands? O inhuman princess! may all the princes of the earth entertain for thee the same sentiments as those with which thou hast inspired me! Instead of being the object of their love, thou wouldest then be their aversion." Saying this, the tutor of the prince of Samarcand retired full of rage, regarding the palace with a furious eye and without speaking another word to the son of Timurtasch. The latter quickly picked up the portrait of Tourandocte, and turned to retrace his steps to the house of the widow; but he missed his way in the darkness, and wandered heedlessly out of the city. He impatiently awaited the daylight to enable him to contemplate the beauty of the princess of China. As soon as the approach of dawn furnished him with sufficient light to satisfy his curiosity, he opened the case which contained the portrait.

Still he hesitated before he looked at it. "What am I about to do?" cried he; "ought I to disclose to my eyes so dangerous an object? Think, Khalaf, think of the direful effects it has caused; hast thou already forgotten what the tutor of the prince of Samarcand has just narrated to thee? Look not on this portrait; resist the impulse which urges thee, it is nothing more than a feeling of idle curiosity. Whilst thou retainest thy reason thou canst prevent thy destruction. But what do I say? prevent," added he, checking himself; "with what false reasoning does my timid prudence inspire me. If I am to love the princess, is not my love already written in indelible characters in the book of fate. Besides, I think that it is possible to look upon the most beautiful portrait with impunity; one must be weak, indeed, to be influenced by the sight of a vain array of colours. Never fear; let us scan these surpassing and murderous features without emotion. I will even find defects, and taste the pleasure of criticizing the charms of this too beautiful princess; and I could wish, in order to mortify her vanity, that she might learn that I have looked upon her portrait without emotion."

The son of Timurtasch had fully made up his mind to look upon the portrait of Tourandocte with an indifferent eye. He now casts his eyes on it, he regards it attentively, examines it, admires the contour of the countenance, the regularity of the features, the vivacity of the eyes,—the mouth, the nose, all appear perfect; he is surprised at so rare a combination of perfect features, and although still on his guard, he allows himself to be charmed. An inconceivable uneasiness takes possession of him in spite of himself; he can no longer understand his feelings. "What fire," said he, "has suddenly kindled itself in my bosom! What tumult has this portrait produced in my thoughts! Merciful Heaven, is it the lot of all those who look upon this portrait to become enamoured of this inhuman princess? Alas! I feel but too surely that she has made the same impression upon me, as she did upon the unhappy prince of Samarcand; I yield to the charms that wounded him, and far from being terrified by his melancholy fate, I could almost envy his very misfortune. What a change, gracious Heaven! I could not conceive a short time ago, how one could be mad enough to despise the severity of the edict, and now I see nothing that frightens me, all the danger has vanished.

"No! incomparable princess," pursued he, devouring the portrait with an enamoured gaze, "no obstacle can stop me, I love you spite of your barbarity; and since it is permitted to me to aspire to your possession, from this day I will strive to win you; if I perish in the bold attempt, I shall only feel in dying the grief of not being able to possess you."

Khalaf, having formed the resolve of demanding the hand of the princess, returned to the widow's house, a journey which cost him no little trouble, for he had rambled to some considerable distance during the night. "Ah! my son," exclaimed his hostess, as soon as she beheld him, "I am so glad to see you, I was very uneasy about you, I feared some accident had befallen you; why did you not return earlier?"

"My good mother," replied he, "I am sorry to have caused you any uneasiness, I missed my way in the darkness." He then related to her how he had met the tutor of the prince whom they had put to death, and did not fail to repeat to her all that he had told him. Then showing her the portrait of Tourandocte; "Tell me," said he, "if this portrait is only an imperfect likeness of the princess of China; for my part, I cannot conceive that it is not equal to the original."

"By the soul of the prophet Jacmouny," cried the widow, after she had examined the portrait, "the princess is a thousand times more beautiful, and infinitely more charming than she is here represented. I wish you could see her, you would be of my opinion, that all the artists in the world who should undertake to paint her as she really is, could never succeed. I will not even make an exception in favour of the famous Many."

"You delight me above measure," replied the prince of the Nagäis, "by assuring me that the beauty of Tourandocte surpasses all the efforts of the artist's power. How flattering the assurance! It strengthens me in my determination, and incites me to attempt at once the brilliant adventure. Oh that I were before the princess! I burn with impatience to try whether I shall be more fortunate than the prince of Samarcand."

"What do you say, my son?" eagerly asked the widow, "what enterprise are you so rashly planning? And do you seriously think of carrying it into effect?"

"Yes, my good mother," returned Khalaf, "I intend this very day to present myself to answer the questions of the princess. I came to China only with the intention of offering my services to the great king, Altoun-Khan, but it is better to be his son-in-law than an officer in his army."

At these words the widow burst into tears. "Ah! sir, in the name of Heaven do not persist in so rash a resolution; you will certainly perish if you are bold enough to aspire to the hand of the princess; instead of allowing her beauty to charm you, let it be the object of your detestation, since it has been the cause of so many frightful tragedies; picture to yourself what the grief of your parents will be when they hear of your death; let the thoughts of the mortal grief into which you will plunge them deter you."

"For pity's sake, my mother," interrupted the son of Timurtasch, "cease to present to my mind such affecting images. I cannot be ignorant, that if it be my destiny to die this day, my sad end will be a source of bitter and inexhaustible grief to my beloved parents; nay, I can conceive their misery being so excessive as to endanger their own lives, for well do I know their extreme affection for me; notwithstanding all this, however, notwithstanding the gratitude with which their love ought to inspire, and indeed does inspire me, I must yield to the passion that consumes me. But, what! Is it not in hopes of making them more happy that I am about to expose my life? Yes, doubtless, their interest is bound up with the desire that urges me on, and I feel sure that if my father were here, far from opposing my design, he would rather excite me to its speedy execution. My resolution is taken; waste no more time in trying to dissuade me; nothing shall shake my determination."

When the widow found that her young guest would not heed her advice, her grief increased. "So it must be, then, sir," continued she; "you will not be restrained from rushing headlong on your destruction. Why was it ordained that you should come to lodge in my house? why did I speak of Tourandocte? You became enamoured of her from the description I gave of her; wretched woman that I am, it is I who have caused your ruin; why must I reproach myself with your death?"

"No, my good mother," said the prince of the Nagäis, interrupting her a second time, "you are not the cause of my misfortune; do not blame yourself because I love the princess; I am to love her, and do but fulfil my destiny. Besides, how do you know that I shall not be able to reply to her questions?

I am not without understanding, and I have studied much; and Heaven may have reserved for me the honour of delivering the king of China from the grief with which his frightful oath overwhelms him. But," added he, drawing out the purse which the khan of Berlas had given him, and which still contained a considerable quantity of gold pieces, "as my success is after all uncertain, and I may chance to die, I make you a present of this purse to console you for my death. You may sell my horse and keep the money, for it will be of no more use to me, whether the daughter of Altoun-Khan become the reward of my boldness, or my death be the mournful forfeit of my audacity."

The widow took the purse from Khalaf, saying, "O my son, you are much mistaken if you imagine that these pieces of gold will console me for your loss. I will employ them in good works, I will distribute a portion among the poor in the hospitals, who bear their afflictions with patience, and whose prayers are consequently acceptable to Heaven; the remainder I will give to the ministers of our religion, that they all may pray together that Heaven may inspire you, and not suffer you to perish. All the favour I ask you is, not to go to-day and present yourself to answer the questions of Tourandocte; wait till to-morrow, the time is not long; grant me that interval to enlist the hearts of the pious in your behalf, and propitiate our Prophet in your favour, after that you can do as you think best. I pray you to grant me that favour; I am bold to say that you owe it to one who has conceived so great a friendship for you, that she would be inconsolable if you were to die."

Indeed Khalaf's appearance had made a favourable impression upon her, for, besides being one of the handsomest princes in the world, his manners were so easy and pleasing that it was impossible to see him without loving him. He was moved by the grief and affection the good lady exhibited. "Well, my mother," said he, "I will do as you desire me; and I will not go to-day to ask the hand of the princess; but, to speak my sentiments frankly, I don't believe that even your prophet Jacmouny will be able to make me forego my determination."

The following morning, the prince appeared more determined than ever to demand Tourandocte. "Adieu, my good mother," said he, to the widow. "I am sorry that you have given yourself so much trouble on my account; you might have spared it, for I assured you yesterday that I should be of the same mind." With these words, he left the widow, who, giving herself up to the deepest sorrow, covered her face with her veil, and sat with her head on her knees, overwhelmed with indescribable grief.

The young prince of the Nagäis, perfumed with rare scents and more beautiful than the moon, repaired to the palace. He found at the gate five elephants, and, on each side, a line of two thousand soldiers, with helmets on their heads, armed with shields, and covered with plate armour. One of the principal officers in command of the troops, judging from Khalaf's air that he was a stranger, stopped him, and demanded his business at the palace.

"I am a foreign prince," replied the son of Timurtasch. "I am come to present myself to the king, and pray him to grant me permission to reply to the questions of the princess his daughter."

The officer, at these words, regarding him with astonishment, said to him, "Prince, do you know that you come to seek death? You would have done more wisely to have remained in your own country, than form the design which brings you hither; retrace your steps, and do not flatter yourself with the deceitful hope that you will obtain the hand of the cruel Tourandocte. Although you may have studied until you have become more learned in science than all the mandarins, you will never be able to fathom the meaning of her ambiguous questions."

"Accept my heartfelt thanks," replied Khalaf; "but, believe me, I am not come thus far to retreat."

"Go on to your certain death, then," returned the officer, in a tone of chagrin, "since it is impossible to restrain you." At the same moment, he allowed him to enter the palace, and then, turning towards some other officers who had been listening to their conversation, he said, "How handsome and well-grown this young prince is. It is a pity he should die so early."

Khalaf traversed several saloons, and, at length, found himself in the hall where the king was accustomed to give audience to his people. In it was placed the steel throne of Cathay, made in the form of a dragon, three cubits high; four lofty columns, of the same material, supported above it a vast canopy of yellow satin, ornamented with precious stones. Altoun-Khan, dressed in a caftan of gold brocade upon a crimson ground, was seated on his throne, with an air of gravity which was in admirable keeping with his long moustache and ample beard. The monarch, after listening to some of his subjects, cast his eyes by chance to where the prince of the Nagäis stood amongst the crowd; he saw, at once, by his noble bearing and splendid dress, that he was not a man of common birth; he pointed out Khalaf to one of his mandarins, and gave an order, in an undertone, to learn his rank, and the reason of his visit to his court.

The mandarin approached the son of Timurtasch, and told him that the king desired to know who he was, and whether he wished to make any request of the king. "You may tell the king, your master," replied the prince, "that I am the only son of a king, and that I am come to endeavour to merit the honour of becoming his son-in-law."

Altoun-Khan no sooner learned the reply of the prince of the Nagäis, than he changed colour; his august countenance became pale as death, he broke up the audience, and dismissed all the people; he then descended from his throne, and, approaching Khalaf, "Rash young man," said he, "are you aware of the severity of my edict, and of the miserable fate of those who have hitherto persisted in their desire to obtain the hand of the princess my daughter?"

"Yes, my lord," replied the son of Timurtasch, "I know all the danger I incur; my eyes have witnessed the just and severe punishment your majesty inflicted upon the prince of Samarcand; but the deplorable end of the audacious youths who have flattered themselves with the sweet, though vain, hope of possessing the princess Tourandocte, only stimulates the desire I have of deserving her."

"What madness!" rejoined the king; "scarcely has one prince lost his life, than another presents himself to share the same fate; it appears as though they took a pleasure in sacrificing themselves. What blindness! Reconsider the step you are taking, and be less prodigal of your blood; you inspire me with more pity than any who have hitherto come to seek their destruction; I feel a growing inclination towards you, and wish to do all in my power to hinder you from perishing. Return to your father's kingdom, and do not inflict upon him the pain of learning from strangers' lips the sad intelligence that he will never more behold his only son."

"My lord," replied Khalaf, "I am overjoyed to hear, from your majesty's own lips, that I have the honour of pleasing you; I draw a happy presage from it. It may be that Heaven, touched by the misfortunes caused by the beauty of the princess, will use me as a means of putting an end to them, and securing you, at the same time, tranquillity for the remainder of your life, which the necessity of authorizing these cruel deeds disturbs. Can you be sure that I shall not be able to answer the questions that may be put to me? What certainty have you that I shall perish? If others have been unable to fathom the depths of the obscure propositions of Tourandocte, is it to be concluded that I cannot penetrate their meaning? No, my lord, their example shall never make me renounce the brilliant honour of having you for a father-in-law."

"Ah! unhappy prince," replied the king, melting into tears, "you wish to die; all the princes who have presented themselves before you, to answer the fatal questions put by my daughter, used the same language; they all hoped that they could penetrate her meaning, and not one was able to do so. Alas! you will be the dupe of your own confidence. Once more, my son, let me dissuade you. I love you, and wish to save you; do not frustrate my good intentions by your obstinacy; whatever confidence you may feel, distrust it. You deceive yourself, if you imagine that you will be able to answer upon the spot what the princess may propose to you; you will, it is true, have seven minutes to answer in; that is the rule. But if in that time you do not give a satisfactory reply, and one that shall be approved of by all the doctors and wise men who are appointed the judges, that moment you will be declared worthy of death, and on the following night will be conducted to execution. So, prince, retire; pass the rest of the day in considering what is your duty in reference to the step you propose to take; consult wise persons, reflect well, and to-morrow let me know your determination." When the king had finished speaking, he dismissed Khalaf, who immediately quitted the palace, much mortified that he was obliged to wait till the next day, for he was no way daunted by what the king had said. He returned to his hostess without exhibiting the least concern about the danger to which he had determined to expose himself. As soon as he presented himself to the widow, and had related all that had passed at the palace, she began to remonstrate with him afresh, and bring every argument she could think of into play to dissuade him from his enterprise; but her efforts were crowned with no better success, and she had the mortification of seeing that they only inflamed her young guest more, and strengthened him in his resolution. The next day the prince returned to the palace, and was announced to the king, who received him in his cabinet, not wishing any one to be present at their interview.

"Well, prince," began Altoun-Khan, "am I to rejoice or grieve at your presence here to-day? What is your determination?"

"My lord," replied Khalaf, "I am in the same mind as yesterday. Before I had the honour of presenting myself then before your majesty, I had thoroughly reflected upon the matter; and I am still prepared to suffer the same punishment as my rivals, if Heaven has not otherwise ordained." At these words the king smote his breast, rent his clothes, and plucked the hairs from his beard.

"Wretched man that I am!" cried he, "that I should have conceived such friendship for him. The death of the others has not caused me half the pain which his will occasion me. Ah! my son," continued he, embracing the prince of the Nagaïs with a tenderness that caused him deep emotion, "yield to my grief, if my arguments are not able to shake thee. I feel that the blow which takes thy life will strike my heart with deadly force. Renounce, I conjure thee, the hope of possessing my cruel daughter; thou wilt find in the world plenty of other princesses whom thou mayst gain with more ease and as much honour. Why persevere in the pursuit of an inhuman creature whom thou wilt never be able to obtain? Remain, if thou wilt, in my court; thou shalt hold the first rank after me; thou shalt have beautiful slaves; pleasures shall follow thee wherever thou goest; in a word, I will look on thee as my own son. Desist from thy pursuit of Tourandocte. Oh! let me at least have the joy of rescuing one victim from the sanguinary princess."

The son of Timurtasch was deeply moved by the friendship which the king of China exhibited towards him; but he replied, "My lord, let me for pity's sake expose myself to the danger from which you seek to deter me; the greater it is, the more do I feel myself tempted to encounter it. I must avow that even the cruelty of the princess stimulates my love. I feel an inward pleasure in the thought that I am the happy mortal who is to triumph over this proud beauty. For Heaven's sake, your majesty," pursued he, "cease to oppose a design which my glory, my repose, my life even render it necessary for me to prosecute; for, truly, I cannot live unless I obtain Tourandocte."

Altoun-Khan, perceiving that Khalaf was not to be moved, was overwhelmed with affliction. "Ah! rash youth," said he, "thy death-warrant is sealed, since thou art still determined to persist in demanding my daughter. Heaven is witness that I have done all in my power to inspire thee with rational thoughts. Thou rejectest my counsel, and lovest rather to perish than follow it; let us say no more; thou wilt receive the reward of thy mad constancy. I consent to thy undertaking to answer the questions of Tourandocte, but I must first pay thee the honour which I am accustomed to bestow upon princes who seek my alliance."

At these words he called the chief of his first band of eunuchs; he ordered him to conduct Khalaf into the princes' palace, and to assign him two hundred eunuchs to wait upon him.

The prince of the Nagäis had scarcely entered the palace to which the eunuch conducted him, before the principal mandarins came to salute him, which they did in the following manner: they placed themselves on their knees before him, bowed their heads to the ground, saying one after the other, "Prince, the perpetual servant of your illustrious race comes to make his obeisance to you." They then all made him presents and retired.

The king, who felt the greatest friendship for the son of Timurtasch, and pitied him, sent for the most learned professor of the royal college, and said to him, "There is a new prince, who has come to my court to demand the hand of my daughter. I have spared no pains to induce him to renounce his intention, but without success. I wish thee to exert thine eloquence in endeavouring to make him listen to reason. It is for this I have sent for thee." The professor obeyed. He went to Khalaf and entered into a long conversation with him; after which he returned to Altoun-Khan, and said, "My lord, it is impossible to dissuade this young prince; he will absolutely deserve the princess or die. When I saw the futility of attempting to conquer his resolution, I had the curiosity to try and ascertain whether his obstinacy did not proceed from some other cause than his love. I interrogated him upon several different subjects, and I found him so well informed that I was surprised at his learning. He is a Moslem, and appears to me perfectly instructed in all that concerns his religion; in fact, to confess the truth to your majesty, I believe if any prince is capable of replying to the questions of the princess it is he."

"O wise man," cried the king, "I am overjoyed at thy report. Heaven grant that he may become my son-in-law. From the moment he appeared before me I felt an affection for him; may he be more fortunate than the others who came to this city only to seek a grave."

After prayers and sacrifices, the Chinese monarch sent his calao to the prince of the Nagäis with notice that he was to hold himself in readiness to reply to the princess's questions on the next day, and to tell him that the proper officers would come at the right time to conduct him to the divan; and that the persons who were to compose the assembly had already received orders to attend.

Notwithstanding his inflexible determination to persevere in this adventure, Khalaf did not pass a quiet night; if at one time he dared to trust to his genius, and promise himself success, at another, losing confidence, he represented to himself the shame he should endure if his replies did not please the divan; at another time he thought of Elmaze and Timurtasch. "Alas!" said he, "if I die, what will become of my father and mother?"

Day surprised him occupied with these conflicting thoughts. Presently he heard the ringing of bells and beating of drums. He concluded that this was to call to the council all those who were ordered to attend. Then raising his thoughts to Mahomet, "O great prophet," said he, "you behold my difficulties and know my doubts. Inspire me, and reveal to me whether I must go to the divan, or must confess to the king that the danger terrifies me!" He had scarcely pronounced these words, before he felt all his fears vanish and his confidence return. He rose and dressed himself in a caftan, and mantle of red silk worked with gold flowers, which Altoun-Khan had sent him, with stockings and slippers of blue silk.

When he had finished dressing, six mandarins, booted and dressed in very wide robes of crimson, entered his apartment, and after having saluted him in the same manner as on the previous day, informed him that they came from the king to lead him to the divan. He immediately rose and accompanied them; they traversed a court between a double file of soldiers, and when they arrived in the first council-chamber found more than a thousand singers and players upon instruments, who performing in concert produced a wonderful noise. From thence they advanced into the hall, where the council was sitting, and which communicated with the interior palace.

All the persons who were to assist at this assembly were already seated under canopies of different colours arranged round the hall. The mandarins of the highest rank were on one side, the calao with the professors of the college on the other, and several doctors, renowned for their erudition, occupied other seats. In the middle were placed two thrones of gold raised upon triangular pedestals.

As soon as the prince of the Nagäis appeared, the noble and learned assembly saluted him with gestures of great respect, but without speaking a word; for every body, being in expectation of the king's arrival, preserved the strictest silence.

The sun was upon the point of rising. As soon as the first rays of that brilliant luminary were perceived, two eunuchs drew aside the curtains which hung before the door of the inner palace, and immediately the king appeared, accompanied by the princess Tourandocte, who wore a long robe of silk and gold tissue, whilst her face was concealed by a veil of the same material. When the king and princess had taken their seats upon their thrones, which they ascended by five steps of silver, two young girls of perfect beauty approached and stationed themselves, one on the side of the king and the other near the princess. They were slaves of the harem of Altoun-Khan; their faces and necks were exposed; they wore large pearls in their ears; and they stood each with pen and paper, ready to transcribe what the king or the princess might desire. All this time the whole assembly, who had risen upon the entrance of Altoun-Khan, stood up with great gravity and their eyes half closed. Khalaf alone looked about him, or rather looked only at the princess, whose majestic demeanour filled him with admiration.

When the powerful monarch of China had ordered the mandarins and doctors to be seated, one of the six nobles who had conducted Khalaf, and who stood with him at fifteen cubits' distance from the two thrones, kneeled down and read a petition, which contained the demand of the stranger prince for the hand of the princess Tourandocte. He then rose and told Khalaf to make three salutations to the king. The prince of the Nagäis acquitted himself with so much grace, that Altoun-Khan could not refrain from smiling and expressing the pleasure he experienced in seeing him.

The calao then rose from his place and read with a loud voice the fatal edict, which condemned to death all the rash lovers who should fail to reply satisfactorily to the questions of Tourandocte. Then addressing Khalaf, "Prince," said he, "you have just heard the conditions upon which alone the princess's hand is to be obtained. If the sense of danger makes any impression upon you, there is still time to retire."

"No, no!" said the prince; "the prize to be carried off is too precious to be lost by cowardice."

The king, seeing Khalaf ready to reply to the questions of Tourandocte, turned towards the princess and said, "My daughter, it is for you to speak; propose to this young prince the questions which you have prepared; and may all the spirits to whom sacrifices were offered yesterday grant that he may penetrate the meaning of your words."

Tourandocte thereupon said, "I take the prophet Jacmouny to witness, that I behold with sorrow the death of so many princes; but why do they persist in desiring to wed me? why will they not leave me to live in peace without making attempts on my liberty? Know then, rash young man," added she, addressing Khalaf, "that you cannot reproach me if you suffer a cruel death; you have the examples of your rivals before your eyes; you alone are the cause of your own destruction; I do not oblige you to come and ask my hand."

"Lovely princess," replied the prince of the Nagäis, "I am fully alive to all that has been said upon this subject; propound, if you please, your questions, and I will endeavour to unravel their meaning."

"Well then," said Tourandocte, "tell me what creature is that which belongs to every land, is a friend to the whole world, and will not brook an equal?"

"Madam," replied Khalaf, "it is the sun."

"He is right," exclaimed all the doctors, "it is the sun."

"What is that mother," resumed the princess, "who, after having brought her children into the world, devours them when they are grown up?"

"It is the sea," replied the prince of the Nagäis; "because the rivers, which draw their sources from the sea, discharge themselves into it again."

Tourandocte, seeing that the prince gave correct replies to her questions, was so vexed that she resolved to spare no effort to destroy him. Exerting all her ingenuity, she next asked, "What tree is that whose leaves are white on one side and black on the other?" She was not satisfied with proposing the riddle alone; the malignant princess, in order to dazzle and confuse him, raised her veil at the same moment, and allowed the assembly to see all the beauty of her countenance, the haughty charms of which were only enhanced by the violence of her emotions. Her head was adorned with natural flowers arranged with infinite art, and her eyes shone more brilliantly than the stars. She was as lovely as the sun in all his splendour, when he emerges from a thick cloud. The son of Timurtasch, at the sight of this incomparable princess, remained mute and motionless; so much so, that all the divan, who were deeply interested in him, were seized with terror; the king himself grew pale, and thought that the prince was lost for ever.

But Khalaf, recovering from the surprise that the beauty of Tourandocte had caused him, quickly reassured the assembly by resuming, "Charming princess, I pray you pardon me if I remained for some moments speechless; I could not behold so much loveliness without being disturbed. Have the goodness to repeat the question, for I no longer remember it; your charms have made me forget every thing."

"I asked you," said Tourandocte, "what tree is that whose leaves are white on one side and black on the other?"

"That tree," replied Khalaf, "is the year, which is composed of days and nights."

This reply was again applauded in the divan. The mandarins and the doctors said that it was correct, and bestowed a thousand praises on the young prince. Altoun-Khan said to Tourandocte, "Come, my daughter, confess thyself vanquished, and consent to espouse thy conqueror; the others were not able to reply to even one of thy questions, and this one, thou seest, has answered them all."

"He has *not* gained the victory," angrily retorted the princess, replacing her veil to conceal her confusion and the tears she was not able to repress; "I have others to propose to him. But I will defer them till to-morrow."

"No," replied the king, "I will certainly not permit you to propose questions without end: all that I can allow you is to ask him one more, and that immediately."

The princess objected, saying that she had only prepared those which had just been answered, and entreated the king, her father, for permission to interrogate the prince on the following day.

"I will certainly not grant it," cried the monarch of China, in a rage; "you are only endeavouring to perplex this young prince, while I am eagerly grasping at the prospect of escaping from the frightful oath I had the imprudence to make. Ah! cruel one, you breathe nothing but blood, and the death of your lovers is a pleasant sight to you. The queen, your mother, touched by the first misfortunes your cruelty caused, died of grief at having brought into the world so barbarous a child; and I, you know well, am plunged into a state of profound melancholy, which nothing can dissipate, whilst I behold the fatal results of the love I entertained for you; but, thanks to the sun, and the moon, and the spirits who preside in the heavens, and by whom my sacrifices have been regarded with a propitious eye, no more of those horrible executions which have rendered my name execrable shall be committed in my palace. Since this prince has answered your questions satisfactorily, I ask all this assembly if it is not right that you should become his wife?"

The mandarins and the doctors expressed their assent in murmurs, and the calao took upon himself to speak. "My lord," said he, addressing the king, "your majesty is no longer bound by the oath you made, to execute your severe edict; it is for the princess to fulfil her engagement. She promised her hand to him who should answer her questions correctly; a prince has answered them, to the satisfaction of the whole divan; she must keep her promise, or we cannot doubt that the spirits who preside over the punishment of perjurers will quickly take vengeance upon her."

Tourandocte kept silence during the delivery of this speech; she sat with her head on her knees, and appeared buried in deep affliction. Khalaf, perceiving this, prostrated himself before Altoun-Khan, and said, "Great king, whose justice and goodness have raised the vast empire of China to such prosperity, I beg of your majesty to grant me a favour. I see that the princess is in despair at my having been so fortunate as to reply to her questions; doubtless she would rather it had so happened that I should have deserved death. Since she exhibits so strong an aversion to me, that, in spite of her promise, she refuses to become my wife, I will renounce my right to her, on condition that she, on her part, replies correctly to a question which I shall propose."

The whole assembly was surprised at this speech. "Is this young prince mad," they whispered one to another, "to risk the loss of that for which he perilled his life? Does he imagine he can propose a question that will be too difficult for Tourandocte to solve? He must have lost his senses." Altoun-Khan was also amazed at the request which Khalaf had the temerity to make. "Prince," said he, "have you reflected upon the words which have just escaped your lips?"

"Yes, my lord," replied the prince of the Nagäis, "and I implore you to grant me this favour."

"I grant it," returned the king; "but, whatever be the result, I declare that I am no longer bound by the oath I made, and that, henceforth, I will not cause another prince to be put to death."

"Divine Tourandocte," resumed the son of Timurtasch, addressing the princess, "you have heard what I said. Although the decision of this learned assembly has awarded to me the prize of your hand, although you are mine, I will give you back your liberty, I will yield up possession of you, I will despoil myself of a treasure precious to me above all things, provided you reply at once to a question I shall ask; but, on your part, swear that if you cannot, you will consent willingly to complete my happiness and crown my love."

"Yes, prince," replied Tourandocte, "I accept the conditions, and I take this assembly as witnesses of my oath."

All the divan awaited, in breathless suspense, the question that Khalaf was to propose to the princess, and there was not one who did not blame the young prince for exposing himself to the risk of losing the daughter of Altoun-Khan; they were all amazed at his temerity. "Lovely princess," said Khalaf, "what is the name of that prince who, after suffering a thousand hardships, and being reduced even to beg his bread, finds himself, at this moment, overwhelmed with glory and joy?"

"It is impossible," said Tourandocte, "for me to reply to that question on the spot, but I promise that to-morrow I will tell you the name of that prince."

"Madam," cried Khalaf, "I asked no time for consideration, and it is not right to grant you any; still, I will grant you your wish; I hope, after that, you will look more favourably on me, and not oppose any further difficulty to your becoming my bride."

"She must make up her mind to that," said Altoun-Khan, "if she cannot reply to the question proposed. Let her not think by falling ill, or pretending to do so, that she will thereby escape. Even if my rash oath should not bind me to grant him her hand, and she were not his according to the tenor of the edict, I would rather let her die, than send this young prince away. Where would it be possible for her to meet with one more perfectly worthy of her?" With these words, he rose and dismissed the assembly. He re-entered the inner palace with the princess, who retired to her own apartments.

As soon as the king had left the divan, all the mandarins and doctors complimented Khalaf upon his wit and understanding. "I admire," said one, "your ready and easy conception." "No!" said another, "there is not a bachelor licentiate, or doctor even, of greater penetration than you. Not one of all the princes who has presented themselves hitherto, in the least degree approached your merit, and we feel the most heartfelt joy at your success." The prince of the Nagäis had no light task to perform in thanking all those who pressed round him to congratulate him. At length, the six mandarins who had conducted him to the council-chamber, led him back to the same palace whence they had brought him, whilst the others, together with the learned doctors retired, not without anxiety about the answer which the daughter of Altoun-Khan would return to the question.

The princess Tourandocte regained her palace, followed by the two young slaves who enjoyed her confidence. No sooner had she entered into her apartment, than she tore off her veil, and throwing herself upon a couch, gave free vent to the grief and rage which agitated her; shame and sorrow were depicted on her countenance; her eyes already bedimmed with tears, overflowed afresh; she tore off the flowers that adorned her head, and allowed her hair to fall about her in confusion. Her two favourite slaves attempted to console her, but she only said bitterly, "Leave me, both of you, cease your useless attentions. I will listen to nothing but my despair; leave me alone to pour forth my tears and lamentations. Ah! how great will be my confusion to-morrow, when I shall be forced to acknowledge before the whole council, and the wisest doctors of China, that I cannot solve the question. Is that, they will say, the transcendent princess who prides herself upon knowing every thing, and to whom the solution of the most difficult enigma presented no difficulty?"

"Alas!" continued she, "they all take an interest in this young prince. I noticed them grow pale with anxiety when he appeared embarrassed. I saw their faces beaming with joy when he penetrated the meaning of my questions. I shall have the bitter mortification of seeing them again rejoice at my confusion, when I shall have to confess myself conquered. How great will be their delight when I make the degrading avowal, and what agony must I endure in making it."

"My princess," said one of her slaves, "instead of afflicting yourself beforehand, instead of picturing to yourself the shame you fear to suffer to-morrow, would it not be better to think of some means of preventing it? Is the question the prince has proposed so difficult, that you cannot answer it? with the genius and penetration you possess, can you not accomplish it?"

"No," said Tourandocte, "it is impossible. He asks me to name the prince who, after suffering a thousand hardships, and being reduced to beg his bread, is, at this moment, overwhelmed with joy and glory? I feel assured that he is himself that prince, but not knowing him, I cannot tell his name."

"Still, madam," rejoined the same slave, "you have promised to name that prince to-morrow; when you made that promise, you hoped, doubtless, to be able to fulfil it."

"I had no hope," replied the princess, "and I only demanded time to die of grief, rather than be obliged to acknowledge my shame, and marry the prince."

"The resolution is a violent one," said the other favourite slave. "I know well that no man is worthy of you, but you must allow that this prince possesses singular merits; his beauty, his noble bearing, and his ready wit ought to plead in his favour."

"I grant it all," interrupted the princess. "If there is any prince in the world who is worthy of my regards, it is he. Indeed, I will not deny it, that I grieved for him, before I put my questions to him; I sighed when I beheld him, and—what has never happened till to-day—I almost hoped he would reply to my questions correctly. It is true that, at the same moment, I blushed at my weakness, but my pride got the better of me, and the apt answers he made excited my abhorrence towards him; all the commendations which the doctors bestowed on him so deeply mortified me, that I then felt, and still feel, the most bitter hatred against him. O unhappy Tourandocte, lay thee down and die of vexation and grief, at having found a man, and he a youth, who has been able to load thee with disgrace, and compel thee to become his wife."

At these words she redoubled her tears, and in the transport of her rage spared neither her hair nor her clothes. She raised her hands more than once towards her cheeks to tear them, and punish them as the prime authors of the disgrace she had endured; but her slaves, who were watching her frenzy, prevented her. They tried, however, in vain to console her; they could not calm the fury of her agitation. Whilst she was in this fearful state of excitement, the prince of the Nagäis, charmed with the result, and overwhelmed with joy, delivered himself up to the hope of bearing off his bride the next day.

The king, having returned from the council-chamber, sent for Khalaf to talk over in private the events which had taken place at the divan. The prince of the Nagäis hastened to obey the orders of the monarch, who, after embracing him with great tenderness, said, "Ah! my son, release me from the anxiety I am suffering. I fear lest my daughter should be able to answer the question you have proposed. Why have you risked the danger of losing the object of your love?"

"Let not your majesty be under the least apprehension," replied Khalaf; "it is impossible that the princess can tell me who the prince is whose name I have asked, for I am that prince, and no one in your court knows me."

"This gives me fresh hope," cried the king in a transport of joy; "I confess I was most anxious about you. Tourandocte is very shrewd; the subtlety of her wit made me tremble for you; but, thank Heaven, you dispel my doubts. However great her facility of penetrating the sense of enigmas, she cannot guess your name. I can no longer accuse you of temerity; and I see what appeared to me a lack of prudence, is an ingenious device you have formed to remove every pretext for my daughter's refusal."

Altoun-Khan, after laughing with Khalaf at the question proposed to the princess, prepared to enjoy the diversion of the chase. He dressed himself in a light and close-fitting caftan, and enclosed his beard in a bag of black satin. He ordered the mandarins to hold themselves in readiness to accompany him, and commanded a hunting-dress to be given to the prince of the Nagäis. They partook of a slight repast, and then quitted the palace. The mandarins, in open palanquins of ivory inlaid with gold, headed the procession, each carried by six men; two men armed with whips of cord marched before each palanquin, and two others followed with tablets of silver, upon which were written in large characters all the mandarin's titles. The king and Khalaf, in an open litter of red sandalwood, carried by twenty military officers, on whose dresses were embroidered in silver the monarch's monogram and badges,—the latter consisting of several figures of animals,—appeared next. After the mandarins, two generals of Altoun-Khan's army marched on either side of the litter, carrying large fans or umbrellas to ward off the heat, and three thousand eunuchs on foot completed the cortége.

When they arrived at the place where the hunters awaited the king with the falcons, the sport began by flying hawks at quails; this diversion lasted till sunset, when the king and the prince, and the persons of their suites, returned to the palace in the same order in which they had left. They found in the court several pavilions of silk of different colours, a great number of small tables, beautifully polished and covered with all sorts of viands ready cut up. As soon as the king had taken his seat, Khalaf and the mandarins sat down, each at a little separate table, near which stood another, which served as a buffet. They all began by drinking several bumpers of rice wine before touching the viands; they then proceeded to eat without drinking any more. The banquet ended, the king, Altoun-Khan, led the prince of the Nagäis into a large hall, brilliantly illuminated, and fitted up with seats arranged for seeing some spectacle, and they were followed by all the mandarins. The king appointed each his place, and made Khalaf sit near him, upon a large ebony throne, inlaid with gold tracery.

As soon as the company had taken their places, singers and musicians entered, who commenced an agreeable concert. Altoun-Khan was delighted with it. Infatuated with the Chinese music, he asked the son of Timurtasch, from time to time, what he thought of it, and the young prince, out of politeness, gave it the highest rank of all the music in the world. The concert finished, the singers and musicians retired, to make room for an artificial elephant, which having advanced by secret springs into the middle of the hall, vomited forth six vaulters, who began by making some perilous leaps. They were attired in very thin dresses; they had on only drawers of Indian cloth, caps of brocade, and light shoes. After they had exhibited their agility and suppleness by a thousand extraordinary performances, they re-entered the elephant, which went away as it came. Next, there appeared players, who performed, impromptu, a piece, the subject of which the king chose. When all these diversions were finished, and the night was far advanced, Altoun-Khan and Khalaf rose, to retire to their apartments, and the mandarins followed their example.

The young prince of the Nagäis, conducted by eunuchs bearing wax candles in gold candelabra, was preparing to taste the sweets of repose as well as his impatience to return to the divan would permit him, when on entering his chamber, he found a young lady, dressed in a robe of red brocade with silver flowers, and adorned with rubies and emeralds; she wore a head-dress of rose-coloured silk, ornamented with pearls and bound by a very light silver border, which only covered the top of her head, and allowed her beautiful hair to escape, which hung down in ringlets, adorned with a few artificial flowers; as to her figure and face it was impossible to see any more beautiful and perfect except that of the princess of China.

The son of Timurtasch was much surprised at meeting a lady alone, and so beautiful, at midnight in his room. He could not have looked upon her with indifference, had he not seen Tourandocte; but as the lover of that princess he had no eyes for any other.

As soon as the lady perceived Khalaf, she rose from the sofa where she was seated, and upon which she had laid her veil, and after making a low inclination of her head, "Prince," said she, "I doubt not that you are surprised to find a woman here; for you cannot be ignorant that it is rigorously forbidden for men and women who inhabit the harem, to have any communication together; but the importance of the matter that I have to communicate to you, has made me disregard all danger. I have had dexterity and good fortune enough to overcome all the obstacles which opposed my design. I have gained the eunuchs who wait upon you. It now only remains for me to tell you what brought me here."

Khalaf felt interested; he could not doubt but that the lady who had taken so perilous a step, had something to communicate worthy his attention; he begged her to resume her seat on the sofa; they both sat down; and the lady then continued in these terms:

"My lord, I believe I ought to begin by informing you that I am the daughter of a khan, one of the tributaries of Altoun-Khan. Some years ago, my father was bold enough to refuse to pay the usual tribute, and, relying too much upon his experience in the art of war, as well as upon the valour of his troops, prepared to defend himself in case he were attacked. What he expected happened. The king of China irritated by his audacity, sent the most experienced of his generals with a powerful army against him. My father, though considerably weaker in numbers, went out to meet him. After a sanguinary battle, which was fought on the banks of a river, the Chinese general remained victorious. My father, pierced with a thousand wounds, died during the battle, but before his death, he ordered all his wives and children to be thrown into the river, to preserve them from slavery. Those who were charged with the generous, though inhuman order, executed it; they threw me, together with my mother, sisters, and two brothers, whose tender age had kept them with us, into the river. The Chinese general arrived at the spot at the very moment when they had cast us in, and when we were about to finish our miserable existence. This mournful and horrible sight excited his compassion; he promised a reward to any of the soldiers who should save any of the vanquished khan's family. Several Chinese horsemen, in spite of the rapidity of the stream, dashed in, and urged their horses wherever they saw our dying bodies floating. They recovered a few, but their assistance was only of use to me. I still breathed when they brought me to shore. The general took great pains for my recovery, as though the glory acquired by my captivity would bestow a fresh lustre on his victory; he brought me to this city, and presented me to the king, after giving an account of his mission. Altoun-Khan placed me with his daughter the princess, who is two or three years younger than I am.

"Although still a child, I could not help reflecting that I had become a slave, and that I ought to have sentiments conformable to my situation. I therefore studied the disposition of Tourandocte, and strove to please her, and I succeeded so well by my compliance with her wishes and my attentions, that I gained her friendship. From that time I have shared her confidence with a young person of illustrious birth, whom the misfortunes of her family have reduced to slavery.

"Pardon, my lord," she continued, "this narrative which does not bear any relation to the subject that has brought me here. I thought it but right to apprize you that I am of noble blood, that you might place more reliance in me; for the important communication I have to make is such, that an ordinary slave might induce you to give but little credence to what she had to say; and I know not, that even I, though the daughter of a khan, shall be able to influence you: would a prince enamoured of Tourandocte give credit to what I am about to say of her?"

"Princess," replied the son of Timurtasch, interrupting her, "keep me no longer in suspense, tell me, I pray you, at once what you have to say concerning the princess of China."

"My lord," replied the lady, "Tourandocte, the barbarous Tourandocte has formed a plot to assassinate you!"

At these words Khalaf, falling back on the sofa, lay for a moment in a state of horror and amazement.

The slave-princess, who had foreseen the astonishment of the young prince, said,

"I am not surprised that you should thus receive this frightful announcement, and I was right when I doubted that you would believe it."

"Merciful Heaven," cried Khalaf, when he recovered from his stupefaction, "did I hear aright? Is it possible that the princess of China could be guilty of such an atrocious attempt? How could she conceive so base a project?"

"Prince," replied the lady, "I will explain to you how she came to take this horrible resolution. When she left the divan this morning, where I had been stationed behind her throne, I saw that she was mortally enraged at what had taken place; she returned into her apartments writhing under the most bitter feelings of mortification and fury; she pondered over the question you asked her for a long time, and not being able to find a suitable answer, she abandoned herself to despair. While she was in the bath, I spared no means, in which I was seconded by the other favourite slave, to calm the violence of her transports; we tried all in our power to inspire her with sentiments favourable to you; we extolled your person and your talents; we represented to her, that she ought to determine to bestow her hand upon you; we pointed out the unseemliness of such immoderate grief; but she imposed silence upon us, with a torrent of injurious words. The most agreeable and handsome make no more impression upon her than the ugliest and most deformed. 'They are all,' said she, 'objects of my contempt, and for whom I shall always entertain the deepest aversion. As regards him who has presented himself last, I entertain a greater hatred towards him than towards the others, and if I cannot rid myself of him by any other means I will have him assassinated.'

"I opposed this detestable design," continued the slave-princess, "and laid before her the terrible consequences of such a deed. I represented to her the injury she would inflict upon herself, the despair she would occasion the king, and the just horror that future ages would entertain for her memory.

"The other favourite slave supported with all her eloquence the arguments I adduced, but all our persuasions were of no avail; we could not turn her from her purpose. She has entrusted her faithful eunuchs with orders to take your life to-morrow morning as you leave your palace to repair to the divan."

"O inhuman princess, perfidious Tourandocte," cried the prince of the Nagäis, "is it thus you prepare to crown the affection of the unhappy son of Timurtasch? Has Khalaf indeed appeared so hateful to you, that you would rather rid yourself of him by a crime that will dishonour you, than unite your destiny with his? Great Heaven! how chequered with strange events is my life! At one moment I seem to enjoy happiness that the greatest might envy, at another I am plunged into a whirlpool of misery."

"My lord," said the slave-princess, "if Heaven ordains that you should suffer misfortunes, it does not will that you should sink beneath their weight, since it warns you of the dangers that threaten you. Yes, prince, it is Heaven that has doubtless inspired me with the thought of saving you, for I come not only to point out the snare laid for your life, I come also to furnish you with means to escape. By the assistance of some eunuchs who are devoted to me, I have gained over the soldiers of the guard, who will facilitate your flight from the serail. As they will not fail to make a searching investigation, when they know of your departure, and discover that I am the author of it, I am resolved to fly with you, and escape from this court, where I have more than one cause for discontent; my state of bondage makes me hate it, and you make it still more odious to me.

"Let us waste no time; come, and let to-morrow's sun, when he begins his course, find us far, far from Pekin.

"In a certain spot in the town," continued she, "horses await us; let us fly, and reach if possible the territory of the tribe of Berlas."

Khalaf replied, "Beautiful princess, I render you a thousand thanks for your wish to save me from the danger with which I am encompassed. Oh! that I could, to prove my gratitude, deliver you from your slavery, and conduct you in safety to the horde of the khan of Berlas your relation. With what pleasure would I place you in his hands! I should thereby repay some of the obligations I lie under to him. But I ask you, princess, ought I thus to steal away from Altoun-Khan? What would he think of me? He would believe that I came to his court for the sole purpose of carrying you off, and at the very time when I should be flying, only that I might save his daughter from perpetrating a fearful crime, he would be accusing me of violating the laws of hospitality. Ah! must I confess it, cruel though the princess of China be, I could never find in my foolish heart to hate her? Whatever misfortune may be in store for me, I cannot consent to so ignominious a flight. I acknowledge that charms like yours would amply repay your liberator, and that my days with you might pass in the greatest bliss, but I am not born to be happy, my destiny is to love Tourandocte; despite the aversion she feels towards me, I should wear out my days in endless sorrow, were they spent away from her."

"Well then, ingrate, remain," cried the lady passionately, interrupting him, "and let the spot in which thy happiness is concentrated be sprinkled with thy blood." Saying these words, she replaced her veil, and quitted the apartment.

The young prince, after the lady had retired, remained upon the sofa in a state of bewilderment. "Must I believe," said he, "what I have just heard? Can she carry her cruelty thus far? Alas! I dare not doubt it, for the slave-princess's expressions of horror at Tourandocte's plot were so natural—the risks she ran in coming herself to warn me of it so great, and the feelings she displayed so unquestionable,—that all are pledges of the truthfulness of her words. Ah! cruel daughter of the best of kings, is it thus that you abuse the gifts with which Heaven has endowed you? O Heaven! how couldst thou confer on this barbarous princess so much beauty, or why adorn so inhuman a soul with so many charms?"

Instead of seeking a few hours' sleep, he passed the night, distracted with the most painful reflections. At length day appeared, the ringing of the bells and beating of drums was again heard, and shortly after six mandarins arrived to conduct him to the council-chamber, as on the preceding day. He traversed the court where the soldiers were arranged in two files: he expected to meet his death at this spot, and that it was here the persons who had been appointed to assassinate him were posted, in order to despatch him as he passed. Far from thinking of defending himself or putting himself upon his guard, he walked on like a man prepared to die; he even appeared to chide the delay of his assassins. He passed through the court, however, without any attack being made upon him, and reached the first hall of the divan. "Ah! doubtless it is here," thought he, "that the sanguinary order of the princess is to be put in execution." He looked around him on all sides, and thought he saw in every one he surveyed a murderer. He nevertheless advanced and entered the hall where the council was sitting, without receiving the deadly stroke which he thought awaited him.

All the doctors and mandarins were already seated under their canopies, and Altoun-Khan was momentarily expected. "What can be the design of the princess?" thought he. "Can she wish to be an eye-witness of my death, and does she desire to have me assassinated before the eyes of her father? Can the king be an accomplice in the deed? What am I to think? Can he have changed his mind, and issued the order for my death?"

Whilst his thoughts were occupied with these doubts, the door of the inner palace opened, and the king, accompanied by Tourandocte, entered the hall. They took their seats upon their thrones, and the prince of the Nagäis stood before them, at the same distance as on the day before.

When the calao saw the king seated, he rose, and demanded of the young prince whether he remembered having promised to renounce the hand of the princess if she answered the question which he had proposed. Khalaf replied that he did, and again declared that in that event, he would renounce all claim to the honour of being the king's son-in-law. The calao then addressed Tourandocte, and said, "And you, great princess, you are aware of the oath that binds you, and of the penalty to which you are subjected if you do not this day declare the name of the prince, which you are required to give."

The king, persuaded that she could not reply to the question of Khalaf, said to her, "My daughter, you have had ample time to consider the question which was proposed to you; but if you had a whole year to think of it, I believe that in spite of your sagacity you would be obliged, at the end of it, to acknowledge that it is something which even you could not reveal. So, as you cannot guess, yield with good grace to the love of this young prince, and satisfy the wish I feel that he should be your husband. He is worthy of being so, and of reigning with you, after my death, over the people of this mighty empire."

"My lord," replied Tourandocte, "why do you think that I shall not be able to reply to the question of this prince? It is not so difficult as you imagine. I suffered the shame of a defeat yesterday, but to-day I look forward to the honour of a victory. I will confound this rash young man who has entertained so mean an opinion of my talents. Let him put the question, and I will answer it."

"Madam," thereupon said the prince of the Nagäis, "I ask, what is the name of that prince who, after suffering a thousand hardships, and being reduced to beg his bread, finds himself at this moment covered with glory, and overwhelmed with joy?"

"This prince," replied Tourandocte, "is named Khalaf, and he is the son of Timurtasch."

When Khalaf heard his name he changed colour, a dark mist seemed to cover his eyes, and he fell senseless to the ground. The king and all the mandarins, judging from this that Tourandocte had answered correctly, and had given the prince's real name, grew pale, and sat in great consternation.

After Khalaf had recovered from his swoon, through the attentions of the mandarins and the king himself, who had quitted his throne to come to his assistance, he thus addressed Tourandocte:

"Beautiful princess, you are mistaken if you think you have given a fitting answer to my question; the son of Timurtasch is not covered with glory, and overwhelmed with joy; he is rather covered with shame, and overwhelmed with grief."

"I agree with you," replied the princess, "that at this moment you are not overwhelmed with glory and joy, but you were so when you proposed this question; so, prince, instead of having recourse to vain quibbles, confess honestly that you have lost your right to Tourandocte. I therefore can, if I choose, refuse you my hand, and abandon you to the regret of having lost your prize; nevertheless, I will acknowledge to you, and declare here publicly, that I entertain different feelings towards you to what I did. The friendship my father has conceived for you, and your own merit, have determined me to take you for my husband."

At these words all etiquette was for a moment forgotten; the council-chamber resounded with shouts of joy. The mandarins and doctors applauded the words of Tourandocte. The king approached her, and kissing her, said, "My child, you could not have formed a decision more agreeable to me; by this act you will efface the bad impression you have made upon the minds of my people, and you confer upon your father a joy to which he has long been a stranger, and which hitherto he had hoped for in vain. Yes, that aversion you entertained for marriage, that aversion so contrary to nature, robbed me of the sweet hope of seeing princes of my own blood spring from you. Happily, that aversion has ceased, and what crowns my wishes is, that you have extinguished it in favour of a young hero who is dear to me. But tell us," added he, "how you have been able to guess the name of a prince who was unknown to you."

"My lord," replied Tourandocte, "it was not by enchantment that I learned it; it was by perfectly natural means. One of my slaves sought the prince Khalaf, and had subtlety enough to rob him of his secret, and I hope he will forgive me for taking advantage of this treachery, since I have made no worse use of it."

"Ah! charming Tourandocte," hereupon cried the prince of the Nagäis, "is it possible that you entertain such favourable sentiments towards me? From what a frightful abyss do you draw me, to raise me to the height of bliss! Alas, how unjust was I! whilst you were preparing such a glorious fate for me I thought you guilty of the blackest of all treachery. Deceived by a horrible fable which darkened my reason, I repaid your good intentions with injurious doubts. Oh! what impatience do I feel to expiate my unjust suspicions at your feet."

Altoun-Khan ordered the preparations for the marriage of Khalaf and Tourandocte to be set on foot, and whilst they were engaged about them he sent ambassadors to the tribe of Berlas, to inform the khan of the Nagäis of all that had taken place in China, and to beg him to come with the princess his wife.

The preparations being concluded, the marriage was celebrated with all the pomp and magnificence which belonged to the high birth of the happy pair. Khalaf was raised to the rank of the highest subject, and the king himself made a public declaration that, to mark his sense of the esteem and consideration he entertained for his son-in-law, he should allow him to dispense with the customary obeisances to his bride. During a whole month nothing was seen at the court but feasting and pageants, and in the city nothing but gaiety and rejoicings.

The possession of Tourandocte did not diminish the love Khalaf entertained for her, and the princess, who had hitherto regarded men with so much contempt, could not but love so perfect a prince. Some time after their marriage the ambassadors whom Altoun-Khan had sent to the country of Berlas returned, bringing with them not only the father and mother of the king's son-in-law, but also prince Almguer, who, to pay honour to Elmaze and Timurtasch, insisted on accompanying them, with the most distinguished of his nobles, and conducting them to Pekin.

The young prince of the Nagäis, apprized of their arrival, immediately rode out to meet them. He found them nearly at the gate of the palace. The joy he felt on seeing his father and mother, and their transports on seeing him, can be scarcely conceived, much less described. They all three embraced each other over and over again, and the tears they shed drew forth corresponding signs of emotion from the Chinese and Tartars who were present.

After these tender embraces, Khalaf saluted the khan of Berlas; he expressed to him how deeply he felt his kindness, and more especially his condescension in himself accompanying his parents to the court of China; the prince Almguer replied that, being ignorant of the rank of Timurtasch and Elmaze, he had not shown towards them the respect that was due to them, and thus to atone for any neglect they might have experienced, he thought it his duty to pay them this mark of honour; the khan of the Nagäis and his wife the princess, however, paid a high tribute to the attentive kindness of the khan of Berlas; they then all entered the palace of the king, to be presented to Altoun-Khan. They found this monarch awaiting them in the first hall. He embraced them all, one after the other, and received them very graciously; he then conducted them into his cabinet, where, after expressing the pleasure he felt at seeing Timurtasch, and his sympathy in his misfortunes, he assured him that he would employ all his power to avenge him on the sultan of Carisma. This was no empty offer, for that very day he despatched orders to the governors of the provinces to march with all speed with the soldiers who were in the towns within their jurisdiction, and to take the route to lake Baljouta, which was chosen for the rendezvous of the formidable army he proposed to assemble there.

For his part, the khan of Berlas, who had foreseen this war, and who wished to assist in the re-establishment of Timurtasch in his dominions, had, previous to his departure from his tribe, ordered the general of his army to be in readiness to take the field at the first summons. He now commanded him also to repair to lake Baljouta with all possible speed.

During the time the officers and soldiers who were to compose the army of Altoun-Khan, and who were dispersed throughout the kingdom, were marching to assemble at the spot indicated, this king spared no pains to express his high consideration for his new guests; he appointed a separate palace to each, with a great number of eunuchs, and a guard of two thousand men. Every day some new fête was contrived for their entertainment, and the king's whole attention seemed turned towards affording them pleasure. Khalaf, although he had now every day a thousand matters to occupy his attention, did not forget his kind hostess; he remembered with gratitude the solicitude she expressed for him; he sent for her to the palace, and begged Tourandocte to receive her amongst her attendants.

The hope that Timurtasch and Elmaze entertained of reascending the throne of the Nagäi-Tartars, by the assistance of the king of China, insensibly made them forget their past troubles; and when Tourandocte gave birth to a beautiful prince, they were quite overwhelmed with joy. The birth of this child, who was named the prince of China, was celebrated in all the cities of this vast empire by public rejoicings.

Whilst these festivities were taking place, news was brought by couriers, sent by the officers who had orders to collect the army, that all the troops of the kingdom, and those of the khan of Berlas, had assembled at lake Baljouta. Immediately Timurtasch, Khalaf, and Almguer set out for the camp, where they found every thing in readiness, and seven hundred thousand men ready to march; they immediately took the read to Kotan, from whence they marched to Raschar, and at length entered the dominions of the sultan of Carisma.

This prince, informed of their numbers, and of the invasion of his territories, by couriers whom the governors of the frontier towns had despatched, far from being alarmed at the number of his enemies, courageously prepared to meet them. Instead even of intrenching himself, he had the boldness to take the field himself, at the head of four hundred thousand men, whom he had hastily collected. The armies met near Cogendi, where they drew up in battle array. On the side of the Chinese, Timurtasch commanded the right wing, prince Almguer the left, and Khalaf the centre. On the other side, the sultan confided the command of his right wing to the ablest of his generals, opposed the prince of Carisma to the prince of the Nagäis, and reserved the left to himself, where the elite of his cavalry were stationed. The khan of Berlas began the attack with the soldiers of his tribe, who, fighting like men who knew the eyes of their master were on them, soon turned the right wing of their enemies; the officer who commanded it, however, succeeded in reforming it almost immediately. Meanwhile the right wing, commanded by Timurtasch, was not so fortunate; the sultan broke them at the first onset, and the Chinese in disorder were on the point of taking flight, in spite of every effort of the khan of the Nagäis, when Khalaf, informed of what had taken place, confided the care of the centre to an experienced Chinese general, and rushed to the assistance of his father at the head of reinforcements. In a short time things assumed a different aspect. The left wing of the Carismians was driven back, and in turn routed; the whole of the ranks fell into disorder and were easily broken—the entire wing was put to flight. The sultan determined to conquer or die, and made incredible efforts to rally his soldiers; but Timurtasch and Khalaf gave them no time, and surrounded them on all sides, whilst prince Almguer having defeated the right wing, victory declared in favour of the Chinese.

There remained but one chance of safety for the sultan of Carisma, and that was to cut his way through the ranks of his enemies, and to take refuge with some foreign prince; but he preferred not surviving his defeat to exhibiting amongst the nations his brow despoiled of the diadem; so rushing blindly into the thickest of the carnage, he fell bravely, fighting to the last, and pierced with a thousand mortal wounds, on a heap of slain. The prince of Carisma, his son, shared the same fate; two hundred thousand of their troops were killed or made prisoners, the rest seeking safety in flight. The Chinese also lost a great number of men; but if the battle had been a bloody one, it was decisive. Timurtasch, after thanking Heaven for this signal success, despatched an officer to Pekin to give an account of the battle to the king of China; he then advanced into Zagatay, and seized upon the city of Carisma.

He made a proclamation in this capital that he would not touch the property, or interfere with the liberty of the Carismians; that Heaven having made him master of the throne of his enemy, he intended to take possession of it, and that henceforth, Zagatay, and the other countries which had been under the sway of the sultan, should acknowledge for their sovereign his son Khalaf.

The Carismians, tired of the harsh rule of their late master, and persuaded that that of Khalaf would be milder, submitted readily, and proclaimed as sultan this young prince, with whose merits they were acquainted. Whilst the new sultan took all necessary measures to strengthen his position, Timurtasch departed with a body of Chinese troops with all possible speed to his own dominions. The Nagäi-Tartars received him like faithful subjects, and were overjoyed to see their legitimate sovereign; but he was not content with regaining his throne; he declared war against the Circassians, in order to punish them for their treachery to prince Khalaf at Jund. Instead of trying to appease him by submission, these warlike people speedily collected an army to oppose him. He attacked them, and cut them nearly all to pieces; after which he caused himself to be proclaimed king of Circassia, and then returned to Zagatay, where he found Elmaze and Tourandocte, whom Altoun-Khan had sent to Carisma in great state.

Such was the end of the misfortunes of prince Khalaf, who gained by his virtues the love and esteem of the Carismians. He reigned long and peacefully over them, and never abated in his love for Tourandocte; he had a second son by her, who became afterwards the sultan of Carisma. As for the prince of China, Altoun-Khan brought him up, and chose him for his successor. Timurtasch and the princess Elmaze passed the rest of their days at Astrachan, and the khan of Berlas, after having received from them and their children all the tokens of gratitude which his generosity merited, retired to his tribe with the remainder of his troops.

IV.

THE WISE DEY.

Chaaban, Dey of Algiers, being dead, the Turkish janissaries bethought themselves of electing a new dey; and their intention was to place in this high station an inert, weak, and indolent man, who would allow them to be their own masters, to act as they pleased either with or without justice, and who would never inflict any punishment upon them. Passing through the streets of Algiers, they beheld Hadgi-Achmet, a man of ripe age, seated peaceably at the door of his dwelling, and carefully mending his old slippers, without taking any part either in the outcries, the conversation, or the gossiping going on all around him. Hadgi-Achmet seemed to them to be just the sort of apathetic man they were in search of, a man who would never interfere with any one, would allow them to do exactly as they pleased, and who, in short, would be but the shadow of a dey. They therefore laid hold of Hadgi-Achmet, tore him from his work, led him to the divan, and elected him dey in spite of himself.

Hadgi-Achmet, thus forced to assume the reins of government, wisely examined into the duties of his new position, and set himself to fulfil them with as much assiduity and zeal as he had employed in the humbler task of mending his old slippers. He watched over the interests of the country, and over those of justice, and punished severely all misdeeds which came under his observation; having a stern, strange habit of knitting his shaggy eyebrows and flashing his brilliant eyes whenever any thing mean or wicked came under his notice. All this was very displeasing to the Turkish janissaries, and to several members of the divan. Four of these latter formed a species of plot with the design of bringing Hadgi-Achmet into contempt in the eyes of the public. Now as it was the pleasure of the dey to administer justice himself, and to enquire into the smallest matter that concerned the interests of the people, they thought to render him ridiculous, by begging him one day to judge four distinct matters, unworthy, in their opinion, to occupy the attention of a great ruler.

"Hadgi-Achmet," said one of the members of the divan to the dey, "my lord, here is a culprit who can only be judged by thee, O sun of justice! He is a Tunisian merchant, who has established himself a short time since at Bab-a-Zoun street, not far from the mosque. At first he carried on his trade with tolerable honesty; but by degrees it has been shown that he is nothing better than a rogue, and has cheated a great number of his customers in the weight, the quality, and the value of his goods. Thou knowest well the law which condemns such offenders to lose an ear. This man was seized, carried before the cadi, and his rogueries being but too apparent, condemned by the cadi to lose his left ear, the right being reserved in the event of fresh misdemeanors. But when the man's turban was removed, it was discovered that his left ear was already gone. The cadi, being informed of the fact, ordered the right ear to be cut off. To execute this order, they had to pull the hand of the culprit away from his right ear, and when this had been done, it was discovered that the Tunisian's right ear was missing as well as the left. The cadi therefore sent to inform me, and I, knowing the pleasure thou takest in resolving grave and important questions, have come to submit this one to thy consummate prudence, to thy glorious justice."

Hadgi-Achmet, having heard these words, knit his brows, his eyes flashed fire upon him who had just spoken, and upon all those who were present at this audience; then, turning towards the man without ears, he said,

"Since thou hast always been a rogue, and that nothing could reform thee, I condemn thee all thy life long to wear neither turban nor any head-dress whatsoever to conceal the mutilation of thy ears. Purchasers, on beholding this mutilation, will shun thee if they are wise, for no one is ignorant that a merchant without ears is nothing else than a rogue."

The earless Tunisian went sadly away. Being compelled to exhibit to every one and at all times the mutilation he had undergone, was a far worse punishment than the loss of five hundred ears, if he had had them.

This judgment pronounced, a second member of the divan addressed the dey,

"Hadgi-Achmet, our lord and master, here are two men who are quarrelling upon a question which thou only canst decide by thy profound wisdom. One of these men is the father of a beautiful and promising boy. He had this son and two others. One day, about ten years ago, Ibrahim, his neighbour, who was childless, said to him, 'Chamyl, give me thy youngest son, I will adopt him; he shall live in my house, inherit my wealth, and be happy. If thou desirest it, I will give thee in exchange for thy son my country-house at Boudjaréah; thou knowest that the north breeze is wafted there in the hottest days of summer.'

"Chamyl consented to give his son, and took the house at Boudjaréah in exchange. Ormed, the son of Chamyl, went to live with Ibrahim, who soon loved him very tenderly, whilst Ormed, if only out of gratitude, soon became much attached to him.

"Chamyl has now lost both his other sons, and having become rich, desires to take back Ormed, saying, 'This child is henceforth the sole hope of my race, the joy of my heart, and I wish him to become my heir.'

"As for Ibrahim, he has lost nearly the half of his fortune, but he has not lost the attachment which he bears to his adopted son. On the contrary, his affection continues daily to strengthen for this child, who is endowed with the finest qualities of mind, and with a grateful and affectionate heart.

"With whom dost thou decree that Ormed shall remain? with his adopted or with his real father?"

Hadgi-Achmet, addressing himself to Chamyl, said, "In what does thy fortune consist?"

Chamyl enumerated his possessions: a house, a ship, several country houses, and merchandise.

"Can these things be removed?" asked Hadgi-Achmet.

"Some of them can," replied Chamyl.

"And the others," replied Hadgi-Achmet; "couldst not thou, if necessary, dispose of them, and buy others with the price?"

"I could," replied Chamyl.

"And the affection which thou hadst for thy sons who are dead, couldst thou transfer it, and bestow it upon other children."

"Ah! that would be impossible," replied Chamyl, sorrowfully.

"Then affection cannot be transferred or exchanged," said Hadgi-Achmet; "and as it forms part of the heart of man, it is of far higher consequence than material things, is it not?"

"Yes, my lord," answered Chamyl.

"So that," continued the dey, "we may say to a man, Sell, or give away, thy possessions; but we cannot, without absurdity, say to any one, Cease to love him whom thou lovest. For which reason, Chamyl, I condemn thee to leave with Ibrahim the child whom he loves, and whom thou voluntarily gavest him when thou hadst affection for thy two sons who are no more. As to thy possessions, thou canst bear them whithersoever thou wilt, for riches are not the heart."

"But I love my son," cried Chamyl, "and I will have him, and him only, for my heir."

"Ah! thou lovest thy son," rejoined Hadgi-Achmet. "It may be so, but thou gavest no proofs of it so long as thy two other children were alive. Moreover, thou hast taken a house in exchange for thy son; it is exactly the same as if thou hadst sold thy child."

"I was poor," murmured Chamyl.

"A lame excuse," said the dey, "for there are many more poor men than rich men, yet we do not see poor men giving up their children for any gain whatsoever."

"No, no! I have not sold my son," cried Chamyl, "and my son is mine."

"No, thy son is no longer thine," said the dey, "for thou art not a father after my heart, and for ten years thy son has been cared for by the man to whom thou gavest him in exchange for a house. Ibrahim has not deserved that the child whom he so tenderly loves should be taken from him, and I order him to be left with him. But since thou wilt have none other than thy son for thine heir, I decree moreover that all thy property shall revert to him after thy death, which is nothing but justice."

Ibrahim then interposed. "My lord," said he to the dey, "Ormed and I have no need of the fortune of Chamyl. What Allah has left to us is sufficient for our wants. Permit Chamyl then to preserve the right of choosing for himself an heir among orphans or poor children, of whom he will now probably adopt one."

"No," replied the dey, "the man who has been able to calmly select one from among his own children and barter him for a house, can never attach himself to the orphan or the unfortunate. I see no reason to alter the judgment I have pronounced. Ormed will have for his inheritance the love of his adopted father and the wealth of his real one."

Chamyl withdrew, greatly incensed at this judgment, which seemed to him unjust, but which appeared highly equitable to the inhabitants of Aldgezaire.

A third member of the divan then addressed Hadgi-Achmet:

"All thy words bear the impress of the wisdom which illuminates thee. It suffices to hear thee, in order to know and venerate thee. If we do not abuse thy patience and thy goodness, it is because both are inexhaustible. Behold," added he, "a woman veiled, according to the law. She accuses her husband of leaving her to perish with hunger, whilst her husband here maintains that the woman tells an infamous untruth, and that he supplies her with ample means for becoming fat and strong; he adds, that the famished locusts from the desert eat not more voraciously than doth this woman, all the while remaining lean and feeble, as thou seest. The woman persists in asserting that her husband scarcely gives her sufficient to languish on like a dying tree, and she claims thy pity and thy justice."

Hadgi-Achmet, having heard these words, knit his brows, his eyes flashed fire upon him who had just spoken, and upon those present at this audience. Then he said, "Mahmoud, dost thou declare that thou affordest sufficient nourishment to thy wife?"

"Yes, my lord," replied Mahmoud.

"And thou, woman," said the dey, "dost thou still maintain that thy husband leaves thee in want of nourishment?"

"Yes, my lord," replied the poor starving woman in a faint voice, and extending her transparent hands and long thin arms, in a supplicating manner towards her master and her judge.

"Art thou poor?" demanded Hadgi-Achmet of Mahmoud.

"No, my lord," replied Mahmoud, "I could support several wives if I wished, but it pleases me to have only this one in my house."

"Ah! thou couldst support several wives," replied the dey; "and why then dost thou not give to this one all she desires, even supposing she devoured as voraciously as the famished locusts of the desert?"

"I never refuse her any thing," said Mahmoud.

The poor veiled woman sighed.

"Well," added Hadgi-Achmet, "since thou art both rich and generous, I will put thee in the position to repel an accusation so disgraceful to thee as that of leaving the woman whom thou hast espoused to perish of hunger. To which end I order that thy wife shall dwell in my palace in the apartments of my women and receive from thee a pension which will enable her to purchase whatever food she may desire. If at the end of a year of peace and plenty she should still possess that feeble voice and that excessive thinness which inspire my compassion, I shall regard her as inflicted with an incurable malady, and will leave her to go and die beneath thy roof; but if, on the contrary, she regains strength and voice, thou shalt be hung, not only for having violated the law which commands the husband to minister to the support of his wife, but still more for having lied before thy lord and thy judge, who knows and ever will know how to punish those who offend him."

Having spoken thus, Hadgi-Achmet cast terrible looks upon all the men present at this audience. Mahmoud withdrew only too sure of being hung next year, and every one preserved a gloomy silence which lasted for several minutes.

Hadgi-Achmet meanwhile resumed: "If there remains any other cause for me to judge, let it be declared."

Then with less self-possession and confidence than his colleagues had displayed, a fourth member of the divan presented himself. "Here, my lord," said he, "is a strange affair which occupies us, and which thou alone canst judge.

"These two men here present are twin-brothers. They have always loved each other, and have never been separated. Their father is just dead. After having deplored his loss, they said to each other: 'The roof of our father's dwelling has sheltered us to this day, let it shelter us still; and let us amicably share all that is left us by our father, arms, vestments, or jewels.'

"But all at once an object presented itself which could not be divided, and for the loss of which nothing else would compensate. The article in question is a holy amulet, which it is said bestows wisdom on him who wears it upon his breast beneath his tunic. Now the two brothers equally desire wisdom, and both would fain possess the precious talisman left them by their father."

Hadgi-Achmet having heard these words, knit his brows, again his eyes flashed fire, as he said to one of the twins:

"Mozza, canst thou not yield to thy brother, who so earnestly desires it, the amulet left you both by your father?"

"No, my lord," replied Mozza, "I could easily reconcile myself to my brother's being richer than myself, but not to his being wiser!"

Hadgi-Achmet turned to the other brother:

"Farzan, canst thou not yield to thy brother the amulet he wishes to possess?"

"No, my lord," replied Farzan, "for wisdom not alone bestows upon its possessor the things of the earth, but those also which belong to heaven, and I desire those above all."

Hadgi-Achmet then ordered Mozza to place upon his breast beneath his tunic the cherished amulet, which being done, he said to the young man:

"I am charmed to find that thou preferrest wisdom to fortune, for wisdom is above all. But dost thou not see that it is wise to be at peace with thy brother, and that to obtain this peace there is no sacrifice too great? To yield to thy brother is the beginning and the end of wisdom; he who yields is ever the best and the wisest. On this ground thou wilt now, I am persuaded, yield cheerfully this amulet to thy brother."

"I repeat, my lord," answered Mozza, "that I will yield every thing to my brother, slaves, diamonds, house—my entire fortune; but I will never willingly give up this sacred amulet: it is the only heritage I covet."

"Ah!" said Hadgi-Achmet, "thou hast not changed thy mind then! well, give me thy father's amulet."

Mozza reluctantly handed the precious talisman to the dey.

"Farzan," said the dey, "place this amulet upon thy breast, and beneath thy tunic."

Farzan obeyed. He had no sooner placed the amulet upon his breast than he felt so lively a joy that he would have embraced his brother had he dared, and his eyes glistened with pleasure.

"Ah!" said Hadgi-Achmet, addressing himself to Farzan, "I perceive that this amulet has great power over thee. Thy heart is opened to wisdom, and thou wilt renounce foolish quarrels, wilt thou not, and yield to thy brother the talisman which he so much desires, and of which he has perhaps greater need than thou?"

"I!" cried Farzan, "rather would I die than part with my father's amulet! I feel myself capable of plunging my dagger into the bosom of any one rash enough to attempt to tear it from me, whoever he might be."

"In truth," rejoined Hadgi-Achmet, "I see that this amulet is far from bestowing all the wisdom of which you young men deem it capable. On the contrary it only seems to me fit to sow dissensions between you, since notwithstanding you have both worn it upon your breast, you have nevertheless preserved your animosity and unjust pretensions in the dispute in question. For which reason I ordain that this precious talisman, of whose real power we are doubtless ignorant, shall remain in my palace and be restored in ten years' time to whichever of you two shall have given by his conduct the most incontestable proofs of piety and virtue."

Having heard this sentence, the two brothers sorrowfully withdrew. But they had no sooner crossed the threshold of the palace, than they were reconciled to each other, avowing that the dey had acted with justice, and thenceforth they lived happy and united as before.

In the mean time, Hadgi-Achmet, having delivered these four judgments, knit his brows once more, and turning to the members of the divan, addressed them as follows:

"Joyfully have I just occupied myself with the smallest things which concern the welfare and repose of my subjects, and I should not regret my time had it been employed in affairs still more trifling. Every thing appears of importance to me which in any way relates to the wellbeing of one of those over whom Allah has made me sovereign. I nothing doubt that you applaud my conduct, and that you would gladly imitate my zeal in the service of the people. Your praises prove it; but I know well that men such as you prefer proving their zeal by actions, rather than by words. I am about therefore to entrust you with a task of great importance to me, since it is for the most interesting class of my subjects, namely, the most unfortunate. I am about to distribute before the Ramadan, four sacks of rice among poor old men and widows. An unskilful hand has contrived in filling these sacks with the rice, to spill amongst it a quantity of *oats*. Now as I do not wish these poor people to think themselves treated with contempt by receiving rice mixed with oats, I wish that pious hands should carefully sift the rice and extract from it these grains. It is on you I rely for the performance of this duty, which awaits you in one of the halls of my palace. I cannot at this moment be an eye-witness of your zeal in obeying me, and serving the people; but before your task is finished, I will be with you."

Having spoken these words, the dey caused the members of the divan to be respectfully conducted by his guards to a large hall, where they found four sacks of rice and several baskets.

The members of the divan feeling persuaded that this was an affair which more nearly concerned their heads than the sacks of rice, set themselves silently to this unexpected work, whilst the guards remained stationary at the entrance of the hall in which the labour was being carried on.

The flight of a musquito might have been heard in this hall where the members of the divan were busily engaged sifting the rice for the poor, all the while vowing to be revenged upon Hadgi-Achmet, if they ever had the power.

Towards the evening the members of the divan were joined by Hadgi-Achmet, who perceiving that one of them had made less progress in his task than his three colleagues, said,

"I would not accuse thee of want of zeal: man knows not always what he wishes, nor knows what he can do; I will therefore aid thee in thy task," and he began gravely to assist the four members of the divan in sifting the rice of the poor.

The tasks being accomplished, the four sacks of rice were carefully closed. Hadgi-Achmet thanked his enemies, and caused them to be conducted with the greatest respect to the gates of his palace.

These men left to themselves, regarded each other with consternation and shame; they then said, "We would fain have laughed at Hadgi-Achmet, and it is he who has mocked us. Let us henceforth abstain from criticizing his scrupulous exactitude in rendering justice, but let us think only of avenging ourselves."

But they sought the opportunity in vain. Hadgi-Achmet, who had commenced his career by so carefully mending his old slippers, held the reins of power with a strong hand, and whilst other deys in those times almost always met a violent death by steel or poison, he died peacefully in his palace, after having lived many long years.

V.

THE TUNISIAN SAGE; OR, THE POWDER OF LONGEVITY.

Selim-ben-Foubi had been twenty years engaged in commerce when he inherited a fortune which greatly surpassed his wants and even his desires.

As he had lost all his children, his great wealth caused him but little joy, and he felt it even embarrassing to possess so much gold and so many precious things, of which he should never be able to make any use.

"I am now fifty," said he, "and were I to live to a hundred, I should not spend half of what I possess. I can only take one meal at a time, dress in a single suit, and sleep in but one bed. Hence if I can but rest in peace in a substantial and commodious house, eat as much as I desire, and invite a friend to partake of my repast, that is all I need wish for. I have therefore resolved to give away the half of my fortune during my lifetime, that I may enjoy the pleasure of beholding happiness of my own creating."

Having formed this generous project, Selim nevertheless wished before putting it into execution to take counsel with two of his friends.

Quitting therefore his country-house at Boudjaréah, he repaired to Aldgezaire, where in the garden of the grand mosque dwelt usually a sage mufti, a grave and reverend man. Seating himself by his side beneath the shade of some flowering pomegranate trees, he thus accosted him:

"Mehemet, I have come to visit thee in order to open my whole heart to thee and take counsel of thy wisdom. I am suddenly become very rich, as thou knowest, and I have no son to inherit my wealth; is it not too great for a single solitary man? speak, answer me."

"That which Allah gives should never be despised," replied the sage.

"I do not disdain my riches," replied Selim, "but I am thinking of sharing them with others, and of keeping only what is necessary to my existence for the remainder of my days."

"Thou knowest not what the number of thy days will be."

"I will suppose that I may enjoy the longest of lives, a hundred years for example, thinkest thou I shall live yet longer?"

"Allah alone knows."

"Let us say five hundred," continued Selim, "surely that covers all chances; well then, during this long course of years, would it not be more agreeable to me to know that my riches are useful, than to feel that they were hidden in some coffer, where they might become an object of envy to the poor, or tempt the cupidity of the ill-doer?"

"May be so," said the mufti.

"My thought is a good one then?"

"It may be; but will it be good in practice? I cannot say. Nothing is more common than to think wisely; nothing more rare than to put wise thoughts into practice."

"Advise me," said Selim, "and I shall then be sure of fulfilling the law, and of doing good. How ought I to distribute the half of my large fortune?"

The mufti reflected profoundly, and then replied:

"I advise thee first to take at least one year to reflect upon thy project. Time is the sun that ripens the thoughts of men. We never repent of having reflected before acting; we often regret not having done so. Reflect then, and afterwards come and consult with me."

Selim quitted the mosque, and repaired to Bab-a-Zoun street, to the house of his other friend, a Moorish merchant, who laboured hard to support himself by his calling. He began thus:

"We have been friends and have known each other these ten years, for which reason I come to put to thee this question: 'In what way, thinkest thou, a man who is both rich and beneficent should employ his fortune, in order to be useful?'"

The Moorish merchant replied: "Thou makest a very singular demand of me. I cannot believe that a man can find any difficulty in giving, if he really possess the desire. He may found a mosque, succour the aged, support the widow and the orphan, enrich his friends, if he have any, and the rich are seldom without friends."

"But thou," rejoined Selim, "if thou hadst aught to give away, what wouldst thou do?"

"I? I cannot fancy myself having any thing to give away, seeing that I can scarcely pay the rent of my poor shop, and fill that shop with a few sacks of rice and a little coffee. If I had money, it is very certain that I should begin by buying a house and goods. It is of no use to say to a poor man like me, 'To whom wouldst thou give thy money?' But I repeat to thee there is no lack of good actions to be done. Happy he who has only to choose."

"Thou art right," said Selim to his friend; and quitting him, he returned to his country-house at Boudjaréah. One of his neighbours, Achmet the Arab, accosted him upon the road thither; and Selim, having stopped to converse with his friend, said to him: "Thou art of a ripe age, and art not wanting in experience of the things of this life. Tell me then if thou considerest that it would be well for a man who is rich and childless to give away, while still living, the half of his fortune, reserving the other half, upon which to subsist honourably the remainder of his days."

Achmet replied, "I cannot say whether it is better in the sight of Allah to give away or to retain the goods with which he has endowed thee. As for myself, I have nothing to give, for I have a very small fortune, and a great many children; but if I were rich and without heirs, I would bury my gold in some corner of my garden, sooner than bestow it to gratify men who are either wicked or ungrateful, and such they almost all are. This gold would sooner or later be discovered by some one whom Allah desired to enrich, and thus I should not be responsible for the use that was made of it."

"Thy idea is not, perhaps, a bad one," said Selim, "and I will certainly reflect upon it."

While Selim and his neighbour were talking together, a Tunisian of miserable aspect approached the spot. This was no other than Hussein Muley, a physician of Tunis. He was already advanced in years, and passed for a man rich in science, but poor in money. Selim requested this man to rest himself in his house, and his invitation being accepted, he saluted his neighbour Achmet, and conducted his guest into one of the fresh and salubrious halls of his smiling abode. Hussein Muley, fatigued by two hours' walk under a broiling sun, threw himself upon a divan, whilst fruits and coffee were abundantly served to him. When he had somewhat reposed and refreshed himself, Selim said to him in a friendly manner, "I am happy to receive thee at my house, because thou art a wise man, and of good renown in thy profession. Thou hast travelled, read, and seen life; thou must of necessity be able to judge wisely of the things which relate to this life. I should therefore be very glad to have thy opinion upon a project which I have formed. I have become very rich by inheritance; and having no children, I think of disposing, while yet living, of a great portion of my wealth. In what way dost thou consider it would be most desirable to employ this wealth?"

Hussein Muley regarded Selim with surprise.

"Thou wouldst give away a great portion of what thou hast," said he. "This is, indeed, a marvellous thing. I have, as thou sayest, travelled, read, and seen life, but never yet have I heard of any man giving away, during his lifetime, the greater part of his fortune."

"Does that prove that it would be wrong to do so?" demanded Selim.

"I know not," replied the Tunisian, falling into a fit of profound meditation, and looking all the while at the tips of his old slippers, instead of contemplating from afar the ever-changing sea and azure sky.

"On what dost thou muse?" at length demanded Selim.

"I was thinking—I was thinking that if the duration of man's life were longer, it would be better both for those who study science, and for those who are the fortunate possessors of great wealth; it would be equally good for the poor, since they might one day hope to enjoy the fruit of their toils, if they took pains to become rich."

"What profits it to meditate so deeply upon a thing which all the reflections of man cannot change?"

"I do not regard the prolongation of human existence as impossible. Hitherto physicians have most frequently been instrumental in abridging it. My aim is to repair the wrongs they have involuntarily committed. I would have succeeding ages regard my memory with gratitude."

"What sayest thou?" cried Selim. "Thou wouldst change the order of things, the whole course of nature?"

"Nothing can convince me that we follow the course of nature by dying at sixty or eighty years of age, when men formerly lived hundreds of years. On the contrary, I am certain that we were created to live longer, much longer, and I consecrate all my days, my nights, and my studies to the pursuit of a discovery which is destined to prolong the existence of mankind, and renew the state of things as they were when men married at a hundred years of age, and lived to see their sons' sons grow up and marry in their turn. Why, have I often asked myself, should our lives be shorter than those of an oak of the forests, of a serpent, or even of a vulture?"

"If we lived as long as an oak," replied Selim, "the cedars and the palm trees would still live longer than we."

"Thou dost but jest, but thy jesting is ill-timed; nothing is more serious than the thought which occupies me. Thou thyself, confess now, wouldst thou not be enchanted to see suns succeed suns, and to contemplate for ages to come the wonders of the heavens and the fecundity of the earth?"

Selim reflected a little, and replied, "Man does not love death, it is true; nevertheless life is not so desirable as thou wouldst fain have us believe."

"Then thou desirest not to prolong thy days upon the earth? For myself, I confess that I desire it greatly; so that besides my days and my nights, I consecrate all that I glean from learned researches to the accomplishment of this great end. I am already upon the track. But unfortunately gold is wanting—this gold which thou despisest, or knowest not how to employ—this gold would in my hands contribute to the happiness of future generations. With gold—with gold you can purchase books of precious value, measure the stars, dig the bowels of the earth, rend metals from her bosom, decompose substances, in short, penetrate into every mystery. Yes, gold which heretofore has been unable to bestow a day, nay an hour upon its possessor, gold in my hands would accomplish a wondrous discovery. I should certainly not keep the secret for myself alone, and I should share it first of all with the man whose wealth had helped me to the means of obtaining it."

"But shouldst thou discover the means of prolonging my life for many centuries, I should not then be rich enough to give away half of my fortune."

"What!" cried the physician of Tunis, "is not life preferable to all the riches in the world? and if at this moment it were said to thee, 'thou shalt die, or give up the whole of thy possessions,' wouldst thou not readily yield them to avoid the thrust of a yataghan, or the discharge of a gun in thy breast?"

"Thou puzzlest me, but I think that in such a case I should give up my property to preserve my life."

"Thou seest then that life is dear, even to the poor. Why not therefore endeavour to prolong thine own? Even if my profound science did not succeed, thou wouldst still be rich enough to enjoy an existence of the shorter duration."

Listening thus to the learned physician, Selim fell by degrees into a profound reverie, and the Tunisian, instead of continuing his discourse, gave himself up to meditation also; so that both these two men became absorbed in their own dreams in presence of each other, but without communicating their ideas, and Allah alone knows of what they were thinking.

After long and silent reflection, Selim said to Hussein Muley, "Before seeing thee I had intended to bestow while yet alive one-half of my fortune in making others happy. It will, I think, be no change of purpose, if I aid thee in pursuing those learned researches which tend to prolong the life of man. For which reason, Hussein Muley, I propose at once to present thee with the gold of which thou hast need. Come with me."

The Tunisian, appearing more astonished than rejoiced at these words, gravely arose, followed Selim into another apartment in the house, and received from him a little casket filled with pieces of gold.

"Employ this wisely," said Selim, "and communicate to me the result of thy labour."

"I will not fail to do so," replied Hussein Muley. And clasping the precious casket to his breast, he exclaimed, "Here then is the means of satisfying my thirst for knowledge, of surmounting all obstacles, of snatching from the past the secret which shall add hundreds of years to the existence of man, and prolong his days to the space of those of his fathers. Selim," added he, "thou dost a meritorious action in giving me this. I need not thank thee, because I am going to work for thee as for myself; nevertheless I do thank thee, and with my whole heart."

Having said these words the learned physician withdrew gravely, and with an air of deep abstraction.

Selim was not less preoccupied. Left to himself, he meditated long and profoundly on long and short lives, and on the prodigies accomplished by science, and he ended by asking himself whether he should confide to the sage mufti, whom he was soon about to see again, what he had done for Hussein Muley, and his hope of beholding the existence of the human species prolonged to an almost indefinite period. His final resolution was to admit no one to his confidence in the matter, but to await in silence the marvellous discovery of his new friend Hussein Muley, the physician of Tunis.

Several months passed by without the reappearance of the latter, but when at length he returned to Boudjaréah he was yellower, leaner, and more attenuated even than a man who had crossed on foot the mighty desert of Sahara. His limbs, in fact, could scarcely support his trembling frame.

"Well," said Selim, "what has befallen thee? art thou sick, or dost thou return to me perishing of hunger?"

"No, but I have travelled night and day beneath the pale light of the stars, and the burning rays of the sun, and have often forgotten to take necessary sustenance, so deeply was I absorbed in my studies."

"Well, and the result?"

"Alas! I have not yet succeeded as I could desire. Thus far have I attained only, that I have secured the power of prolonging our days fifty years."

Having uttered these words, Hussein Muley sorrowfully clasped his withered hands upon his breast, and then added:

"I know that such a discovery would afford intense joy to any other but myself, but it is far from satisfying me. To live fifty years longer than usual, what is that?"

"It is something, nevertheless," replied Selim, "and wilt thou tell me what is necessary to be done, in order to add fifty years to one's existence?"

"Will I tell thee?" cried the Tunisian; "I am come expressly for that purpose, and to give thee this powder. It must be taken every morning fasting, for one year, three months, a week, and a day, without fail."

"I must write down these directions," said Selim.

He wrote them down at once, and then asked, "Dost thou not think thou shouldst rest satisfied with thy discovery, and begin to live well, and sleep well, in order to enjoy the remaining years of thy life?"

"I have no desire to repose yet from my labours. Of what account are fifty years added to sixty or eighty, soon to be over for me? No, no, I would live two centuries at the least, to enjoy the fruits of my toil, and make the fortunes of my children, and my children's children. For thou dost not imagine we shall at first give to every one for nothing this magnificent secret, which has cost us so much. It is this secret which will procure us the means of living in splendour to the end of our days. Thou canst, for heavy sums of money, dispose of the powder which I shall have composed to whomsoever thou pleasest, while I on my part equally will part with it for gold; and when at length we die, surfeited with life, we will leave our secret to the multitude that survives us."

"This arrangement seems to me just, and well conceived. Nevertheless, I desire not to sell the powder, but may I bestow it, and at once, upon one or two men whom I esteem highly?"

"No, let us not yet draw attention to our happy fortune; let us wait until my discovery shall be completely perfected."

"Agreed; but I lament to see thee yellow, thin, and attenuated, as thou art."

"Oh! that is nothing," said the Tunisian, striking his forehead with his hands; "do not let my haggard appearance disturb thee. I would rather have nothing but skin upon my bones, and keep my secret to myself. I shall soon regain my flesh and my complexion. No, my health causes me no uneasiness. I merely suffer from anxiety, which arises from not having money sufficient for the prosecution of my studies."

"Dost thou require much?" demanded Selim.

"Ah! yes, much," replied Hussein with a sigh; "and if I fail in procuring it, instead of living fifty years longer than the usual course of things, I will either starve myself to death, or drown myself in the well of my house."

"Beware of acting thus," said Selim. "I can still give thee something; make use of that, and afterwards follow my advice, and sell to some rich man thy powder, in order to meet the expenses of thy lengthened researches."

Hussein Muley appeared to meditate profoundly with his forehead buried in his hands, and seemed not to listen to Selim, but it is not improbable that he heard him very well.

"Thou dost not listen to me," continued Selim. "Hussein! Hussein! I will give thee another little casket of gold; but after this casket I have nothing more to give thee. There will only remain just sufficient for me, during the time that I hope to live, thanks to thy powder. If thou discoverest another still more marvellous, thou wilt give it me, at least for my own use, wilt thou not?"

Hussein Muley seemed suddenly to come to himself, and exclaimed:

"Oh! I have at length found that of which I was in search! Yes, one herb alone is now wanting; I will go in quest of it, were it at the other end of the earth, and I will resolve the great problem which has occupied me for more than thirty years. Selim! Selim! entrust to my keeping what thou canst still consecrate to the happiness of mankind, and rest assured that thou wilt merit the admiration and the gratitude of ages to come."

"I desire neither the one nor the other," replied Selim; "I only wish to do a little good, that is all. Shall I succeed in my purpose? I will confess to thee, Hussein Muley, that I have more than once regretted devoting my fortune to a discovery which may prove more fatal than useful to the world; for the world is already peopled enough, and what would it be, if men lived for several centuries? Would they not kill each other for want of room?"

"Do they not already kill each other by sea and by land?" said Hussein Muley with a strange smile. "Come," continued he, "do not disquiet thyself about what will some day happen upon the earth; profit by what fate offers thee, and prolong thy days in peace."

Having thus spoken, he took the second casket proffered him by Selim, put it under his arm, and said in a grave tone:

"I am about to undertake a journey into Asia. There, near the Indies, is a high mountain, Mount Himalaya—dost thou not know it?"

"No," answered Selim.

"Well, nor I either; but I go to cull from its summit, covered with perpetual snows, a plant, which will complete the discoveries I have already made."

"I thought that no plant was ever to be found on those mountain tops covered with perpetual snow and frost?"

"There grows none, but that of which I have immediate need; I am going in quest of it, and will show it thee on my return."

"It is well," said Selim, and they separated.

Hussein Muley retreated with rapid strides.

Selim carefully placed in a small box the powder which he was to take fasting, during one year, three months, a week, and a day, and he began from the very next day to administer to himself this drug, which happily he did not find to be very nauseous to the taste.

Meanwhile the Tunisian set out from Aldgezaire with his wife, his children, and several chests, containing no doubt his books, and the papers necessary for his studies; but Selim never saw him more. He awaited his return, three, five, ten years, and, as he judged that ten years should suffice to go to Asia, and scale the highest mountain there, he began to think that the yellow, thin, and learned Tunisian was either dead, or else had taken advantage of his credulity and ignorance.

Whilst these thoughts occupied his mind, an epidemic broke out in Aldgezaire; Selim was attacked by it.

He therefore begged the wise mufti, who was still alive, to come and visit him; and then with that burst of confidence which seizes men in the hour of danger, he opened his heart to him, and related how he had given two caskets full of gold to Hussein Muley, in the hope of prolonging the existence of mankind for many centuries.

The wise mufti stroked his venerable beard and exclaimed:

"Selim, Selim, thou hast been played upon by a swindler, to whom thou hast imprudently confided thy generous thoughts. This proves the truth of what I one day said to thee, 'With the best intentions we may commit the most foolish actions.'"

"Ah!" said Selim sorrowfully, "my misfortune has been in not spontaneously following the first impulse of my heart, for I had really the wish to do good, but in taking counsel of one and another I have followed the worst I received."

"Yes," replied the mufti, "thou mightest perhaps have acted wisely in following thy first idea; at the same time, if thou hadst, in accordance with my advice, reflected longer upon thy projects of benevolence, it is certain that thou wouldst not have given thy gold to a cheat who has done nothing but laugh at thy credulity."

Selim willingly consented to acknowledge his fault. He confessed that it is useless to take the opinion of the wise and learned, if we do not mean to profit by it; then he prostrated himself devoutly before Allah, recovered his health by degrees, and caused a large sum of money to be distributed among the poor of the mosques, for he relied no longer on the hundreds of years of existence which were to come to him from Mount Himalaya, any more than on the powder of longevity.

VI.

THE NOSE FOR GOLD.

Mohammed and Yousouf, young Moors, born in Aldgezaire, had loved each other from infancy, and increasing years only served to strengthen the bonds of their attachment. Besides the happiness they enjoyed in their mutual affection, their friendship tended also to elevate their characters, and make them remarkable, for every body knows that constant friendships are never the lot of vulgar minds. These two young men, therefore, raised themselves above the level of the vulgar herd by the fidelity of their affection; they were cited as models in their native city; people smiled with pleasure on seeing them pass, always together, ever in good humour; and although they were far from being rich, yet their fate was envied by every one.

Mohammed and Yousouf generally dressed alike, and they had recourse to the same trade to gain their living. Their only trouble,—there must always be some in this world,—arose from the shops in which they were engaged during the day being separated from each other; evening, it is true, reunited them in the same dwelling, but that was not enough for them. When they married even, they contrived that it should be to each other's relatives. One family established itself on the first floor of the house, the other immediately above, and the two friends continued to love as heretofore, and to rejoice in their common felicity.

Over and over again, during their long conversations, they would repeat with the reiteration usual to those to whom a subject is dear, some such sentiments as these:

"The restless periods of youth, marriage, and commercial affairs have tried our friendship without altering it; it is henceforth secure from all changes; old age will only serve to render us dearer to each other, and we shall leave to our families the record and example of an affection which a future day will doubtless see renewed in our sons."

"It is probable," they would often say, "that Allah, touched by our friendship upon earth, will reunite us eternally in the paradise of true believers, beneath fresh shades, and by the side of bubbling fountains, surrounded by flowers of sweet perfume."

At this prospect of an eternal union, an eternal happiness, both would smile in anticipation, and such expressions as these they were never weary of repeating to each other.

These two friends were about thirty years of age, when a lucky chance gave them the opportunity of accomplishing the dearest wish of their hearts, that of occupying together two small shops adjoining each other.

An old Israelite, without family and without children, had inhabited them for twenty years. In one he slept and ate, not having any other house; in the other he displayed his merchandise; essences, amber, pastilles, necklaces and bracelets for the rich Moors, small looking-glasses, and beads of coral for the slaves; all of which he sold at the dearest possible price, as if he had a dozen children to support, and as many of his co-religionists.

Mohammed and Yousouf established themselves with lively satisfaction in these shops, the possession of which they had so long coveted, without at the same time desiring the death of the old Jew. They were incapable of a wicked action; but the Jew being dead, as they could not restore him to life, they saw no harm in lawfully taking possession of his domicile. This event seemed to complete their happiness.

But who can say or know what is really a good or an evil? who can foresee the consequences of things?

Mohammed one day, while knocking a nail into the partition wall between his shop and that of Yousouf, discovered that this wall was hollow, and that it contained some pieces of metal. His first impulse was to call, "Yousouf! Yousouf! there is gold or silver in our wall;" but the next moment he thought, "I will first assure myself of what this part of the wall contains, and if I really make a fortunate discovery, I shall give Yousouf such an agreeable surprise by calling him to partake of it."

Accordingly he waited until Yousouf should be out of the way for an hour or two to give him the opportunity of exploring further into his wall, but it so happened that Yousouf was never absent at all for several days following.

Mohammed then said to his friend:

"I fancy that something has been stolen from my shop during the night. I shall sleep there to-night, in order to surprise the thief, if he should reappear."

"I shall not leave thee alone here all night," replied Yousouf, "but shall sleep also in my shop by the side of thee."

Mohammed in vain strove to oppose the resolution of his friend; he could not revisit his shop alone in the evening, and for several days following, Yousouf seeing that he appeared pensive and uneasy, quitted him less than ever, and said to him with the solicitude of true friendship:

"Thou seemest sad! Thy wife and thy sons, are they ill? Regrettest thou what has been taken from thy shop? Compensate thyself for thy loss by selecting whatever thou wilt from that which I possess."

Mohammed thanked Yousouf, and replied with a smile:

"Rest satisfied, I have no grief." He dared not add, "I have no secret," for he had one.

In order however to put an end to the feeling of intense anxiety that filled his mind, he came to his shop one night unknown to Yousouf, and hastily detaching from the partition wall first one stone, then two or three more, he discovered a hundred Spanish doubloons, and eight four-dollar pieces. This was a perfect treasure to Mohammed, who had never in his life possessed more than the half of a small house, and the few goods exposed for sale in his shop.

"We are rich," said he. "Yousouf and I can now purchase a country house by the sea-side, as we have so often wished. Our wives and our children will disport themselves in our sight. My son Ali, that beautiful child whom I so tenderly love, will be delighted to run among the trees and climb up into their topmost branches. Ah! how rejoiced I am, if only for his sake."

Thus thinking, Mohammed took his gold and his silver, replaced, as well as he was able, the stones in his wall, and returned to his home, his mind occupied with delightful visions, and already beholding himself in imagination enjoying the pleasures of a delightful habitation by the sea-shore, with his beautiful Ali, that dear child whom he so tenderly loved. During two days he put off from hour to hour the disclosure which he had to make to Yousouf; and during those two days he revolved all sorts of ideas in his mind.

"If I made the fortune of my son, instead of that of my friend," said he at length to himself, "should I be guilty? Is not a son nearer and dearer than all the friends in the world? Yes; but then the gold and silver which I have discovered belong by rights as much to Yousouf as to myself, for the wall whence I have taken them belongs as much to his shop as to mine."

Unable to resolve either to share his treasure with his friend or to keep it for himself alone, he took the resolution of carefully concealing it in the chamber in which he slept, and of waiting until the agitation caused in his mind by so important an event should have somewhat subsided, to which end he hastened to secure his newly acquired possession.

"Reflection is no crime," said he. Consequently he gave himself time to reflect, instead of following the first impulse of his heart and remaining faithful to that devotion of friendship which had hitherto constituted his pride and glory, and which still bore the promise of so rich a harvest in the future.

He passed all his time then, extended during the heat of the day upon a mat by the side of his merchandise, and with closed eyes feigning to sleep, while in reality he was thinking of nothing but his treasure, and of what he ought to do with it.

Yousouf meanwhile, impressed with the idea that his friend was sleeping, took every care to guard his slumbers from interruption, thinking as he gently fanned his fevered brow of nothing but Mohammed, and what he could possibly invent to divert him and render him happy.

One day as Yousouf and Mohammed were reposing after their labours, an old hump-backed Jew with a sallow complexion and an enormous nose accosted Yousouf, saying:

"Was it not here that Nathan Cohen, the son of David, lived about two years since?"

"Speak low," replied Yousouf to the Jew. "My friend is asleep, and I would not that his slumbers should be disturbed."

The Jew seated himself on the edge of Yousouf's little counter, and repeated his inquiry, at the same time lowering the harsh and hollow tones of his voice.

"Yes, it was here that Nathan Cohen, the son of David, dwelt," replied the young Moor.

"Ah!" said the old Jew, working his large and flexible nostrils, "I was sure of it—that is why I scent gold hidden here."

"Indeed!" said Yousouf, regarding somewhat incredulously the extraordinary nose of his interlocutor. "Thou dost well to talk of smelling gold or silver either. Thy olfactory nerves are of the strongest no doubt, nevertheless I fear me they are at fault in this dwelling, where gold and silver but seldom make their appearance."

"They are not often to be seen here," replied the Jew; "I know that full well; they are not heard here either, for the earth conceals them both from sight and sound. But remove them from the envious ground that covers them, and they will dazzle thine eyes and charm thine ears."

"Indeed!" said Yousouf, laughing. "Thou art the bearer of good news. How much dost thou demand for thy reward?"

"I would have thee share with me all that I shall cause to be discovered in thy house by means of the marvellous sense of smelling with which I am endowed, and at which thou now jestest."

"Share with thee!" exclaimed Yousouf. "Oh no, indeed! If I were fortunate enough to discover a treasure, it is with my friend Mohammed that I should hasten to share it."

"But thou wilt have nothing to share with him if I do not disclose to thee the spot where thy treasure lies concealed."

"Perhaps so. But if I put any confidence in thy nose, what prevents me from turning my whole shop topsy-turvy, digging up the floor, and pulling down the walls and the shelves?"

The Jew slowly regarded the ground, the walls, and the shelves, as they were severally named by Yousouf; then he said in an ironical manner:

"Thou wouldst not do much harm if thou wert to demolish all around thee; but to save thyself so much trouble and labour, thou hadst far better give me at least one-third of what I shall discover in thy dwelling. The other two-thirds can be for thyself and thy friend, if thou art fool enough not to wish to keep all for thyself."

"Ah, it may suit such a man as thou to call him who prefers friendship to money a fool! But in spite of all thy arguments I shall never change, and I shall love Mohammed better than all the money in the world."

"As you please. It remains to be seen if Mohammed would do the same for you."

"I have not the slightest doubt of it," replied Yousouf.

The Jew uttered a suppressed laugh.

"And I have every doubt of it," said he. "I doubt even *thy* future disinterestedness, notwithstanding the warmth of thy discourse. Yousouf! Yousouf! thou hast not yet beheld the dazzling brilliancy of gold! It is the lustre of this metal which charms the eyes and wins the heart of man. Once let him see gold before him, and know that he has the power to possess himself of it, and adieu to every other thought. Gold! why it is the thing to be most desired in the world. Possessed of gold, what can we not enjoy? a fine house, smiling pasturage, blooming gardens, rich stuffs, divans, perfumes, all, in short, that renders life desirable!"

"That is very true," replied Yousouf. "We can procure many things with gold; but still gold cannot purchase youth, gaiety, friendship, or even a good appetite or sound sleep. Leave me then in peace with thy discoveries, and if thou art so skilled in the art of scenting gold, learn also to scan the disposition of him to whom thou addressest thyself."

"Then thou wilt not consent to give me the third of what I know to be here, hidden though it may be?"

"Decidedly not," replied Yousouf. "I have no faith in thy ridiculous pretensions; moreover, I do not know thee, and have never seen thee either in the public walks, the streets, or elsewhere."

"I have just returned from a long journey," replied the old man; "my name is Ephraim. When I quitted this city, thou wert but sixteen years of age; my friend Nathan Cohen, son of David, was then very old: he has been dead, they say, these two years."

"And so thou comest to exercise thy sense of smelling in thy accustomed haunt," said Yousouf gaily; "and seest thou not then that there is some power in friendship, since it is the memory of a friend that brings thee hither?"

"Ah! it is not the memory of the past, but hope for the future," replied the old Jew. "So long as our friends are alive they may be useful, though that is a thing that very rarely happens; but when they are dead, what is the use of thinking any more of them?"

Yousouf, wearied out with so much discussion, said at length to Ephraim:

"Come, come, enough of this! Leave this place; thy voice will, I am sure, awaken my friend, and prevent him from sleeping, as he delights to do during the heat of the day."

"Do not let us awaken him," replied the Jew, "but let us remove the ground there beneath thy feet. I will hope that a feeling of gratitude may induce thee to bestow upon me a portion of what I shall discover for thee."

So saying, the Jew drew a long iron pickaxe from beneath his dirty brown tunic, and began to break up the ground around the feet of Yousouf. The latter regarded the old man—his prodigious nose inflated by the hope of gain—with a smile of derision. But in a short space of time their eyes were dazzled by a sight of the precious metal. The Jew had, indeed, succeeded in disinterring a veritable treasure.

"Let us now count this gold and silver," said he.

They took it, and counted it, and found that Yousouf had suddenly become the possessor of five hundred Spanish doubloons, and sixty four-dollar pieces. He could scarcely believe his eyes.

"Well," said the Jew, "what sayest thou? have I lied to thee, or deceived myself? Come, let us see now what thou art going to give me in reward for my pains."

"I will awaken Mohammed," said Yousouf, "and he and I will certainly give thee something as a recompense."

"Yousouf!" said the Jew, arresting the young Moor by the arm, "reflect a moment before awakening thy friend. Would it not be better to keep this treasure for thyself and for thy sons? Hast thou not children, and are not children much dearer than a friend?"

"If I have children," replied Yousouf, "Mohammed has them also. We loved each other before they were born, and we know how to be good fathers without being faithless friends."

At this moment Mohammed, who had not awaked, for the very sufficient reason that he had not been asleep, started as if he had been stung by a thousand mosquitoes at once, and rose with a sudden bound. The concluding words of Yousouf had awakened a feeling of remorse within his breast.

"Yousouf! Yousouf!" said he to his friend, "I have heard all. Yes, every thing, and thy sincere friendship, tried by time and tried by gold, is now the sole treasure I desire."

"I know for how long a time thou hast thought thus," replied Yousouf. "But since Allah has chosen to make us rich, let us not disdain the blessing which he sends. He it was who first inspired us with the wish for these two little shops, and who has bestowed them upon us. It is he who has conducted hither this Jew who has been the instrument of our discovering this treasure. Let us offer our thanks to Allah, and let us give to Ephraim that which is meet and right."

"Be that as thou only wilt," said Mohammed with a preoccupied air. "Thou art just and righteous, and thy thoughts are pure in the sight of Allah."

Yousouf paid no great heed to this friendly eulogium, but continued gaily:

"Since thou permittest me to be the sole arbiter in the affair, this is my decision."

Then, turning towards Ephraim: "Thou shalt be more or less recompensed," said he, "according to the candour with which thou repliest to my question. Come, then, answer me truly, hast thou really, thanks to the singular form of thy nose, so fine a sense of smell as to be able to trace any metal whatever, either under ground or elsewhere?"

"Yes," said the Jew, "I possess this rare faculty, thanks to my nose; and to give thee a farther proof of it, I declare that I can again scent in this spot in the wall a sum of gold and silver, the exact amount of which I cannot enumerate."

Mohammed turned pale at these words. "In this wall?" said he.

"Yes. Suffer me to make a little hole with this gimlet here, and you will see if I speak falsely."

"Dig where thou wilt," replied Yousouf; "we have no right to prevent thee after the discovery thou hast just made here."

The Jew instantly set to work at the wall, but it was now his turn to be astonished, for the wall, hollow it is true, was guiltless of gold or silver either.

Yousouf burst out laughing at the disconcerted and stupified look of the old Jew.

"Never mind," said he, "thy nose has deceived thee for once; but thou must not let that discourage thee. Still, hadst thou frankly told me that as a friend of old Nathan Cohen thou knewest where he had hidden his treasure, in return for thy confidence I should have given thee a quarter of what thou hast found; but since thou hast persisted in assuring me that thy nose is gifted with supernatural powers, I shall give thee much less. Besides, with such a nose as thine no one can doubt but thy fortune is made."

"Ah!" cried the Jew, clasping his withered and wrinkled hands, "Yousouf! Yousouf! since thou art good and just, as Mohammed says, take pity on my poverty; it impelled me to deal falsely with thee; I confess it now; and spite of its singular form, my nose has nothing but what is common to other noses. Accord then to my tardy sincerity that which thou wouldst at first have given me."

Yousouf consulted Mohammed again, who replied thus:

"Thou art just and pious; act according to thy own desire."

Yousouf then counted out to the old Jew the fourth part of what he had just found, thus rendering him happy for the remainder of his days.

Then, finding himself alone with his friend, he began to divide into two equal parts the gold and silver which remained.

"Give me none! give me none, Yousouf!" exclaimed Mohammed, "I am no longer deserving of thy friendship."

"Thou!" said Yousouf, "art thou mad? what sayst thou?"

"I speak the melancholy truth," cried Mohammed; "I have not a noble heart like thine. Some time since I discovered in the wall the gold and silver which the Jew thought to find there; but instead of saying as thou hast done, 'I will share it with my friend,' I put off from day to day the fulfilment of this sacred duty. Ah, Yousouf, I am unworthy of thy friendship, and am very unhappy!"

Yousouf remained silent for a few moments, but soon his brow grew clear, and a pleasing smile diffused itself over his features and illuminated his fine dark eyes.

"What man," said he, "is entirely master over his own thoughts? Thou didst hesitate, sayst thou, before confiding to me the discovery thou hadst made. That may be, but thou wouldst not have failed to do so at last. Thou wouldst never have been able to behold thyself rich, knowing me to be poor, and to sit at a feast whilst I lived upon black bread. Thou didst not thoroughly understand the wants and feelings of thy heart: that is all. Thou didst not at once perceive wherein lies true happiness, for which reason thou hast caused thyself much uneasiness. It is over now; our friendship has been tried by gold; nothing remains for us but to enjoy the good fortune that has befallen us. Let us seek to do so like wise men, and never let us forget to set apart for the poor a portion of that which Allah has bestowed upon us."

The two friends agreed therefore to give a hundred doubloons to the poor of the great mosque. Then with the rest of their treasure they purchased a beautiful country house not far from the sea, on the coast of Punta Pescada. There they lived happily for many long years, always admired and esteemed for their mutual affection, and for the goodness of their hearts; for, strange to say, their sudden and unexpected change of fortune never served to render them callous to the poor, nor indifferent to the wants and troubles of their fellow-creatures.

VII.

THE STORY OF THE TREASURES OF BASRA.

All historians agree that the caliph Haroun-al-Raschid would have been the most perfect prince of his time, as he was also the most powerful, if he had not so often given way both to anger and to an insupportable vanity. He was always saying that no prince in the world was so generous as himself. Giafar, his chief vizir, being at last quite disgusted with his boasting, took the liberty to say to him one day, "Oh, my sovereign lord, monarch of the world, pardon your slave if he dares to represent to you that you ought not thus to praise yourself. Leave that to your subjects and the crowds of strangers who frequent your court. Content yourself with the knowledge that the former thank heaven for being born in your dominions, and that the latter congratulate themselves on having quitted their country to come and live under your laws." Haroun was very angry at these words; he looked sternly at his vizir, and asked him if he knew any one who could be compared to himself in generosity.

"Yes, my lord," answered Giafar, "there is in the town of Basra a young man named Aboulcassem, who, though a private individual, lives in more magnificence than kings, and without excepting even your majesty, no prince is more generous than this man."

The caliph reddened at these words, his eyes flashed with anger. "Do you know," he said, "that a subject who has the audacity to lie to his master merits death?"

"I have said nothing but the truth," replied the vizir. "During my last visit to Basra I saw this Aboulcassem; I stayed at his house; my eyes, though accustomed to your treasures, were surprised at his riches, and I was charmed with the generosity of his manners."

At these words the impetuous Haroun could no longer contain his anger. "You are most insolent," he cried, "to place a private individual on an equality with myself! Your imprudence shall not remain unpunished."

So saying, he made a sign for the captain of his guards to approach, and commanded him to arrest the vizir Giafar. He then went to the apartment of the princess Zobeide his wife, who grew pale with fear on seeing his irritated countenance.

"What is the matter, my lord?" said she; "what causes you to be thus agitated?"

Haroun told her all that had passed, and complained of his vizir in terms that soon made Zobeide comprehend how enraged he was with the minister. This wise princess advised him to suspend his resentment, and send some one to Basra to ascertain the truth of Giafar's assertion; if it was false, she argued, the vizir should be punished; on the contrary, if it proved true, which she could not believe, it was not just to treat him as a criminal. This discourse calmed the fury of the caliph.

"I approve of this counsel, madam," said he, "and will acknowledge that I owe this justice to such a minister as Giafar. I will do still more; as any other person I charged with this office might, from an aversion to my vizir, give me a false statement, I will myself go to Basra and judge of the truth of this report. I will make acquaintance with this young man, whose generosity is thus extolled; if Giafar has told me true, I will load him with benefits instead of punishing him for his frankness; but I swear he shall forfeit his life if I find he has told me a falsehood."

As soon as Haroun had formed this resolution he thought of nothing but how to execute it. One night he secretly left the palace, mounted his horse, and left the city, not wishing any one to follow him, though Zobeide entreated him not to go alone. Arriving at Basra, he dismounted at the first caravansary he found on entering the city, the landlord of which seemed a good old man.

"Father," said Haroun, "is it true that there is in this city a young man called Aboulcassem, who surpasses even kings in magnificence and generosity?"

"Yes, my lord," answered the landlord; "and if I had a hundred mouths, and in each mouth a hundred tongues, I could not relate to you all his generous actions." As the caliph had now need of some repose, he retired to rest after partaking of a slight refreshment. He was up very early in the morning, and walked about until sunrise. Then he approached a tailor's shop and asked for the dwelling of Aboulcassem. "From what country do you come?" said the tailor; "most certainly you have never been at Basra before, or you would have heard where the lord Aboulcassem lives; why, his house is better known than the palace of the king."

The caliph answered, "I am a stranger; I know no one in this city, and I shall be obliged if you will conduct me to this lord's house."

Upon that the tailor ordered one of his boys to show the caliph the way to the residence of Aboulcassem. It was a large house built of stone, with a doorway of marble and jasper. The prince entered the court, where there was a crowd of servants and liberated slaves who were amusing themselves in different ways while they awaited the orders of their master. He approached one of them and said, "Friend, I wish you would take the trouble to go to the lord Aboulcassem and tell him a stranger wishes to see him." The domestic judged from the appearance of Haroun that he was no common man. He ran to apprise his master, who coming into the court took the stranger by the hand and conducted him to a very beautiful saloon. The caliph then told the young man, that having heard him mentioned in terms of praise, he had become desirous of seeing him, and had travelled to Basra for that purpose. Aboulcassem modestly replied to this compliment, and seating his guest on a sofa, asked of what country and profession he was, and where he lodged at Basra.

"I am a merchant of Bagdad," replied the caliph, "and I have taken a lodging at the first caravansary I found on my arrival."

After they had conversed for a short time there entered twelve pages bearing vases of agate and rock crystal, enriched with precious stones, and full of the most exquisite beverages. They were followed by twelve very beautiful female slaves, some carrying china bowls filled with fruit and flowers, and others golden caskets containing conserves of an exquisite flavour. The pages presented their beverages to the caliph; the prince tasted them, and though accustomed to the most delicious that could be obtained in the East, he acknowledged that he had never tasted better. As it was now near the hour for dinner, Aboulcassem conducted his guest to another room, where they found a table covered with the choicest delicacies served on dishes of massive gold. The repast finished, the young man took the caliph by the hand and led him to a third room more richly furnished than the two others. Here the slaves brought a prodigious quantity of gold vases, enriched with rubies, filled with all sorts of rare wines, and china plates containing dried sweetmeats. While the host and his guest were partaking of these delicious wines there entered singers and musicians, who commenced a concert, with which Haroun was enchanted. "I have," he said to himself, "the most admirable voices in *my* palace, but I must confess they cannot bear comparison with these. I do not understand how a private individual can live in such magnificence."

Amongst the voices there was one in particular the extraordinary sweetness of which attracted the attention of the prince, and whilst he was absorbed in listening to it Aboulcassem left the room and returned a moment after holding in one hand a wand, and in the other a little tree whose stem was of silver, the branches and leaves emeralds, and the fruit rubies. On the top of this tree was a golden peacock beautifully executed, the body of which was filled with amber, essence of aloes, and other perfumes. He placed this tree at the caliph's feet; then striking the head of the peacock with his wand, the bird extended its wings and tail, and moved itself quickly to the right and left, whilst at each movement of its body the most odoriferous perfumes filled the apartment. The caliph was so astonished and delighted that he could not take his eyes off the tree and the peacock, and he was just going to express his admiration when Aboulcassem suddenly took them away. Haroun was offended at this, and said to himself, "What does all this mean? It appears to me this young man does not merit so much praise. He takes away the tree and the peacock when he sees me occupied in looking at them more than he likes. Is he afraid I want him to make me a present? I fear Giafar is mistaken in calling him a generous man." He was thus thinking when Aboulcassem returned accompanied by a little page as beautiful as the sun. This lovely child was dressed in gold brocade covered with pearls and diamonds. He held in his hand a cup made of one single ruby, and filled with wine of a purple colour. He approached the caliph, and prostrating himself to the ground, presented the cup. The prince extended his hand to receive it, but, wonderful to relate, he perceived on giving back the cup to the page, that though he had emptied the cup, it was still quite full. He put it again to his lips and emptied it to the very last drop. He then placed it again in the hands of the page, and at the same moment saw it filling without any one approaching it. The surprise of Haroun was extreme at this wonderful circumstance, which made him forget the tree and the peacock. He asked how it was accomplished. "My lord," said Aboulcassem, "it is the work of an ancient sage who was acquainted with most of the secrets of nature;" and then, taking the page by the hand, he precipitately left the apartment. The caliph was indignant at this behaviour. "I see how it is," said he, "this young man has lost his senses. He brings me all these curiosities of his own accord, he presents them to my view, and when he perceives my admiration, he instantly removes his treasures. I never experienced treatment so ridiculous or uncourteous. Ah, Giafar! I thought you a better judge of men."

In this manner they continued amusing themselves till sunset. Then Haroun said to the young man, "Oh, generous Aboulcassem, I am confused with the reception you have given me; permit me now to retire and leave you to repose." The young lord of Basra not wishing to inconvenience his guest, politely saluted him, and conducted him to the door of the house, apologizing for not having received him in a more magnificent style. "I quite acknowledge," said the caliph on returning to his caravansary, "that for magnificence Aboulcassem surpasses kings, but for generosity, there my vizir was wrong in placing him in comparison with myself; for what present has he made me during my visit? I was lavish in my praises of the tree, the cup, and the page, and I should have thought my admiration would have induced him to offer me, at least, one of these things. No, this man is ostentatious; he feels a pleasure in displaying his riches to the eyes of strangers. And why? Only to satisfy his pride and vanity. In reality he is a miser, and I ought not to pardon Giafar for thus deceiving me." Whilst making these disagreeable reflections on his minister, he arrived at the caravansary. But what was his astonishment on finding there silken carpets, magnificent tents, a great number of servants, slaves, horses, mules, camels, and besides all these, the tree and the peacock, and the page with his cup? The domestics prostrated themselves before him, and presented a roll of silk paper, on which were written these words, "Dear and amiable guest, I have not, perhaps, shown you the respect which is your due; I pray you to forget any appearance of neglect in my manner of receiving you, and do not distress me by refusing the little presents I have sent you. As to the tree, the peacock, the page, and the cup, since they please you, they are yours already, for any thing that delights my guests ceases to be mine from that instant." When the caliph had finished reading this letter, he was astounded at the liberality of Aboulcassem, and remembered how wrongly he had judged the young man. "A thousand blessings," cried he, "on my vizir Giafar! He has caused me to be undeceived. Ah, Haroun, never again boast of being the most magnificent and generous of men! one of your subjects surpasses you. But how is a private individual able to make such presents? I ought to have asked where he amassed such riches; I was wrong not to have questioned him on this point: I must not return to Bagdad without investigating this affair. Besides, it concerns me to know why there is a man in my dominions who leads a more princely life than myself. I must see him again, and try to discover by what means he has acquired such an immense fortune."

Impatient to satisfy his curiosity, he left his new servants in the caravansary, and returned immediately to the young man's residence. When he found himself in his presence he said, "Oh, too amiable Aboulcassem, the presents you have made me are so valuable, that I fear I cannot accept them without abusing your generosity. Permit me to send them back before I return to Bagdad, and publish to the world your magnificence and generous hospitality." "My lord," answered the young man with a mortified air, "you certainly must have had reason to complain of the unhappy Aboulcassem; I fear some of his actions have displeased you, since you reject his presents; you would not have done me this injury, if you were satisfied with me."

"No," replied the prince, "heaven is my witness that I am enchanted with your politeness; but your presents are too costly; they surpass those of kings, and if I dared tell you what I think, you would be less prodigal with your riches, and remember that they may soon be exhausted."

Aboulcassem smiled at these words and said to the caliph, "My lord, I am very glad to learn that it is not to punish me for having committed any fault against yourself that you wished to refuse my presents; and now to oblige you to accept them, I will tell you that every day I can make the same and even more magnificent ones without inconveniencing myself. I see," added he, "that this astonishes you, but you will cease to be surprised when I have told you all the adventures which have happened to me. It is necessary that I should thus confide in you."

Upon this he conducted Haroun to a room a thousand times richer and more ornamented than any of the others. The most exquisite essences perfumed this apartment, in which was a throne of gold placed on the richest carpets. Haroun could not believe he was in the house of a subject; he imagined he must be in the abode of a prince infinitely more powerful than himself. The young man made him mount the throne, and placing himself by his side, commenced the history of his life.

HISTORY OF ABOULCASSEM.

I am the son of a jeweller of Cairo, named Abdelaziz. He possessed such immense riches, that fearing to draw upon himself the envy or avarice of the sultan of Egypt, he quitted his native country and established himself at Basra, where he married the only daughter of the richest merchant in that city. I am the only child of that marriage, so that inheriting the estates of both my parents I became possessed on their death of a very splendid fortune. But I was young, I liked extravagance, and having wherewith to exercise my liberal propensities, or rather my prodigality, I lived with so much profusion, that in less than three years my fortune was dissipated. Then, like all who repent of their foolish conduct, I made the most promising resolutions for the future.

After the life I had led at Basra, I thought it better to leave that place, for it seemed to me my misery would be more supportable among strangers. Accordingly I sold my house, and left the city before daybreak. When it was light I perceived a caravan of merchants who had encamped on a spot of ground near me. I joined them, and as they were on their road to Bagdad, where I also wished to go, I departed with them; I arrived there without accident, but soon found myself in a very miserable situation. I was without money, and of all my large fortune there remained but one gold sequin. In order to do something for a living I changed my sequin into aspres, and purchased some preserved apples, sweetmeats, balms, and roses. With these I went every day to the house of a merchant where many persons of rank and others were accustomed to assemble and converse together. I presented to them in a basket what I had to sell. Each took what he liked, and never failed to remunerate me, so that by this little commerce I contrived to live very comfortably. One day as I was as usual selling flowers at the merchant's house, there was seated in a corner of the room an old man, of whom I took no notice, and on perceiving that I did not address him, he called me and said, "My friend, how comes it that you do not offer your merchandise to me as well as the others? Do you take me for a dishonest man, or imagine that my purse is empty?"

"My lord," answered I, "I pray you pardon me. All that I have is at your service, I ask nothing for it." At the same time I offered him my basket; he took some perfume, and told me to sit down by him. I did so, and he asked me a number of questions, who I was, and what was my name.

"Excuse me satisfying your curiosity," said I, sighing; "I cannot do so without reopening wounds which time is beginning to heal."

These words, or the tone in which I uttered them, prevented the old man from questioning me further. He changed the discourse, and after a long conversation, on rising to depart he took out his purse and gave me ten gold sequins. I was greatly surprised at this liberality. The wealthiest lords to whom I had been accustomed to present my basket had never given me even one sequin, and I could not tell what to make of this man.

On the morrow, when I returned to the merchants, I again found my old friend; and for many days he continued to attract my attention. At length, one day, as I was addressing him after he had taken a little balm from my basket, he made me again sit by him, and pressed me so earnestly to relate my history, that I could not refuse him. I informed him of all that had happened to me; after this confidence he said:

"Young man, I knew your father. I am a merchant of Basra; I have no child, and have conceived a friendship for you; I will adopt you as my son, therefore console yourself for your past misfortunes. You have found a father richer by far than Abdelaziz, and who will have as much affection for you." I thanked the venerable old man for the honour he did me, and followed him as he left the house. He made me throw away my basket of flowers, and conducted me to a large mansion that he had hired. There I was lodged in a spacious apartment with slaves to wait on me, and by his order they brought me rich clothes. One would have thought my father Abdelaziz again lived, and it seemed as if I had never known sorrow. When the merchant had finished the business that detained him at Bagdad,—namely, when he had sold the merchandise he brought with him,—we both took the road to Basra. My friends, who never thought to see me again, were not a little surprised to hear I had been adopted by a man who passed for the richest merchant in the city. I did my best to please the old man. He was charmed with my behaviour. "Aboulcassem," he often said to me, "I am enchanted that I met you at Bagdad. You appear worthy of all I have done for you." I was touched with the kindness he evinced for me, and far from abusing it, endeavoured to do all I could to please my kind benefactor. Instead of seeking companions of my own age, I always kept in his company, scarcely ever leaving him. At last this good old man fell sick, and the physicians despaired of his life. When he was at the last extremity he made all but myself leave him, and then said, "Now is the time, my son, to reveal to you a most important secret. If I had only this house with all its riches to bequeath, I should leave you but a moderate fortune; but all that I have amassed during the course of my life, though considerable for a merchant, is nothing in comparison to the treasure that is concealed here, and which I am now about to reveal to you. I shall not tell you how long ago, by whom, or in what manner it was found, for I am ignorant of that myself; all I know is, that my grandfather, when dying, told the secret to my father, who also made me acquainted with it a few days before his death. But," continued he, "I have one advice to give you, and take care you do not slight it. You are naturally generous. When you are at liberty to follow your own inclinations, you will no doubt be lavish of your riches. You will receive with magnificence any strangers who may come to your house. You will load them with presents, and will do good to all who implore your assistance. This conduct, which I much approve of if you can keep it within bounds, will at last be the cause of your ruin. The splendour of your establishment will excite the envy of the king of Basra, and the avarice of his ministers. They will suspect you of having some hidden treasure. They will spare no means to discover it, and will imprison you. To prevent this misfortune, you have only to follow my example. I have always, as well as my grandfather and father, carried on my business and enjoyed this treasure without ostentation; we have never indulged in any extravagance calculated to surprise the world."

I faithfully promised the merchant I would imitate his prudence. He told me where I should find the treasure, and assured me that whatever idea I might have formed of its splendour, I should find the reality far exceed my expectations. At last, when the generous old man died, I, as his sole heir, performed for him the last offices, and, taking possession of his property, of which this house is a part, proceeded at once to see this treasure. I confess to you, my lord, that I was thunderstruck. I found it to be, if not inexhaustible, at least so vast that I could never expend it, even if heaven were to permit me to live beyond the age of man. My resolution therefore was at once formed, and instead of keeping the promise I made to the old merchant, I spend my riches freely. It is my boast that there is no one in Basra who has not benefited by my generosity. My house is open to all who desire my aid, and they leave it perfectly contented. Do you call it *possessing* a treasure if it must not be touched? And can I make a better use of it than by endeavouring to relieve the unhappy, to receive strangers with liberality, and to lead a life of generosity and charity? Every one thought I should be ruined a second time.

"If Aboulcassem," said they, "had all the treasures of the commander of the faithful, he would spend them."

But they were much astonished, when, instead of seeing my affairs in disorder, they, on the contrary, appeared every day to become more flourishing. No one could imagine how my fortune increased, while I was thus squandering it. As the old man predicted, a feeling of envy was excited against me. A rumour prevailed that I had found a treasure. This was sufficient to attract the attention of a number of persons greedy of gain. The lieutenant of police at Basra came to see me.

"I am," said he, "the daroga, and am come to demand where the treasure is which enables you to live in such magnificence."

I trembled at these words, and remained silent. He guessed from my confused air that his suspicions were not without foundation; but instead of compelling me to discover my treasure, "My lord Aboulcassem," continued he, "I exercise my office as a man of sense. Make me some present worthy of my discretion in this affair, and I will retire."

"How much do you ask?" said I.

"I will content myself with ten gold sequins a day."

"That is not enough—I will give you a hundred. You have only to come here every day or every month, and my treasurer will count them out to you."

The lieutenant of police was transported with joy at hearing these words. "My lord," said he, "I wish that you could find a thousand treasures. Enjoy your fortune in peace; I shall never dispute your possession of it." Then taking a large sum of money in advance he went his way.

A short time after the vizir Aboulfatah-Waschi sent for me, and, taking me into his cabinet, said:

"Young man, I hear you have discovered a treasure. You know the fifth part belongs to God; you must give it to the king. Pay the fifth, and you shall remain the quiet possessor of the other four parts."

I answered him thus: "My lord, I acknowledge that I *have* found a treasure, but I swear to you at the same time that I will confess nothing, though I should be torn in pieces. But I promise to give you every day a thousand gold sequins, provided you leave me in peace."

Aboulfatah was as tractable as the lieutenant of police. He sent his confidential servant, and my treasurer gave him thirty thousand sequins for the first month. This vizir, fearing no doubt that the king of Basra would hear of what had passed, thought it better to inform him himself of the circumstance. The prince listened very attentively, and thinking the affair required investigating, sent to summon me. He received me with a smiling countenance, saying:

"Approach, young man, and answer me what I shall ask you. Why do you not show me your treasure? Do you think me so unjust, that I shall take it from you?"

"Sire," replied I, "may the life of your majesty be prolonged for ages; but if you commanded my flesh to be torn with burning pincers I would not discover my treasure; I consent every day to pay to your majesty two thousand gold sequins. If you refuse to accept them, and think proper that I should die, you have only to order it; but I am ready to suffer all imaginable torments, sooner than satisfy your curiosity."

The king looked at his vizir as I said this, and demanded his opinion.

"Sire," said the minister, "the sum he offers you is considerable—it is of itself a real treasure. Send the young man back, only let him be careful to keep his word with your majesty."

The king followed this advice; he loaded me with caresses, and from that time, according to my agreement, I pay every year to the prince, the vizir, and the lieutenant of police, more than one million sixty thousand gold sequins. This, my lord, is all I have to tell you. You will now no longer be surprised at the presents I have made you, nor at what you have seen in my house.

CONCLUSION OF THE STORY OF THE TREASURES OF BASRA.

When Aboulcassem had finished the recital of his adventures, the caliph, animated with a violent desire to see the treasure, said to him, "Is it possible that there is in the world a treasure that your generosity can never exhaust? No! I cannot believe it, and if it was not exacting too much from you, my lord, I would ask to see what you possess, and I swear never to reveal what you may confide to me." The son of Abdelaziz appeared grieved at this speech of the caliph's. "I am sorry, my lord," he said, "that you have conceived this curiosity; I cannot satisfy it but upon very disagreeable conditions."

"Never mind," said the prince, "whatever the conditions, I submit without repugnance."

"It is necessary," said Aboulcassem, "that I blindfold your eyes, and conduct you unarmed and bareheaded, with my drawn scimitar in my hand, ready to cut you to pieces at any moment, if you violate the laws of hospitality. I know very well I am acting imprudently, and ought not to yield to your wishes; but I rely on your promised secrecy, and besides that, I cannot bear to send away a guest dissatisfied."

"In pity then satisfy my curiosity," said the caliph.

"That cannot be just yet," replied the young man, "but remain here this night, and when my domestics are gone to rest I will come and conduct you from your apartment."

He then called his people, and by the light of a number of wax tapers, carried by slaves in gold flambeaux, he led the prince to a magnificent chamber, and then retired to his own. The slaves disrobed the caliph, and left him to repose, after placing at the head and foot of his bed their lighted tapers, whose perfumed wax emitted an agreeable odour. Instead of taking any rest, Haroun-al-Raschid impatiently awaited the appearance of Aboulcassem, who did not fail to come for him towards the middle of the night. "My lord," he said, "all my servants are asleep. A profound silence reigns in my house. I will now show you my treasure upon the conditions I named to you."

"Let us go then," said the caliph. "I am ready to follow you, and I again swear that you will not repent thus satisfying my curiosity."

The son of Abdelaziz aided the prince to dress; then putting a bandage over his eyes, he said, "I am sorry, my lord, to be obliged to treat you thus; your appearance and your manners seem worthy of confidence, but—"

"I approve of these precautions," interrupted the caliph, "and I do not take them in ill part."

Aboulcassem then made him descend by a winding staircase into a garden of vast extent, and after many turnings they entered the place where the treasure was concealed. It was a deep and spacious cavern closed at the entrance by a stone. Passing through this they entered a long alley, very dark and steep, at the end of which was a large saloon, brilliantly lighted by carbuncles. When they arrived at this room the young man unbound the caliph's eyes, and the latter gazed with astonishment on the scene before him. A basin of white marble, fifty feet in circumference and thirty feet deep, stood in the middle of the apartment. It was full of large pieces of gold, and ranged round it were twelve columns of the same metal, supporting as many statues composed of precious stones of admirable workmanship. Aboulcassem conducted the prince to the edge of the basin and said to him, "This basin is thirty feet deep. Look at that mass of gold pieces. They are scarcely diminished the depth of two fingers. Do you think I shall soon spend all this?"

Haroun, after attentively looking at the basin, replied: "Here are, I confess, immense riches, but you still may exhaust them."

"Well," said the young man, "when this basin is empty I shall have recourse to what I am now going to show you."

He then proceeded to another room, more brilliant still, where on a number of red brocaded sofas were immense quantities of pearls and diamonds. Here was also another marble basin, not so large or so deep as that filled with gold pieces, but to make up for this, full of rubies, topazes, emeralds, and all sorts of precious stones. Never was surprise equal to that of the caliph's. He could scarcely believe he was awake, this new basin seemed like enchantment. His gaze was still fixed on it, when Aboulcassem made him observe two persons seated on a throne of gold, who he said were the first masters of the treasure. They were a prince and princess, having on their heads crowns of diamonds. They appeared as if still alive, and were in a reclining posture, their heads leaning against each other. At their feet was a table of ebony, on which were written these words in letters of gold: "I have amassed all these riches during the course of a long life. I have taken and pillaged towns and castles, have conquered kingdoms and overthrown my enemies. I have been the most powerful monarch in the world, but all my power has yielded to that of death. Whoever sees me in this state ought to reflect upon it. Let him remember that once I was living, and that he also must die. He need not fear diminishing this treasure: it will never be exhausted. Let him endeavour so to use it as to make friends both for this world and the next. Let him lead a life of generosity and charity, for in the end he must also die. His riches cannot save him from the fate common to all men."

"I will no longer disapprove of your conduct," said Haroun to the young man on reading these words; "you are right in living as you now do, and I condemn the advice given you by the old merchant. But I should like to know the name of this prince. What king could have possessed such riches? I am sorry this inscription does not inform us."

The young man next took the caliph to see another room in which also there were many rarities of even greater value than what he had seen, amongst others several trees like the one he had given the prince. Haroun would willingly have passed the remainder of the night admiring all that was contained in this wonderful cavern, but the son of Abdelaziz, fearing to be observed by his servants, wished to return before daybreak in the same manner as they came, namely, the caliph blindfolded and bareheaded, and Aboulcassem with his scimitar in his hand, ready to cut off the prince's head if he made the least resistance. In this order they traversed the garden, and ascended by the winding stairs to the room where the caliph had slept. Finding the tapers still burning, they conversed together till sunrise; the caliph then, with many thanks for the reception he had received, returned to the caravansary, from whence he took the road to Bagdad, with all the domestics and presents he had accepted from Aboulcassem.

Two days after the prince's departure, the vizir Aboulfatah, hearing of the magnificent gifts that Aboulcassem made to strangers when they came to see him, and above all astonished at the regularity of his payments to the king, the lieutenant, and himself, resolved to spare no means to discover the treasure from which he drew such inexhaustible supplies. This minister was one of those wicked men to whom the greatest crimes are nothing, when they wish to gain their own ends. He had a daughter eighteen years of age, and of surpassing beauty. She was named Balkis, and possessed every good quality of heart and mind. Prince Aly, nephew of the king of Basra, passionately loved her; he had already demanded her of her father, and they were soon to be married. Aboulfatah summoned Balkis one day to his presence and said: "My daughter, I have great need of your assistance. I wish you to array yourself in your richest robes, and go this evening to the house of the young Aboulcassem. You must do every thing to charm him, and oblige him to discover the treasure he has found."

Balkis trembled at this speech; her countenance expressed the horror she felt at this command. "My lord," said she, "what is it you propose to your daughter? Do you know the peril to which you may expose her? Consider the stain on your honour, and the outrage against the prince Aly."

"I have considered all this," answered the vizir, "but nothing will turn me from my resolution, and I order you to prepare to obey me."

The young Balkis burst into tears at these words. "For heaven's sake, my father," said the weeping girl, "stifle this feeling of avarice, seek not to despoil this man of what is his own. Leave him to enjoy his riches in peace."

"Be silent, insolent girl!" said the vizir angrily, "it does not become you to blame my actions. Answer me not. I desire you to repair to the house of Aboulcassem, and I swear that if you return without having seen his treasure, I will kill you."

Balkis, hearing this dreadful alternative, retired to her apartment overwhelmed with grief; she called her women, and made them attire her in the richest apparel and most costly ornaments, though in reality she needed nothing to enhance her natural beauty. No young girl was less desirous to please than Balkis. All she feared was appearing too beautiful in the eyes of the son of Abdelaziz, and not sufficiently so to prince Aly.

At length, when night arrived and Aboulfatah judged it time for his daughter to go, he secretly conducted her to the door of the young man's house, where he left her, after again declaring he would kill her if she returned unsuccessful. She timidly knocked and desired to speak to the son of Abdelaziz. A slave led her to a room where his master was reposing on a sofa, musing on the vicissitudes of his past life. As soon as Balkis appeared Aboulcassem rose to receive his visitor; he gravely saluted her, and, taking her hand with a respectful air, seated her on a sofa, at the same time inquiring why she honoured him by this visit. She answered, that hearing of his agreeable manners, she had resolved to spend an evening in his company.

"Beautiful lady," said he, "I must thank my lucky star for procuring me this delightful interview; I cannot express my happiness."

After some conversation supper was announced. They seated themselves at a table covered with choice delicacies. A great number of officers and pages were in attendance, but Aboulcassem dismissed them that the lady might not be exposed to their curious looks. He waited on her himself, presenting her with the best of every thing, and offering her wine in a gold cup enriched with diamonds and rubies. But all these polite attentions served but to increase the lady's uneasiness; and at length, frightened at the dangers which menaced her, she suddenly changed countenance and became pale as death, whilst her eyes filled with tears.

"What is it, madam?" said the young man much surprised; "why this sudden grief? Have I said or done any thing to cause your tears to flow? Speak, I implore you; inform me of the cause of your sorrow."

"Oh, Mahomet!" exclaimed Balkis, "I can dissimulate no longer; the part I am acting is insupportable. I have deceived you, Aboulcassem; I am a lady of rank. My father, who knows you have a hidden treasure, wishes me to discover where you have concealed it. He has ordered me to come here and spare no means to induce you to show it me. I refused to do so, but he has sworn to kill me if I return without being able to satisfy his curiosity. What an unhappy fate is mine! If I was not beloved by a prince who will soon marry me, this cruel vow of my father's would not appear so terrible."

When the daughter of Aboulfatah had thus spoken, Aboulcassem said to her, "Madam, I am very glad you have informed me of this. You will not repent your noble frankness; you shall see my treasure, and be treated with all the respect you may desire. Do not weep, therefore, or any longer afflict yourself."

"Ah, my lord," exclaimed Balkis at this speech, "it is not without reason that you pass for the most generous of men. I am charmed with your noble conduct, and shall not be satisfied until I have found means to testify my gratitude."

After this conversation Aboulcassem conducted the lady to the same chamber that the caliph had occupied, where they remained until all was quiet in the dwelling. Then blindfolding the eyes of Balkis he said, "Pardon me, madam, for being obliged to act thus, but it is only on this condition that I can show you my treasure."

"Do what you please, my lord," answered Balkis; "I have so much confidence in your generosity that I will follow wherever you desire; I have no fear but that of not sufficiently repaying your kindness."

Aboulcassem then took her by the hand, and causing her to descend to the garden by the winding stairs, he entered the cavern and removed the bandage from her eyes. If the caliph had been surprised to see such heaps of gold and precious stones, Balkis was still more so. Every thing she saw astonished her. But the objects that most attracted her attention were the ancient owners of the treasure. As the queen had on a necklace composed of pearls as large as pigeons' eggs, Balkis could not avoid expressing her admiration. Aboulcassem detached it from the neck of the princess, and placed it round that of the young lady, saying her father would judge from this that she had seen the treasure; he then, after much persuasion, made her take a large quantity of precious stones which he himself chose for her.

The young man then, fearing the day would dawn whilst she was looking at the wonders of the cavern, again placed the bandage over her eyes, and conducted her to a saloon where they conversed together until sunrise. Balkis then took leave, repeatedly assuring the son of Abdelaziz that she would never forget his generous conduct.

She hastened to her father's and informed him of all that had passed. The vizir had been impatiently awaiting his daughter's return. Fearing she might not be sufficiently able to charm Aboulcassem, he remained in a state of inconceivable agitation. But when he saw her enter with the necklace and precious stones that Aboulcassem had given her, he was transported with joy.

"Well, my daughter," he said, "have you seen the treasure?"

"Yes, my lord," answered Balkis, "and to give you a just idea of its magnitude, I tell you that if all the kings of the world were to unite their riches, they could not be compared to those of Aboulcassem. But still, however vast this young man's treasures, I am less charmed with them than with his politeness and generosity." And she then related to her father the whole of her adventure.

In the mean time Haroun-al-Raschid was advancing towards Bagdad. As soon as he arrived at his palace he set his chief vizir at liberty, and restored him to his confidence. He then proceeded to relate to him the events of his journey, and ended by asking, "Giafar, what shall I do? You know the gratitude of monarchs ought to surpass the pleasures they have received. If I should send the magnificent Aboulcassem the choicest and most precious treasure I possess, it will be but a slight gift, far inferior to the presents he has made me. How then can I surpass him in generosity?"

"My lord," replied the vizir, "since your majesty condescends to consult me, I should write this day to the king of Basra and order him to commit the government of the state to the young Aboulcassem. We can soon despatch the courier, and in a few days I will depart myself to Basra and present the patents to the new king."

The caliph approved of this advice. "You are right," he said to his minister, "it will be the only means of acquitting myself towards Aboulcassem, and of taking vengeance on the king of Basra and his unworthy vizir, who have concealed from me the considerable sums they have extorted from this young man. It is but just to punish them for their violence against him; they are unworthy of the situations they occupy."

He immediately wrote to the king of Basra and despatched the courier. He then went to the apartment of the princess Zobeide to inform her of the success of his journey, and presented her with the little page, the tree, and the peacock. He also gave her a beautiful female slave. Zobeide found this slave so charming that she smilingly told the caliph she accepted this gift with more pleasure than all his other presents. The prince kept only the cup for himself; the vizir Giafar had all the rest; and this good minister, as he had before resolved, made preparations for his departure from Bagdad.

The courier of the caliph no sooner arrived in the town of Basra than he hastened to present his despatch to the king, who was greatly concerned on reading it. The prince showed it to his vizir. "Aboulfatah," said he, "see the fatal order that I have received from the commander of the faithful. Can I refuse to obey it?"

"Yes, my lord," answered the minister; "do not afflict yourself. Aboulcassem must be removed from hence. Without taking his life I will make every one believe he is dead. I can keep him so well concealed that he shall never be seen again; and by this means you will always remain on the throne and possess the riches of this young man; for when we are masters of his person we can increase his sufferings until he is obliged to reveal where his treasure is concealed."

"Do what you like," replied the king; "but what answer shall we send the caliph?"

"Leave that to me. The commander of the faithful will be deceived as well as others. Let me execute the design I meditate, and the rest need cause you no uneasiness."

Aboulfatah then, accompanied by some courtiers who were ignorant of his intention, went to pay a visit to Aboulcassem. He received them according to their rank, regaled them magnificently, seated the vizir in the place of honour, and loaded him with presents without having the least suspicion of his perfidy. Whilst they were at table and partaking of the most delicious wines, the treacherous Aboulfatah skilfully threw unperceived into the cup of the son of Abdelaziz a powder which would render him insensible, and cause his body to remain in a state of lethargy resembling that of a corpse long deprived of life. The young man had no sooner taken the cup from his lips than he fainted away. His servants hastened to support him, but soon perceiving he had all the appearance of a dead man, they placed him on a sofa and uttered the most lamentable cries. The guests, struck with sudden terror, were silent from astonishment. As for Aboulfatah, it is impossible to say how well he dissimulated. He not only feigned the most immoderate grief, but tore his clothes and excited the rest of the company to follow his example. He ordered a coffin to be made of ivory and ebony, and while they were preparing it, he collected all the effects of Aboulcassem and placed them in the king's palace. The account of the young man's death soon spread abroad. All persons, men and women, put on mourning, and came to the door of the house, their heads and feet bare; old and young men, women and girls, were bathed in tears, filling the air with their cries and lamentations. Some said they had lost in him an only son, others a brother or a husband tenderly beloved. Rich and poor were equally afflicted at his death; the rich mourned a friend who had always welcomed them, and the poor a benefactor whose charity had never been equalled. His death caused a general consternation.

Meanwhile the unhappy Aboulcassem was enclosed in the coffin, and a procession having been formed, the people, by order of Aboulfatah, carried him out of the town to a large cemetery containing a number of tombs, and amongst others a magnificent one where reposed the vizir's father and many others of his family. They placed the coffin in this tomb, and the perfidious Aboulfatah, leaning his head on his knees, beat his breast, and gave way apparently to the most violent grief. Those present pitied and prayed heaven to console him. As night approached the people returned to the town, but the vizir remained with two of his slaves in the tomb, the door of which he shut and double locked. They lit a fire, warmed some water in a silver basin, and taking Aboulcassem from the coffin, bathed him with the warm water. The young man by degrees regained his senses. He cast his eyes on Aboulfatah, whom he at once recognized. "Ah, my lord," said he, "where are we, and to what state am I reduced?"

"Wretch!" answered the minister, "know that it is I who have caused your misfortune. I brought you here to have you in my power, and to make you suffer a thousand torments if you will not discover to me your treasure. I will rack your body with tortures—will invent each day new sufferings to render life insupportable: in a word, I will never cease to persecute you until you deliver me those hidden treasures which enable you to live with even more magnificence than kings."

"You can do what you please," replied Aboulcassem; "I will never reveal my treasure."

He had scarcely uttered these words, when the cruel Aboulfatah, making his slaves seize the unfortunate son of Abdelaziz, drew from his robe a whip made of twisted lion's skin, with which he struck so long and with such violence that the young man fainted. When the vizir saw him in this state, he commanded the slaves to replace him in the coffin, and leaving him in the tomb, which he firmly secured, returned to his palace.

On the morrow he went to inform the king of what he had done. "Sire," said he, "I tried yesterday, but in vain, to overcome the firmness of Aboulcassem; however, I have now prepared torments for him which I think he cannot resist."

The prince, who was quite as barbarous as his minister, said, "Vizir, I am perfectly satisfied with all you have done. Ere long, I hope, we shall know where this treasure is concealed. But we must send back the courier without delay. What shall I write to the caliph?"

"Tell him, my lord, that Aboulcassem, hearing he was to occupy your place, was so enchanted, and made such great rejoicings, that he died suddenly at a feast."

The king approved of this advice, and writing immediately to Haroun-al-Raschid, despatched the courier. The vizir, flattering himself that he should at length be able to force Aboulcassem to reveal his treasure, left the town, resolving to extract the secret or leave him to perish. But on arriving at the tomb, he was surprised to find the door open. He entered trembling, and not seeing the son of Abdelaziz in the coffin, he nearly lost his senses. Returning instantly to the palace, he related to the king what had occurred. The monarch, seized with a mortal terror, exclaimed, "Oh, Waschi! what will become of us? Since this young man has escaped, we are lost. He will not fail to hasten to Bagdad, and acquaint the caliph with all that has taken place."

Aboulfatah, on his part, in despair that the victim of his avarice was no longer in his power, said to the king his master, "What would I now give to have taken his life yesterday! He would not then have caused us such uneasiness. But we will not quite despair yet; if he has taken flight, as no doubt he has, he cannot be very far from here. Let me take some soldiers of your guard, and search in all the environs of the town; I hope still to find him."

The king instantly consented to so important a step. He assembled all his soldiers, and dividing them into two bodies, gave the command of one to his vizir, and placing himself at the head of the other, prepared with his troops to search in all parts of his kingdom.

Whilst they were seeking Aboulcassem in the villages, woods, and mountains, the vizir Giafar, who was already on the road to Basra, met the courier returning, who said to him, "My lord, it is useless for you to proceed further, if Aboulcassem is the sole cause of your journey, for this young man is dead; his funeral took place some days past; my eyes were witnesses of the mournful ceremony."

Giafar, who had looked forward with pleasure to see the new king, and present his patents, was much afflicted at his death. He shed tears on hearing the sad news, and, thinking it was useless to continue his journey, retraced his steps. As soon as he arrived at Bagdad, he went with the courier to the palace. The sadness of his countenance informed the king he had some misfortune to announce.

"Ah, Giafar!" exclaimed the prince, "you have soon returned. What are you come to tell me?'

"Commander of the faithful," answered the vizir, "you do not, I am sure, expect to hear the bad news I am going to tell. Aboulcassem is no more; since your departure from Basra the young man has lost his life."

Haroun-al-Raschid had no sooner heard these words than he threw himself from his throne. He remained some moments extended on the ground without giving any signs of life. At length his eyes sought the courier, who had returned from Basra, and he asked for the despatch. The prince read it with much attention. He shut himself in his cabinet with Giafar, and showed him the letter from the king of Basra. After re-reading it many times, the caliph said,

"This does not appear to me natural; I begin to suspect that the king of Basra and his vizir, instead of executing my orders, have put Aboulcassem to death."

"My lord," said Giafar, "the same suspicion occurred to me, and I advise that they should both be secured."

"That is what I determine from this moment," said Haroun; "take ten thousand horsemen of my guard, march to Basra, seize the two guilty wretches, and bring them here. I will revenge the death of this most generous of men."

"We will now return to the son of Abdelaziz, and relate why the vizir Aboulfatah did not find him in the tomb. The young man, after long remaining insensible, was beginning to recover, when he felt himself laid hold of by powerful arms, taken from the coffin, and gently laid on the earth. He thought it was the vizir and his slaves come again on their cruel errand.

"Executioners!" he cried, "put me to death at once; if you have any pity spare me these useless torments, for again I declare that nothing you can do will ever tempt me to reveal my secret."

"Fear not, young man," answered one of the persons who had lifted him from the coffin; "instead of ill-treating you, we are come to your assistance."

At these words Aboulcassem opened his eyes, and, looking at his liberators, recognized the young lady to whom he had shown his treasure.

"Ah, madam!" he said, "is it to you I owe my life?"

"Yes, my lord," answered Balkis; "to myself and prince Aly, my betrothed, whom you see with me. Informed of your noble behaviour, he wished to share with me the pleasure of delivering you from death."

"It is quite true," said prince Aly; "I would expose my life a thousand times, rather than leave so generous a man to perish."

The son of Abdelaziz, having entirely recovered his senses by the help of some cordials they had given him, expressed to the lady and the prince his grateful thanks for the service they had rendered him, and asked how they had been informed he still lived.

"My lord," said Balkis, "I am the daughter of the vizir Aboulfatah. I was not deceived by the false report of your death. I suspected my father in this affair, and, bribing one of his slaves, was informed of all concerning you. This slave is one of the two who were with him in the tomb, and as he had charge of the key he confided it to me for a few hours. I no sooner made this affair known to prince Aly than he hastened to join me with some of his confidential domestics. We lost not a moment in coming hither, and, thanks be to heaven, we did not arrive too late."

"Oh, Mahomet!" said Aboulcassem, "is it possible so unworthy and cruel a father possesses such a daughter?"

"Let us depart, my lord," said prince Aly; "the time is precious. I doubt not but that to-morrow the vizir, finding you have escaped, will seek you in all directions. I am going to conduct you to my house, where you will be in perfect safety, for no one will suspect me of giving you an asylum."

They then covered Aboulcassem with a slave's robe, and all left the tomb. Balkis proceeded to her father's, and returned the key to the slave, whilst prince Aly took the son of Abdelaziz to his own palace, and kept him so well concealed, that it was impossible his enemies could discover him. Aboulcassem remained some time in prince Aly's house, who treated him most kindly, until the king and his vizir, despairing of finding him, gave up their search. The prince then gave him a very beautiful horse, loaded him with sequins and precious stones, and said to him:

"You can now safely depart; the roads are open, and your enemies know not what is become of you. Hasten to seek a place where you will be secure from harm."

The young man thanked this generous prince for his hospitality, and assured him he should ever gratefully remember it. Prince Aly embraced him, and prayed heaven to protect and watch over him on his journey. Aboulcassem then took the road to Bagdad, and arrived there in safety a few days afterwards. The first thing he did on entering the city was to hasten to the place where the merchants usually assembled. The hope of seeing there some one he had known at Basra, and of relating his misfortunes, was his only consolation. He was vexed at being unable to find this place, and traversing the town, sought in vain for the face of a friend amongst the multitudes he met. Feeling fatigued, he stopped before the caliph's palace to rest a little: the page whom he had given to his former guest was then at a window, and the child looking by chance that way, instantly recognized him. He ran to the caliph's apartment.

"My lord," he exclaimed, "I have just seen my old master from Basra!"

Haroun put no faith in this report. "You are mistaken," he said; "Aboulcassem no longer lives. Deceived by some fancied resemblance, you have taken another for him."

"No, no, commander of the faithful; I assure you it is he: I am certain I am not mistaken."

Though the caliph did not believe this assertion, still he wished to fathom the mystery, and sent one of his officers with the page to see the man the boy declared was the son of Abdelaziz. They found him in the same place, for, imagining he had recognized his little page, he waited till the child reappeared at the window. When the boy was convinced he was not deceived, he threw himself at the feet of Aboulcassem, who raised him, and asked if he had the honour of belonging to the caliph.

"Yes, my lord," said the child; "it was to the commander of the faithful himself—he it was whom you entertained at Basra—it was to him that you gave me. Come with me, my lord; the caliph will be delighted to see you."

The surprise of the young man at this speech was extreme. He allowed himself to be conducted into the palace by the page and the officer, and was soon ushered into the apartment of Haroun. The prince was seated on a sofa. He was extremely affected at the sight of Aboulcassem. He hastened towards the young man, and held him long embraced without uttering a word, so much was he transported with joy. When he recovered a little from his emotion he said to the son of Abdelaziz:

"Young man, open your eyes, and recognize your happy guest. It was I whom you received so hospitably, and to whom you gave presents that kings could not equal."

At these words Aboulcassem, who was not less moved than the caliph, and who from respect had drawn his cloak over his head, and had not yet dared to look up, now uncovered his face, and said:

"Oh, my sovereign master! oh, king of the world, was it you who honoured your slave's house?" And he threw himself at the feet of Haroun, and kissed the floor before him.

"How is it," said the prince, raising him, and placing him on a sofa, "that you are still alive? Tell me all that has happened to you."

ABOULCASSEM AND THE PAGE

Aboulcassem then related the cruelties of Aboulfatah, and how he had been preserved from the fury of that vizir. Haroun listened attentively, and then said:

"Aboulcassem, I am the cause of your misfortunes. On my return to Bagdad, wishing to repay my debt to you, I sent a courier to the king of Basra, desiring him to resign his crown to you. Instead of executing my orders, he resolved to take your life. Aboulfatah, by putting you to the most frightful tortures, hoped to induce you to reveal your treasures; that was the sole reason he delayed your death. But you would have been revenged. Giafar, with a large body of my troops, is gone to Basra. I have given him orders to seize your two persecutors, and to bring them here. In the mean time you shall remain in my palace, and be attended by my officers with as much respect as myself."

After this speech he took the young man by the hand, and made him descend to a garden, filled with the choicest flowers. There he saw basins of marble, porphyry, and jasper, which served for reservoirs to multitudes of beautiful fish. In the midst of the garden, supported upon twelve lofty pillars of black marble, was a dome, the roof of sandal wood and aloes. The spaces between the columns were closed by a double trellis-work of gold, which formed an aviary containing thousands of canaries of different colours, nightingales, linnets, and other harmonious birds, who mingling their notes formed the most charming concert. The baths of Haroun-al-Raschid were under this dome. The prince and his guest took a bath, after which the attendants rubbed them with the finest towels, which had never before been used. They then clothed Aboulcassem in rich apparel. The caliph conducted him to a chamber where refreshments awaited them, such as roasted fowls and lamb, white soups, pomegranates from Amlas and Ziri, pears from Exhali, grapes from Melah and Sevise, and apples from Ispahan. After they had partaken of these delicacies, and drunk some delicious wine, the caliph conducted Aboulcassem to Zobeide's apartment. This princess was seated on a throne of gold, surrounded by her slaves, who were ranged standing on each side of her; some had tambourines, others flutes and harps. At that moment their instruments were mute, all being attentively engaged in listening to a young girl whose charming voice rang through the saloon like the warblings of a nightingale. As soon as Zobeide perceived the caliph and the son of Abdelaziz, she descended from her throne to receive them.

"Madam," said Haroun, "allow me to present to you my host of Basra."

The young man prostrated himself before the princess. At this moment the vizir Giafar was heard returning with the troops, and bringing with him Aboulfatah securely bound. As for the king of Basra, he was left behind dying of grief and fright at not finding Aboulcassem. Giafar had no sooner rendered an account of his mission, than the caliph ordered a scaffold to be erected before the palace, to which the wicked Aboulfatah was conducted. The people knowing the cruelty of this vizir, instead of being touched with his misfortune, testified the utmost impatience to witness his execution. The executioner was already prepared, sabre in hand, to strike off the guilty man's head, when the son of Abdelaziz prostrating himself before the caliph, exclaimed, "Oh, commander of the faithful, yield to my prayers the life of Aboulfatah! Let him live to witness my happiness, to behold all the favours you are conferring upon me, and he will be sufficiently punished."

"Oh, too generous Aboulcassem," replied the caliph, "you, indeed, deserve a crown! Happy the people of Basra to have you for their king."

"My lord, I have one more favour to ask. Give to the prince Aly the throne you destined for myself. Let him reign, together with the lady who had the generosity to avert from me the fury of her father; these two lovers are worthy this honour. As to myself, cherished and protected by the commander of the faithful, I have no need of a crown; I shall be superior to kings."

The caliph assented to this proposal, and to recompense prince Aly for the service he had rendered the son of Abdelaziz, sent him the patents, and made him king of Basra; but finding Aboulfatah too guilty to accord him liberty as well as life, he ordered the vizir to be shut up in a dark tower for the remainder of his days. When the people of Bagdad were informed that it was Aboulcassem himself who had begged the life of his persecutor, they showered a thousand praises on the generous young man, who soon after departed for Basra, escorted by a troop of the caliph's guards, and a great number of his officers.

VIII.

THE OLD CAMEL.

Eggadi-ben-Yousouf, a merchant at Miliana, was a mere lover of gain; he never gave away any thing in alms; his heart was dry as the earth in the hottest days of summer, and never open to pity for the unfortunate. To amass, to amass for ever was the sole desire of Eggadi. But in what did his riches consist? None could say, for he concealed them with the utmost care.

One day one of his camels having died, he bought to replace it the only camel of Ali-Bénala, a poor dealer in mats. This camel was the sole heritage of which Ali came into possession at the death of his father. He sold it for much less than its value;—Eggadi, who was an adept at bargaining, depreciating it in every possible way, especially on account of its extreme age.

On his next journey Eggadi added this camel to his little caravan. As he was passing a solitary place, he was surprised to see the camel betake itself with hasty steps to a spot at some distance behind some rocks, and on its arrival there kneel down and groan, as camels usually do when they expect to be unloaded. A negro, having run after the animal, brought it back to its place in the caravan.

Eggadi soon took a second journey on the same road, and on this occasion too the camel sold him by Ali-Bénala again quitted the rank, and was again observed to kneel down and groan at the same place. This time Eggadi followed it, and saw with surprise that the spot at which it stopped was one where no merchant of any country had been ever known to unload his merchandise. He reflected deeply on this circumstance, and in the end resolved to revisit the spot alone with the camel, who, faithful perhaps to some recollection, might, he thought, be the means of disclosing to him some mysterious act, or perhaps the place where a treasure lay concealed.

Eggadi returned, in short, soon after, to this solitary spot. He had brought with him a spade, and proceeded to dig with care around the camel, who had invariably knelt in the same place. He had scarcely laboured ten minutes ere he discovered traces of another spade; this redoubled his zeal, and soon after, to his intense satisfaction, he came upon some bags of money, then a coffer firmly shut, but which contained, he could not doubt, objects of costly value. He first took the bags, which were filled with good and true Spanish doubloons; with these he loaded his camel, who thus had gained nothing but a double burden for his pains; then, having re-covered with stones and sand the precious coffer, which he resolved upon examining another time, he returned with his mind greatly preoccupied, asking himself whether it must not have been the old father of Ali-Bénala to whom all the wealth he had just discovered formerly belonged.

This question, which he could not help addressing to his conscience over and over again, prevented him from fully enjoying the possession of his treasure. Although he dearly loved money, yet Eggadi to obtain possession of it had never yet plundered the widow and the orphan. The first step in the road to evil is not accomplished without difficulty and without remorse; Eggadi painfully experienced the truth of this. "And yet," said he to himself, "I made a fair bargain with poor Ali for this very camel which has been the means of my finding a treasure."

Before going to take possession of the coffer left underground behind the rocks, Eggadi, impelled by his conscience, approached the miserable shop where Ali carried on the sale of his mats, and said to him:

"How comes it, Ali, that your father, rich as it is said he was, left you no fortune, only an old camel and a house in ruins?"

"Ah!" replied Ali, "my father was good to the poor. Not only did he call every poor man his brother, but assisted him to the utmost of his power. At times, however, I have suspected that my father may have had riches concealed in some spot, and that he intended to bestow them upon me before he died. And I will tell you what led me to suppose so.

"A few moments before his death he sent for me, and said: 'I have a great secret to confide to thee. Come close to me that my voice may reach thy ear alone: but before our conversation, my son, let us pray to Allah to grant us on this solemn day that which is best for us.'

"We prayed, and in ten minutes my father was no more. Allah, no doubt, judged that that which was best for me was poverty. Allah be praised."

Ali bowed his head profoundly, laying his hand upon his breast. Eggadi, much disturbed at the virtuous resignation of Ali-Bénala, rejoined:

"But thinkest thou, that if good fortune befel thee, thou wouldst know how to make good use of it?"

"Allah alone knows," said Ali. "Should he ever see fit to make me rich, he will know how to fit me for the change. For myself, I cannot succeed in improving the poverty of my estate. I work incessantly, but nothing succeeds with me. My oxen, if I have any, drown themselves in crossing a torrent; my goods either do not sell or are damaged. I am destined to possess upon this earth nothing but this miserable hut, which has been my only home for ten years, But what matters it, provided I fulfil the law of the prophet? I shall see Abraham, in heaven. If at times my poverty renders me uneasy, it is only for the sake of my poor children, who live miserably in a house as open to the wind and the rain as though it were without a roof."

"Well," said Eggadi, "it is certainly not just that such an honest man as thou should be in such a wretched state of poverty."

"How! not just!" replied Ali. "Are there not, then, many honest men who are no richer than myself?"

"That may be," said Eggadi. "Nevertheless, since thy father was rich, it seems to be but just that thou shouldst be so too, and I come to propose to thee to enter into partnership with me. I have two good houses outside the town; one shall be for thy family, the other for mine. We will live as brothers, and unite our children as in the time of the patriarchs."

Ali remained greatly astonished at such a proposition, coming especially from Eggadi-ben-Yousouf, who had never had any friendship for him, and who so far from evincing any generosity towards him, had bargained with him for his poor camel like the veriest Jew in the world.

He therefore remained silent, neither accepting nor refusing the offer, but looking with an abstracted air upon the mats in his miserable dwelling.

"Well," said Eggadi, ashamed at the bottom of his heart at making this show of generosity to one whom he was secretly despoiling, "well, thou dost not reply to me?"

"Grant me time to imitate the example of my father by invoking Allah before taking a resolution," said Ali. "Allah alone can know whether it will be best for me to keep at once my poverty and the freedom of all my actions, or to accept opulence and with it the necessity of being always of thy opinion; for bringing into our partnership nothing but my two stout arms, I should be an ingrate if I did not yield in every thing to thy wishes."

Eggadi involuntarily cast down his eyes before this poor man who spoke with so much wisdom.

"Well," said he again, "reflect till to-morrow, and come to me in the morning under the palm trees in front of my house; I will there await thee."

Then these two men separated. Ali, praying in the mosque, thought he heard his father pronounce these words. "Never associate thyself save with him who has no more than thyself, and who already knows the right way. The good are spoilt by associating with the rogue and the miser, whilst neither rogue nor miser is reformed by association with one better than himself."

The next morning Ali repaired to the palm trees which grew before the house of Eggadi, where the latter awaited him uneasy and fatigued after a sleepless night. After the usual Mussulman salutation, Ali-Bénala said to the rich Eggadi:

"How comes it that thou appearest sad, thou who possessest fine houses, coffers of gold, and merchandise, whilst I, I who have nothing, rise with a joyous heart, and smoke my pipe all day with pleasure, seated on the threshold of my poor shop?"

"The weight of business overwhelms me," replied Eggadi; "I have great need of some one to share it."

"Then why not diminish thy transactions, and live in peace?" inquired Ali.

"No, no, it is impossible to set limits to one's purchases and sales. A fortunate speculation balances an unlucky one. You must accept all if you would grow rich. But come, hast thou decided? Wilt thou enter into partnership with me?"

"I have reflected and prayed," said Ali. "I am very grateful for thy offers, and Allah will doubtless recompense thee; but prudence forbids me to accept them. I will never enter into partnership but with one who is as poor as myself."

"Indeed!" exclaimed Eggadi-ben-Yousouf, "be no longer then surprised at thy poverty, since thou refusest the opportunity of enriching thyself. The traveller who does not stop beneath the first trees he meets runs the risk of not finding another upon his road, and of performing the whole journey without enjoying their refreshing shade. Such a man would have no right to complain of the dust of the roads, or the heat of the sun."

"I do not complain," replied Ali, "I come, on the contrary, to tell thee that I live and sleep in peace."

"It is well, it is well," said Eggadi, who had not closed his eyes till the morning, "it is well, remain as thou art. Instead of gold pieces, be content to receive rain-drops through thy roof, eat bread when thou hast any, and go fasting oftener; it concerns me no more."

"I should be a fool," added he internally, "to trouble myself any longer about the poverty of this man." And he remembered his fine house, where gilded cakes, a delicious repast, and rich and rare fruits awaited him.

He ate his meal in company with his sons; then he washed his beard and hands, rose from the table, and called his wife, his daughters, his mother, and his grandmother, and said to them, "Women, eat in your turn; this is for you."

The women respectfully kissed his hands, and proceeded to make their meal, whilst he went and sat down out of doors, and smoked with his sons, to whom he spoke as follows whilst a negro waited upon him with coffee:

"I am about to take another journey. During my absence see to such and such things, and do not forget any of my orders, if you would not run the risk of becoming poor, poor—" he was going to say, "as Ali, the seller of mats," but this name excited too keenly his remorse; he could not venture to pronounce it.

So that in spite of the good repast of which he had just partaken, Eggadi felt ill at ease, for the thought was ever recurring to him, "Ali is poor, his father was rich, and it is I who have unjustly taken possession of his father's wealth." Meanwhile Eggadi had this very moderate relief, he might still enjoy the benefit of a doubt as to whether the father of Ali was really the possessor of the discovered treasures. However, the coffer left behind the rocks would doubtless throw a light upon this matter. Eggadi proceeded at once in search of this coffer; he opened it, and his eyes, dazzled though they were by the precious objects that met their gaze, were constrained to perceive at the same time a sheet of parchment, upon which the following words were very distinctly inscribed:

"All the treasures buried in this spot have been lawfully acquired, or received in heritage by me, Mustapha Selim. I bequeath them to my only son, Ali-Bénala, who has ever been a faithful servant of Allah, and respectful towards me. May he, and his children, and his children's children inherit and enjoy these possessions, to which I add my benediction."

As soon as Eggadi had read these words a profound sadness took possession of him, for he could no longer doubt that these hidden riches were the inheritance of Ali-Bénala. If therefore he appropriated them, he was a despoiler of the poor and the orphan. It would have been so delightful to have been able to keep up the illusion, and to say to himself: "This wealth was without an owner; Allah has been pleased to bestow it on me!" But if Eggadi had never as yet committed any very culpable actions, he had never done any good ones, and did not merit the protection of heaven. He dared not doubt that by keeping unlawful possession of the property of Ali he should incur the wrath of heaven; at the same time he could not bring himself to renounce it. He took the coffer, carried it home, meditating by turns on the uses to which he might turn his great fortune, and on what might be done by way of compromising his conscience for poor Ali, his children, and his children's children.

Arrived at his own house, he placed his treasures in a large chest, which he kept thenceforth in the chamber where he passed his nights. By day, too, this coffer often served him for a seat; whilst scarce a day passed without his opening it, to assure himself that nothing had disappeared. He kept it carefully fastened with the aid of several locks and a master key, of which he never gave up the possession.

Eggadi contemplated a thousand times these treasures acquired with so little trouble; if we can call that gained with little trouble which is purchased at the price of our peace of mind. And each time after having contemplated them, he would repeat to himself the words of Ali, "Allah will no doubt recompense thee." "Ah! if he recompenses me as I deserve," he could not help reflecting, "he will send me great disasters indeed."

Pursued by the dread of a heavy chastisement, Eggadi became so miserable in the midst of his fine family and his treasures, that he formed the project of quitting his country, where the sight of Ali, his humble house and miserable shop, haunted him incessantly. So he adjusted his affairs, collected his merchandise, and then communicated his intention to his children and his servants.

But whilst, spurred on by a secret terror, he was hastening the preparations for his departure, Allah, on whose will depend all things on earth and in heaven, visited him with a severe fever, accompanied with delirium, during which he spoke incessantly of the old camel of Ali, of concealed treasures, and the vengeance of Heaven.

Salmanazar, an old Jew doctor, had charge of Eggadi; he heard the incoherent ravings of his patient, and immediately divined them to be the result of preceding mental anguish. Thanks to the skill acquired by medical science, and still more to the intuition engendered by the desire of self-enrichment, the old Jew was not slow in comprehending that there was a secret relating to a treasure unjustly acquired, and he saw no reason, moreover, why he should not be a partaker in the booty.

He found means therefore to remove all the attendants, and constituting himself sole guardian of the sick man, seated himself by his bedside and patiently awaited the auspicious moment which should deliver into his merciless keeping a soul harassed by the stings of remorse.

This moment at length arrived; Eggadi ceased to be delirious, and as though awakening from a painful dream, drew a long breath, and cast looks of inquiry around him.

Salmanazar, who had been watching for this opportunity, then exclaimed: "Eggadi! Eggadi! you Mussulmans cry, 'God is great,' but you do not believe it, for if you did, how could you dare enrich yourselves at the expense of the poor man and his children? Thou art rich, Eggadi, and Ali is poor."

"What sayst thou?" cried the sick man, distending his eyes with terror as dismal recollections thronged upon him.

"I say that thou hast a treasure which should not belong to thee, and that this is why thou hast the fever, and why moreover thou wilt die, unless I save thy life by my profound science. Restitution must be made; nay, if indeed thou wert to do good with this treasure to poor Jews like me, God would perhaps pardon thee, but thou takest care to give us nothing. If I cure thee what will be my profit? a few miserable doubloons, which I shall have all the same if thou diest; for thy sons will give them me, and if they refused to pay me, I should summon them before the cadi. Thus, whether thou livest or whether thou diest is much the same to me. Nevertheless, if I had a mind I could easily cure thee, and cause thee still to live, that thy days might be long upon the earth. But what profit would this be to me?"

"Cure me, cure me," cried the sick man, "and I will give thee far more than my sons would give thee, far more than the cadi would grant thee did my children refuse thee payment. I will give thee twenty doubloons; nay, fifty. That would be a fine thing for thee."

"It would be a much better thing for thyself," chuckled Salmanazar. "Of what use will thy doubloons be to thee when thou art dead? I demand five hundred doubloons for curing thee, and I will have them at once, for in an hour's time I shall demand a thousand, and if you then delay deciding there will be no longer any time to choose."

"A thousand doubloons!" exclaimed the patient; "I will not even give thee five hundred. If I did,—Allah would not pardon me the more, even supposing I really am guilty of what thou suggested."

"Well, then, thou wilt die," rejoined Salmanazar, settling himself again in his chair.

The chamber of the sick man was gloomy. A small lamp cast a fitful light upon one corner, while the rest seemed inhabited by nothing but dim shadows. An odour of fever and its remedies pervaded the atmosphere; out of doors,—for it was night,—the dismal cry of the jackals seeking food resounded, whilst the deep baying of the neighbouring dogs was heard without intermission. The weather was windy and tempestuous. All this but served to increase the deep depression which filled the soul of Eggadi. He threw a wistful look around his shadow-haunted room; it fell upon the old Jew who was watching him askance, his large dark eyes dimmed by ophthalmia, and he asked himself whether the old man with his prominent nose, yellow visage, long, lean and withered arms, habited in a scanty and dirty garment, were not some evil genius come thither to curse him for his crime, and drag him to the bottomless pit of perdition.

Nevertheless, Eggadi contrived to raise himself up in a sitting posture on his bed. He collected all his strength, drew a long breath, sighed feebly, and said:

"Well, I have decided, Salmanazar; give me the remedy which will make my days long upon the earth."

"Give me first the five hundred doubloons," said Salmanazar.

"I have them not here," replied the sick man.

"Tell me where they are, I will go and get them."

"That is impossible," said Eggadi; "but summon Bankala, my black slave, he will bring me the key of my coffer, and the coffer itself which contains my treasures."

"Well and good," replied Salmanazar; and he summoned Bankala.

Eggadi gave some orders to the slave in a language unknown to Salmanazar, and he disappeared. He returned shortly with two other slaves, whom he placed like two sentinels by the side of his master's bed.

"Send away those men," said Salmanazar to the sick man. The latter replied, "They are needed to go and bring the coffer as soon as Bankala shall have given us the key; he and I alone know where it is hidden."

"It is well," said the Jew; and he held his peace, looking alternately at the sick man and the two slaves.

"What wilt thou do to effect my cure?" began Eggadi to inquire of the Jew in a doleful tone.

"Thou shalt see—thou shalt see," replied the latter. And they both awaited the return of the slave with an equal anxiety, which they in vain strove to conceal.

Bankala made them wait a long time, but when at length he did return, Ali, the poor seller of mats, followed upon his footsteps. "Arise quickly," had been the summons of the slave to him; "Eggadi my master summons thee in the name of Allah, and desires to see thee before he dies." Ali had hastened to obey. At sight of him the Jew trembled. Eggadi, on the contrary, felt himself happy and reassured.

"Come hither, Ali," said he; "come and behold a man guilty but repentant. The example of thy virtues did not suffice to bring me back to the path of duty: it was necessary that I should be struck by misfortune. Thanks to Heaven misfortune has befallen me. Ali! Ali! it was I who bought of thee the old camel which was left thee by thy father. That camel no doubt aided him in concealing the great wealth he would fain have bestowed upon thee ere he died. I discovered this wealth, and I conceived the iniquitous design of keeping it, instead of restoring it to thee in accordance with the demands of justice. I was on the point of quitting my country to avoid the further sight of thy poverty, the unceasing reproach to my crime, when Allah visited me with a terrible malady, and a still more terrible physician. This physician, whom thou there beholdest, having discovered my secret, instead of urging me to the restitution of my ill-acquired fortune, dreamt only of sharing it with me, and threatened me with death if I refused the division of the plunder.

"His horrible conduct, his avarice and cruelty combined, have inspired me with horror, and have shown me to what lengths an inordinate love of gold may lead. I have mourned for my fault, and have taken a sudden resolution to repair it. By deceiving this skilful man, I have been enabled to send for thee, and before him I declare that I render thee up joyfully all the treasures which are enclosed in the chest upon which Salmanazar is seated."

Salmanazar started up on hearing these words. How! he had been actually sitting upon the treasure and had not divined it.

Eggadi continued:

"Consider, Ali, what will be most suitable to bestow upon this Jew. He demanded of me five hundred doubloons down, or a thousand in an hour's time, if I desired to live. I think that five hundred blows with a stick should be his recompense; at the same time I am unworthy to judge any man in this world. Thou who art just, act towards him as thou thinkest best, but deign, above all things, to grant me thy forgiveness."

Ali was of course greatly surprised at all he had just heard. He took a moment to collect his thoughts and then said:

"Eggadi-ben-Yousouf, I pardon thee willingly; and to prove it, I say to thee as thou once saidst to me:

"Let us enter into partnership, let us live as brothers, and unite our children as in the time of the patriarchs. As for Salmanazar, let his only punishment be to behold the riches he would have forced thee to share with him, and after having seen them, let him return home without money and without blows."

The wish of the wise Ali was put into execution. The coffer, the key of which Eggadi had about him, was opened; and the Jew, though still trembling with the fear of receiving the blows, could not help eagerly regarding the gold and precious stones which were revealed to his cupidity. Then he departed, filled with grief at having missed his aim, and at not having been himself the fortunate purchaser of the old camel of Ali. This event was engraven on his memory, and caused him to regard with looks of eager anxiety all the old camels whom he chanced to meet. He often stopped before them, and seemed to endeavour to trace in their movements some mysterious sign which might lead to the discovery of hidden treasures.

Eggadi, having his conscience at ease, regained his health without the aid of any other physician. He became the adopted brother of Ali, who insisted on sharing with him his newly-acquired fortune; and these two men, their children, and their children's children, continued to live together wealthy and united.

IX.

THE STORY OF MEDJEDDIN.

Many hundred years ago there lived in the famous city of Bagdad a retired merchant named El Kattab. The earlier part of his life had been assiduously devoted to commercial pursuits, in the prosecution of which he had made many a long journey, and crossed many a sea. In the course of his wanderings he had not only amassed the wealth he sought, but, what was better, had stored his mind and memory with the treasures of wisdom and general information. The property he had acquired was far from immense, yet it was amply sufficient to enable him to live in a style of substantial comfort and respectability, and to devote himself to the darling object of his declining years, the education and training of his only son.

El Kattab's beard was grey, yet he had not very long passed the prime of life, and still retained most of the vigour and elasticity of his earlier years. He was wise enough to be content with the quiet enjoyments of a moderate affluence, and had no desire to wear out the rest of his life in the feverish labour of constant acquirement, for the mere sake of amassing a splendid fortune; therein differing from too many of his friends, who seemed to forget in their headlong pursuit of enormous riches, that by the time these might be acquired, life would be nigh spent, and at any rate all its charms gone, unless some higher and nobler object had been substituted for that of mere wealth-getting.

The city of Mossul had been El Kattab's home in his earlier days; but he quitted it, and took up his abode in Bagdad, partly in order to be near his friend Salek, with whom he had been on the most intimate terms from his youth; partly, too, for the sake of his son's education, as he expected that a residence in the latter city would produce good and lasting impressions on the mind of the young man; for the great city of Bagdad was at this time under the rule of the far-famed caliph Haroun al Raschid, and was the resort of strangers from all parts of the globe; and here artists and sages of all countries mingled with each other. Nor had El Kattab conceived a vain expectation. His son, whose name was Medjeddin, was a young man gifted with good natural abilities, and endowed with a pure and noble heart. He used every opportunity to extend his knowledge and improve his disposition; nor was he deficient in bodily exercises and warlike accomplishments: so that through good discipline he became powerful in body and strong in mind. He was not only, therefore, as was natural enough, the joy and pride of his father, but was loved and esteemed by all who knew him, and was often pointed out by the elders, to others of his own age, as an example worthy of imitation.

As the father saw his greatest treasure in the person of his son, so the latter, with all the fervour of a well-directed mind, clung affectionately to his father.

Some years passed over them in this mutual love, rendered still more delightful by the companionship of their friend Salek, and their happiness was full and uninterrupted. It chanced one day that El Kattab and Salek were taking their accustomed walk in the gardens adjoining the city in front of the gate. The heat of the summer's day had been diminished by a gentle rain, and the two strolled on, in happy conversation, and extended their walk beyond its usual length. They passed the last garden, and wandered on over some green meadow-land, behind a little wood, at the entrance of which stood high palms, whose shadows invited to repose, while a fresh spring gushed from a neighbouring rock, and meandered among the verdant herbage and variegated flowers.

The two friends lay down in the shade, and conversed on the perils to which even the most virtuous men are subject, particularly enlarging on the danger of an over-confidence in the rectitude of our own intentions, and on the comparative ease with which a sudden impulse will sometimes hurry even the best of men, who possesses an overweening reliance on his own firmness of purpose, into a false or even fatal step in life.

"I have known men," observed Salek, "who, although among the best and noblest I have ever met in the course of my life, have been led unawares, by too great self-confidence, into an action which they might easily have avoided by moderate caution, but which has proved the beginning of a long chain of evils, ending at last in their complete ruin."

El Kattab, on the contrary, maintained that a heart accustomed from early youth to virtue, would not be easily led to commit a serious fault; and even if this should happen, that it would readily find its way back from a slight error to the right road. They continued to talk on these subjects, each endeavouring to confirm his assertions by examples, whilst Medjeddin, stretched beside them, listened with attention to their conversation. Suddenly he sprang to his feet, and ran quickly up the woody hill, at the foot of which they were reposing. His father and Salek looked after him surprised, as they could not comprehend what had occasioned his sudden disappearance. They then saw that a little bird, as white as snow, was flying before him, which he was trying to catch. He was soon lost to their view among the bushes; they called to him to come back; but in vain. They waited for a quarter of an hour, and still Medjeddin did not return. Growing uneasy about him, they advanced in the direction in which he had disappeared, but could discover nothing. At last the sun set; then Salek said, "Let us return home: your son is a strong, active young man; he will easily find his way back to the city. Perhaps he has gone home some other way, and will be there before us."

After much opposition, the father was persuaded to return without his son; but he was still full of anxiety which no arguments could overcome. When they arrived at the city, his friend accompanied him to his house. They entered hastily, and inquired for Medjeddin: but he had not returned. Salek's cheering suggestions were of no more avail; El Kattab would no longer listen to him, but threw himself weeping on his couch. Salek rebuked him for this weakness, and represented to him that it might easily have happened that the young man had lost his way in the pursuit of the bird, and could not recover the track all at once.

"He has no doubt found a shelter where he will remain till morning," continued he; "he will return here early to-morrow, and will laugh heartily at your fears."

When Salek was gone, El Kattab gave free scope to his feelings. He wept aloud, tore his beard, and dashed himself upon the ground, like a madman. The slaves stood around in motionless astonishment, surprised to see their master exhibiting such passionate emotion; others sought to console him, but fruitlessly; at length they all began to cry and bewail with him for his dear son, who was beloved by them all. After a sleepless night, the afflicted father rose not at all quieted. He wished early in the morning to send messengers in all directions; but Salek, who had come to inquire if the lost one had returned home, explained to him how foolish this step would be.

"Consider," said he, "that your Medjeddin has most probably found a night's lodging, and slept better than you. Supposing him, therefore, to be at any probable distance, even if he had set out on his way at daybreak, he could hardly be here now: if you send these messengers after him, he may perhaps come home by a shorter path, while they will be searching for him in vain; wait at least till mid-day."

El Kattab yielded; he appointed the messengers to be ready at noon, and in the meanwhile walked through the gardens and in the country around the city, where they had been on the preceding day. His friend accompanied him, although he pointed out that Medjeddin might, in the interval, have reached home while they were walking, and that El Kattab was thus perhaps giving himself more trouble than was necessary.

"I have yielded to you in the rest," replied El Kattab; "let me at least in this instance have my own will, and walk here."

They went together to the fountain in the rock near the palms; they climbed the neighbouring heights; they called the name of the lost one in all directions; but no sound was heard in reply. At noon they went home, and asked all they met if they had seen a young man, whom they accurately described. Nobody could give them any information about him. El Kattab now sent out his messengers in all directions; promising a rich reward to the one who should lead his lost son back to his arms. The messengers returned on the tenth day, and reported that all their researches had been without success. At this the parent's grief knew no bounds. His friend Salek remained almost constantly with him, comforting him; and all his friends held a consultation on the possible means of gaining tidings of Medjeddin. They agreed that he could not have been killed, for then his corpse would have been found: that he had no cause to conceal himself: that he could not have been attacked by enemies, as he had none: might he, they suggested, in the pursuit of the bird, have been led to the brink of the river, and have thrown himself in, and been carried away by the stream? scarcely had this idea presented itself, ere two messengers were despatched to each side of the river to search, from its junction with the Euphrates above Balsora to the spot where it flows into the Arabian Sea, and ascertain if the corpse of Medjeddin had been washed ashore. But these messengers also returned to the anxious parent, without having found what they sought. The parent and his friend now gave up Medjeddin for lost; El Kattab's spirit was broken; grief for his lost son shortened his life; he soon became old: all joy fled from his mind; and his sorrow was only a little alleviated when his faithful friend Salek sat by him in the evening, talking with him of his son, relating the virtues by which he had been distinguished, and telling him how it had been his darling wish that this excellent young man should marry his daughter Maryam.

A few days afterwards the caliph Haroun al Raschid went, as he was accustomed, in disguise, with his grand vizier Giafar, and Mesrur his chamberlain, through the streets of Bagdad, to see with his own eyes and to hear with his own ears how justice and order were maintained by his servants, and whether his people were happy and prosperous. He had, as usual, chosen the last hour of the evening for this walk, because he thought that at this time he could look deeper into the joys and pleasures of his subjects, as they had then ended their daily toils, and were seeking comfort and repose in the bosoms of their families. In the course of his progress he came to a street remarkable for its peculiar quiet. As he approached a house, before the door of which two men were standing whispering, Haroun al Raschid addressed them with these words: "Why do you whisper, as if you were concerting a crime? is not this street lonely enough, that you cannot hold your discourse aloud? Can you tell me why this street is so quiet, as though every inhabitant were dead?"

"I can easily tell you, my lord," answered one of the whisperers; "here, in the next house, lives the unfortunate El Kattab; and, as usual at this hour, his friend Salek is sitting with him to console him. Now all the inhabitants of this street respect this man, and wish not to remind him, by any outburst of joy, that happier men than himself live in his neighbourhood."

Before the caliph could answer him, the man turned away, and entered the house, and the other followed him.

"Have you ever heard of this unfortunate El Kattab before?" asked Haroun al Raschid of his grand vizier; and as he answered in the negative, the caliph proceeded, "Let us make an inspection of the house where this El Kattab dwells; perhaps we may discover the cause of his sorrow."

They drew near, and saw the light from the inner court shining through a crevice. The caliph applied his eye to the aperture, and after he had watched for some time, beckoned his followers to him, and said, "Two grey-headed men are sitting in this court by the light of a lamp, and one seems to be comforting the other; but this latter continues to weep all the more bitterly, the more his companion endeavours to console him: both appear to be of the same rank. I am desirous of knowing what sorrow oppresses the unfortunate El Kattab: order him to appear at my palace early to-morrow morning; perhaps it may be in my power to lighten his calamity."

The next day the grand vizier executed his commission. El Kattab was alarmed when he heard that his presence was required at the palace. He was led into the great hall where the divan usually assembled; but there the attendants left him quite alone. He reviewed the whole of his past life, to see if he had sinned in any way, so as to bring on him the displeasure of the caliph; for he knew that Haroun al Raschid often, in a mysterious manner, discovered the faults of his subjects, and punished them accordingly. But he could not call to mind any deed of which he felt ashamed, nor any that deserved punishment. Whilst he was thus meditating, a curtain was drawn back, and the caliph entered, followed by his vizier and his chamberlain. El Kattab rose from the ground, and bowed his head down to the carpet on which the caliph stood.

"El Kattab," said the caliph, "a heavy weight of grief seems to oppress you; and by the anxiety which your neighbours manifest to show respect for your sorrow, I must consider you as a man of worth: I wish then to know the cause of your despondency; have you any objection to inform me of it before these two witnesses, or would you rather confide to me alone the reason of your tears?"

"Ruler of the faithful," answered El Kattab, "sorrow is great and deep in my soul; but still the cause of it is unworthy to distract for a moment the attention of the caliph from the cares of his kingdom."

The caliph replied, "That which fills the heart of the meanest of my subjects with such grief that it consumes his life, is not unworthy of my care. If I am careful for my whole kingdom, this care none the less extends to each individual; and, if I am careful for one, this one is a member of the whole, and thus my care is not lost. But speak, what is the cause of your affliction?"

El Kattab then recounted the mysterious disappearance of his son; how he had sought for him every where, and how all his messengers had returned home without the least trace of him. "I must therefore weep for him as one that is dead,"—thus he ended his relation; "and in tears perhaps my sorrow might expend itself, if at the same time a spark of hope did not live in my heart, that possibly he is still alive: but ah! where? This spark of hope keeps the wound in the father's heart always open."

"You have, indeed, real cause for grief," answered the caliph, "and I comprehend that the uncertainty of your son's fate must be as terrible to bear, as would be the mournful certainty of his death. You did wrong in not applying to me before; my power extends not only over believers, but also into foreign lands: other kings and rulers I have as my servants, whose eyes see for me, whose ears hear for me, and whose hands perform what is necessary in order to do my pleasure. That which was not possible to yourself, your friends, and your servants to accomplish, may perhaps prove easy for me. Now go home, and believe that you shall obtain news of your son, if he live on the earth, in any land where my power can reach."

With these words he dismissed him, after he had first inquired the marks by which his lost son might be recognised.

When El Kattab was sitting again with his friend Salek in the evening, he related to him the gracious and comforting words of the caliph. Salek perceived that hope was revived in his friend's heart, and that he confidently trusted to find his son. He thought it his duty, therefore, to damp somewhat this hope, and said, "Beloved friend, I have once heard a speech, which sunk deeply in my memory: it is, 'Trust not in princes; they are but men.' In truth, the mightiest on earth are subject to destiny. If the caliph have influence in distant lands, it must still be within a comparatively confined and narrow limit; whilst what is in the farthest regions of the earth, as well as what is but a span distant, are all equally under the control of all-governing fate, even from the meanest slave to the ruler of the faithful."

Haroun al Raschid meanwhile resolved to do all he could to fulfil the hope he had raised in El Kattab's heart. He gave a commission to all his servants in the kingdom, high and low, and to his ambassadors in the neighbouring kingdoms, and even sent into distant lands, with the princes of which he was on terms of friendship, at the same time despatching messengers with the charge to search for Medjeddin with all diligence, giving them a description by which they might recognise him if they found him. But week after week, and month after month passed away; even a whole year elapsed, without any intelligence being received either of the life or death of the lost one. So that all hope of finding him deserted the father for ever.

Medjeddin, meantime, had not perished—none of the accidents suggested by his father's advisers had befallen him; he still lived, but in such complete concealment that it was impossible for any one to discover him. He had followed the snow-white bird till evening, without clearly knowing why: he was induced to think he could catch the curious creature, particularly as it flew at such a moderate height from the ground, and at the same time so slowly. The tardiness of its flight made him conjecture that it must have hurt one of its wings; several times he succeeded in getting quite close to it, but just as he stretched out his hand to seize it, the bird again raised its wings, and flew a little in advance. Medjeddin now felt himself tired, and would have given up the pursuit, but the bird also seemed fatigued; he approached it, but again the bird flew a little farther off. In this chase he climbed a hill, and soon after found himself in a narrow meadow-valley, down which he ran; twilight came, but the snow-white colour of the bird still lighted him on. At last the pursued bird perched in a thicket; he hastened to it, but when he closed his hand to seize his prisoner, it flew away, leaving only one of its tail-feathers tightly grasped in his hand: still he saw it through the twilight flying before him, and still he hastened after it. The bird seemed now to quicken its pace; but as he had so nearly caught it once, he continued the pursuit with more eagerness; he ran through the high grass, with his strained sight fixed on this glimmering white object, he saw nothing else. Thus he came unexpectedly on a small but deep pool of water, which lay across his path; he jumped in, swam across, and tried to climb the other side, but it was so steep that he fell in with some of the crumbling earth: the water closed over his head, and he lost all consciousness. When he came to himself, he found himself lying on the turf, and a tall, grey-headed man of strange appearance by him, clothed in a long black robe reaching to his ancles, and fastened by a glittering girdle of a fiery colour. Instead of a turban, he wore a high pointed cap on his head, with a tassel of the same hue as the girdle.

"Has your life returned to you?" he asked: "you deserved to be suffocated in the mud. Come, we must go farther before daylight quite leaves us."

With these words the stranger raised him from the ground, passed his left arm round his body, and flew with him through the air with the speed of an arrow. Medjeddin again soon lost recollection, and did not know how long he remained in this condition. He awoke at last as from a deep sleep; and looking around, the first thing he observed was a cage of gold wire, hanging from the ceiling by a long golden chain, and within was the snow-white bird he had so long followed. He found himself alone with this bird in a hall, the roof of which was supported on pillars of white marble, and the walls were built of smooth pale-green stones. The openings which served as windows were protected by lattices so skilfully contrived with winding tracery, that even the white bird could have found no space to pass through, even if it had escaped from the cage. Beside one wall stood a crystal urn; and from this fell a stream of clear water, which passing over the curved brim of the urn, was received in a white basin beneath, from which it disappeared unseen. Whilst he was observing this, and wondering what had happened to him, and how he came there, suddenly the old man in the black robe entered from behind a curtain. He carried a small golden box in his hand, and approached him with these words: "You have now caught the white bird, and have it safe in a cage; in this box is food for it, and there is water; take diligent care of it, and mind that it does not escape."

As he said this he disappeared. Medjeddin now arose and walked round the hall: he looked through the windows, and ascertained that he must be in a foreign land, as the forms of the mountains and trees were quite different from any he had before seen. The hall seemed to be high in the air, as if it were the upper story of a lofty tower. No other edifice was to be seen, and from the windows he could not distinguish what shrubs and plants bloomed beneath. He drew the curtain aside, and discovered a doorway; but there was a thick metal door which he could not open. He was now very much embarrassed, for he began to feel hungry, and could find nothing that would serve him for food. He examined the walls to see if he could discover any concealed outlet; he tried to open the lattices, that he might put his head out, and see if there were any body beneath, to whom he might cry out. There was no door; he could not open the lattices; and as far as he could strain his sight in every direction, he could see nobody: he threw himself in despair on the pillow, wrung his hands, and wept, and cried: "I am then imprisoned— imprisoned in a dungeon where splendour and riches are lavished around! Of what avail is it that these walls are built of precious stones? that this lattice is of fine gold, that this cage is of gold, and hangs on a golden chain? I am as much a prisoner behind golden lattices as I should be behind a grating of iron." Then he rose and shouted through the lattices, in hopes that his voice might be heard, and aid brought; but nobody appeared, and no one answered him. When he again threw himself weeping on his couch, after these useless efforts, he observed that the white bird fluttered restlessly in its prison, and pecked at the golden dish for its food, without finding any.

"Poor brother in misfortune," said Medjeddin, "you shall not suffer want; I will take care of you; come, I will bring you what you want."

He took the pans from the cage, filling one with water from the urn, and the other with grain from the gold box which the old man had given him. Scarcely had he hung the last on the cage, when, on turning round, he saw a table behind him covered with costly viands. He was astonished, and could not understand how this had happened; still it was not long before he attacked the meats with the zest of a young man who had fasted nearly all day. Although these viands were altogether different from those he had been accustomed to taste in his father's house, they all appeared excellent. He ate till he was fully satisfied, and then took from the table a golden cup, and quenched his thirst with pure water from the urn. After this he threw himself on a couch and fell asleep. When he awoke he felt strong and well. He arose and began to make another tour of the hall, and he then observed that the table with the meats had disappeared. This was a disappointment, as he had thought to make a good supper of the remainder. He did not allow this, however, to trouble him much, as he now felt pretty sure that he was not to die of hunger. He next proceeded to scrutinise his prison more closely: he examined all anew, pillars, walls, and floor; but could no where find a crevice or a fissure: all was fast and whole. His view from the windows did not allow him to make any further discovery; he only saw that he was very far above the earth, and in a spacious valley; mountains were to be seen in the distance, with curiously-pointed summits. As soon as he had completed this examination, and found there was nothing to occupy him, he turned his attention to the white bird in the cage. Here was still life; and if the cage was narrow, yet the prisoner could hop about on the different perches. Soon it remained still and gazed at him with its bright eyes, which seemed as if sense and speech lay in them, the interpretation only was wanting.

Night put an end to these reflections. Next morning he observed that the bird again wanted food. He filled its seed-pan with grain from his golden box, and gave it fresh water from the urn. Scarcely had he done this, when the table covered with meats again stood in the same place as the day before. This day passed like the former, and the following in the same manner; Medjeddin wept and mourned, took care of the little bird, fed it, and was every time rewarded in the same manner with the table covered with dishes as soon as he had filled the bird's seed-pan. He could not perceive who brought the table, nor how it disappeared. It always came whilst he stood beside the cage with his back turned, and without any noise. On the ninth day the old man suddenly appeared to him, and said, "To-day is a day of rest for you; you have performed your duty during the preceding days in giving the bird its food, you may now amuse yourself in the garden till evening." He led him through a door into a narrow passage, at the end of which they descended twenty steps; he then opened a small metal trap-door, and then Medjeddin descended twenty steps more: they next came to a similar door, and descended twenty more steps to a third, and so on, till, after passing the ninth door, they found themselves in the open air.

"Remain here till you are called," said the old man, who went back into the building through the same doors, which he shut after him. Medjeddin was very curious to examine more closely the building in which he had been imprisoned: he therefore went round it, and narrowly observed it. It was a tower of nine stories, each about fifteen feet in height. The tower was nine-sided, with a window in the third side of each story, so arranged that no window was directly over another, and that consequently only three altogether appeared in each side of the tower from bottom to top. This distribution of regularity and order reigned throughout the whole building. The walls were made of large pieces of gold, quite as smooth as glass; and these were so skilfully put together that, even when closely looked at, the joints could not be discovered. The lattices of the windows were all of gold, like those in the upper hall, and the lower doors through which he had passed were of a yellow metal, inclining to green. All these considerations were not calculated to lessen his conviction that no man could possibly find him out in such a prison. Suddenly a new hope awoke in him: "I am no longer shut up in the tower," said he to himself; "here I am in the open air, in a garden: I can clamber and jump like a monkey; I may possibly find some outlet from this garden, by which I can escape." He immediately turned from the tower, and hastened through the gardens, seeking freedom; but he soon discovered that this hope was vain. He found the gardens surrounded on all sides by a lofty wall, constructed of the same materials, and quite as glassy, as the tower. After making the whole circuit of the garden, he at length found a gate, consisting of a grating of strong iron bars, polished to the highest degree of smoothness, and so close together, that he could scarcely pass his arm through. He tried to climb it by holding by the upper bars with his hands; but his feet slipped on the smooth iron, and he hurt his knee so much, that he lost his hold and fell backwards on the earth. He next examined the grating closely to see if there were no means of escape; but all was in vain: every where the bars were high, thick, and like polished glass. Sorrowfully he wandered round the garden; the sun's rays darting down scorched up the grass, and he sought some shade where he might screen himself from their influence. He lay down on a mossy bank, and meditated anew on his fate. Besides his own grief at his imprisonment, the thought of his father's sorrow at his loss pained him. The exhaustion consequent on tears and loud lamentations, joined with the noontide heat, at last caused him to fall into a deep sleep. When he awoke, the table covered with meats was again before him; he ate, and wandered again mournfully through the garden, meditating whether he could not make a ladder from the trees around him, to aid him in his escape over the grating. But there was something wanting for this work; he had not even a dagger or a knife. As he thus thought, the old man appeared, and said, "Evening is drawing on; follow me in." He led him again to the upper room of the tower, and locked the metal door upon him.

There was no change observable in his prison, only the bird seemed harassed and mournful; it sat quiet and still on the lowest perch, its plumage was rough, and its eyes dull. "Poor creature," said Medjeddin, "what is the matter?

are you ill?" It seemed as if the bird was affected by these sympathising questions, but it soon sank again into its former dejection. He mused long upon this. The next day and the following ones passed like the former; but on the ninth the old man again appeared, led him into the garden, and at night conducted him back into the hall. He took care of the bird; and as soon as he had given it food and water, he always found the table covered with meats behind him. In the intervals he stood at the lattice of one of the three windows looking on the plain below, earnestly hoping to catch sight of some person to free him from his captivity. In such monotonous employment many months passed away: every ninth day the old man appeared, and gave him leave to walk in the garden; but he did not derive much amusement from his strolls in this narrow enclosure. In the mean time he asked the old man many times the reason of his imprisonment, and how long it was to last. No answer was vouchsafed but these words: "Every man has his own fate; this is thine."

One day the old man appeared and led him into the garden as usual; but he had not been there more than a quarter of an hour, when he returned, called him in, and then quickly retired with marks of disquietude. Medjeddin also remarked that the white bird, which he had learnt to love more every day, sat at the bottom of its cage, more mournful than it usually was after the old man's visit. He drew near, and observed a little door in the cage which he had never before seen. He examined it closely, and found a fine bolt which passed into a ring of gold wire. These were made so skilfully, and worked into the ornamental parts of the cage so cunningly, that nobody could have discovered them if his attention had not been drawn to them by design or accident. Medjeddin pushed back the bolt and opened the door; the bird started up as if some sudden joy had seized it, hopped out, and as soon as it touched the floor was transformed, and in its stead a young maiden stood before Medjeddin, clothed in a white silk robe; beautiful dark locks streamed over her neck and shoulders, and a thin fragrant veil fell over them, confined by a fillet set with precious stones; her finely-formed countenance was as white as ivory, relieved by the softest shade of the rose. Surprised and astonished, Medjeddin started back and said, "By the beard of the prophet, I conjure you to tell me whether you are of human race, or whether you belong to the genii?"

"I am a helpless maiden," said she, "and implore you to deliver me from the hands of this cruel magician; I will reward you handsomely for it: know, I am the only daughter of Omar, king of Zanguebar; and this wicked enchanter has cunningly carried me off from my father's palace, and shut me up in this cage. He has one son, as ugly as night, whom he wishes me to take for my husband. Every ninth day he comes, brings his son with him, and praises his excellent qualities. This he has done regularly for many months past, tormenting me at every visit for my consent to this odious union; and he now threatens me with cruel tortures if I give it not by the next new moon. On that day he will have kept me a year in imprisonment, and longer than a year he says he will not continue to entreat: then will the time of my punishment begin; I conjure you therefore to help me." At these words she burst into a flood of tears.

"Noble maiden," answered Medjeddin, "how willingly would I free you! but, alas, I am as helpless as yourself, and cannot even free myself. But tell me how is it? you say the enchanter brings his hateful son with him—why, then, have I never seen him?"

"He always sends you away when he comes," answered the princess.

"But even then," pursued Medjeddin, "the son could not conceal himself from me on the stairs, or in the narrow passage."

"Quite true," she answered, "but he carries him in his pocket."

"What," exclaimed Medjeddin in astonishment, "in his pocket!—how can that be?"

The princess informed him that the young man became on the occasion of each visit a white bird, like herself: that the enchanter put him into the cage with her, and that she felt such a dislike to him that she always fluttered about the cage to avoid getting near him; but that he, with the pertinacious obstinacy of a brutal affection, would follow her and settle confidingly near her. "You must," she continued, "have remarked how tired and mournful I always was on the ninth day when you returned."

Medjeddin, astonished at this explanation, assured her of his willingness to free her, but bewailed his helplessness. The princess, however, would not give up hopes of their success. "It seems to me," said she, "a good omen that the enchanter has to-day received a message which caused him to leave so early, and in such haste that he did not securely close the cage, and that you returned so early to-day from the garden; this day is my birthday, the only day I can be delivered from the magician's power; on any other day I should still have remained a dumb bird, even if you had freed me from my cage; only on this day has my touching the floor had power to restore me to my natural form; the enchantment lies in the cage."

Medjeddin instantly seized the cage, exclaiming, "If it be so, we will break the enchantment." He threw the cage to the ground, stamped on it with his feet till it was quite flat, and its shape no longer distinguishable, then he rolled it together, and threw it into a corner of the hall.

At this moment a frightful noise like thunder resounded through the air. The whole building shook as with a furious tempest, the doors flew open with a crash, the curtains were drawn aside, and the magician stood before them with a countenance full of anger. "Ah," cried he, "weak worms, what have you presumed to do? how did you learn to break my charm in this manner? who bid you destroy the cage?"

Medjeddin was so terrified he could answer nothing. The enchanter then turned to the maiden and cried, "And you, you thought this miserable worm could defend you against my power: I will show you how useless it is to oppose me."

He felt in the pocket of his black robe, and pulled out thence a small box; this he opened, and a white bird flew out and perched on the table. He then took a smaller box from his girdle and opened it,—it was filled with grains of millet; from these he took one, and laid it before the bird, who had scarcely eaten it before such a distorted man stood in its place, that both Medjeddin and the princess screamed aloud. His head was large and thick, his eyes red and dark, his nose small and quite flat, his lips thick and blueish red, his chin broad and projecting, and on his head grew a few stiff white hairs; a hump grew out in front, and a similar one behind; his shoulders were quite drawn up, and his head so jammed between them that his ears could not be seen. The upper part of his body was so unwieldy, and his legs so weak and thin that it was wonderful how they supported him; he tottered about incessantly, balancing himself first on one leg, then on the other.

"Come forward, my son," said the enchanter to this deformed creature; "behold, there is your bride; she does not wish to wait till the new moon which I fixed upon for your betrothal: to-day she has effected her own change by the help of this friend. Go, my son, give your bride a kiss, and then thank this young man."

The deformed creature approached the princess with a horrible fiendish laugh; she averted her face with disgust, and stretched out her arms to motion him away. But by this time Medjeddin's courage had returned: resolving to venture all, he stepped before the princess and gave the deformity such a blow that he reeled and fell backwards. His head struck in the fall on the corner of the pedestal of one of the marble pillars with such violence, that his skull was broken: a stream of blood flowed from the wound, and the monster gave a hollow groan. Medjeddin thought of nothing but the father's rage and revenge, and gave up his life for lost. But the enchanter stood quite confounded as he observed his son's mortal wound, and appeared stupified with horror and amazement. Presently he threw himself down beside him, examined the injury, and wrung his hands, forgetting his revenge in his sorrow. Medjeddin quickly seized the hand of the princess, and led her through the door and down the stairs: all the doors were open, and they found their way without any obstacle into the garden. Soon they stood before the grating of the iron gate, which was closed.

"Of what use is our flight?" said Medjeddin despondingly; "we are still as much as ever in the power of the enchanter; and even if we were on the other side of the gate, and concealed in the deepest cavern, he would discover us by his knowledge, and wreak his vengeance on us."

"I am of a different opinion," said the princess; "I know many of the things on which the superior power of this magician depends, and I believe that if we could only get out of this place, we should be safe."

They went on a little further, and came to a spot where a number of trees had been uprooted by the hurricane; one of these lay overturned with its summit resting on the top of the wall, and its boughs and branches hanging far over the other side. At this sight the young man rejoiced; he climbed quickly on to the trunk, pulling the princess after him, and guiding her with great care and tenderness into the top of the tree. They then clambered over the wall in spite of a formidable row of spikes, and let themselves down on the other side by the overhanging branches of the tree. These did not quite reach to the ground, but near enough for them to leap down; they let go accordingly, and fell gently to the earth; then jumping up, they proceeded as rapidly as the strength of the princess and the difficulties of the way would allow them, through thickets, underwood, and plains studded with prickly plants, towards the distant mountains.

After the two fugitives had continued their flight for several hours without looking back on the scene of their imprisonment, the princess felt her strength exhausted, and that she could go no further; she begged her companion, therefore, to stop and rest for a short time. Medjeddin sought a place free from bushes, and clad with moss and long grass; they seated themselves there, and Medjeddin entreated the princess to relate her history. She was too much exhausted at first, but after a short pause recovered her strength and commenced thus:

"My early history is very simple. I am called Jasmin, the only daughter of the sultan of Zanguebar. My mother was brought over the wide-stretching sea, from beyond Arabia and Mount Caucasus, and was sold to him as a slave. Soon attracted by her beauty and manners, he raised her to the dignity of wife. My earliest youth was spent in happy sports under my mother's eyes, who died, however, before I had passed the age of childhood, as the change from the mild climate of her land to the heat of my father's shortened her days. My father loved me as his greatest treasure, and confided me to a careful nurse. Every evening I passed several hours with him, as soon as he was released from the cares of government, and one whole day in each week he devoted to conversation with me. On that day we always went together in a light bark to a neighbouring promontory, where he had a beautiful palace and gardens. The air there was cooler and more refreshing, the trees and shrubs were clothed with fresher green than in the shut-up garden in the capital, and we passed the whole day in the open air. In the mean time I had outgrown childhood, and was beloved by a prince, the son of a neighbouring king, to whom I was betrothed, and who was to succeed my father in his kingdom. This prince, whose name was Mundiana Mesoud, often accompanied us in these visits to the castle on the promontory.

"It happened one day, as we were sitting on a terrace by the sea, that a foreign ship anchored just below us. A stranger caused himself to be landed in a little boat, and asked us permission to appear before us, as he had many costly wares to offer for sale. I was desirous to see his wares, and begged my father to admit him. The man laid many costly trinkets of gold and precious stones before us; and my father bought some which pleased me the most. I remarked that the merchant watched me closely, but he did this with such evident pleasure that my vanity ascribed it to his admiration of my charms, and found no harm in it. Whilst he showed his goods, he let fall some words which intimated that he had left his most precious articles behind in the ship; he had there, he said, many curious birds, particularly a snow-white bird which was the most beautiful of all creatures of this kind. He managed thus to excite my curiosity so much that I begged my father to allow me to go with the stranger to his ship to see these rarities. My father was weak enough to comply with this unreasonable wish. A suitable train ought to have accompanied me, but the stranger prevented this; he said his boat had only room in it for three people, and that he should not like to show his wares if many strangers came into his ship. 'They are only things fit for the royal princess,' he said; 'there is no fear that I should expose her to danger. I can never forget that a powerful king has entrusted his only daughter to my care. However, the prince may accompany you as a watchful protector.' We accompanied the merchant to the ship; there we found an immense number of extraordinary things and unknown animals. In the place where in other ships the rowers sat, were great apes; on high on the mast sat an eagle; in the cabins were many large and small cages of smooth ebony with thick gold bars, behind which moved a confused multitude of animals.

"My desire was now directed to the snow-white bird, about which I made inquiry. He showed it me high up in a sort of box; and as I could not see it distinctly, he took it out and placed it in my hand. 'The most wonderful circumstance,' said he, 'connected with this bird is, that, being a native of a far distant country, when removed to this it can only remain a few days alive, but I have found the corn of life of which I give it some grains each week, and it is then refreshed for nine days.' We asked for the corn of life, of which we had never heard; and he opened a little box and took out three grains. He gave me one to give the bird, the other I was to try, and the third prince Mesoud. When I offered the grain to the bird, it refused it; and when I pressed my hand closer, drew back, lost its balance and fell down with outspread wings. I hastened to it, picked it up perhaps somewhat roughly, and as it tried to escape, I held some of its tail-feathers fast, so that it lay fluttering in my hand. I was very much frightened, and the merchant seemed so also. He soon laughed, however, with a sort of malicious joy, and said that I should swallow the corn, because it would prevent the flight of the frightened prisoner; he said the same to the prince; and we swallowed the grains at the same moment. I felt a wonderful transformation pass over me, and found that I was changed into a snow-white bird; and when I looked towards the prince, in his stead I saw a black bird. Upon this the stranger, who was no other than the enchanter, seized me, and shut me up in the golden cage which you have trodden to pieces. The apes began to ply the oars, and the ship moved with unusual swiftness over the sea. I still saw my father and the attendants on the terrace, and could distinguish their gestures of wonder as they saw the ship depart; I believed even that I heard their voices calling us back. But what could I do in my cage? The black bird flew to the promontory; and from that moment I have neither heard nor seen any thing of prince Mesoud.

"When my home was far in the distance, and even the summit of the mountains which overhung it could no longer be distinguished, the enchanter rose with my cage high in the air, leaving his ship behind, and bore me into the hall of the tower. How he brought the other white bird, I do not know; I only know that he took it out of his pocket and put it into the cage. 'Now you have a companion,' said he. As I took him for a real bird, I considered myself, though unfortunate, superior to him, and drew myself back into a corner. But the bird came nearer and followed me round the cage. At last I lost patience, and pecked his eyes. When the enchanter saw this, he took out a little box and took from it a grain which he laid before the bird, who picked it up immediately. It was then changed into a man, the same ugly wretch you saw in the tower. He desired me, as I have already told you, to take that deformity for my husband; and promised me that, on my consent, I should be immediately restored to my proper form, and assured me that otherwise I should always remain as a bird, except on my birthday. It was also part of my enchantment to be obliged to allure you here. I have now no other wish than to return to my father in Zanguebar, because I know he is living in great affliction."

This relation vividly reminded Medjeddin of his own father; he knew, from the great love he had always shown him, that he must have pined for his loss, and his mournful countenance and bowed-down form presented themselves before his mind. "Princess," said he, "your desire cannot be greater than mine. Still, I swear to you, that I will not return to my father till I have safely conducted you to your native land, or have seen you safe into the hands of those who will bring you to your father; if I do not, may Heaven not grant my father life to receive this joy!"

They journeyed on with renewed vigour. But evening was drawing near, and it was necessary to find a resting-place for the night; fortune was favourable; they soon found a nook overhung by a large and lofty bush. Medjeddin broke away the boughs, so as to form a hedge which fenced round a small spot in which he concealed the princess, leaving only a narrow entrance, before which he lay down to watch. Night passed without danger. However anxiously Medjeddin strove against sleep in order to watch over his companion, it at last weighed down his eyelids; and they both awoke with the first rays of the sun. They wandered the whole day, resting occasionally; at every step the journey became more hazardous; the thickets became thicker and higher; they were often obliged to creep between the boughs, and their clothes hung in rags. On the fourth day they reached the foot of the mountains. There they found cultivated land and human habitations. Medjeddin inquired where they were, and asked the way to the sea. The people told them the name of the country, which was unknown to Medjeddin and to the princess Jasmin, and added, that on the other side of the high mountains lay a large flat land, bordering on the sea. They received this information with great joy, and, tired and footsore as they were, addressed themselves, without loss of time, to the task of crossing the mountains, and at last, after a wearisome journey, during which they had seen the sun rise and set seven times, they arrived at the flat country and the sea-coast of which they had been told. A ship lay ready at anchor; and when they inquired its destination, the steersman answered, "We are going to Zanguebar, to fetch a cargo of cinnamon." To Medjeddin's question where they came from, and the name of the land where they were, he received for answer, "that the ship belonged to a merchant of Balsora, and that it had been cast on these unknown shores by a violent storm."

When the princess perceived that the ship was going towards her native land, she was very much rejoiced. She took one of the precious stones out of the fillet on her forehead, and gave it for the passage money of herself and her companion. The following morning they weighed anchor, and, after a prosperous voyage, reached the very same place where the enchanter's ship had formerly lain at anchor, when he carried off the princess.

They were landed in a small boat, and Jasmin led her deliverer through the beautiful leafy walks of the imperial gardens. In this way they came to a terrace, from which they could see the ship. Instead of pressing hastily forwards, they concealed themselves behind a bush, for on the terrace sat a venerable and noble-looking man, with the profoundest melancholy stamped on his features; he was looking seawards, and the vessel had just caught his eye; a flood of tears ran down his face, "Ah!" cried he, "it was just so on the day that my sorrows began! There lay the ship of the robber; there landed the boat which carried away my beloved daughter and her betrothed. It was even at the same hour of the day. I have sent messengers into all the neighbouring lands; I have caused the opposite sea-coasts to be searched; but all has been in vain. I must die, and never see my child again."

He pronounced these words aloud, and covered his face, as he bowed himself forward on his hands.

The princess Jasmin was rushing towards him, but Medjeddin held her back, and said, "Let me first prepare him for your arrival, for otherwise joy may kill him." And he came forward, and bowed himself before the sorrowing old man.

The king then said, "Who are you? Are you a beggar, and do you need any gift? It shall be given you; go to my palace."

Medjeddin stood up and answered, "From my appearance, you might well take me for a beggar, O great king Omar. But know that under these ragged clothes is concealed a magician, who is able to change your tears into smiles, your sobs into transports of joy."

"Can any man on earth do this?" asked Omar.

"I have only to speak three words," answered the other, "and it will happen. Are you strong enough to support the highest joy that your heart can feel or conceive?"

At these questions, a ray of hope kindled in the soul of the mourning father. "What is it? Who are you who can promise this?" asked he; and, on Medjeddin repeating his question, he answered, "I think so," regarding him, at the same time, with eager looks.

"Approach, princess Jasmin," cried the youth; and she sprang forward into her father's open arms.

Medjeddin's promise was indeed fulfilled; the aged monarch's tears were changed into smiles of joy. Their embrace continued long. At last Omar raised himself, beckoned Medjeddin to approach, and said, "You are indeed a magician such as I have never seen before. By your words you have changed the mournful course of my life into the brightest sunshine. I will not now ask you who you are, and what I have to thank you for, nor inquire what chance brought you to my daughter; I shall only give myself up to joy at her return."

They went back to the capital in the king's barge, and soon the joyful news of the unexpected reappearance of the princess spread every where. Crowds assembled at the palace to ascertain if the news were true, and the princess at length went out of the principal gate of the palace, and showed herself at the head of the flight of steps which led up to it. Then arose a shout of joy from ten thousand voices, and loud wishes for her health and happiness.

The next day, after the king had heard from his daughter the history of her imprisonment, and of the devotion with which Medjeddin had watched over her and when Medjeddin had in turn narrated his history Omar became very thoughtful, and caused his council to assemble, to deliberate how they should reward him. "If he were not so young," said some of them "he might be made grand vizier, the next in dignity to the king, or be appointed governor of a province. But his youth prevents his being placed over the people next to the king."

After longer consultation, the eldest of the councillors rose, and said, "Omar, my king and lord, the youth has certainly performed a great service to you and the princess Jasmin; it seems to me, therefore, that his reward ought to come from you. It is fitting that the king, having received from him a great benefit in his family, should reward him from his family. Were I in such a case, I would constitute him Mundiana, and give him for a wife the daughter whom he has restored."

The whole assembly were of the same opinion, and the king gave them to understand that this was also his wish. "I am old," said he, "and can easily perceive that the cares of this land will soon need other hands to support them. I shall be much pleased to see my daughter with so good a husband. The prince Mundiana Mesoud, whom I had before chosen, has disappeared; and this youth, although of lower birth, is of noble soul, and will soon, under my guidance, acquire the necessary experience to enable him to promote justice and order in my kingdom."

He did not delay, but immediately caused Medjeddin to be called. A costly band of gold and silver was fastened round his forehead, and the king then said, "I herewith appoint you Mundiana;" and the assembled councillors immediately added their congratulations.

Medjeddin expressed his gratitude in becoming terms, but inquired, smiling, what was the precise nature of the dignity conferred on him.

The eldest councillor stepped forward and said, "This name points out the highest post of honour which the king can bestow. You are found worthy of this honour, and no other lives who bears the title, because the Mundiana Prince Mesoud has disappeared."

An elephant covered with costly trappings was now brought in by its keeper, and upon it was a richly ornamented seat. On this the new officer was placed, and led through the streets. Heralds went before him, and cried aloud,

"Listen to what Omar makes known to all people. This youth has restored to him his dearest jewel, which he had lost. In gratitude, the king has nominated him Mundiana, and has appointed his daughter Jasmin for his wife. To-morrow the betrothal will be celebrated; and every body is invited to the court of the palace to partake of the general joy."

Medjeddin hardly knew how all this had come about. He had received clothes and rich arms as a present from the king, and the king so highly favoured him, that he was not only to be husband of the princess Jasmin, but was to succeed Omar on the throne, and to reign over that beautiful and rich land. In his happiness he forgot his early life, his father's sorrow, and even his playfellow Maryam and his father's faithful friend Salek, and thought no more of his home or his father-land. The next day his betrothal with the princess was celebrated with great pomp.

The princess had willingly yielded to her father's wish, without manifesting any particular joy, although, she felt a very sincere friendship for her intended husband, and treated him with great respect and attention, as she did not forget in her prosperity how much she had owed to him in the time of misfortune. The first days and weeks after the ceremony of betrothal were devoted to recreation and amusement, after which he was formally introduced by the king to the council, and instructed in the business of the state. The king and councillors had soon reason to wonder at the acuteness of his judgment in difficult cases, and above all, at his quick perception of right and order. Throughout the country, the justice and wisdom of the king's future son-in-law were praised, and it was hoped that fortune would permit him to rule over the land. A whole year had now elapsed, and the day was fast approaching when he was to marry the princess and ascend the throne. One day, as usual, he sought his betrothed, the princess Jasmin, in her apartments. He happened to enter very rapidly after his announcement by the attendant, and saw the princess hastily wiping her eyes; and as he drew nearer, he perceived the traces of her tears. Sympathising with her, he asked the cause of her grief; she tried to avoid answering him, but as he continued to urge her, she at last said, "I dare tell you why these tears flow, because you are good and compassionate, and will not consider it a crime that I have a feeling and constant heart. You know that I was formerly beloved by prince Mesoud, the son of the neighbouring king; I related to you that this prince was changed into a black bird by the enchanter, and flew from the ship to the promontory of the island where our country seat was situated. Now I must tell you that I grieve so much the more about this prince's fate, as from my own change I can compassionate his mournful condition. I could not repress the desire to ascertain his fate, and I have obtained certain news of his present condition, by the secret knowledge of a certain wise man. I have learned that he still lives in his new form, and that he has flown away, from fear of the machinations of the demon hunter, called among us Dolda Waldas, and is now in far distant regions; and that it is ordained by fate that he shall never regain his human form if I give my hand to another husband. Sorrow at his mournful destiny has drawn these tears from my eyes, the traces of which you observed."

This narrative made a deep impression on Medjeddin; he discovered that Jasmin had acceded to her father's wish only from gratitude and filial obedience, whilst her affections were still fixed on the absent prince. He saw that he could purchase the good fortune of being the husband of the noble princess, and son-in-law of the great king Omar, and after him king of Zanguebar, only by the misfortunes of prince Mesoud. He asked himself if this were right, and was obliged to confess that justice and honour were opposed to it. He saw that the intoxication of good fortune had hitherto blinded him. Then the remembrance of his father came before him, and his imagination pictured him pining away at the uncertainty of his son's fate. He bitterly reproached himself for his long forgetfulness, and for not having sent an embassy to announce his safe arrival in Zanguebar. Scarcely had these thoughts and feelings arisen in his breast, than he made up his mind: he went to the king, told him all, and begged him to let him go and fulfil a son's duty to a father whom he had too long neglected. Omar sighed deeply at these disclosures of his expected son-in-law; he proposed to send a ship to bring his father, so that he might spend the rest of his life in sharing his son's good fortune and companionship. Upon this Medjeddin declared to him, with determination, that he could never be his son-in-law or successor to the throne. "I cannot purchase such good fortune at another's expense," said he; "it was otherwise before I knew the decision of fate; but now that I know that the prince Mesoud must, through my happiness, always remain in his present condition, if I thus take away the possibility of his ever returning to his human form, I should be in the highest degree culpable, if I did not voluntarily give up my good fortune."

All the persuasions and arguments of Omar were useless. The councillors also, and the grand vizier and the governors of the provinces, begged him to continue in the land, and to take still more share in the government. He remained firm in his resolution; he promised the princess, who was astonished at his honourable spirit, that, as soon as he had seen and comforted his father, he would seek information about prince Mesoud from all the sages and magicians of his native land, and that he would try all means to restore him to his former condition. As he was determined to set out, the king gave him costly presents, including many precious stones from his treasury, and provided him with a ship, and all necessaries for the voyage.

The heavens seemed to favour the resolution of the returning son: the finest weather and most favourable winds seconded his journey, and the ship anchored in the harbour without accident. He took some servants, bought some camels, which he loaded with the king's presents, and so went through Balsora along the river to Bagdad. One beautiful evening he came near the city, and recognised the very place where he had lain at the feet of his father and Salek, and listened to their conversation; their last discourse there returned to his memory. "Well," said he to himself, "my own experience has indeed proved how true it is that it is easy for a man to be seduced from virtue into one false step, if he be not watchful, but relies on his own power: I thought that my heart was sure to be always right, and neglected the practice of weighing carefully each action beforehand. In this manner have I so much forgotten my love for my father, and had nearly committed a great wrong, having been about to sacrifice to my vanity, in the intoxication of good fortune, the happiness of the princess and her betrothed. And you, my father, were also right when you maintained that a heart accustomed to virtue from early years would only for a short time wander from the right road. I have myself experienced the truth of these words, and I therefore thank you with tears that you brought me up to what was good." As he spoke, he espied a small solitary hut where the palm-trees used to stand. A venerable man, much marked by sorrow, appeared at the door; he stood still before the threshold, and regarded the youth with astonishment; the young man gazed earnestly at him. Then suddenly recognising the features of the old man, he threw himself on his knees before him, seized his hand, and covered it with kisses.

"My father," cried he, "is it so indeed? have you become so much altered in the course of so few years? that is my fault. Father, forgive your offending son, who forgot you in the height of prosperity."

El Kattab extended his other hand to him, blessed him, and said: "Rise up, my son, rise; he who feels repentance is forgiven." He rose and threw himself into his father's arms.

When he looked up again, he saw a man approaching, accompanied by a maiden, whose features he recognised. It was Salek and his daughter Maryam, Medjeddin's playfellow. After welcoming him, they sat down, and Medjeddin related to them all that had happened to him since the memorable evening. He related, truly and candidly, how he had forgotten his father, and nearly fallen into greater crimes, because he had been blinded by fortune, by greatness, and by honours. As they were sitting and conversing, they observed three birds coming up from a distance, and who seemed to be chasing one another. They soon perceived that one of them was a black bird flying in great fright from a large hawk. It was obvious that the hawk would soon have seized his prey, had he not been pursued in turn by a larger bird, to avoid which, he was often compelled to dart from side to side: at last they came to close conflict. The pursued black bird fell into Medjeddin's lap; the hawk, struck by his pursuer, fell to the ground at their feet, and was, by the strong hooked bill and sharp claws of his adversary, soon killed and torn to pieces. Scarcely had this taken place, when the conqueror changed into a venerable-looking sage. He turned to Medjeddin, who was quite astonished, and said: "Dip quickly your forefinger in the blood of this slain bird, and anoint with it the beak of the black one."

Medjeddin obeyed immediately; and scarcely had he touched the black bird's beak with the blood, ere it was transformed, and a handsome youth in kingly dress stood before them.

"Guess who this is," said the genius.

"The prince Mesoud?" asked Medjeddin.

The genius answered, "It is he!" And as he stood looking at the young prince with astonishment, added, "You do not perceive how and why all this has happened. I could explain to you all these mysteries; but to what purpose? It is not necessary for weak men to know the threads by which their fates are linked together: suffice it to know that it was necessary for you to perform all this, that you might be tried: you are found worthy, and Heaven rewards you with Maryam, the early companion of your youth, now to be your wife."

Then Medjeddin turned towards Maryam, and looked inquiringly at Salek, her father. This latter said, "With joy I listen to the will of fate; the highest wish of my heart will now be fulfilled."

"Know," continued the genius, "that the slain bird was the enchanter who transformed the princess Jasmin and the prince Mesoud. They were also to pass through trials; thus it was decreed by fate. Because the enchanter only fulfilled the will of fate from selfish motives, and carried his revenge beyond it, and contrary to it, the king of the genii commanded me to slay him."

With these words he disappeared from their sight. They returned now in happy union to the city; and El Kattab, who had built his hut at the edge of the wood to be always near the place of his sorrow, dwelt again in his house with his children. The prince proceeded to Zanguebar in the same ship that had brought Medjeddin. He was received there with great joy, and was soon married to his early love. But Medjeddin's name lived long in their memory, and in that of all the inhabitants of that island.

When the caliph Haroun al Raschid heard of Medjeddin's return, he had him called before him, and made him relate his history. The caliph was so pleased with him that he took him into his palace, and gave him an important post in his court. His history he caused to be inscribed in the records of his kingdom. And when Giafar, his aged vizier, expressed a wish to end his life in quietness, the caliph raised Medjeddin to the grand viziership; and he continued long in this office, to the pleasure of his friends and the happiness of the people, by whom he was greatly beloved.

VIII.

THE STORY OF KING BEDREDDIN-LOLO AND HIS VIZIR ATALMULC.

The city of Damascus is one of the most populous and flourishing cities of the East, and to this capital of a rich kingdom travellers and caravans arrive from all the countries of the world. Its sovereigns bear the title of "Prince of the Believers," and their person is sacred.

Bedreddin-Lolo, king of Damascus, had for his grand vizir a man celebrated in history for his goodness. This minister, whose real name was Aswad, but whose great virtues had acquired for him the surname of Atalmulc[9], was in every way worthy of the high name he had so obtained; uniting to an indefatigable zeal for the king's service a vigilance that nothing could deceive, a penetrating and capacious mind, and a disinterestedness that was universally admired. But he was surnamed the "sorrowful" vizir, because he appeared to be always plunged in a profound melancholy. Whatever he did at court was performed in a grave and serious manner, and he never smiled at the wittiest remark that was made in his presence.

[9] A gift to the kingdom.

One day the king entertained this vizir and Sedif-Elmuloak, his favourite, and related to them, laughing immoderately all the while, the following misfortunes that happened to a rich old miser.

THE OLD PAIR OF SLIPPERS.

There was at Bagdad a merchant very notorious for his avarice, and his name was Abou-Cassem-Tambouri. Although he was enormously rich, his clothes were constantly in rags and tatters, and his turban, made of coarse stuff, was so dirty that its colour could no longer be distinguished. Of all his garments, however, his slippers were the most remarkable; the soles were kept together by large, clumsy nails, and the upper leathers were pieced in every direction. The famous ship Argo was not made up of a greater number of separate fragments. During the ten years of their existence as slippers, the cleverest cobblers of Bagdad had exerted their utmost skill to tag together their remains, and had only succeeded by adding piece on piece, by which means they had become so heavy, that they had passed into a proverb; and when any one wished to describe something weighty, the slippers of Cassem were always the object of comparison.

One day, when this merchant was taking a walk in the great bazaar of the city, a proposal was made to him to buy a considerable quantity of glass; he agreed to the offer, because it was an advantageous one; and having heard a few days afterwards, that a perfumer who had fallen into difficulties had nothing left but some rose-water, which he would of course be obliged to sell as speedily as possible, Cassem took advantage of the poor man's misfortune, and purchased it at less than half its value. This successful stroke of business had put him into good humour, and instead of giving a great feast, according to the custom of Eastern merchants, when they have made an excellent bargain, he thought it better to take a bath, a luxury which he had not enjoyed for a long time.

Whilst he was taking off his clothes, one of his friends, or at least one who pretended to be a friend—for it is a rare thing for a miser to have one—remarked to him that his slippers made him the laughing-stock of the whole city, and that he certainly ought to purchase a new pair.

"I have long thought of doing so," replied Cassem; "but my old ones are not so very bad, and will last me for some time even yet." While talking, he stripped off his clothes, and entered the bath.

At this juncture the cadi of Bagdad came also to take one. Cassem, having finished his bath before the judge, went into the first apartment, where he found his clothes, but not his slippers, which had disappeared, and in their place was a new pair, which our miser was convinced were a present from the man who had made him such a friendly remonstrance about them. With that he made no more ado, but put the new pair on his own feet, thus sparing himself the pain of buying new ones, and left the bath overjoyed with his prize.

When the cadi had finished his bath, his slaves looked about in vain, for their master's slippers, and finding only a wretched pair, which were immediately recognized as Cassem's, the police ran after the supposed sharper, and brought him back with the stolen goods upon his feet. The cadi, after having exchanged the slippers, sent Cassem to prison; and, as he was well known to be rich as well as avaricious, he was not allowed to come out of prison until he had paid a handsome fine.

On returning home the afflicted Cassem threw his slippers, in a rage, into the Tigris, which flowed beneath his windows. A few days after, some fishermen, drawing up a net heavier than usual, found in it Cassem's slippers. The nails, with which they had been patched, had broken the meshes of the net. The fishermen, out of spite to Cassem and his slippers, threw them into his room by the open window, and in their passage they struck the bottles containing the rose-water, and knocking them down, the bottles were broken and the water totally lost.

The grief and wrath of Cassem on seeing this may easily be conceived. He cursed his slippers, and tearing out the hair from his beard, vowed that they should cause him no more mischief; and so saying, he took a spade, and digging a hole in his garden, buried them there.

One of his neighbours, however, who had borne him a grudge for a long time, perceived him turning up the earth, and ran and told the governor that Cassem had dug up a treasure in his garden. This was enough to excite the cupidity of the officer, and he sent forthwith for Cassem. In vain our miser declared that he had not found money, that he was only employed in burying his slippers. The governor had calculated on his bribe, and the afflicted Cassem could only regain his liberty by paying down a second large sum.

Our friend, in an extremity of despair, consigned his slippers to Shitan[10], and went and threw them into an aqueduct at some distance from the city, thinking that this time he should hear no more of them. But as though the evil spirit he had invoked was determined to play him a trick, the slippers somehow found their way just to the very pipe of the aqueduct, by this means preventing the flowing of the water. The persons who had the care of the aqueduct having gone to ascertain the cause of the stoppage, and to remove it, carried Cassem's slippers to the governor of the city, declaring them to be the cause of all the injury. Their unfortunate owner was thrown again into prison, and condemned to pay a larger fine than before. The governor who had punished the offence, and who pretended to be indebted to no one for any thing, returned Cassem's precious slippers to him again most faithfully; and Cassem, in order to free himself from all the evils which they had brought upon him, resolved to burn them. As they were saturated with water, he first of all put them out to dry in the sun on the terrace of his house. But Cassem's evil genius had not yet quite done with his tricks, and the last which he played him was the worst of all.

[10] The Devil.

A neighbour's dog prowling along the terrace on the housetops spied out the slippers, and, darting at them, carried off one of them. As, however, the dog was playing with it, and tossing it about, he contrived to let it fall off the terrace on to the head of a woman who happened to be passing below. The fright and the violence of the blow together, made the poor woman quite ill; and her husband having carried his complaint before the cadi, Cassem was condemned to pay a fine proportionate to the misfortune of which he had been the cause. Going home, he took up his slippers, and returned to the cadi with them in his hands.

"My lord," he exclaimed with a vehemence which excited the judge's laughter, "my lord, look at the fatal cause of all my troubles! These abominable slippers have at length reduced me to poverty; be pleased now to issue a decree, in order that the misfortunes which they will, no doubt, still continue to occasion, may not be imputed to me."

The cadi could not refuse to comply with this request, and Cassem learned, at great expense, the danger there is in not changing one's slippers often enough.

The vizir listened to this story with such a serious countenance that Bedreddin was astonished.

"Atalmulc," he said, "you are of a strange disposition; you seem always sad and melancholy. During ten years that you have been in my service I have never seen the slightest sign of pleasure on your countenance."

"May it please your majesty," replied the vizir, "you need not be surprised at it; all have their secret sorrows; there is no man on earth who is exempt from them."

"Your remark is surely untrue," replied the king. "Do you mean to say that all men have some secret anxiety preying on their minds, because you appear in that state? Do you really believe this to be the truth?"

"Yes, your majesty," replied Atalmulc; "such is the condition of all the children of Adam; our bosoms are incapable of enjoying perfect ease. Judge of others by yourself. Is your majesty quite contented?"

"Oh, as to me," exclaimed Bedreddin, "that is impossible! I have enemies to deal with—the weight of an empire on my hands—a thousand cares to distract my thoughts, and disturb the repose of my life; but I am convinced that there are in the world a vast number of persons whose days run on in unruffled enjoyment."

The vizir Atalmulc, however, pertinaciously adhered to what he had stated, so that the king, seeing him so strongly attached to his opinion, said to him:

"If no one is exempt from vexation, all the world, at any rate, is not like you, wholly overcome by affliction. You have made me, however, very curious to know what it is that has rendered you so pensive and sorrowful; tell me therefore the reason of your melancholy."

"I shall comply with your majesty's wish," replied the vizir, "and reveal the cause of my secret cares to you, by relating the history of my life."

THE HISTORY OF ATALMULC, SURNAMED "THE SORROWFUL VIZIR," AND THE PRINCESS ZELICA.

I am the only son of a rich jeweller of Bagdad. My father, whose name was Cogia Abdallah, spared no expense in my education; having from my earliest infancy hired masters, who taught me the various sciences, philosophy, law, theology, and more particularly the different languages of Asia, in order that they might be useful to me in my travels, if I should ever make any in that part of the world.

Shortly after this my father died, and when the funeral ceremony, which was magnificent, was over, I took possession of all his immense property. Instead of giving myself up to the pursuit of pleasure, I resolved to devote myself to my father's profession. Being well versed in the knowledge of precious stones, I had reason to believe that I should succeed in business, and accordingly I went into partnership with two merchant jewellers of Bagdad, friends of my father, who were about to undertake a trading expedition to Ormus. At Basra we hired a vessel, and embarked on our enterprise from the bay which bears the name of that city.

Our companions on board were agreeable; the ship wafted by favourable winds glided swiftly through the waves. We passed the time in festive mirth, and our voyage promised to end as pleasantly as we could desire, when my two associates gave me a startling proof that they were not the honourable characters I had supposed. We were just at the end of our voyage, and being in good spirits on that account, we held a sort of farewell feast, and did ample justice to some exquisite wines which we had laid in at Basra. For my part, being in the highest spirits, I made copious libations, and, on retiring to rest, lay down on a sofa, without taking off my clothes. In the middle of the night, while I was buried in profound slumber, my partners took me up in their arms, and threw me over-board through the cabin window. Death would seem inevitable under the circumstances, and in truth it is still impossible for me to imagine how I was fortunate enough to survive such a catastrophe. The sea was running high at the time, but the waves, as if Heaven had commanded them to spare me, instead of overwhelming me, bore me to the foot of a mountain, and cast me violently on shore. As soon as I recovered the shock, I found myself safe and sound on the beach, where I passed the remainder of the night in thanking God for my deliverance, at which I could not sufficiently wonder.

At break of day I clambered up with great difficulty to the top of the mountain, which was very steep, and met there with some peasants of the neighbourhood, who were occupied in collecting crystal, which they afterwards sold at Ormus. I related to them the danger in which my life had been placed, and my escape seemed miraculous to them, as well as to myself. These worthy people took pity on me, gave me part of their provisions, which consisted of honey and rice, and as soon as they had finished gathering their crystal, acted as my guides to the great city of Ormus. I put up at a caravansary, where the first object that met my eyes was one of my associates.

His surprise was great at seeing a man whom he no doubt believed to be safely housed in some marine monster's stomach, and he ran off instantly to find his companion, in order to acquaint him with my arrival, and to plan how they should receive me. They soon settled as to their course of proceeding, and, returning to the place where I was, they took no notice of me, and studiously conducted themselves as though they had never seen me before.

"O traitors!" I exclaimed, "Heaven frustrated your murderous intentions, and in spite of your cruelty I am still alive; give me back instantly all my precious stones; I will no longer associate with such vile wretches."

On hearing these words, which ought to have overwhelmed them with shame and remorse, they had the impudence to reply:

"O thief and rogue! who are you, and where do you come from? What precious stones do you speak of that we have belonging to you?"

So saying, they set on me, and gave me several blows with a stick. I threatened to complain to the cadi, but they anticipated me by going to that judge themselves. Bowing down before him, after having previously taken care to present him with some valuable brilliants, which no doubt belonged to me, they said to him:

"O lamp of justice! light which dispels the darkness of deceit! We have recourse to you. We are poor strangers, come from the ends of the earth to trade here; is it right that a thief should insult us, and will you permit that he should deprive us by an imposture of what we have acquired at the risk of our lives, and after running a thousand dangers?"

"Who is the man of whom you make this complaint?" asked the cadi.

"My lord," they replied, "we do not know him, we never saw him before this morning."

At this moment I presented myself before the judge, to make my own complaint, but as soon as they saw me they exclaimed:

"Here is the man—here is the wretch, the arrant thief! He is even impudent enough to venture into your palace, and show himself before you, the very sight of whom ought to frighten the guilty. Great judge, condescend to protect us."

I now approached the cadi, in order to address him, but having no presents to make to him, I found it impossible to get him to listen to my story. The calm and unmoved aspect with which I spoke to him, proceeding from the testimony of a good conscience, was thought by the cadi's prejudiced mind to arise from impudence, and he ordered his archers to convey me instantly to prison, an order which they lost no time in executing. So that while I, an innocent man, was loaded with chains, my partners departed, not only unpunished but in triumph, and well persuaded that a new miracle would require to be wrought to deliver me from the hands of the cadi.

And, indeed, my escape from my present difficulty might not have been of so fortunate a nature as that from drowning, had not an incident occurred which showed the goodness of Heaven still visibly displayed on my behalf. The peasants who had brought me to Ormus, having heard by chance that I had been put in prison, moved with compassion, went to the cadi, and told him in what way they had fallen in with me, together with all the details which they had heard from myself on the mountain.

This recital began to open the eyes of the judge, and caused him to regret that he had not listened to me. He forthwith resolved to investigate the matter; and first of all sent to the caravansary to inquire for the two merchants, but they had hastily decamped, and returned on board the ship, which had put to sea; for in spite of the bias of the cadi in their favour they had taken the alarm. Their rapid flight effectually convinced the judge that I had been committed to prison unjustly, and he gave orders to set me at liberty. Such was the termination of the partnership I had entered into with the two honest jewellers.

As one saved from drowning, and the hands of justice, (or rather injustice,) I might well have considered myself eminently bound to return thanks to the Almighty. My situation, however, was such as to render me rather indifferent as to what might happen to me; for I was without money, without friends, without credit, and reduced either to subsist on charity, or to perish of hunger. I quitted Ormus, without knowing what would become of me, and walked in the direction of the prairie of Lar, which is between the mountains and the Persian Gulf. On arriving there, I met a caravan of merchants from Hindostan, who were setting out for Schiras, and, joining myself to them, I gained a subsistence by rendering myself useful on trifling occasions. On our arrival at Schiras, where the shah Tahmaspe held his court, I stopped for some time in that city.

One day, when returning from the great mosque to the caravansary where I lodged, I saw an officer of the king of Persia, richly dressed and very handsome; looking at me attentively, he came up to me and said, "Young man, from what country do you come; for I see you are a stranger, and evidently not in a very prosperous condition?" I replied, that I came from Bagdad, and that his conjecture was but too well founded. I then related my history more at length, to which he listened attentively, and with much feeling for my misfortunes. He next asked me how old I was; and when I told him that I was nineteen years of age, he desired me to follow him, and walking before me proceeded to the king's palace, which I entered along with him. Conducting me into a very elegant apartment, he asked me, "What is your name?" I replied, "Aswad;" he then asked many other questions, and being satisfied with my replies, said at last:

"Aswad, your misfortunes have affected me greatly, and I wish to assist you as a father: I am the capi-aga[11] of the king of Persia; there is now a place vacant for a new page, and I have appointed you to it. You are young and handsome, and I cannot make a better choice, for there is not one among the present pages who surpasses you in good looks."

[11] Captain of the door of the king's chamber.

I thanked the capi-aga for his kindness, and he forthwith took me under his command, and caused me to be equipped in the dress of a page. I was made acquainted with my duties, which I soon learned to discharge in such a manner as to gain the esteem of the zuluflis[12], and to confer honour on my protector.

[12] The officer in command of the pages.

There was a rule that no page of the twelve chambers should, under pain of death, remain in the gardens of the seraglio after a certain hour, when the women were accustomed occasionally to walk there. The same rule extended to all the officers of the palace and the soldiers of the guard. Being in the gardens one evening quite alone, and musing on my misfortunes, I became so lost in thought that I did not perceive that the proper time for men to leave the gardens was already past: knowing that no time was to be lost, I quickened my pace in order to enter the palace, when just as I was turning the corner of one of the walks, a lady appeared before me. She was of a majestic stature, and in spite of the darkness I could see that she was both young and beautiful. "You are in a great hurry," she remarked; "what can it be that obliges you to walk so fast?"

"I have very good reasons for doing so," I replied, "and if you belong to the palace, as doubtless you do, you cannot be ignorant of them. You know that men are forbidden to appear in the gardens after a certain hour, and that whoever breaks this rule suffers death."

"You have been rather slow in remembering the rule," replied the lady, "for the hour is long past; however, on another account you may thank your stars you have loitered, for if you had not, you would not have met with me."

"How unfortunate for me that I should have mistaken the time," I exclaimed, thinking only that I had placed my life in danger.

"Don't reproach yourself," said the lady; "if you do, I shall feel offended. You ought to look on your misfortune to be rather a source of congratulation. It is very true that the danger in which you are placed presents ideas disagreeable enough, but it is not quite so certain that you will be beheaded, for the king is a good prince, who may be induced to forgive you. Who are you?"

"I am one of the pages," I replied.

"Indeed!" she exclaimed, "you make very wise observations for a page; the grand vizir could not make better. Well, don't distress yourself about what may happen to-morrow, the events of which are hidden from you, and are only known to Heaven, which has perhaps even now prepared a means of escape for you. Leave then the future to take care of itself, and think only of the present. If you knew who I am, and the great honour conferred upon you by this adventure, instead of poisoning the precious moments by bitter reflections, you would esteem yourself the most fortunate of mortals."

By such animating language the lady at length dispelled my fears: the idea of the punishment which threatened me vanished from my mind as I abandoned myself to the flattering ideas which she held out to me, and I proceeded somewhat over ardently to ingratiate myself with my companion. The next moment, however, as if at a signal from her, I found myself surrounded by ten or a dozen women who had concealed themselves close by, in order to listen to our conversation. It was easy now to see that the woman who had played me this trick was laughing at me. I supposed she was one of the female slaves of the princess of Persia who was desirous of having a little amusement at my expense. All the other women ran quickly to her assistance, and, bursting into laughter, began to surround me, and to joke with me. One remarked that I was of a lively character, and well fitted for an amusing companion. "If I should ever walk all alone at night," said another, "I hope I shall meet with somebody quite as clever as this page." Their pleasantries put me quite out of countenance, while every now and then they laughed outrageously, and I felt as ashamed as if they had rallied me for being too bashful. They even made themselves merry at my having permitted the hour for leaving the gardens to escape me, and said that it would be a pity if I were to die on that account; and that I well deserved to live since I was so devoted to the service of the ladies. The first one then, whom I had heard addressed as Cale-Cairi, said to another, "It is for you, my princess, to determine respecting his lot: is it your wish that he should be abandoned to his fate, or shall we lend him our assistance?"

"He must be saved from the danger he is in," replied the princess: "I give my consent for him to live; and, indeed, to the end that he may remember this adventure of his for a long time to come, we must make it still more agreeable to him; let him come to my apartments."

When I entered the chamber of Zelica Begum—for such was her name, and she was the princess of Persia—she inquired my name, and how long I had been a page. When I had satisfied her curiosity on these points she said:

"Well, Aswad, make yourself at home, and forget that you are in an apartment which is forbidden to be entered by any man: forget that I am Zelica: speak to us as if you were with a party of young ladies, the daughters of plain citizens of Schiras: look attentively at all these young women, and tell me frankly which one among us all you like best."

Although Zelica's slaves were perfectly beautiful, and the princess herself might be considered to have a just claim to the preference, my heart decided at once in favour of the charming Cale-Cairi; but concealing sentiments which would seem to cast Zelica into the shade, I said to her that she ought not to place herself in the same rank with the others, or contend with her slaves for the possession of my heart, for that her beauty was such that wherever she was seen, all eyes must be directed to her, and her alone. While speaking thus, however, I could not resist looking at Cale-Cairi in a way which would make her think that my language had been dictated by courtesy alone, and not by the real feelings of my breast. Zelica noticing this, said, "Aswad, you flatter me too much: you must be more candid: I am certain that you have not spoken your real sentiments, and you must really answer me truly in reply to my question: open your inmost soul to us: we all beg you to do this, and you cannot confer a greater pleasure both on myself and all my slaves." Yielding at last to their urgent requests, I threw off my timidity, and addressing myself to Zelica, I said:

"I will then endeavour to comply with your highness's wishes: it would be difficult to decide which of the exquisitely beautiful assemblage before me is the most beautiful, but I will avow to you that the amiable Cale-Cairi is the lady for whom the inclinations of my heart plead the most strongly."

Zelica, instead of being offended by my boldness, replied: "I am well pleased, Aswad, that you have given the preference to Cale-Cairi; she is my favourite, and that is sufficient to prove that your taste is not bad. You do not know the full worth of the fair lady whom you have chosen: we unite in owning that she excels us all."

The princess and her slaves now began to banter Cale-Cairi on the triumph which her charms had achieved—and she received all their witticisms in very good part. Zelica then ordered a lute to be brought, and placing it in Cale's hands, said to her, "Show your lover what you can do with it," and she played upon it in a style which enchanted me, accompanying it at the same time with her voice in a song which indicated that when a lover has made choice of a suitable object, he ought to love that dear one for ever. An old slave at length came to inform us that daylight was approaching, and that there was no time to be lost, if it were intended that I should quit the apartments in safety. Zelica then told me to follow the slave, who led me through many galleries, and by many windings and turnings, until we reached a little gate of which she had the key; and on the door being opened, I went out, and as it was now daylight, I saw that I was no longer in the palace. A few hours after I rejoined my companions.

Eight days after this, an eunuch came to the door of the king's apartments, and said that he wished to speak with me. I went to him and inquired what he wanted.

"Is not your name Aswad?" he asked.

I replied that it was. He then put a note into my hands, and went away. The letter stated that if I felt inclined to pay a visit to the gardens of the seraglio next night, and would be at the same place as before, I should there see a lady who was very sensibly touched with the preference I had given to her over all the princess's women. Although I suspected that Cale-Cairi had taken a fancy to me, I had no idea of receiving such a letter as this from her. Intoxicated with my good luck, I asked leave from the oda-baschi to pay a visit to a dervise—who was a countryman of my own, and who had just arrived from Mecca. Leave being granted me, I ran, or rather flew, to the gardens of the seraglio, as soon as night was come. If, on the first occasion time fled too swiftly and surprised me into stopping after the hour for leaving the gardens, it seemed now too slow in bringing me the promised pleasure, and I thought the hour of retreat would never come. It did come, however, and I could see, shortly afterwards, approaching the place where I was concealed, a lady whom I recognized by her stature and air to be Cale-Cairi. Transported with delight, I drew near, and throwing myself at her feet, I remained for some time prostrate on the ground without speaking a word, so completely had I lost all self-possession.

"Rise, Aswad," she said, "I am enraptured at having inspired you with such feelings towards me, for I will confess to you that for my part I have not been able to resist a friendly regard for you. Your youth, good looks, and lively and brilliant wit, but more than all, perhaps, your preferring me to other ladies of great beauty, have endeared you to me. My conduct proves this sufficiently; but, alas! my dear Aswad," she added, sighing, "I scarcely know whether I ought to be proud of the conquest I have made, or rather to regard it as an event which will embitter the whole course of my life."

"But, madam," I replied, "why give way to such gloomy presentiments at the very time when your presence brings me such delight?"

"It is not," she replied, "a foolish fear that now, at such a moment as this, causes me annoyance and disturbs the pleasure of our meeting; my fears are only too well founded, and you are ignorant of the cause of my grief. The princess Zelica loves you, and when she has freed herself, as she will do soon, from the splendid bondage in which she is held, she will inform you of your happiness. When she confesses to you that you are dear to her, how will you receive such a glorious avowal? Will your love for me hold out against the honour of having the affections of the first princess in the world?"

"Yes, charming Cale-Cairi," I said, interrupting her; "I would prefer you even to Zelica. Were it to please Heaven that you should have even a still more formidable rival, you would see that nothing could shake the constancy of a heart that is devoted to you."

"Unhappy Aswad!" exclaimed the lady, "whither does your love carry you? What a fatal assurance you are giving me of your fidelity! You forget that I am a slave of the princess of Persia. If you were to repay her kindness by ingratitude you would draw down her anger upon us both, and we should perish. Better it were that I should yield you up to so powerful a rival; it would be the only means of saving ourselves."

"No, no," I replied hastily; "there is another means which I should rather choose in my despair, and that would be to banish myself from the court altogether. After my retreat you would be safe from the vengeance of Zelica, and you would regain your peace of mind: by degrees you would forget the unfortunate Aswad, who would retire into the deserts to seek for rest in his misfortunes."

I spoke with such deep feeling and truth that the lady was herself overcome with my grief, and said:

"Cease, Aswad, to yield to a needless affliction. You are mistaken; your merits are such that it would be wrong to keep you longer in the dark. I am Zelica herself, and not her slave. That night when you came to my apartment I personated Cale-Cairi, and you supposed my attendant to be myself."

Zelica then called one of her women, who ran to her from amidst some cypress trees where she was concealed, and I perceived that she was the slave whom I supposed to be the princess of Persia.

"Aswad," said the princess to me, "you now see the true Cale-Cairi; I give her back her name and take my own: I have no wish to disguise myself any longer. Although your love is greater than your ambition, I am certain that it will be a source of new pleasure to you to know that the lady who loves you is a princess."

We passed nearly the whole night in walking about and conversing, and daylight would no doubt have found us in the gardens, had not Cale-Cairi, who was with us, taken care to inform us that it was time to withdraw. It was needful then that we should separate, but before I parted from Zelica the princess said to me:

"Adieu, Aswad! do not forget me. We shall see each other again, and I will soon let you know how dear you are to me." I threw myself at her feet to thank her for so flattering a promise, after which Cale-Cairi took me out by the same winding passages as before, and I then left the seraglio.

Beloved by the august princess whom I idolized, and forming an enchanting image of what she had promised me, I abandoned myself to the most pleasing fancies that the mind could depict, when an unlooked-for event deprived me all on a sudden of my proud hopes. I had heard a report that the princess Zelica was ill, and two days afterwards the rumour of her death was circulated in the palace. I was unwilling to give credit to this fatal intelligence, and refused to do so until I saw preparations going for the funeral ceremony. I did not see the whole of it, because excessive grief threw me into a succession of dangerous fainting fits which lasted for a long time. One of the officers of the palace gave directions for me to be carried into the pages' room, where great care was taken of me; my limbs were rubbed with a balm of exceeding virtue, and in spite of my overwhelming misery, such was the progress I made, that in two days my strength was restored. A stay in Schiras, however, having become insupportable, I secretly left the court of Persia three days after the interment of my beloved princess. Overwhelmed with grief, I walked all night without knowing whither I was going or where I ought to go. Next morning, having stopped to rest myself, a young man approached who was dressed in a very extraordinary manner. Coming up to me he saluted me and presented me with a green branch which he held in his hand, and after having civilly made me accept it, he began to recite some Persian verses to induce me to bestow my charity upon him. As I had no money I could not give him any. Thinking that I was ignorant of the Persian language he recited some Arabic verses, but seeing that he had no better success this way than the other, and that I did not do what he wanted, he said to me, "Brother, I cannot persuade myself that you are deficient in charity, but rather in the means wherewith to exercise it."

"You are right," I said, "I have not a farthing in the world, and I know not even where to shelter my head."

"Unfortunate man," he exclaimed, "what a sad plight you are in; I really pity you, and wish, moreover, to assist you."

I was not a little astonished to be thus addressed by a man who had been asking alms of me a moment before, and I supposed that the assistance he offered was merely that of his prayers, when he went on to say:

"I am one of those merry fellows they call fakirs; and I can tell you, that though we subsist entirely on charity, we fare none the less sumptuously for that, as we have discovered the secret of exciting the compassion of well-meaning people by an appearance of mortification and penance which we well know how to impart to ourselves. It is true there are a few fakirs fools enough to be really what they seem, and who lead a life of such austerity as sometimes to go ten whole days without the least nourishment. But we are a little less rigorous than these ascetics; we make no pretensions to the reality of their virtues, only to the appearance of them. Will you become one of our fraternity? I am now on my way to meet two of them at Bost; if you have a fancy to make the fourth, you have but to follow me."

"I am afraid," I replied, "that not being accustomed to your religious exercises I shall acquit myself but clumsily."

"Pray don't trouble yourself," he broke in, "on that head; I repeat to you that we are not fakirs of the austere order; in short, we have really nothing of the fakir about us but the dress."

Although I guessed from what the fakir had told me, that he and his companions were in reality three libertines in disguise, I nevertheless did not hesitate to join them; for besides being reckless from sheer misery, I had not learned among the pages of the court many lessons of scrupulousness on the score of morality. As soon as I had signified to the fakir my consent, he set out with me at once for Bost, feeding me on the road with abundance of dates, rice, and other good things, which people presented to him in the towns and villages through which we passed; for the moment his little bell and his peculiar cry became heard, the good Mussulmans came running to him with provisions from all quarters.

In this way we arrived at the large town of Bost; we made our way to a small house in the suburbs, where the two other fakirs resided. They received us with open arms, and appeared delighted with my resolution of joining them. They soon initiated me into their mysteries; that is to say, they showed me how to perform their antics. As soon as I was well instructed in the art of imposing on the populace, they sent me into the town to present respectable citizens with flowers or branches, and to recite verses to them. I always returned home with some pieces of silver, which enabled us to live merrily enough.

I passed nearly two years with the fakirs, and should have lived there much longer had not the one who had induced me to join them, and whom I liked the best, proposed to me to travel.

"Aswad," said he one day, "I am sick of this town; I begin to long to roam a little. I have heard wonderful accounts of the city of Candahar; if you will accompany me we will put the truth of these reports to the test."

I consented at once, for I had a curiosity to see some new country, or rather, I was impelled by that superior power which guides our destinies.

Accordingly we both quitted Bost, and passing through many cities of Segestan without stopping, we reached the noble city of Candahar, surrounded with its strong fortifications. We betook ourselves to a caravansary, where our dresses, the most commendable thing about us by the way, procured us a kind and hearty reception. We found the inhabitants of the city in a great bustle, as they were going to celebrate the feast of Giulous on the following day. We learned that at court they were no less busy, as every one was anxious to show his attachment for the king Firouzshah, who had earned by his justice the love of all good men, and still more by his rigour the fear of the wicked.

The fakirs going where they please without hindrance, we proceeded next day to court to witness the festival, which however had few charms for the eyes of a man who had seen the Giulous of the king of Persia.

Whilst we were attentively watching what passed, I felt myself pulled by the sleeve, and turning round, perceived close to me the very eunuch who, in the shah's palace, had been the bearer of Cale-Cairi's, or rather Zelica's letter.

"My lord," he whispered, "I recognized you at once in spite of your strange dress; but indeed, though I flatter myself I am never mistaken, I am not quite sure whether on the present occasion I ought not to doubt the evidence of my own eyes. Is it possible that it is you I have met here?"

"And pray," I asked in reply, "what are you doing at Candahar, and why have you left the court of Persia? Can the death of the princess Zelica have driven you away as it did me?"

"That," replied he, "is exactly what I cannot tell you at this moment, but I will amply satisfy your curiosity if you will meet me here to-morrow alone at the same hour. I have a few things to tell you which will astonish you, and which—let me add—concern you not a little."

I promised to return alone to the same spot the following day, and took care to keep my word. The eunuch was there, and coming up to me, proposed that we should leave the palace and seek some place better adapted for conversation. We accordingly went out into the city, and after traversing several streets, stopped at last at the door of a good-sized house, of which he had the key. We entered, and I observed suites of apartments magnificently furnished, delicious carpets and luxurious sofas, whilst through the windows I perceived a garden beautifully laid out, with a delightful piece of water in the middle, bordered with variegated marble.

"My lord Aswad," said the eunuch, "I trust the house pleases you."

"I am delighted with it," I replied.

"I am glad to hear you say so," he returned, "for I yesterday took it, just as you see it, for *you*. You will next want slaves to wait on you. I will go and purchase some whilst you take a bath."

So saying, he conducted me to a chamber, where I found baths all ready.

"In Heaven's name," I exclaimed, "tell me for what purpose you have brought me here, and what the news is you have promised to tell me."

"At the proper time and place," he rejoined, "you shall learn all; for the present be content to know that your lot is materially changed since I met you, and that I have my orders for every thing I am doing."

As he spoke, he assisted me to undress—a process which did not take long— I entered the bath and the eunuch left me, enjoining patience.

All this mystery furnished ample food for conjecture, but I wearied myself fruitlessly in endeavouring to fathom it. Schapour left me a long time in the bath, and my patience was beginning to be exhausted, when he returned, followed by four slaves, two of whom carried towels and garments, and the others all sorts of provisions.

"I beg your pardon, my lord," said he, "I am extremely sorry I have kept you waiting so long."

At the same time the slaves placed their bundles on the sofas and proceeded to wait on me: they rubbed me with towels of the finest texture, and then dressed me in rich garments, with a magnificent robe and turban.

"What on earth is all this to end in?" said I to myself; "and by whose orders can it be that this eunuch treats me in such a manner?"

My impatience to be enlightened became so lively that I could not conceal it. Schapour soon perceived it, and said:

"It is with the deepest regret that I see you so restless and uneasy, but I cannot yet relieve you. Even supposing I had not been expressly forbidden to say a word, or even supposing that I betrayed my trust, and told you every thing I am now concealing from you, I should not succeed in tranquillizing you in the least; anxieties still more harassing would take the place of those which now worry you—you must wait till night, and you shall then learn all you desire to know."

Though I would not but augur well from what the eunuch said, yet it was impossible to help being for the rest of the day in a state of cruel suspense. I really believe that the expectation of evil causes less real suffering than that of some great pleasure. The night however came at last, and the slaves proceeded to light up the whole house, and particularly the principal apartment, with wax candles. In this apartment I took my seat with Schapour, who, to assuage my impatience, kept saying to me, "They will be here in a moment—have but a little more patience." At last we heard knocking at the door, the eunuch went himself to open it, and returned with a lady whom, the moment she raised her veil, I recognized as Cale-Cairi. My surprise was extreme, for I believed her to be at Schiras.

"My lord Aswad," said she, "however astonished you may be to see me, you will be much more so when you hear the story I have to tell you."

At these words Schapour and the slaves quitted the apartment, leaving me alone with Cale-Cairi; we both sat down on the same sofa, and she commenced her narration as follows:

"You recollect well, my lord, that night on which Zelica made herself known to you, nor can you yet have forgotten the promise she made you on leaving. The following day I asked her whether she had come to any resolution what course to pursue in the matter; I represented to her the absurdity of a princess of her rank dreaming of exposing herself to disgrace and death for the sake of a mere page; in short, I used every effort to overcome her passion; and you may well pardon me for doing so, as all my reasoning served but to strengthen her attachment. When I saw I was utterly unable to prevail with her, 'Madam,' I said at length, 'I cannot contemplate without shuddering the danger into which you are rushing, but since no consideration seems powerful enough to detach you from your lover, we must endeavour to contrive some plan for you to meet without endangering either your life or his. I have thought of one which would doubtless be gratifying to your affection, but it seems to me so daring that I hardly like to propose it.'

"'Let me hear it at once, Cale-Cairi,' said the princess; 'whatever it may be, pray do not keep it from me.'

"'If you put it in practice,' replied I, 'you must make up your mind to quit the court and live as though you had been born to the humblest lot in life. You must renounce all the honours of your rank. Do you love Aswad sufficiently to make so great a sacrifice?'

"'*Do* I love him?' returned she, drawing a deep sigh. 'Ah! the very humblest lot with him would please me far more than all the pomp and luxury with which I am now surrounded. Only point out to me what I can do in order to enjoy his society without constraint and without impropriety, and I am ready to do it without a moment's hesitation.'

"'Well, madam,' I replied, 'since I perceive it is useless to endeavour to overcome your attachment, I will do all in my power to favour it. I am acquainted with the properties of a herb of singular power. One leaf of it placed in your ear will in an hour bring on so lethargic a sleep that you will appear quite dead; they will then perform the funeral rites, and carry you to your tomb, from which at nightfall I can easily release you—'"

Here I interrupted Cale-Cairi, "Great Heavens!" I exclaimed, "is it possible that the princess Zelica did not die after all—what then has become of her?—"

"My lord," said Cale-Cairi, "she is still alive. But pray listen patiently to my story, and you will learn all that you desire to know. My mistress," she continued, "threw herself into my arms with joy, so clever did my plan appear to her; presently, however, she began to perceive many difficulties connected with the rites and observances usual at funerals. I removed all her doubts, and thus we set about the execution of our plan.

"Zelica complained of a terrible pain in her head, and went to bed. The next morning I spread a report that she was dangerously ill; the royal physician was sent for; it was no difficult matter to deceive him. He sent some remedies which of course were never taken. From day to day the princess's illness increased; and as soon as, in my judgment, her last moments ought to approach, I placed in her ear a leaf of the herb I have mentioned. I immediately after ran to the shah, and told him the princess had but a few moments to live, and desired anxiously to speak to him. He came to her at once, and, observing that, as the herb began its work, her face changed rapidly, he was deeply moved, and began to weep.

"'My lord,' said his daughter, in faint accents, 'I implore you, by the love you have always borne me, to order my last wishes to be carried out to the letter. My wish is, that when I am dead, no one but Cale-Cairi shall be permitted to wash my body, and that none of my other slaves shall share that honour with her. I also beg that none but she shall watch my tomb the first night, that no tears but hers shall fall on it, and that her prayers alone shall ascend to the prophet, to avert from me the assaults of evil spirits.'

"Shah Tahmaspe promised his daughter that I alone should perform for her these last sad duties.

"'But this is not all, my lord,' continued she; 'I also implore you to give Cale-Cairi her liberty the moment I am no more, and to give her, with her freedom, presents worthy of yourself and of the affection she has always evinced towards me.'

"'My child,' replied the shah, 'make yourself perfectly easy on all the matters you have commended to my notice; should it be my misfortune to lose you, I swear that your favourite slave, loaded with presents, shall be at liberty to go whither she pleases.'

"He had hardly done speaking when the herb completed its work. Zelica lost all consciousness, and her father, supposing her to be dead, retired to his own apartments in deep grief. He gave orders that I alone should wash and embalm the body, which I pretended to do, and then wrapping it in a white cloth, laid it in the coffin. The princess was then carried in great pomp to the tomb, where by the shah's express orders I was left alone for the first night. I made a careful survey all round, to assure myself that no one was on the watch, and, not having discovered any one, I roused my mistress at once from her sleep in the coffin, made her put on a dress and veil I had concealed under my own, and we both repaired to a spot where Schapour was in waiting. The faithful eunuch conducted the princess to a small house which he had taken, and I returned to the tomb to pass the remainder of the night. I made up a bundle to represent the corpse, covered it with the same cloth in which I had previously wrapped Zelica, and placed it in the coffin. The next morning the princess's other slaves came to take my place, which I took care not to leave without previously indulging in all the expressions of inconsolable grief usual on such occasions. A faithful account of this exhibition of woe was duly carried to the king's ear, who was induced by it to make me presents far beyond what he had determined on. He ordered me ten thousand sequins out of his treasury, and granted me permission, the moment I asked it, to quit the court and carry with me the eunuch Schapour. I immediately proceeded to join my mistress, and congratulate her on the complete success of our stratagem. Next day we sent the eunuch to the royal apartments with a note asking you to come and see me. But one of your attendants told him you were ill, and could see no one. Three days after we sent him again; he brought back word that you had left the palace, and that no one knew what had become of you. We caused search to be made for you all through the city; Schapour left nothing undone in order to discover you; and when at last we gave up the search in despair and left Schiras, we took the road to the Indus, because we thought it just possible that you might have turned your steps in that direction;—and, stopping at every town on our route, we set on foot the most careful inquiries, which nevertheless proved entirely useless.

"One day, on our road from one city to another, though we were travelling with a caravan, a vast horde of robbers surrounded us, and, in spite of a vigorous defence, swept down the merchants and plundered their goods. Of us, of course, they soon made themselves masters, robbed us of our money and jewels, carried us to Candahar, and sold us to a slave merchant of their acquaintance. This merchant had no sooner secured Zelica, than he resolved to show her to the king of Candahar. Firouzshah was charmed the moment he saw her, and asked her whence she came. She told him Ormus was her native place, and answered the prince's other inquiries in a similar manner. In the end he purchased us, and placed us in the palace of his wives, where the handsomest apartments were assigned to us. Passionately though she is loved by the king of Candahar, she cannot, nevertheless, forget you; and, though he sighs at her feet, he has never succeeded in obtaining the slightest proof of any return of attachment. No one ever saw any thing like the joy she exhibited yesterday when Schapour informed her he had met with you. She was quite beside herself all the rest of the day. She ordered Schapour instantly to engage a furnished house for you, to conduct you there to-day, and to suffer you to want for nothing. I am now here by her orders to inform you of the several things I have communicated, and to prepare you to see her in the course of to-morrow night. We shall leave the palace unobserved, and let ourselves in here by a small door in the garden wall, of which we have had a key made for us." As she uttered these last words the favourite slave of the princess of Persia rose and quitted the apartment, in order to return to her mistress, and Schapour accompanied her.

I could do nothing all that night but think of Zelica, my love for whom seemed to return with tenfold ardour. Sleep never approached my eyelids, and the following day seemed a century. At last, as I almost began to think I should fall a victim to the agonies of suspense, I heard a knocking at the door; my slaves ran to open it, and the next moment I saw my princess entering the room. How shall I describe the feelings which her presence excited in me! and for her part what was her delight to see me once more! I threw myself at her feet and for some time could do nothing but embrace them without uttering a syllable. At length she forced me to rise, and seating me next her on the sofa, "Aswad," said she, "I render thanks to Heaven for reuniting us; let us now hope that the goodness of Providence will not stop here, but will remove the new obstacle which hinders our union. In expectation of the arrival of that happy hour we will live here in contentment; and if circumstances prevent our meeting unconstrainedly, we can at least enjoy the consolation of hearing daily news of each other, as well as of occasional secret interviews." In such conversation we passed the greater part of the night. Next day, in spite of the happy thoughts which now filled my mind, I did not forget the fakir in whose company I had come to Candahar; and picturing to myself his uneasiness at not knowing where I was, I determined to go and find him out. I met him by accident in the street and we embraced each other.

"My friend," said I, "I was on my way to your caravansary to inform you of what has happened to me, and to set your mind at ease. No doubt I have occasioned you some uneasiness."

"That is true enough," replied he; "I was in no small trouble about you. But what a change! What clothes are these you appear in? You seem to have been in luck. Whilst I was worrying myself about what had become of you, you were passing your time, as it seems to me, pleasantly enough."

"I confess it, my dear friend," replied I; "and I can assure you, moreover, that I am a thousand times happier than it is possible for you to conceive. I want you not only to be witness of my good fortune, but to profit by it as well. Quit your caravansary and come and live with me."

So saying, I led him to my house and showed him all over it. He admired the rooms and the furniture amazingly, and every now and then would exclaim, "O Heaven! what has Aswad done more than other men to deserve such an accumulation of good fortune?"

"What, now, fakir," asked I, "do you view my happy condition with chagrin? It seems to me that my good fortune is positively annoying to you."

"On the contrary," returned he, "it affords me the liveliest satisfaction; so far from envying my friends' happiness, I am never so happy as when I see them flourishing."

As he concluded this speech he embraced me ardently, the better to persuade me of the sincerity of his words. I believed him sincere, and acting towards him myself in the most perfect good faith, betrayed myself without the least mistrust into the hands of the most envious, the most cowardly, and the most treacherous of men.

In this way we continued to live for some time. Schapour or Cale-Cairi brought me daily intelligence of my beloved princess, and an occasional stolen interview elevated me to the seventh heaven of happiness. The fakir expressed the liveliest interest in the progress of my attachment, and I confided to him, as to my bosom friend, every particular of my life.

One day, as I was reposing on a sofa and dreaming of Zelica, I was aroused by a great noise in my house. I rose in order to ascertain the cause, and to my great dismay, found that it was occasioned by a body of Firouzshah's own guards.

"Follow me," said the officer in command; "our orders are to conduct you to the palace."

"What crime have I committed?" asked I; "of what am I accused?"

"We have not been informed," replied the officer; "our orders are merely to carry you before the king; we know nothing about the cause: but I may tell you for your comfort, that if you are innocent you have nothing whatever to fear, for you have to do with a prince of the strictest justice, who never lightly condemns any one who is brought before him. He requires the most convincing proofs before he will pass an adverse sentence; but it is true at the same time that he punishes the guilty with the utmost rigour, so that, if you are guilty, I pity you."

There was no help for it; I was obliged to follow the officer. On my way to the palace I said to myself, "Firouzshah has no doubt discovered my correspondence with Zelica; but how can he have learned it?" As we crossed the court-yard of the palace I observed that four gibbets had been erected there. I made a shrewd guess at their destination, and apprehended that this kind of death was the least part of the punishment I had to expect from the wrath of Firouzshah. I raised my eyes to heaven and prayed that at least the princess of Persia might be saved from this. We entered the palace; the officer who had charge of me conducted me into the king's apartment. That prince was there, attended only by his grand vizir and the fakir. The moment I perceived my treacherous friend I saw that I had been betrayed.

"It is you, then," said Firouzshah to me, "who has secret interviews with my favourite. Wretch! you must be bold indeed to dare to trifle with me! Speak, and reply exactly and truly to my questions:—When you came to Candahar, were you not told that I was a severe punisher of criminals?"

I replied that I was informed of it.

"Well," he continued, "since you knew that, why have you committed the greatest of all crimes?"

"Sire," I answered, "may your majesty's days last for ever. You know that love gives courage to the dove: a man possessed by a violent passion fears nothing: I am ready to be a victim to your just wrath; and as to any tortures that may be reserved for me I shall not complain of your severity, provided you grant a pardon to your favourite. Alas! she was living peacefully in your palace before I came here, and would soon have been contented with rendering a great king happy, while gradually forgetting an unfortunate lover whom she never thought to see again. Knowing that I was in this city, her former attachment returned. It was I that separated her from your affection, and your punishment should fall on me alone."

While I was thus speaking, Zelica, who had been sent for by the king's order, entered the apartment, followed by Schapour and Cale-Cairi, and hearing the last words I uttered, ran forward and threw herself at the feet of Firouzshah.

"Great prince!" she exclaimed, "forgive this young man: it is on your guilty slave, who has betrayed you, that your vengeance ought to fall."

"Traitors that you both are!" exclaimed the king "expect no favour either of you: die! both of you. This ungrateful woman only implores my kindness in behalf of the rash man who has offended me; while his sensibilities are only alive to the loss of her whom he loves; both of them thus parading in my very sight their amorous madness; what insolence! Vizir!" he cried, turning to his minister, "let them be led away to execution. Hang them up on gibbets, and after their death, let their carcasses be thrown to the dogs and the vultures."

The officers were leading us away, when I resolved on one more desperate effort to save the princess.

"Stop, sire!" I shouted at the top of my voice, "take care what you do, and do not treat with ignominy the daughter of a king! Let your jealousy even in its fury have respect to the august blood from which she has sprung!"

At these words Firouzshah appeared thunderstruck, and then addressing Zelica, he inquired, "Who then is the prince who is your father?"

The princess looked at me with a proud countenance, and said:

"Alas! Aswad, where was your discretion? how is it that you have told what I wished to conceal, if it were possible, even from myself? I should have had the consolation in death of knowing that my rank was a secret, but in disclosing it, you have overwhelmed me with shame. Learn then who I am," she continued, addressing herself to Firouzshah; "the slave whom you have condemned to an infamous death is the daughter of shah Tahmaspe!" She then related her whole story, without omitting the slightest circumstance.

When she had concluded her recital, which increased the king's astonishment, she said to him, "Now I have revealed a secret which it was my intention to bury in my own breast, and which nothing but the indiscretion of my lover could have wrung from me. After this confession, which I make with extreme humiliation, I beg that you will instantly give orders for my immediate execution. This is the only favour I now ask of your majesty."

"Madam," replied the king, "I revoke the order for your death: I have too great a love for justice not to honour your faithfulness: what you have told me makes me look upon you in a different light; I have no complaint to make against you, and I set you at liberty. Live for Aswad, and may the happy Aswad live for you! Schapour also and your friend have life and liberty granted to them. Go, most faithful lovers, and may you pass the rest of your days in the enjoyment of each other's society, and may nothing interrupt the course of your happiness. As for you, traitor," he continued, turning to the fakir, "you shall be punished for your treason, for your base and envious heart, which could not endure to see the happiness of your friend, and led you to deliver him up yourself to my vengeance. Miserable wretch! You shall yourself be the victim of my jealousy!"

While this villain was being led to the gallows, Zelica and I threw ourselves at the feet of the king of Candahar, and bathed them with tears of gratitude and joy. We assured him that we should ever retain a grateful sense of his generous goodness. And at length we left his palace, accompanied by Schapour and Cale-Cairi, with the intention of taking up our lodging at a caravansary. We were just about to enter, when an officer sent by the king accosted us. "I come," he said, "from my master, Firouzshah, to offer you a lodging: the grand vizir will lend you a house of his, situated at the gates of the city, where you will be very commodiously lodged. I will be your conductor thither, if you will allow me, and will take the trouble to follow me." We accompanied him, and soon arrived at a house of imposing appearance, and elegant architecture: the interior corresponded to the outside appearance. Every thing was magnificent, and in good taste. There were more than twenty slaves, who told us that their master had desired them to supply us with every thing that we wanted, and to treat us as they would himself all the time that we remained in the house.

Here my marriage with the princess was duly celebrated, though with the strictest privacy. Two days after we received a visit from the grand vizir, who brought an immense quantity of presents from the king. There were bales of silk and cloth of India, with twenty purses, each containing a thousand sequins of gold. As we did not feel ourselves quite at our ease in a house which was not our own, and as the king's bounty enabled us to go elsewhere, we joined ourselves to a great caravan of merchants, who were proceeding to Bagdad, where we arrived without encountering any disaster.

We took up our lodgings at my own house, where we remained for a few days after our arrival, for the purpose of recovering ourselves from the fatigue of our long journey. I then went into the city and visited my friends, who were astonished to see me, as they had been told by my associates on their return, that I was dead. As soon as I knew that they were at Bagdad, I hastened to the grand vizir, threw myself at his feet, and related their perfidious conduct towards me. He gave orders for their immediate arrest, and commanded them to be interrogated in my presence. "Is it not true," I asked them, "that I awoke when you took me up in your arms, that I asked what you intended doing with me, and that without replying you threw me out through the porthole of the ship into the sea?"

They replied that I must have been dreaming, and that I must certainly have thrown myself into the sea when asleep.

"Why then," said the vizir, "did you pretend not to know him at Ormus?"

They replied that they had not seen me at Ormus.

"Traitors!" he replied, eyeing them with a threatening aspect, "what will you say, when I show you a certificate from the cadi of Ormus, proving the contrary?"

At these words, which the vizir only made use of to put them to the proof, my associates turned pale and became confused. The vizir noticed their altered looks, and bade them confess their crime, that they might not be compelled to do so, by being put to the torture.

They then confessed every thing and were conveyed to prison, until the caliph should be informed of the matter, and give his orders respecting the kind of death which they were to undergo. In the mean time, however, they contrived to make their escape, either by bribing their guards, or deceiving their vigilance, and concealed themselves so carefully in Bagdad, that all search after them proved ineffectual. Their property, however, was confiscated to the caliph, excepting a small part which was bestowed upon me, by way of some compensation for the robbery.

After this all my ambition consisted in living a quiet life with the princess, with whom I was perfectly united in love and affection. My constant prayer to Heaven was, that such a state of felicity might be continued to us; but alas! how vain are the wishes and hopes of man, who is never destined to enjoy unruffled repose for a long time, but whose existence is continually disturbed by contending cares and sorrows! Returning home one evening from partaking of an entertainment with some friends, I knocked at the door of my house, but could get no one to admit me, although I knocked loudly and repeatedly. I was surprised at this, and began to form the gloomiest conjectures. I redoubled my knocks at the door, but no slave came to admit me. What can have happened? I thought; can this be some new misfortune that has befallen me? Such were my surmises. At the noise I made several neighbours came out of their houses, and being as astonished as myself at none of the domestics appearing, we broke open the door, and on entering found my slaves lying on the floor, with their throats cut, and weltering in their blood. We passed from them to Zelica's apartment, and here another frightful spectacle presented itself, for we found both Schapour and Cale-Cairi stretched lifeless on the ground, bathed in their blood. I called on Zelica, but received no reply. I searched every room and corner in the house, but without finding her. Such a blow was too much for me, and I sank back in a swoon in the arms of my neighbours. Happy would it have been for me had the angel of death at that moment borne me away; but no! it was the will of Heaven that I should live to see the full horror of my fate.

When my neighbours by their attentions had succeeded in recalling me to life, I asked how it was possible that so terrible a slaughter could have taken place in my house, and not the slightest sound of it have been heard by them. They replied that they were as astonished as I was at the circumstance. I then ran to the cadi, who despatched his nayb[13] into all the surrounding country with all his asas[14], but their inquiries were fruitless, and every one formed his own conjecture respecting this horrible tragedy. As for myself, I believed, as well as many others, that my former partners were the perpetrators of the crime. My grief was so intense that I fell ill, and continued in a languishing state at Bagdad for a long time. When I recovered I sold my house, and went to reside at Mossoul, carrying with me the wreck of my fortune. I adopted this course because I had a relation there of whom I was extremely fond, and who belonged to the household of the grand vizir of the king of Mossoul. My relation received me very cordially, and in a short time I became known to the minister, who, thinking that he saw in me good business talents, gave me some employment. I endeavoured to discharge effectively the duties entrusted to me, and I had the good fortune to succeed. His satisfaction with me daily increased, and I became insensibly initiated into the most secret state affairs, the weight of which I even assisted him to bear. In a few years this minister died, and the king, who was perhaps too partial to me, appointed me to his place, which I filled for two years, to the satisfaction of the king, and the contentment of the people. To mark, also, how much he was pleased with my conduct as minister, he first gave me the name of Atalmulc. And now envy soon began to be excited against me. Some of the chief nobles became my secret enemies, and plotted my ruin. The better to secure their ends, they instilled suspicions respecting me into the mind of the prince of Mossoul, who, being influenced by their unfavourable insinuations, asked the king, his father, to deprive me of power. The king at first refused, but yielded at last to the urgent requests of his son. I thereupon left Mossoul, and came to Damascus, where I had soon the honour of being presented to your majesty.

[13] Lieutenant.

[14] Archers.

I have now related to you, sire, the history of my life, and the cause of the deep grief in which I seem to be buried. The abduction of Zelica is ever present to my mind, and renders me insensible to every kind of pleasure. If I could learn that she was no more in life, I might, perhaps, lose the recollection of her, as I did before; but the uncertainty of her fate brings her ever back to my memory, and constantly feeds my grief.

CONTINUATION OF THE STORY OF KING BEDREDDIN-LOLO AND HIS VIZIR.

When the vizir Atalmulc had concluded the recital of his adventures, the king said to him:

"I am no longer surprised at your melancholy, for you have, indeed, good reason for it; but every one has not, like you, lost a princess, and you are wrong in thinking that there is not one man in the world who is perfectly satisfied with his condition."

For the purpose of proving to his grand vizir that there are men in this state, the king of Damascus said, one day, to his favourite Seyf-Elmulouk, "Go into the city, walk before the shop of the artisans, and bring me here immediately the man who seems the gayest of the gay." The favourite obeyed, and returned to Bedreddin in a few hours. "Well," said the monarch, "have you done what I commanded you?"

"Yes, sire," replied the favourite, "I passed in front of several shops, and saw all descriptions of workmen who sung while at their various occupations, and seemed quite contented with their lot. I noticed one among them, a young weaver, named Malek, who laughed with his neighbours till I thought he would have split his sides, and I stopped to have some chat with him. 'Friend,' I said, 'you appear to be very merry.' 'Yes,' he replied, 'it is my way: I don't encourage melancholy.' I asked his neighbours if it was true that he was of such a happy turn of mind, and they all assured me that he did nothing but laugh from morning till night. I then told him to follow me, and I have brought him to the palace. He is now at hand: does your majesty wish him to be introduced to your presence?"

"By all means," replied the king, "bring him here, for I wish to speak with him."

Seyf-Elmulouk immediately left the king's cabinet and returned in an instant, followed by a good-looking young man, whom the favourite presented to the king. The weaver threw himself down at the monarch's feet, who said to him, "Rise, Malek, and tell me truly if you are as happy as you seem to be: I am told you do nothing but laugh and sing the live-long day while at your work: you are thought to be the happiest man in my dominions, and there is reason to believe that such is really the case. Tell me whether or not this is a correct judgment, and if you are contented with your condition. This is a matter that I am concerned to know; and I desire that you will speak without disguise."

"Great king," replied the weaver, standing up, "may your majesty's days last to the end of the world, and be interwoven with a thousand delights, unmixed with the slightest misfortune. Excuse your slave from satisfying your curiosity. If it is forbidden to lie to kings, it must also be owned that there are truths that we dare not reveal. I can only say that a false idea is entertained respecting me: in spite of my laughter and songs, I am perhaps the most unfortunate of men. Be contented with this avowal, sire, and do not compel me to relate my misfortunes to you."

"I am resolved to have them," replied the king. "Why should you be afraid to tell them? Are they not creditable to you?"

"Of this your majesty must judge," replied the weaver. "I had resolved to keep them to myself, but since it is necessary I will proceed with my story."

The weaver then began as follows:—

THE STORY OF MALEK AND THE PRINCESS SCHIRINE.

I am the only son of a merchant of Surat, who left me at his death considerable wealth, most of which I squandered away in a very short time. I was nearly at the end of my property, when one day a stranger, who was going to the island of Serendib, happened to be dining with me. The conversation turned on voyages and travels: some who were present praised the advantages and the pleasure attending them, and others expatiated on their dangers. Among the guests there were a few persons who had travelled extensively, and who gave us detailed accounts of their experience in this adventurous kind of life. Between their accounts of the strange and curious scenes which they had witnessed and of the dangers which they had encountered, my mind was kept in suspense, as I conceived a strong desire to travel, and yet felt afraid of the accompanying risks. After listening to all that was related, I remarked:

"It is impossible to hear your striking account of the pleasure experienced by you in travelling over the world without feeling a strong wish to travel also; but the dangers to which a traveller is exposed deprive me of all inclination for visiting foreign countries. If it were possible," I added, smiling, "to go from one end of the earth to the other, without meeting with any bad accident by the way, I would leave Surat to-day."

These words excited universal laughter, but the stranger before alluded to remarked:

"O Malek! if you have a desire to travel, and if nothing prevents you but the fear of encountering robbers and other dangers, I will teach you whenever you have a mind, a method of travelling at your pleasure, and without peril, from one kingdom to another."

I thought he was joking, but after dinner he took me aside, and told me that he would pay me a visit the following morning and show me something extraordinary. He was true to his word, for the next day he came to see me, and said, "I mean to keep my promise, but some days must elapse before you can see the effect, for what I have to show you is a piece of workmanship which cannot be constructed in a day. Send therefore for a carpenter; let one of your slaves go for him, and let them both return with planks and other materials according to this list." I immediately complied with his request. When the slave and the carpenter returned, the stranger directed the latter to construct a box in the form of a bird, six feet in length and four in breadth, the upper part open, so as to admit a man to sit in it. The artisan immediately set to work, and the stranger on his part was not idle, for he made or brought from his lodging several parts of the machine, such as wings, wheels, and springs. For several days the carpenter and he worked together, and afterwards the former was dismissed, while the stranger spent one day in putting together the machinery and finishing the work.

At length on the sixth day the box was finished, and covered with a Persian carpet. I observed that in this box there were several apertures, as well to admit air as to serve for look-outs. At the stranger's desire I then ordered some of my slaves to carry it into the country, whither I followed with the stranger. When we arrived at the spot he said to me, "Send away your slaves and let no one be here but ourselves. I do not wish to have other persons present beside yourself to see what I am about to do."

I ordered my slaves to return home, while I remained alone with the stranger. I was very anxious to know what he intended to do with this machine, and eagerly watched his movements. He removed the carpet, and stepped inside. In a moment the box began to ascend above the earth and soared into the sky with incredible swiftness, carrying him rapidly to a great distance in the clouds; before I had recovered from my astonishment he was down again on the ground. I cannot express to you my amazement at witnessing this miracle of art.

"You behold," said the stranger to me, as he stepped out of the machine, "a very quiet carriage, and you must admit that in travelling in it there is no fear of being robbed on the journey. This is the method I spoke of, and I now make you a present of the machine to be employed by you if ever you should take a fancy to visit foreign countries. Do not suppose that there is any magic or black art in what you have seen: it is neither by cabalistic words nor by virtue of a talisman that the box rises above the earth: its motion is produced merely by an ingenious adaptation of machinery. I am perfectly conversant with the mechanical arts, and know how to construct other machines quite as surprising as this one."

I thanked the stranger for such a rare gift, and as a mark of my gratitude presented him with a purse of sequins. I then requested him to instruct me how to set the machine in motion. "It is very easily done," he said, and requested me to step into the box along with him: he then touched a spring and we immediately mounted up into the air; when there, he next showed me how to steer the machine. "By turning this screw," he said, "you will go to the right, and that other screw will take you to the left; by touching this spring you will ascend, and the same operation applied to another spring will cause you to descend." I wanted to make the experiment myself: I turned the screws and touched the springs, and the machine, obedient to my hand, went whither I pleased; I quickened its movements, or slackened them, just as I wished. After having taken several turns in the air, we directed our flight towards my house and alighted in the garden.

We reached home before my slaves, who were astonished beyond measure when they found we had returned. I shut up the box in my room, where I watched it more carefully than any heap of gold; and the stranger departed as well satisfied with me as I was with him. I continued to amuse myself in the society of my friends until I had eaten and drunk all my fortune—was compelled to borrow money, and eventually got over head and ears in debt. As soon as it was known in Surat that I was a ruined man, I lost all credit; no one would trust me, and my creditors being impatient to get their money, sent me summonses to pay them. Finding myself almost penniless, and consequently exposed to all kinds of insults and mortifications, I had recourse to my machine, and dragging it out one night from my room into the open air, I stepped into it, taking with me some provisions and the little money I had left. I touched the spring which caused the machine to ascend; and then moving one of the screws, I turned my back upon Surat and my creditors, without any fear of their sending the officers after me. I put on as much propelling power as possible all night, and it seemed to me that my flight was swifter than the winds. At daybreak I looked out of one of the apertures in the carpet to see whereabouts I was. I could see nothing but mountains, precipices, a barren country, and a frightful desert. Wherever I looked I could discover no signs of human habitations. During all that day and the following night I continued my aërial tour, and next day I found myself above a very thick wood, near which was a fine city situated in an extensive plain. I stopped here in order to take a view of the city, as well as of a magnificent palace which I saw at some distance from it at the extremity of the plain. I was extremely anxious to know where I was, and began to ponder in what way I could satisfy my curiosity, when I observed a peasant at work in a field. I descended in the wood, left my box there, and going up to the labourer, asked the name of the city. "Young man," he replied, "it is easy to see that you are a stranger, since you do not know that this is the renowned city of Gazna, where the just and valiant king Bahaman resides."

"And who lives," I asked, "in the palace at the end of the plain?"

"The king of Gazna," he replied, "has built it in order to keep his daughter, the princess Schirine, shut up there; for the princess's horoscope declares that she is threatened with being deceived by a man. Bahaman, for the purpose of evading this predicted danger, has erected this palace, which is built of marble, and surrounded by a deep ditch. The gate is formed of Indian steel, and while the king himself keeps the key, a numerous body of troops keep watch round it day and night to prevent any man from gaining entrance. The king goes once a week to see his daughter, and then returns to Gazna. Schirine's only companions in the palace are a governess and a few female slaves."

I thanked the peasant for his information, and directed my steps towards the city. When I was near to it, I heard the noise of an approaching multitude, and soon espied a vast crowd of horsemen magnificently attired, and mounted on very fine horses richly caparisoned. I perceived in the midst of this splendid cavalcade a tall individual, with a crown of gold on his head, and whose dress was covered with diamonds. I concluded that this person was the king of Gazna, going to visit the princess his daughter; and, in fact, I learned in the city that my conjecture was correct.

After having made the circuit of the city, and somewhat satisfied my curiosity, I bethought me of my machine; and although I had left it in a spot which seemed to promise security, I became uneasy on its account. I left Gazna and had no peace of mind until I reached the place where I had left the box, which I found quite safe. I then became tranquil, and partook with a good appetite of the food which I had brought with me, and as night was coming on, I resolved to pass it in the wood. I had reason to hope that a profound sleep would soon overpower me, for latterly my debts, as well as the general complication of my affairs, had naturally caused me much uneasiness and many sleepless nights: but my wishes were in vain, I could not sleep; for what the peasant had told me respecting the princess Schirine was constantly present to my mind. The more I thought of her and her peculiar situation, the more did I become possessed with the desire of effecting an interview; at length my inclinations became ungovernable, and I resolved to convey myself to the roof of the princess's palace and endeavour to obtain an entrance into her chamber. "Perhaps," thought I, "I may have the happiness to please her, perhaps to dispel the *ennui* she must suffer under: perhaps even I may be the mortal whose fortunate audacity was foretold by the astrologers." I was young and consequently thoughtless, and I was not deficient in courage, or such a scheme would not have occurred to me. However, having formed the rash resolution, I instantly proceeded to execute it. I raised myself up in the air and steered my machine in the direction of the palace: the night was as dark as I could wish. I passed without being seen over the heads of the soldiers, who were dispersed around the palace fosse, keeping watch, and descended on the roof near a spot where I saw a light; quitting my box I then slipped in at a window which had been left open to admit the cool night breeze. The room was furnished with the utmost magnificence; and I saw, reposing in slumber on a sofa, a young lady who, from the splendour and luxury with which she was surrounded, I could not doubt was the princess Schirine herself. I gazed for some time on her and found her to be of such dazzling beauty as exceeded the highest idea I had formed of her. I drew nearer in order to gaze upon her more intently: I could not, without an overwhelming emotion of rapture, contemplate such charms. I was quite overcome; and hardly knowing what I was about, knelt down beside her to kiss one of her beautiful hands. She awoke at that instant, and seeing a man near her, though in an attitude of respect which need have excited no alarm, uttered a cry which soon brought her governess, who slept in an adjoining room.

"Help, Mahpeiker!" exclaimed the princess: "here is a man! how was it possible for him to get into my room? You must surely have admitted him, and are an accomplice in his crime."

"I his accomplice!" exclaimed the governess: "the bare idea is an insult to me! I am as astonished as you can be, to see here this rash young man. Besides, if I had even been inclined to favour him in his bold attempt, how was it possible for me to deceive the vigilance of the guards who keep watch around the palace? You know also that there are twenty gates of burnished steel to be opened before any person can get in here; the seal royal is on every lock, and the king, your father, keeps the keys. I cannot imagine how this young man has been able to overcome all these obstacles."

All this time I remained kneeling, overwhelmed with confusion: the governess's long speech, however, gave me time to collect my thoughts, and it occurred to me that I would endeavour to persuade them that I was a being of a superior order.

"Beautiful princess," I said to Schirine, rising from my knee and making her a profound obeisance, "do not be surprised at seeing me here. I am not a lover who lavishes gold, and resorts to nefarious tricks to accomplish his wishes; far be from me any unworthy intention: I have not a wish at which your virtuous mind need be ashamed. Know then that I am the king of the genii: for a long time I have been aware of your singular position, and could not without pitying you see you condemned to pass your best days in a prison. I am come here to throw myself at your feet, and to ask you in marriage from Bahaman: as my bride it will be in my power to shield you from the danger alluded to by the prediction which has terrified your father. Deign, therefore, beautiful princess, to look kindly on my suit, and then let both your father and yourself be at rest respecting your future fate, which cannot fail to be both glorious and happy; for as soon as the news of your marriage is spread abroad in the world, all the kings of the earth will stand in awe of the father-in-law of so powerful a monarch, and every princess will envy your fate."

Schirine and her governess looked at each other during this speech as if desirous of consulting together whether they should give credit to it. I confess I had reason to believe that they would give no heed to such a fable, but women are fond of the wonderful, and both Mahpeiker and her mistress believed me.

After passing the greater part of the night in delightful conversation with the princess of Gazna and her governess, I left her apartment before daybreak, promising to return next day. I lost no time in getting into my machine, and ascended to a great height that I might not be seen by the soldiers. I alighted in the wood, left the box there, and went into the city, where I purchased a stock of provisions for eight days, magnificent robes, a turban of Indian woof surrounded with a golden circlet, darting forth rays of light, and a rich girdle. At the same time I did not forget the costliest perfumes and essences. I spent all my money in these purchases without troubling my head about the future; for I thought that after such a pleasant adventure as had befallen me, I should never more want for any thing. I remained all day in the wood employed in dressing and perfuming myself with the utmost care and attention. When night came on, I entered the machine and set off for the roof of Schirine's palace, where I introduced myself into her apartment as before, and spent another delightful evening in conversation with the princess and her attendant. I left the palace when night was waning, for fear lest my imposture should be discovered. I returned next day, and always conducted myself so cleverly that the princess and Mahpeiker had not the least idea that I was an impostor. True it is that the princess by degrees had acquired such a fondness for me that, on this account, she gave a more ready belief to what I said; for love is blind and, when such feelings exist in favour of a person, his sincerity is never doubted. I, too, had become deeply enamoured of the beautiful princess, and more than once regretted the imposture I was practising on her; but what was I to do? To discover it was certain destruction, and I could not summon up courage to undeceive her.

After some days had elapsed, the king of Gazna, attended by some of his officers, paid his weekly visit to his daughter's palace, and finding the gates securely fastened, and his seal on the locks, said to the vizirs who accompanied him:

"Every thing goes on as well as possible: so long as the palace gates continue in this state I have little fear of the evil with which my daughter is threatened."

He went up to her apartment alone and unannounced, and at seeing him she could not help betraying some emotion, which he noticed and required to know the reason of. His curiosity added to her perplexity; and, finding herself at last compelled to satisfy him, she related all that had taken place. Your majesty may conceive the astonishment of king Bahaman when he learned that, without his knowledge, a proposal of marriage had been made by the king of the genii. But he was not so easily duped as his daughter. Suspecting the truth, he exclaimed:

"Alas! my child, how credulous you are! O Heaven! I see that it is hopeless to endeavour to avoid the misfortunes destined for us; the horoscope of Schirine is fulfilled; some villain has deceived her!"

So saying, he left the princess's room in a state of great agitation, and went over all the palace, from the top to the bottom, searching every where, and strictly examining all the attendants, but I need hardly say without success, for he found no trace of any stranger, nor the slightest circumstance to lead to the supposition that bribery had been resorted to, which increased his astonishment. "By what means," he said, "can any person, however ingenious and daring, enter this fortress? To me it is inconceivable."

He resolved to get at the truth of the matter somehow, but being desirous of setting to work prudently, and of speaking himself alone, in the first instance, and without witnesses, to the pretended genius, he sent back his vizirs and courtiers to Gazna. "Withdraw," he said to them, "and I will remain alone at the palace this night with my daughter; and do you return here to-morrow."

They all obeyed the king's orders: they returned to the city, and Bahaman set about questioning the princess afresh until night drew on. He asked her if I had eaten with her. She replied that I had not, for that she had in vain offered me refreshments, and that she had not seen me either eat or drink any thing since I came to her. "Tell me the whole occurrence again," he said, "and conceal nothing." Schirine related to him her story all over again, and the king, who was attentive to her recital, weighed every circumstance of it carefully.

Night had now set in; Bahaman seated himself on a sofa, and ordered tapers to be lit and to be placed before him on the marble table. He then drew his sabre, to be employed, if necessary, in wiping out with my blood the insult he conceived to have been offered to his honour. He sat thus, expecting me every moment; and the idea of seeing me appear instantaneously probably agitated him not a little.

That night it happened that the atmosphere was highly charged with electric matter. A brilliant flash of lightning darted across the sky before him and made him start. Approaching the window at which Schirine had told him I should enter, and observing the heavens to be on fire with vivid flashes, his imagination was excited, although nothing was taking place but what was quite natural: he thought he saw in the clouds fanciful forms, among which was prominently conspicuous that of a venerable old man, such as the prophet is represented to us. As he gazed he forgot to reflect that these meteors arose merely from exhalations of an inflammable nature that exploded in the air, and came to regard them as brilliant lights announcing to the world the descent of the king of the genii. In such a state of mind the king was disposed to receive me as really bearing the character to which I pretended, and therefore when I appeared at the window, instead of exhibiting the fury he had contemplated, he was overcome with respect and fear; he dropped his sabre, and, falling at my feet, kissed them, and said, "O great king! what am I, and what have I done to deserve the honour of being your father-in-law?"

From these words I could guess what had passed between the king and the princess, and discovered that the worthy monarch was almost as easily imposed upon as his daughter. We sat down together on the sofa and conversed. I now formally renewed to him my suit for the hand of the princess. He believed all I told him, and feeling delighted at the prospect of being allied to me, again prostrated himself at my feet in sign of gratitude for my kindness. I raised him up, embraced him, and assured him of my protection, for which he could not find language sufficiently strong to thank me. It was arranged that the marriage should take place the following day. I stopped with Schirine and her father for a few hours, but however pleased I might be with our interview, I did not forget how time was flying; I was apprehensive of daylight surprising us, and of my box being seen on the roof of the palace. I therefore made haste to leave in good time and to reseat myself in the machine.

The following day, on the return of the vizirs and great officers of state, a magnificent banquet was prepared at the palace, and immediately on my arrival in the evening the marriage was celebrated with great pomp and rejoicing.

A month had nearly passed during which I continued to be looked on and treated as the king of the genii, and I was leading a most agreeable life, when there arrived in the city of Gazna an ambassador from a neighbouring monarch to demand Schirine in marriage. On being admitted to an audience, and detailing the object of his embassy, Bahaman said to him:

"I am sorry that I am unable to give my daughter in marriage to the king, your master, for I have already bestowed her hand on the king of the genii."

From such a reply the ambassador supposed that king Bahaman had lost his senses; he therefore took leave and returned to his master, who also at first thought Bahaman was mad, but on reconsidering the answer began to look on the refusal as a studied insult; he therefore raised troops, and forming a large army, entered the kingdom of Gazna in a hostile manner. This king, whose name was Cacem, was more powerful than Bahaman, who also was so slow in preparing to oppose his enemy that he could not prevent him from making great progress. Cacem defeated some troops which opposed him, and advancing rapidly towards the city of Gazna, found the army of Bahaman intrenched in the plain before the castle of the princess Schirine. The design of the irritated lover was to attack Bahaman in his intrenchments; but as his troops had need of rest, and he had only arrived that evening in the plain after a long forced march, he delayed his attack until the following morning.

The king of Gazna, having been informed of the numbers and valour of Cacem's soldiers, began to tremble for the result. He assembled his privy council and asked for their advice, when one of its members spoke in the following terms:

"I am astonished that the king should appear to be at all uneasy on this occasion. What alarm can all the princes of the world, to say nothing of Cacem, occasion to the father-in-law of the king of the genii? Your majesty need only address yourself to him, and beg his assistance, and he will soon confound your enemies. It is his duty to do this, indeed, since it is on his account that Cacem has come to disturb the quiet of your majesty's subjects."

This speech did not fail to inspire king Bahaman with confidence.

"You are right," he said to the courtier; "I shall at once go and beg of him to repulse my proud enemy, and I venture to hope that he will not reject my supplication."

So saying, he went to visit his daughter, and said to her:

"Schirine, to-morrow at daybreak it is Cacem's intention to attack us, and I am afraid he will carry our intrenchments. I wish to entreat of the king of the genii that he would undertake our defence. Let us unite our prayers that he would be favourable to us."

"My lord and father," replied the princess, "there will be no great difficulty in engaging the king on our side; he will soon disperse the enemy's troops, and all the kings of the world will learn, at Cacem's expense, to respect you."

"But," resumed king Bahaman, "night is coming on, and still the king of the genii does not appear; can he have forsaken us?"

"No, no, my father," replied Schirine; "do not fear that he will fail us in time of need. He sees the army which is now besieging us, and is perhaps at this moment preparing to carry disorder and terror into all its ranks."

And this, in fact, was what I was desirous of doing. I had watched during the day Cacem's troops; I had observed their arrangement, and taken particular notice of the head-quarters of the king. I collected a quantity of stones and pebbles, both large and small, with which I filled my box, and at midnight I mounted aloft. Advancing towards the tents of Cacem, I easily discovered that in which the king was reposing. It was very lofty, richly adorned with gilding, and in the form of a dome, supported on twelve columns of painted wood, fixed deep in the ground; the spaces between the columns were intertwined with branches of different kinds of trees, and towards the summit there were two windows, one at the east, and another at the south side.

All the soldiers around the tent were asleep; and this circumstance permitted me to descend near one of the windows without being perceived. Through it I saw the king lying on a sofa, with his head supported on a satin cushion. Rising a little in my box, I hurled a large stone at Cacem; I struck him on the forehead, and wounded him dangerously; he uttered a cry, which soon awoke his guards and officers, who, running up to him, found him covered with blood, and almost insensible. Immediately loud cries were heard, and the alarm was communicated to the whole quarter, every one asking what had happened. A report was soon circulated that the king was wounded, and it was not known by whom the blow had been struck. Whilst the culprit was being searched for, I ascended high up among the clouds, and discharged from an immense height a shower of stones on the royal tent and all near it. The stones cut through the silk of the tent, and severely wounded the attendants; many of the soldiers who surrounded it, too, were very badly hit, and began to cry out that stones were being rained down on them from heaven. The news soon spread, and to confirm it I scattered my stony artillery in all directions. Terror took possession of the army; both officers and soldiers thinking that the Prophet was enraged with Cacem, and that his anger was too evidently declared by this miraculous interference. In short, Bahaman's enemies took to flight in a panic, and with such precipitation, that they abandoned their tents and baggage to their foes, crying out, "We are lost; Heaven is destroying us!"

When day dawned the king of Gazna was not a little surprised to find, that, instead of advancing to the attack, the enemy was in full retreat. Seeing this, however, he pursued the fugitives with his best troops, who made prodigious carnage, and took prisoner Cacem himself, whose wound prevented his making a sufficiently speedy flight.

"Why," asked Bahaman, when his enemy was brought before him, "why have you advanced into my dominions against all right and reason? What provocation have I given you for making war against me?"

"Bahaman," replied the vanquished monarch, "I thought you had refused me your daughter out of contempt for me, and I thirsted to be revenged upon you. I believed the story of the king of the genii being your son-in-law to be a mere pretext. I have now, however, good reason to be sure of its truth, for it is he who has wounded me and dispersed my army."

When the pursuit was ended Bahaman returned to Gazna with Cacem, who, however, died of his wound the same day. The spoil was divided, and it was so considerable, that even the common soldiers returned home laden with booty; and prayers were offered up in all the mosques thanking Heaven for having confounded the enemies of the state.

When night arrived, the king repaired to the princess's palace.

"My daughter," he said, "I have come to thank the king of the genii for a success I owe entirely to him. The courier whom I despatched to you has informed you of all that he has done for us, and I am so profoundly grateful for it, that I am dying with impatience to embrace his knees."

This satisfaction was soon granted him. I entered Schirine's room by the usual window, and there, as I indeed expected, I found him.

"O great king!" he exclaimed, "language is wanting to express to you what I feel on this occasion. Read yourself in my countenance the full measure of my gratitude."

I raised up Bahaman, and kissed his forehead.

"Prince," I said to him, "could you possibly think that I would refuse to help you in the embarrassing situation in which you were placed on my account? I have punished the proud Cacem who intended to make himself master of your kingdom, and to carry off Schirine, to place her among the slaves of his seraglio. No longer fear that any potentate on the earth will dare to make war against you; but if any one should be so bold, be assured that I will rain a fiery shower upon his troops, which will reduce them to ashes."

After having again assured the king of Gazna that I would take his kingdom under my protection, I related how the enemy's army had been terrified at seeing stones showered down upon their camp. Bahaman, for his part, repeated to me what Cacem had told him, and then took his departure, leaving Schirine and myself to ourselves. The princess was as sensible as her father of the important service I had rendered to the country, and manifested the greatest gratitude, caressing me a thousand times over.

Two days after the interment of Cacem, on whom, although a foe, a magnificent funeral was bestowed, the king of Gazna commanded that rejoicings should take place in the city for the defeat of the enemy's troops. I thought that a festival prepared in my honour ought to be signalized by some wonderful prodigy; and for this purpose I purchased in Gazna some combustible materials. With these I manufactured fireworks, which I let off at as great a height as possible, while the people in the streets were celebrating their victory with great rejoicings. My pyrotechnic display was very successful; and as soon as daylight appeared I left my machine, and went into the town to have the pleasure of hearing what people said about me. I was not deceived in my expectations. A thousand extravagant accounts were current among those who had been spectators of my display. Some said that the king of the genii had illuminated the whole heavens expressly to show his satisfaction with the festival; and others asserted that they had even seen him in the sky, surrounded by a blaze of meteors.

All these speeches amused me exceedingly. But alas! while I was indulging in these pleasurable sensations, my box—my dear machine—the instrument by which I had worked all my wonders—was burning to ashes in the wood. A spark, which I had not perceived, had set fire to it in my absence, and consumed it, and in this state I found it on my return. A father who enters his house, and finds his only son pierced with a thousand mortal wounds, and lying bathed in his blood, could not suffer more than I did on this occasion. I tore my hair and garments, while the wood resounded with my cries and lamentations; I even wonder that I did not lay violent hands upon myself in the paroxysm of my despair. However, by degrees I became calmed, and reflecting that there was no help for my disaster, I at the same time perceived that some resolution must be formed immediately. Only one course seemed open to me, and that was to seek my fortunes elsewhere.

Leaving, therefore, Bahaman and Schirine, doubtless in the deepest distress about me, I left the city of Gazna, and falling in with a caravan of Egyptian merchants, returning to their own country, I joined myself to them, and travelled to Grand Cairo, where I became a weaver in order to gain a subsistence. I lived there for some years and afterwards came to Damascus, where I have followed the same occupation. In appearance I am very well satisfied with my condition, but in reality I am not at all happy, I cannot forget my former fortunate condition, Schirine is ever present to my thoughts, and although I would wish to banish her from my recollection, and in truth make every effort to do so, yet the attempt, as painful as useless, merely causes me constant uneasiness.

I have now, may it please your majesty, performed what you required of me. I know very well that you do not approve the deceit I practised towards the king of Gazna and the princess Schirine, for I have perceived oftener than once, that my story was repugnant to your feelings and that your piety shuddered at my sacrilegious audacity. But be pleased to remember that you demanded a true account from me, and condescend to forgive the confession I have made of my adventures, in consideration of the necessity I was under of obeying you.

CONCLUSION.

The king of Damascus made a suitable reply, and dismissed the weaver, whose story afforded a new argument in favour of the grand vizir's opinion that there is no man who is perfectly happy: however, the king would not desist.

"Atalmulc," he said, "with the exception of yourself, there is no man approaches me but with a smiling countenance; it cannot be that not one of all these is perfectly happy; I shall ask my generals, courtiers, and all the officers of my household. Go, vizir, and summon them all into my presence in succession."

He had the patience to speak to them all individually, and they all made the same reply; namely, that they were not exempt from grief. One complained of his wife, another of his children; the poor accused their poverty as the cause of all their misfortunes, and the rich either did not enjoy good health, or laboured under some other source of affliction.

Bedreddin having questioned so many persons, not one of whom was contented with his lot, came at last to be of the same mind with Atalmulc, and was obliged to admit to his favourite vizir that perfect felicity is not to be looked for in the present life; that every lot and every station has its cares, its anxieties, and its misfortunes; and that we approach the condition of complete happiness only as we conscientiously discharge those duties which our position daily and hourly requires of us.

THE END.

Milton Keynes UK
Ingram Content Group UK Ltd.
UKHW042302170324
439575UK00004B/432